Swallow the Ghost

Swallow the Ghost

Eugenie Montague

MULHOLLAND BOOKS

LITTLE, BROWN AND COMPANY

NEW YORK BOSTON LONDON

Mulholland Books / Little, Brown and Company
Hachette Book Group
1290 Avenue of the Americas, New York, NY 10104
mulhollandbooks.com

First Edition: August 2024

Mulholland Books is an imprint of Little, Brown and Company, a division of Hachette Book Group, Inc. The Mulholland Books name and logo are trademarks of Hachette Book Group, Inc.

The publisher is not responsible for websites (or their content) that are not owned by the publisher.

The Hachette Speakers Bureau provides a wide range of authors for speaking events. To find out more, go to hachettespeakersbureau.com or email hachettespeakers@hbgusa.com.

Little, Brown and Company books may be purchased in bulk for business, educational, or promotional use. For information, please contact your local bookseller or the Hachette Book Group Special Markets Department at special.markets@hbgusa.com.

ISBN 9780316568067
LCCN 2023952180

Printing 1, 2024

LSC-C

Printed in the United States of America

For Ed and Dianne

Heart weeps.
Head tries to help heart.

— *Lydia Davis, "Head, Heart"*

GROUNDHOG DAY 2!

WHEN JANE WAKES UP, her throat hurts. She reaches for the glass of water she keeps by the bed. The glass is solid and cold from the room, and it has made the water cold. It's too harsh on her throat, which is raw and scratchy, and she wishes the water were a few degrees warmer. It is still dark outside, and cold, she knows. She can almost feel it from the color of the sky. She wants to skip her run, make coffee, sit on her bed, and read things on her phone until it's time to go to work. The coffee will feel good on her throat, and the words on her phone will float upward with the touch of her finger. But she had woken up with the feeling that something was wrong, that she had done something wrong. She waits for the shame to loose its hold on her, to realize it belonged to some dream, but then she remembers, and the dread she perceived, which felt like a heavy but lifeless presence, transforms into something restless and grasping. In her dresser, she finds clothes warm enough to run in.

Outside, the air hits her lungs like she is breathing hand sanitizer. Jane runs fast, except she slows down around corners, because she has run into too many people, and it seems to her that her body remembers now even when she forgets, as if it retains somewhere inside it the memory of slamming hard into another person, the bloody knees and the guilt, picking someone up off the sidewalk with palms torn from concrete, too tender to close properly around the outstretched hand. Though as she rounds a corner to turn toward the river, both her mind and body forget, and she has to leap out of the way of a woman and her dog. The woman glares at her, the dog barks, and Jane says sorry and runs even faster so she can reach the jogging path.

Up ahead, she can see the guy with the green running shoes. They are the same brand as hers but newer, and she wonders if he actually buys things like sneakers and toothbrushes on the schedules they suggest, backs up his work, replaces the vacuum bag. Jane's nose is running when she passes him. She sniffs at the wetness above her lip. Some days, she pretends not to notice him. Today, she smiles. Last week, the smile was more like a nod: *I recognize you.* Now it's something different: *Oh, hi. Oh, hi.* She smiles, and then she can see FDR Drive, dull and loud. The cars are out in numbers before the people on the streets. She jogs in place until she can cross, and when she does, it feels like her run properly starts. She can hear the gentle lapping of the East River. The streetlamps are still on and make patterns on the water. The path is laid out before her, wide and gray.

At home, Jane straightens up her room, showers, and pulls a pair of sweater tights from her drawer. She tugs them over one foot and then the other. She has small feet, and the tights remind her of being a child, a memory assembled from pictures of herself as a toddler, mittens hanging from her coat, her mom holding her on her hip so Jane's pinafore dress is hiked up and the tights are on full display. She almost remembers the feeling, crying as her mom put them on her, how scratchy they were. They don't feel scratchy now. Jane has them in six different colors. She hangs them to dry so they will retain their shape longer, and after laundry day, the bookshelf in the corner of her room resembles the kind of tree Dr. Seuss might have thought up or the yarn-bombed fence surrounding a construction site she passes every day on her way to work. A neon weeping willow.

On the subway, she plays a word scramble, two geography puzzles, and then a mini-crossword, which she tries to finish before the train gets to her stop. When she makes it, she thinks it will be a better day than it was yesterday, that she will be better.

At work, the client team meets in the conference room with mugs of coffee and a plate of croissants and fruit, because one of their clients is here. The conference room is at the back of their mostly open office space, cordoned off from the rest with frosted-glass walls. There is a black metal table on a colorful Moroccan rug. The walls are blank so they can be projected on from any angle, except the wall facing the street, which has a series of large windows from which Jane can see brick, tree branches hitting the glass, a slice of sky, and more brick. She is nervous, so she looks at how the tree branches move with the wind.

Her boss likes to bring clients in periodically for presentations by the project leader. Much of what Jane does, if she does it right, should be invisible, so in these meetings, it is her job to show her work so the client can see it. The client group is twice as big as it was when Jane started, and her boss has asked the whole team to come in, as well as a few people from Creative. The fact that Tom has asked so many people to sit in is a compliment, though he hasn't said that. He comes in after everyone is already seated, walking slowly through the door because he is reading something on his phone. He shakes the client's hand, finds an open seat, and sits down. Jane tries to catch his eye because she is not sure if she is supposed to start or if he wants to say something, but he is cleaning his glasses, then leaning forward to grab a piece of fruit, then back on his phone.

"Jane, will you take everybody through it?" Tom asks, his mouth full of apple.

Jane smooths her skirt by rubbing her palms down her thighs three times, then she stands up, smiling. Her heels sink into the rug.

Their client is a young author named Jeremy who wrote a literary thriller on Twitter. All of the characters have different fake Twitter accounts, including Rita Hadzic (@ritahadzic), a twenty-one-year-old student at Hunter, though she has stopped tweeting since she went missing. Rita wanted to be an urban planner and was a nanny for a Brooklyn family when she wasn't in class. She paid a monthly fee at Hunter to use the ceramic studio and posted pictures of her finished bowls and vases on her Instagram account, bowls and vases that are actually made by Jane's friend Amelia. For four months starting at the end of 2018, Rita tweeted like a person addicted to Twitter—somewhere between twenty and forty times a day, more if she decided to live-tweet a TV show or a protest or discuss an article she was reading in school. As Rita tweeted, so did a number of other characters Jeremy created—an ex-boyfriend, the mother and father in the family Rita nannied for, friends from Hunter, a city council commissioner. Rather, Jeremy created most of the characters, but as Jeremy and Jane met to discuss how to make them come alive on Twitter, they changed slightly—or sometimes a lot—as Jane brought up the possibilities and limitations of the platform. Jeremy knew who the characters were and what he wanted to happen in the investigation, but Jane was the one who knew how to use their tweeting habits as characterization: who would retweet what, who would engage with trolls, who would apologize and who would double down. And so the characters they'd invented tweeted and retweeted and followed and unfollowed—each other, but also real people. They had opinions about current events; they piled on where it would be appropriate to pile on; they made jokes that didn't come off and deleted them. Then, when Jeremy and Jane were sure they had sufficient material for the coming investigation, Jane used her background in social media marketing to make Rita go viral, and they disappeared her.

Rita's followers have grown by thousands since she disappeared; her final post, a picture of a blue ceramic bowl with the caption *Big news soon. Watch this space!* The follower counts for the rest of the characters who populate her world have likewise continued to grow exponentially. They, of course, have continued to tweet—looking for her, mourning her, writing earnest and mostly ill-advised threads in the middle of the night that are "accidentally" self-incriminating. Or incriminating of someone else. Joshua—Jeremy's alter ego, a writer figure who stumbled across the Rita mystery researching something for his own novel—continues to document his findings: interviews he conducts with campus security guards, live-tweets of stakeouts he undertakes where he follows whoever is at the top of his suspect list at the moment, successful attempts to trick the police into showing him witness statements. Every once in a while, he uploads blurry photographs of someone he believes might be Rita riding her bike but who is actually Jane's friend Amelia.

It was Jane's idea, the Twitter mystery. Jeremy had come to them looking to increase his follower count before sending out his recently finished manuscript, a book he planned to pitch to agents as a novel of ideas that utilized and subverted the tropes of detective fiction. Her boss often shakes his head at her when they walk by each other in the office. She loves working with Jeremy. They both sign their emails *J,* and it does feel like that, that the project is theirs, impossible without the two of them, so dependent on both their labor that it would be difficult to separate her contribution from his. Sometimes she feels like she has disappeared into his project, but not in a way that feels deficient. Like they both know exactly what they are good at and slotted into each other like pieces of IKEA furniture. The bespoke tool made for their particular product is the internet.

Jane walks the team through the various Reddits and subreddits dedicated to Jeremy's mystery; a writer from BuzzFeed who has started collecting relevant Twitter threads; an article on Medium analyzing the various leads; biographical sketches of the suspects. Even some fan fiction. Mutually beneficial, Jane tells the group. Keeping in line with the dead and absented author. Some of what Jane tells the group about, she made happen— reached out to journalists she knew, @ed the right people, created the first meme off a cringey tweet posted by one of the characters (the father in the family Rita used to nanny for, an unfortunate "tribute" to Rita that Jane wrote deliberately, making sure it was cringey enough to meme). Then she watched it multiply, sucking in a larger and larger audience—some of whom would never understand that a fictional character was the original source material but a significant amount who did or who went back to find out what the original said and why and got caught up in the mystery. But some of what Jane shares with the group has happened without her doing anything at all. More and more each day, it has a life of its own.

After the meeting, a smaller group decides to go to lunch across the street at Mika's and they all drink wine. Jane is lightheaded after her salad. Jeremy is smart; he didn't have an agent for his book before he hired them. His first book was published in a contest run by a respected indie publisher, a slim novel that centered on a man whose wife went missing and where the primary action consisted mostly of the man wandering through his house, thinking about things. It was experimental, received critical praise from the small indie reviewers who covered it, and sold two hundred copies. He was paid one thousand dollars. When he finished another book, he came to Stile looking for a way to increase his follower count before he sent it to agents. Now agents are contacting him. He fingers Jane in the bathroom, her sweater tights pulled down to her ankles. She had wondered if he was flirting with her. Sometimes she reread his emails, trying to discern what kind of energy was in them. In the past week, they talked on the phone before bed almost every night, but she hadn't been sure until today. When they are done, she makes him leave before she pulls her tights up so he doesn't see her yank them up to her breasts, the reverse karate chop necessary to move the crotch back up between her legs. She fixes the ribbing that snakes around her calves, lines straight down her shins into ankle boots with uneven soles.

After lunch, she works, scrolling through various feeds, tracking analytics, editing tweets, uploading Instagram stories, following links, changing her music, texting with Jeremy—which makes her feel pointed and alive until around three, when he stops writing her back. She reads through the Twitter account of a young Vulture reporter, scrolls through Instagram, reads a profile of an actress she likes written by a profiler she likes. There is threat all around her.

At four, Kaya comes for her, and they put on their coats and gloves and walk to get coffee. Usually, she and Kaya talk about work on their walk, but today they talk about Jeremy. Jane can't look at her.

"What?" Kaya screeches as something hot bursts at the back of Jane's throat. "Jeremy fingerbanged you while I had to listen to Tom explain how to grow basil? He and his wife are trying to make the perfect tomato sauce or something." Kaya shakes her head, laughing. "That bathroom has seen a lot of action," she continues, because Kaya is sleeping with one of the waiters there. The restaurant is across the street from their office and when Billy works the lunch shift, Kaya goes over to see him. Sometimes when Jane is in the bathroom looking at herself in the mirror, she imagines she sees Kaya's back in the reflection, Billy's determined face over her shoulder. When she orders from him now, she looks just to the right of him.

Kaya is staring at her, and Jane knows she is imagining Jeremy's finger inside her. Kaya is always coming to her desk and asking questions like "Do you think Tom has sex with his wife in the shower?" and other things Jane doesn't want to think about. It is because of this, and because of the fact that Jeremy stopped texting her, that Jane hadn't planned to tell Kaya about what happened. But she couldn't help it. With every passing moment, it became more uncomfortable to keep inside her. Both unreal and painful. A dream that hurt. When Kaya came to get her, she barely got into the street before it all came tumbling out of her, a relief, the words hot and streaming. Her breath makes her scarf wet where she'd wrapped it around her mouth.

Now Kaya is scrolling through Jane and Jeremy's text exchange, her glove hanging from her mouth from when she tugged it off with her teeth.

"No, you're good," she says, handing Jane her phone back. "Just make sure to be the one who goes dark first next time."

"But what if there isn't a next time?"

"There will be."

Kaya is dismissively confident. It's Jane's favorite kind of confident. She allows it to seep into her.

At the coffee shop, Kaya laughs with the baristas, a skateboarder with gauges in his earlobes and a slight female drummer who wears platform high-tops. Kaya is funny; Jane always goes to her when she needs to use humor for a client. Jane has spent years trying to understand humor. What happens when we laugh? How does humor make us trust people online and in real life? What is funny? People tell Jane she is funny too sometimes, but it makes her nervous that she can't pinpoint the source of it, the same way she can never tell why men want to kiss her. It feels scary to have important things like that both inside her and also completely out of her control.

Kaya and Jane live in the same neighborhood and they often walk home from work together, reach Jane's block, and keep going.

"I have to go to the pharmacy," Kaya will say, "do you want to come?" and they'll turn away from Jane's apartment, run errands, grab dinner, take Kaya's dog to the dog park, suit up for a run or a yoga class until it is past dark. Jane has spent full Saturdays at Kaya's, the sky darkening outside the window, their positions changing on the couch, sweaters added or discarded. A surprising absence of memories; hours, days, where she has retained nothing but the sense of a surprised laugh warming her chest on the way out—or the sense she is about to say something funny, the knowledge of it shaping her mouth, altering the tone of her voice, the satisfaction of Kaya's laughter, the whole body of joy of it, like hot summer nights with no rain, only lightning.

Kaya pays for their coffees and says something to the drummer that makes the young woman laugh. Kaya can do it with anyone, but Jane can do it comfortably only with Kaya. Jane makes Jeremy laugh too, but she feels nervous.

The rest of the workday is marked by waiting for a text she does not expect to come. Still, every few minutes, she notices the absence of it. She switches screens back to her computer. She wants to create a Tumblr for Rita, the presumably murdered college senior at the center of Jeremy's Twitter mystery. It's supposed to be her old Tumblr, something she stopped using in high school. Jane's experimenting with another Tumblr now—song lyrics scrawled across pictures of empty subway stations—backdating posts versus manipulating the HTML code to hide when the posts were uploaded, both of which Tom had just taught her to do. She sends various versions to him to see if he can find the date anywhere using web browsers or applications.

Rita's about to reveal her teenage self as a soulbonder. Jane had needed to explain the concept to Jeremy, but he'd immediately gravitated to it.

"So they think they're a fictional character?" he'd asked.

"No, it's more an intense bond with a fictional character to the point where they exist in your own head," she told him. "That thing that happens when you're a kid reading books but times a million so you think they were written for you, exist inside you."

"Like multiple personalities?"

"No. The character is still the character, and they have their own life, but they also exist in your head. Or some people believe there's a soulscape where your soul and theirs meet, but it feels like it's in your head. Plus soulbonds don't front, for the most part."

"Front?"

"A multiple personality fronts—becomes dominant. Soulbonds don't do things like that."

"And how do they meet? Why do they bond?"

"Well, they meet in fiction. And it can get a little convoluted after that. Some people believe it's essentially just a soulmate situation. Some SBs believe it's related to the multiverse—where, of all the possible worlds, there is one world where the fictional character exists and lives the life they lived in the book. There's something about reading that opens the portal between the worlds—possibly because to write the book in the first place, someone from this world had access to that world. Somehow."

"SBs?"

"Soulbonders. It was a Tumblr thing. I guess you were never on Tumblr?"

"No."

"So you hate it?"

"No."

"Really?" The relief she felt was palpable, troubling. "I thought it worked on a few levels, because there's all these people identifying with Rita—who's not real—and she does the same thing, so there's a sense of unreality/reality all the way down."

"It's perfect," he said. "There's also this concept of the double in mysteries."

"Why?"

"Because we can only see what we are."

"So you really like it?"

"No, I love it," he said. "And this is a real thing that people believe in?"

"Yeah. Well, some people. Mostly on Tumblr."

"What about you? Do you have one?"

"No. I just like to eavesdrop on people on the internet. They'll tell you anything."

"So, then, is the bond part of them or something they want to fuck?"

"It's unclear. Both, either. It can be a romantic interest or a part of yourself you're too scared to express. Sometimes, it's more like a guardian angel."

"Amazing."

When Jane got home that night, Jeremy followed up with texts full of links. He'd been on a deep dive into the soulbond universe and had some questions. It was the first time they'd texted all night, sending possibilities for Rita's soulbond back and forth, watching snippets of movies, quoting from books they'd loved as teenagers. She came to work bleary-eyed and ecstatic.

At the end of the day, Kaya gets her for yoga. Amanda is teaching, and they love Amanda. She is less earnest than the other teachers, and her classes are hard, but she never seems like she is trying to make people fail, which they both agree Leslie does. Jane has fallen on her face in Leslie's class, her arms buckling after the nine hundredth chaturanga. In Amanda's class, Jane's arm balances have gotten longer and steadier. Most days, she's sure she's never experienced progress like this before in her life.

During savasana, the sweat chills on Jane's body. She feels rooted to the floor. Amanda comes by and pulls gently on all her limbs like she is trying to make her a little bit taller. Kaya is asleep, snoring lightly. Jane is not asleep, but still, when Amanda begins speaking again to guide them through the end of class, she feels as if she is pulling herself up from under something heavy.

They eat at the Whole Foods salad bar with their yoga mats rolled up by their feet. Kaya buys a small bag of Mexican wedding cookies and eats them with one leg pulled up on her chair, powdered sugar on her fingers.

A couple from their yoga class is wandering the aisles. They plan their meals for the week and grocery shop according to this menu. Jane and Kaya have seen them do this after Amanda's class for the past six months. They are reading the ingredients on a bottle of salad dressing.

"How often do you think they have sex?" Kaya asks.

"God. Why do you do this?"

"How do you not do this? I picture people having sex within the first minute of meeting them."

"That is not normal."

"He seems like the kind of guy who would make sex all about flexibility. Like, 'Let's see how far we can bend each other.'"

"He is pretty flexible," Jane concedes as the images populate her mind. "Fuck. I'm never going to be able to unsee this now."

"It makes class go by faster," Kaya says. She pushes her cookies across the table at Jane. "Please, eat the rest. I've already eaten three."

Jane peeks in the small paper bag at the remaining cookies. "I'm full."

"Well, take them for later, at least. I can't take them or I'll eat them."

"Okay, sure."

It's almost ten by the time they get to their neighborhood, but Jane doesn't really feel like going home, so she sits on the stairs of Kaya's building while Kaya gets her dog, and then they walk around the block together. Kaya's dog is strong, barrel-chested. He yanks Kaya toward cracks in the sidewalk, tree stumps, cockroaches, feral cats. A rat crosses their path, running nimbly over the broken sidewalk. He disappears somewhere near the stairs of a brownstone.

"Randy," Kaya says, nodding at the rat's retreating back.

"And a good evening to you, sir," Jane adds. "Give our best to your family."

At home, Jane showers and puts on an extra-large hooded sweatshirt that makes her feel like she is disappearing. Jeremy has not texted her, but he has sent her an email about work, drafts of some possible tweets, an outline of upcoming plot points. Regular tone. No signaling about the bathroom except for the final line: Hope you were able to get some work done after all that wine. I basically passed out—J.

She smiles, relieved that he has alluded to it at all and then a little elated, because if he passed out, that could explain why he suddenly stopped writing her back. But the more she rereads it, she wonders if it's meant to imply that he was very drunk, and what happened was the result of that drunkenness and not anything else, like mutual attraction. Wonders also whether he is giving her the opportunity to cosign this interpretation so they can move on, egos intact, without the need to talk about it ever again. She forwards the email to Kaya with a question mark, then clips her nails as she waits for her to write back, but she doesn't. Jane puts the clippers away, washes her hands in the bathroom, searches for Kaya's leftover cookies in her purse, and eats them while composing her response. She licks the sugar off her fingers and rubs them on her arm to dry them before typing.

Me too, she writes, and includes a GIF of Nicolas Cage loading bottles into a shopping cart. Then she reads what he has sent her and starts editing. When they began, after Jane pitched Jeremy the idea of the Twitter mystery, he would go home and write it, consulting with her occasionally about how it could be accomplished online. Slowly that had changed, because Jeremy didn't really understand the internet—he just knew he needed it. They met once in the beginning to discuss ideas for how they could position the ex-boyfriend as a suspect—what Jeremy had planned for him and what they could do before and after Rita went missing to lay the proper foundation. Jeremy came to the meeting with some cryptic tweets the ex-boyfriend could post as well as a list of incriminating information his alter ego, Joshua, would discover after Rita disappeared (it looked like he was reading her emails; some indications he was cheating on her before they broke up; explosive fights described by a witness; a temper—maybe they could upload a photo of Rita's cracked phone and somehow insinuate he had done that). Jane told him these all sounded like good ideas but suggested another possibility: They could upload a picture the boyfriend took at a concert and post it some night before Rita disappeared. On the same night, they would upload a picture of the same concert from a similar angle—under the account of one of Rita's best friends. Rita's tweets from that night, meanwhile, would show she was at the library. Jeremy didn't see the point but agreed Jane could do it, so she and Kaya went to see Billy's band play and Jane took a hundred pictures on her phone. When she got home, she deliberated for hours about which two to use and how to crop them. After Rita went missing, Jane used another fake Twitter account they had created to "notice" the angle of the two photographs they'd posted months earlier; thousands of people argued online for three days about whether you could tell from the pictures if Rita's ex and Rita's best friend had been at the concert together.

Now Jeremy talks to her about everything he is thinking, sends her whatever he writes, and she figures out how to make it move on Twitter, tweaking the language so it fits the medium, retweeting real tweets that she thinks the characters would retweet, commenting on posts, responding when people @ them. Jeremy does this too, but Jane does far more of it than she did in the beginning because Jeremy didn't understand how much energy was needed to make each of the characters a presence, what it took to be real and coherent in a place like Twitter. So slowly, without it ever really being discussed, it became more of a collaboration. Or like a director and cinematographer, him telling her what shots he wanted, Jane the one with the camera making it happen. She feels indispensable.

She goes to the kitchen and finds a bag of pretzels and brings them back into her room after extricating herself from a conversation with one of her roommates by pleading work. She reads the replies to her various posts, chooses particularly funny or emphatic ones to amplify. She opens a document on her computer and begins a list to show her colleagues at check-in tomorrow: teenage girls and their videos, a meme based on the detective figure, a website that simply tracks the minutes since Rita's last post, a gushing stan tweet from a mildly famous Hollywood actor asking if he can play Joshua in the movie. The pretzels feel a little bland, a little empty. She watches the likes accumulate on the Hollywood actor's post and wonders if she has any cream cheese. She does, and that makes the pretzels feel more substantial but saltier, and suddenly she is craving something sweet to break through. She has some peanut butter and, she thinks, maybe some chocolate chips, but she can hear, now, both her roommates, and she does not want to talk to them or take food in front of them. She searches her room, but all she finds is an old pack of Halls that tastes like Listerine. She sucks on one until she hears the voices die outside her door.

In the kitchen, she leaves the water running as she rummages in her drawer, locates the peanut butter, the chocolate chips. Because she doesn't want to have to come back out and risk seeing her roommates, she also takes a knife and four pieces of bread from the refrigerator. She wishes she had something more sugary than chocolate chips, something where chocolate was just one element of the sweetness. Briefly, she considers running to the store, but she knows she has to respond to the Hollywood actor. She brings the food and her laptop back to her bed, creates a little spread on her comforter. She sucks the peanut butter off the knife, wipes the crumbs off her hands, and writes from one of the accounts she's been using for the project.

@ChrisOke I'd see that movie. How about @edithdellman for Rita?

She waits. Edith Dellman has a substantial fan base and a public crush on Chris Oke. Also, she'd just retweeted something. Jane felt struck by inspiration when she thought of her, how Newton must have felt when he understood gravity, like he could perceive a blue-tinted schematic overlaying a force that nobody could see but everyone felt. Pressing down on them.

Time on the internet was excruciating. Too fast. A complete standstill. Forever. It has been seconds since she tagged Edith Dellman, but Jane feels like she might run out of breath soon. Peanut butter stuck in a tooth. She digs at it with her tongue.

Thirty minutes later, Edith Dellman replies: Omg @ChrisOke, what is this? Where is @ritahadzic? Her fans start retweeting. The traffic to @joshtweeting spikes. Chris Oke responds to Edith Dellman, and Jane thinks she might faint. She texts Kaya: Omg I made a ship. Please help. Kaya doesn't respond. Jane adds the new developments to her document for the check-in and sends the thread to Jeremy—not in a text, the way she probably would have done it the night before, but in an email. She regrets it immediately.

He writes her back: !!

Jane feels the adrenaline draining out of her. Time returns to normal, the pointed quality to each second flattening out so there is no distinction between one moment and the next. Her ears are ringing slightly, like she's been at a loud concert. Her computer whirs audibly and is hot to the touch. Her bed is covered in crumbs. There's a typo in her last post. She's retweeted someone who, she sees now, tweets frequently about how his ex-girlfriend is a fucking bitch. Jane goes into the bathroom and turns on the shower. She thinks, as she often does, her head over the toilet, her finger touching the back of her throat, that she doesn't really have the right personality for her job. It all happens too fast. She never has any time to think about things except when it's all done and irreversible and all she can do is see—over and over—everything she's done wrong.

When Jane wakes up, her throat hurts. She reaches for the glass of water she keeps by the bed. The glass is solid and cold from the room, and it has made the water cold. It's too harsh on her throat, which is raw and scratchy, and she wishes the water were a few degrees warmer. It is still dark outside, and cold, she knows. She can almost feel it from the color of the sky. She wants to skip her run, make coffee, sit on her bed, and read things on her phone until it's time to go to work. The coffee will feel good on her throat, and the words on her phone will float upward with the touch of her finger. But she had woken up with the feeling that something was wrong, that she had done something wrong. She waits for the shame to loose its hold on her, to realize it belonged to some dream, but then she remembers, and the dread she perceived, which felt like a heavy but lifeless presence, transforms into something restless and grasping. In her dresser, she finds clothes warm enough to run in.

Outside, the air hits her lungs like she is breathing hand sanitizer. Jane runs fast, except she slows down around corners, because she has run into too many people, and it seems to her that her body remembers now even when she forgets, as if it retains somewhere inside it the memory of slamming hard into another person, the bloody knees and the guilt, picking someone up off the sidewalk with palms torn from concrete, too tender to close properly around the outstretched hand. Though as she rounds a corner to turn toward the river, both her mind and body forget, and she has to leap out of the way of a woman and her dog. The woman glares at her, the dog barks, and Jane says sorry and runs even faster so she can reach the jogging path.

Up ahead, she can see the guy with the green running shoes. They are the same brand as hers but newer, and she wonders if he actually buys things like sneakers and toothbrushes on the schedules they suggest, backs up his work, replaces the vacuum bag. Jane's nose is running when she passes him. She sniffs at the wetness above her lip. Some days, she pretends not to notice him. Today, she smiles. Last week, the smile was more like a nod: *I recognize you.* Now it's something different: *Oh, hi. Oh, hi.* She smiles, and then she can see FDR Drive, dull and loud. The cars are out in numbers before the people on the streets. She jogs in place until she can cross, and when she does, it feels like her run properly starts. She can hear the gentle lapping of the East River. The streetlamps are still on and make patterns on the water. The path is laid out before her, wide and gray.

At home, she straightens up her room, throwing away the pretzel bag and pushing it down under the Q-tips, strands of hair, discarded Post-it notes. There are a few chocolate chips left in the bag, so she rolls down the plastic and places these too at the bottom of the trash. She pushes the covers off her bed and brushes the crumbs off with her hand. There is a smear of chocolate on her pillow, and she realizes she must have dropped a chocolate chip that melted there from the warmth of her body as she slept. She washes the pillowcase in the sink, scrubbing with soap and her hands, stretching out the stained area until the discoloration disappears and the fabric is translucent with water. She wrings it out over the sink until not a single drop emerges, then hangs it over the laundry hamper in her room. She finds another pillowcase in her closet, but it's a bright green that clashes with the pink sheets, so she takes the pink sheets off her bed and makes it with the green sheets that match the pillowcase. The knife is wrapped in a paper towel on her nightstand, and she brings it and the jar of peanut butter into the kitchen after making sure her roommates aren't there. From the kitchen, she takes the broom and sweeps the crumbs on the floor around her bed. With her bed made and her floor clean, she removes the plastic bag from her small trash can and ties it in a knot. After listening to make sure she can't hear her roommates outside her door, she walks quickly and quietly through their apartment, stops at the front door to listen for neighbors, then walks quickly and less quietly to the trash chute at the end of the hall. When she reenters her bedroom, it feels like a metal coat is falling off her shoulders. She yearns to stay standing where she is.

On the subway, she plays a word scramble, two geography puzzles, and then a mini-crossword, which she tries to finish before the train gets to her stop. When she makes it, she thinks it will be a better day than it was yesterday, that she will be better.

At the office, they meet in the conference room with mugs of coffee.

"Jane, will you take everybody through it?" Tom asks.

She smooths her skirt by rubbing her palms down her thighs three times, then she stands up, smiling. Her heels sink into the rug.

She walks everyone through the Chris Oke/Edith Dellman updates. Tom smiles but lacks the enthusiasm from yesterday. Kaya has a giant calendar that covers her entire desk, and she marks on it the days she thinks Tom has sex with his wife before coming into the office. Today, Jane knows, the Tom-sex icon will go undrawn.

"It's too soon to track real engagement," Jane says, "but we did pick up a few thousand new followers."

Jeremy was clear when he hired them he was interested in investment, not merely likes. He wanted people to care for Rita as if she were one of their own friends, their favorite television character. He wanted people to actually look for her. Not on the streets, like Pokémon. But on the internet where she was born. Every time Jeremy spoke, Jane felt a frisson of something she couldn't quite identify. Not excitement. Not lust. Devotion.

Miriam speaks up from behind her phone. "Edith Dellman is following Jeremy! They were tweeting at each other at, like, four in the morning."

Jane, standing in front of the group, tries to look happy about this development, not as if every cell inside her has been cleaved in half. She thinks that might be the sound roaring in her head, the broken cells attempting to reconfigure themselves into something viable.

"Way to go, stud," she says.

The group laughs. She can't look at Kaya, because Kaya might see her.

After the check-in, she reads around on the internet. She tells herself she needs to read the Jeremy/Edith Dellman tweets for work, but she would

have read them anyway. She is so pretty. He is so charming. The leftover croissants from yesterday's meeting are still in their box in the break room, and she
takes one back to her desk, pulls up the flaky, slightly stale bread. It leaves a
buttery sheen on her fingertips. Edith tweets about weed, social justice. Two
weeks ago, she and her fans paid someone's medical debt. The impulse to continue down her feed feels yawning, insatiable, like an emptiness but also a
pressure. Sometimes Jane thinks this is the only feeling she recognizes. She
returns for two more croissants and eats them, breaking off big chunks and
stuffing each one in her mouth while she is still chewing the previous bite.

In the bathroom, she places her travel toothpaste on a paper towel on
the counter and throws up quickly. The bread comes back in large pieces.

They go to happy hour at Mika's, because Billy is working. He always goes
behind the bar and makes them at least two free drinks, which is sweet but means
Jane is tipsy by the time she leaves, and all her plans to go to a yoga class or get
some work done or call her parents never seem like a good idea, because she only
wants to sit very still and experience the altered state. Here but not here. Jane but
not Jane. A feeling like she is unclenching a fist she didn't realize she had clenched.
Once, walking home after the bar with Kaya, she tried to explain it.

"It's like I'm ceding control to something, but it's a relief, the abdica-
tion. But the really weird part is I never feel like I'm in control. The opposite, really. I'm always doing something I can't help, so why would this loss
of control feel so appealing?"

"I heard this guy on a podcast," Kaya had said, "who was afraid of death,
and then he did mushrooms and hallucinated that he was dead, and when he
sobered up, he was basically cured. Maybe it's like that."

"Maybe," Jane had said.

Billy brings them two highball glasses, clear and sickly smelling. He follows mixologists on Instagram.

"Any bathroom trysts planned for today?" he asks Jane.

Her hand shakes slightly as she brings the drink to her lips. She doesn't know if he knows because Kaya told him or because she and Jeremy were so obvious yesterday that everybody knows. She'd thought they were subtle. Jane's gotten so good at recognizing this on the internet—the division between what someone thought they'd said and how people read it, how a person wanted to come across and how they actually came across—that she'd almost forgotten it happened in real life too.

The restaurant begins to fill up around them, and Billy disappears. Kaya explains something new she is working on, an AI thing for one of their clients. Jane can't decide if she wants Kaya to bring up the Edith Dellman thing or not. She asks an appropriate number of questions about Kaya's project—three—and then says:

"Jeremy hasn't texted today."

Kaya tips her glass. Her mouth fills with ice cubes. Cracking.

"That makes sense," she says. "It happened yesterday. You said he wrote last night."

"But not anything."

"Still, he did. That was the gesture. He'll be back soon. Trust."

Jane stirs her drink with her straw. There is bruised fruit at the bottom of the glass. "Even after the Edith Dellman thing?"

"Edith Dellman lives in LA and has a boyfriend. Jeremy is, like, unknown-indie-author cute, not Hollywood-actress-dating cute."

Jane starts to feel better, but then Kaya says, "I mean, if a bunch of Edith Dellmans start showing up, then yeah. But also, it's kind of your job to make that happen."

Billy rushes up to the bar to collect drinks for his table. He puts the ticket on his tray and loads the drinks around it.

"Damn," Kaya says. "He's slammed. That means we'll have to buy our next drink."

"Maybe I'm done," Jane says, because there is a yoga class she can go to on the way home, but she doesn't really want to leave Kaya. "Do you want to go to a yoga class?"

"No," Kaya says. "I ran before work."

Being still is uncomfortable. "Well, let's walk home. We can drink wine at your place."

"Maybe," Kaya says.

Jane's phone buzzes on the bar.

What color are your tights today?

Jane wears pretty much the same thing every day: a top, a black or brown skirt, and one of her different colors of tights. It helps her in the morning.

"It's from Jeremy," she tells Kaya.

"Told you."

Jane wonders how Kaya always knows, if she is that much better at read-ing people or if she is simply more confident. Once, Kaya gave her number to a man at a bar who never called her. "When he was putting the number in his phone," she said, "I could tell he was doing it wrong."

Jane had no idea if this was true—it was true that most people Kaya gave her number to did call her. Still, Jane couldn't believe this was the narrative Kaya's mind provided, that it didn't need to worry the edges. As far as Jane knew, Kaya never thought about that guy again, not even when Tom told her he thought they might be having an emotional affair, and out of respect for his wife, he thought they should stop communicating with each other unless it was about work.

Over Jeremy's shoulder, Jane reads the notes he's posted for himself around his studio. The room is small enough that from where they are sitting on his bed, she can look across the room to his desk and see the index cards he has taped to the wall behind his computer. *Fix park scene. Silent movies?* A map labeled EDIR'S WORLD. A pencil drawing of a young boy working on a puzzle. Big black Sharpie on an index card: *Do the work, asshole.* She doesn't recognize the prints on his wall and is nervous to ask about them. She tries to internalize one of the paintings so she can input a description into Google later, but it's only a wash of greens and reds and blues.

He has left empty water glasses everywhere. On his desk, the windowsill, the stove. He is using a cardboard box for a trash can, but his bookshelves have leaded-glass doors on them. Jane can't read the titles. Jeremy's mouth is on her shoulder. She turns her head and stares down into his hair dispassionately. His focus captivates her. A singular purpose. When he comes to the office or when they are talking or when he is sitting at a table across from her, his mind often seems to be elsewhere. Floating. But now—she's not sure she has ever felt what he is feeling. Even when he moves his hand down and a warm fluttering rushes through her body, she is still thinking of something else. His demeanor. The notes on the wall. When he puts his hand on her stomach, the fluttering stops. His hand brushes up against the place where her tights have started to roll back on themselves. Edith Dellman is lanky. In interviews, she has expressed dismay about the rumors of an eating disorder that swirl around her. Once, on a late show, she ate a box of doughnuts while the audience clapped. Jeremy is taking her tights off. They get stuck at her ankles. He bends her body into unflattering angles.

"Do you want a blow job?" she says.

"Really?"

She places her hand on his chest and pushes him down. She ties her tights around his eyes like a blindfold. He is breathing heavy. He shudders when she finally touches him. She can tell by his face he's trying to think of something else to make it last longer. Maybe, when it is over, she will ask him what it was.

But she doesn't. He cracks the window near the bed. Cool air and noise from the street seep into the room. Outside, she can see the fire escape and electrical wires. Jeremy gets his laptop and they sit propped up in his bed watching *Blow-Up,* drinking red wine out of coffee mugs. Her mouth feels full, swollen. The models are angular and awkward, perfect, in the way only the really thin can be. She's not sure which one she wishes she looked like more. She wants to rewind to the scene with the first model, the aggressive way he photographs her, how hard she's working, every movement a pose.

"I love how quiet this movie is," Jeremy says when it ends. "All these scenes where no one says a word, and no soundtrack, nothing tinny and electronic in the background letting you know you're supposed to feel on edge."

When she thinks of the photographer walking through the park, she can hear the wind in the trees. It feels more real than wind she's experienced in real life.

"Watching this movie," he says, "I think the world will never be that quiet again."

"And it ends with the mimes," she says.

He smiles at her happily, which makes her want to pull the sheet over her head.

"Yes," he says. "And starts with screaming."

"It's odd, though, in the final scene, with the mimes playing tennis, at the end, you can hear the tennis ball. Do you think—" she starts but he is already kissing her.

Later, he writes while she works lying on his bed. She watches him take a notebook and pen from the drawer of his desk. He writes a full page, tears it from the seam, walks across the room to the trash, throws it out, then opens his computer and begins to work on his book.

"What was that?" she asks.

"Getting the crap out of my head."

"You always do that?"

"Yeah."

This makes her think about how Rita always reads facing east, which she tells him.

"I always give my characters rituals."

"Why?"

"Because we need them, and, generally, we don't believe in God or country anymore, so we make them."

Most of the time when Jane is around Jeremy, she feels as if she can't sit in her own skin, but there are other times she feels like he is inside her.

"I go to church," he says, "to watch the priest bless the wine, the way he breaks the wafer above the altar."

"I thought we didn't believe in God."

"We don't. But some people do, and I watch them. Everyone standing and kneeling in unison. After, I go to brunch and smell the incense on myself."

"Brunch is a ritual."

Sometimes when he smiles at her, she feels like she's won a prize.

"Absolutely brunch is a ritual. 'The primeval terror under the rites from time immemorial'—now with mimosas." He climbs back into bed beside her. "Cortázar wrote that," he says. She draws a champagne flute on his back with her finger. Goose bumps break out on his skin. "He also wrote *Blow-Up*. Or the story Antonioni's movie is based on."

"Do you find out why he died in the story?"

"Oh, there's no murder in the story."

"What?"

"Right? It's amazing what we do."

She erases the champagne flute with the palm of her hand. Draws eggs Benedict now. Two perfect orbs, smothered.

"So let me make sure I have this right: You crumple up a piece of paper before you write because of primeval terror?"

"That's why I do a lot of things," he says. "What are your rituals? Well, your clothes. I noticed that immediately. What else?"

The light from the streetlamp hitting her naked stomach feels like it's been refracted through stained glass.

"I don't know," she says. "I'd have to think about it."

She has to take two trains to get back from Jeremy's. She gets off three stops early and walks to Rocco's, where she buys a slice of pizza and a Diet Coke and eats at one of the two tables near the window. The paper plate turns translucent with grease. At the other table, two men are shoving pizza into their mouths without speaking and a third has his head on the table, passed out. The restaurant is warm from the ovens, spiced. From Rocco's, she walks to Nico's and orders another slice. It's so hot when they bring it to her, the cheese is still bubbling. The crust burns her hands. After Nico's, Rosa's. She orders two slices and takes two to go. She realizes she's walked to Kaya's instead of her own apartment. Briefly, she thinks about going up, but it's late and she doesn't want Kaya to get sick of her. She is rationing herself. She eats another slice on a bench near Kaya's building. The night is frigid—frozen snow, red nose.

"Randy," Jane says with a full mouth as a rat runs past.

It's too cold to take off her gloves. Pizza stains the fingers. The sauce has lost its heat, turned thick and pasty. She feels like she's choking. She wonders if this might be something like what Jeremy felt earlier. The body taking over, erasing the mind. But she is not seeking pleasure—the release—even when she throws up in the toilet at home. It's more like she is cutting her own hair, taking a little from one side and then the other, trying to get the two sides in balance. But each time she takes off a little too much, and, at the end, she has balded herself.

When Jane wakes up, her throat hurts. She reaches for the glass of water she keeps by the bed. The glass is solid and cold from the room, and it has made the water cold. It's too harsh on her throat, which is raw and scratchy, and she wishes the water were a few degrees warmer. It is still dark outside, and cold, she knows. She can almost feel it from the color of the sky. She wants to skip her run, make coffee, sit on her bed, and read things on her phone until it's time to go to work. The coffee will feel good on her throat, and the words on her phone will float upward with the touch of her finger. But she had woken up with the feeling that something was wrong, that she had done something wrong. She waits for the shame to loose its hold on her, to realize it belonged to some dream, but then she remembers, and the dread she perceived, which felt like a heavy but lifeless presence, transforms into something restless and grasping. In her dresser, she finds clothes warm enough to run in.

Outside, it is dark still, and icy, and she runs fast in tight, sweat-wicking clothes and a furry band of fabric that covers her ears. The air hits her lungs like she is breathing hand sanitizer. It is early. The streets are mostly empty; occasionally, a bundled shape walking a dog. Trash trucks with young men in dark leggings hanging from the back. No sounds except gears shifting, the hydraulic cylinders compacting trash, dumpsters returned to the ground with a crash. She has been running for an hour already, and when she reaches her apartment, she doesn't slow down; she rounds the corner and keeps going. Her nose is running when she passes him. She sniffs at the wetness above her lip. She is slow. Her upper body is wilting. She is breathing heavy. She can hear it in the quiet morning, his lack of breath. She wants to tell him this is her tenth mile on no sleep, but she can't. Not only because she is already past him (looking hard at the ground so he can't see what effort does to her face), but also because that would break the illusion that they are the same.

At home, she straightens up her room, making her bed, throwing away a piece of tinfoil dotted with hardened cheese, pushing it down under the Q-tips, strands of hair, discarded Post-it notes. There is a smear of tomato sauce on the shirt she was wearing last night. She washes it in the sink, scrubbing with soap and her hands, stretching out the stained area until the discoloration disappears and the fabric is translucent with water. She wrings it out over the sink until not a single drop emerges, then hangs it over the laundry hamper in her room. With that task completed and her bed made and her floor clean, she removes the plastic bag from her small trash can and ties it in a knot. After listening to make sure she can't hear her roommates outside her door, she walks quickly and quietly through their apartment, stops at the front door to listen for neighbors, then walks quickly and less quietly to the trash chute at the end of the hall. When she reenters her bedroom, it feels like a metal coat is falling off her shoulders.

On the subway, she plays a word scramble, two geography puzzles, and then a mini-crossword, which she tries to finish before the train gets to her stop. When she makes it, she thinks it will be a better day than it was yesterday, that she will be better.

At the office, they meet in the conference room with mugs of coffee and a plate of doughnuts because it is Miriam's birthday.

"Jane, will you take everybody through it?" Tom asks.

He is grinning from ear to ear. Jane catches Kaya's eye. Kaya touches her nose. This means not morning sex but coke, which she marks on her calendar with an illustration of a polar bear. She is cataloging Tom's moods and habits. Jane swallows the laugh bubbling in her throat. When she stands up, her heels sink into the rug.

For lunch, Jane eats a salad she brought from home and works on Rita. Tom has tested her code on Tumblr, and no one will be able to see when the posts were written. Jane has to write it, hide it, then lead people to it as if it's always been there. She and Jeremy have decided on Rita's soulbond: a ghost from a YA novel who solves her own murder.

> Noelle told me the strangest part of being dead was how she didn't know it. It felt like falling and then she woke up. I told her I've felt that so many times, I have no idea if I'm alive. It's dangerous for her to come visit me. I can feel she is unsafe and beg her to leave, but she says she has something to tell me.

Jane rereads sections of the YA novel lying on the floor of the break room, drafting a few more posts they might include on the Tumblr when they reveal it, texting with Jeremy and Kaya until Kaya comes and gets her for yoga. They spread their mats in the back corner and stretch, discussing work and then Tom, who has started writing to Kaya again. They eat large salads out of floppy containers at the Whole Foods salad bar and watch the couple from their class snipe about kombucha.

"If you had to have sex with him," Kaya says, pointing at the male portion of the couple, "would you do it from behind or the front?"

"Why do you do this?"

"Behind, right?"

"I don't want to have sex with him at all."

"But if you had to."

"Yeah, behind, I guess."

"Yeah. That's what I thought at first, but then I sort of pictured how his back looks in dolphin pose. It's so pretty. I'd like to look down on it."

"Well, if he was in dolphin pose, how would you be looking down on it? Oh, Jesus—you're making me picture this way too much."

"I think you probably look really lovely during sex," Kaya says. "Maybe a bit timid. Like a puppy biting someone's finger."

"Stop."

"Don't you ever think about what I look like having sex?"

Jane thinks of Kaya's back reflected in the mirror at Mika's. Her head lolled back. Sleepy eyes. "Flashes," Jane says. "Then I make it stop."

"You don't have to stop. I don't mind."

It's almost ten by the time they get to their neighborhood, but Jane doesn't really feel like going home, so she sits on the stairs of Kaya's building while Kaya gets her dog, and then they walk around the block together. Kaya's dog is strong, barrel-chested. He yanks Kaya toward cracks in the sidewalk, tree stumps, cockroaches, feral cats. A rat crosses their path, running nimbly across the broken sidewalk. He disappears somewhere near the stairs of a brownstone. The rat path—Kaya has been reading a book on rats—has never bothered them. It's oddly comforting to see rats at night, always the same route, just like Kaya and Jane. Only the dog seems to crave chaos.

"Randy," Kaya says, nodding at the rat's retreating back.

"And a good evening to you, sir," Jane adds. "Give our best to your family."

At home, Jane showers and puts on an extra-large hooded sweatshirt that makes her feel like she is disappearing. In bed, she scrolls through the internet contrapuntally. Instagram. Twitter. Comedians riffing on a meme. Picture of a drowned child. Effortful commentary by someone with forty followers. Offhand joke by someone with three million. Edith Dellman. Jeremy. Pretzel. Chocolate. A man announces his wife has died. A video of a fat baby playing with a bunny. A writer announces he is one year sober. An influencer makes coasters out of lobster crates. Edith Dellman. Jeremy. Tortilla chip. Milk Dud. Thinspo. Body positivity. Salty. Sweet. Tenant unions take over vacant houses. A photo tour of a church converted into an Airbnb. Edith. Jeremy. Lit Twitter. Film Twitter. Snapchat. WhatsApp. Edith. Jeremy. Twitter. Twitter. Twitter. Jane feels like a flat line.

She decides to focus on Rita for a while. She works on a few cryptic tweets from the ex; a post by the Brooklyn dad about how his children miss her; some more for Rita's Tumblr. When she's done, she sends it all to Jeremy to see if he has any notes. They hadn't talked about the whole shape of the Tumblr, but Jane thinks he will like what she's doing. She closes her computer but then opens it again and starts clicking on each of Rita's new followers, all the new people—mostly young women—who are trying to find her. After she puts her laptop away, she runs the water for a shower and throws up until she feels hollow.

When Jane wakes up, her throat hurts. She reaches for the glass of water she keeps by the bed. The glass is solid and cold from the room, and it has made the water cold. It's too harsh on her throat, which is raw and scratchy, and she wishes the water were a few degrees warmer. It is still dark outside, and cold, she knows. She can almost feel it from the color of the sky. She wants to skip her run, make coffee, sit on her bed, and read things on her phone until it's time to go to work. The coffee will feel good on her throat, and the words on her phone will float upward with the touch of her finger. But she had woken up with the feeling that something was wrong, that she had done something wrong. She waits for the shame to loose its hold on her, to realize it belonged to some dream, but then she remembers, and the dread she perceived, which felt like a heavy but lifeless presence, transforms into something restless and grasping. In her dresser, she finds clothes warm enough to run in.

Outside, the air hits her lungs like she is breathing hand sanitizer. Jane runs fast, except she slows down around corners, because she has run into too many people, and it seems to her that her body remembers now even when she forgets, as if it retains somewhere inside it the memory of slamming hard into another person, the bloody knees and the guilt, picking someone up off the sidewalk with palms torn from concrete, too tender to close properly around the outstretched hand. Though as she rounds a corner to turn toward the river, both her mind and body forget, and she has to leap out of the way of a man and his dog. The dog lunges at her, the man yells at his dog, and Jane says sorry and runs even faster so she can reach the jogging path.

Her nose is running when she passes him. She sniffs at the wetness above her lip. She pretends not to notice him. She picks up her pace, her knees. Her back is straight. She looks like she never gets tired.

"Hi," he says, but she is already past him.

At home, she straightens up her room, throwing away the empty bags of pretzels, chips, the box for the Milk Duds. She pushes it all down under the Q-tips, strands of hair, discarded Post-it notes. There is a smear of chocolate on her pillow, and she realizes she must have dropped a Milk Dud and it melted there from the warmth of her body as she slept. She washes the pillowcase in the sink, scrubbing with soap and her hands, stretching out the stained area until the discoloration disappears and the fabric is translucent with water. She wrings the pillowcase out over the sink until not a single drop emerges, then hangs it over the laundry hamper in her room. She changes the sheets, from green to light blue. Her hamper is stuffed with bedding. She has to go to the laundromat. With her bed made and her floor clean, she removes the plastic bag from her small trash can and ties it in a knot. After listening to make sure she can't hear her roommates outside her door, she walks quickly and quietly through their apartment, stops at the front door to listen for neighbors, then walks quickly and less quietly to the trash chute at the end of the hall. When she reenters her bedroom, it feels like a metal coat is falling off her shoulders. A brief communion with the sacred clean. She yearns to stay standing where she is.

She takes a long shower. She gives a presentation at work. She eats salad out of Tupperware at her desk for lunch. She walks with Kaya to get coffee. She texts with Jeremy. She tweets, posts pictures, sends messages, screenshots, links. She works on Rita's Tumblr:

> *Last night, Noelle came to me in my dreams. She was running from something.*

She walks to yoga with Kaya. She falls doing an arm balance. She wipes her yoga mat down with a wet cloth. She eats at Whole Foods. She walks Kaya's dog. She says good night to Randy. She stops at a corner store on the way home. She texts with Jeremy. She sends him a picture of her breasts, then deletes it from her photos, along with the thirty she took trying to make them look good. He calls her to tell her he's coming. She puts on an extra-large hoodie that makes her feel like she is disappearing. She eats. She throws up. She brushes her teeth and keeps eating.

When Jane wakes up, her throat hurts, and she reaches for the glass of water she keeps by the bed. Outside, it is dark still, and cold. Snow makes the path narrow, and he steps out of the way so she can pass, jogging in place.

"I'm Aaron," he says, and she smiles as she runs past him, looks back once over her shoulder.

At work, she reads Rita's DMs. Where are you? Are you safe? What happened to you? Were you on the L train on Saturday night around 11? I feel like I know you. I feel like you are me. I feel like you need me. And @theblessing, who claims he killed her, writes about it in great detail, how he stalked her from the subway station, how he followed her for three weeks before he grabbed her, pushed her into a small park, hedges four feet tall around a green space. How he slapped her after he stepped in dog shit. How beautiful she looked when she finally stopped talking.

He writes every day. The way he kills her changes, but there are a few versions he returns to again and again, a few details he never alters. The dog shit and the way her cheek bloomed red where he hit her. The way he had never noticed before how her bangs hid her large forehead. They've decided not to block anyone so they can measure engagement more accurately, so Jane reads a new message from him every day.

At lunch, she eats salad out of Tupperware. Jeremy emails her some new content for Rita. It's different than they discussed. He's changed what she sent him for Rita's Tumblr. Her head feels squeezed, her chest heavy.

Did you not like it? she texts him. I thought you liked the soulbond concept.

No, it's great. But it's all very high-school-girl-doesn't-know-herself. Not the most interesting on its own...

What you sent me doesn't sound very much like her.

Exactly, right? A series of projections depending on who the audience is.

Who's the audience?

Exactly.

He calls her then, talks fast. She can almost picture him pacing around his small room, perhaps walking up and over the bed. She's very aware that she doesn't understand why he's excited and that it feels like he's been cleaved from her, so she doesn't know what he wants—more Tumblrs, more accounts, deleted tweets emerging from somewhere, Rita looking for herself before the world started looking for her. What interests him is not Rita, she's only language spread across technological platforms—and at the center, an absence, only the different ways she presents herself—but a new way to think about form and function and what it means to construct one-self and what it means to be a reader, encountering pieces of her that have been constructed but that are separated in place and in time.

"That sounds very interesting," Jane says carefully. "But it's hard for people to connect to an absence."

"No," he says, "people do it all the time."

"No," she says, "only for a little while."

The silence extends. She doesn't remember ever having a silence like this with Jeremy.

"Well, if you want Edith Dellman to play her in a movie," she says finally, "Rita has to be more than an absence."

"I don't care about a fucking movie."

"Oh, it seemed like you did, kind of."

"You don't get it," he says, which makes her feel lost in black space.

"Well, you did hire us."

"Because I want to write, and that's only possible if someone eventually pays me more than a thousand dollars for something that took three years of my life. Some writers pay to get their MFAs. Some spend their money on contests or conferences, hoping someone who matters will notice them. This seemed like a better use of my money."

"Okay, I'm sorry. I get it."

"It's fine."

"Really, I do," Jane says. "With Rita. It's like that Bob Dylan movie with all the different actors playing him."

"Right," Jeremy says, and she is relieved to hear the thrill come back into his voice. "Right, but now there's nothing holding it all together. Not the medium of the movie—or two hours of time—because different people are going to see different parts of her at different times and take different paths to see her. Part *I'm Not There,* part *Hopscotch.* Part something new, hopefully."

"But we're holding it together. It's still made by us. And Jack Dorsey, I guess."

"Are we holding it?"

"Aren't we?"

"I don't know. Maybe we're all Antonionis now. Well, lesser Antonionis. Taking someone else's story and putting a murder in it."

Kaya Slacks to see if she wants to get coffee, but Jane says no because Kaya might see her. And @theblessing has written again: I wish I had kept your body. There are four croissants in the break room, and Jane grabs three of them and puts them on a plate. When she sees Miriam coming down the hall, she veers toward Kaya's desk, but as soon as Miriam passes, Jane returns to the empty conference room and eats the croissants sitting cross-legged on the floor under the table. Her fingers are oily. Crumbs fall and stick in her sweater tights. She brushes at them, but they break apart into smaller pieces. She picks each crumb out. When her tights are finally clean, they are crooked, snaking diagonally over her shins. She can't get them straight; she pulls them, tread by tread, into a line, follows it with her finger from ankle to midthigh, where the tights become hidden by her skirt.

Kaya is putting makeup on in the bathroom. "Guess who I heard from again last night?" she says. Without waiting for an answer, she asks, "What do you think his wife is like? Weird that we've never met her."

Kaya examines her eye shadow and shakes her head, wets a small piece of paper towel. Jane's so uncomfortable, she feels like she might explode, like monsters in movies. Gunk on the walls. No center. Kaya is putting containers of makeup back into a small pink bag. Jane concentrates on keeping her face impassive. When the door to the bathroom opens, she can feel tears behind her eyes, and when the building's housekeeper pushes her cart into the room, Jane knows she is going to cry, so she tells Kaya she's late for a phone call and rushes from the room. At her desk, she finds the Tupperware she used for her salad. Crouching behind the table in the conference room, she empties herself into it. She seals the red plastic top around the edges and runs back to her desk for her bag. Back in the conference room, she carefully retrieves the Tupperware from underneath the table, balances it in the bottom of her bag, returns to her desk, fits her earbuds in her ears, selects music, pulls on her gloves, and leaves the office. At a small park, she sits on a metal bench. When she is sure no one is looking at her, she discards the Tupperware in a garbage can, leans back on the bench, and turns her music up.

When Jane wakes up, her throat hurts, and she reaches for the glass of water she keeps by the bed. Outside, it is dark still, and cold. Snow makes the path narrow, and he steps out of the way so she can pass, jogging in place.

"Jane," she says, and he smiles.

At the office, she tweets, posts pictures, videos, screenshots, links. She works on Rita's Tumblr. They want to reveal it soon, and it has to be complete when they upload it. She plays around with the ideas Jeremy sent her for a while. Then she deletes them and writes:

> *Last night Noelle told me the story of how she died. There were things she had never told anyone, she said, but then her face turned pale, and she went silent. "You can tell me," I said. "I promise." But she said it wasn't safe.*

She reads Rita's DMs. Were you on the 6 train on Saturday night around 11? I feel like we belong together. And of course, @theblessing—dog shit and the way her cheek bloomed red where he hit her. The way he'd never noticed before how her bangs hid her large forehead. She eats salad out of Tupperware at her desk. She walks to the coffee shop with Kaya. Their ears burn from the cold. The drummer laughs at something Kaya says. Jane loses her balance doing crow. Her chin hits the wood floor. They eat dinner at the Whole Foods salad bar. She has sex with Jeremy on his desk looking at the Post-its on the wall.

"'Do the work, asshole,'" she reads, and he looks up from where he'd been licking the sweat off her shoulder and laughs. It feels better than his mouth.

They lie in bed looking at their phones.

"Here," Jeremy says.

He's typed out some ideas for upcoming tweets for a few characters. Some verbatim, some general themes. The ex, the dad, her best friend, Sophie. The ex's tweets go on and on. The dad a mix of social justice–themed threads and quippy observations about parenting. Jane feels both distress and admiration. It's perfect; it's exactly what a forty-something Brooklyn dad would retweet, down to the earnest platitudes and self-owns. Jeremy is getting better at the internet.

None of them mention Rita except Sophie.

"What is this?" Jane asks.

"It's been months. They can't tweet about her all the time. It doesn't make sense anymore."

Jane can see it unfold, how Rita will disappear again without explanation, absented from her own narrative. "What about yesterday? You said you wanted all this new content from her."

"Right. From her from before. Other people move on."

"People are probably going to want something concrete soon."

"People are probably going to be disappointed."

Jane feels tenuous. It was her idea, the whole Twitter mystery, and now he's telling her she's doing it wrong. He goes to his desk, pulls out his notebook, fills one page, rips the paper from the seam, balls it up, drops it in the trash, and comes back to sit with her on the bed.

"In a classic detective story," he tells her, "the reader is led to believe if you can find the clues, you can find the answer. But everything you encounter is a clue—has meaning—because it's been designed that way, with a few red herrings dropped in to keep you guessing. But it doesn't transfer—if everything were a potential clue in real life, you'd go mad. Except the internet is kind of like that. Link after link after link after link."

"I find things on the internet all the time."

"Sure. We find things on the internet sometimes, just as in real life we sometimes find Ritas, and we sometimes find out who killed them. But these people—they don't want to find her; they want to be looking. But not even really looking, because it's a path we designed. They want to walk on it and see something interesting."

"It's not a path, it's a hole."

"Either way," Jeremy says.

"No. The depth is important," she says. Here but not here. Jane but not Jane. The sacred clean. "The feeling that there's something under, a truth you can't quite reach."

"You're right," he acknowledges, pulling a small bag of weed out of his bedside dresser. "You're right."

"You know some people really do want to find her."

He lights his pipe, shrugging.

"People aren't going to like this," Jane says.

"Some, maybe. But some will, because it's more true."

"No, not the people who are following Rita."

"How do you know?"

"Because I know who's following her. It's my job, and they're not going to like it."

"I don't care what people like," he says. "I don't write fantasies."

When Jane wakes up, her throat hurts, and she reaches for the glass of water she keeps by the bed. They smile at each other at the place where the sidewalk narrows. Aaron yells something at her, but she has her headphones on, and she is too afraid to look back and ask him what he said. She straightens her room, gives an update at the office. She works on Rita's Tumblr:

"I know who killed me," Noelle told me yesterday. "Who?" I asked, but she wouldn't answer. "You have to be careful" was the only thing she would say. "Am I dead?" I asked her, because maybe that was why we came to know each other. She laughed. All day, I kept putting my hands on things to make sure I could touch them.

She works on some new characters that Jeremy didn't write. An eyewitness whose memory suddenly revealed something before unseen. Rita's college counselor. A manic rant by her ex that is not what Jeremy gave her to post. Then she works on some of his new projects. She spends a few hours creating a screenshot of Rita's now-defunct LiveJournal. Rita in middle school, earnest and afraid. Then back to the backpack that might be Rita's. Her Tumblr. Someone writing strange eulogies on her Instagram. Sometimes when Jane is scattering pieces of Rita over the internet for people to find, she feels like a high-fashion photographer cutting women into sections. An eye here. A calf there. The suggestion of an ass.

She walks to the coffee shop with Kaya. Their ears burn from the cold. Jeremy texts her:

??????

But she doesn't write him back.

They go to happy hour at Mika's. Billy makes them a drink that he sets on fire. And then one with chili pepper on the rim, pieces of jalapeño. Variations on a theme. Kaya leaves, but Jane decides to stay for one more. A Bloody Mary so spicy her eyes water, which is why she is not sure when she first sees him whether it is him. She feels heavy and light at the same time. Blurry. She wipes at the wetness on her cheeks.

"Hi," he says. "I always wondered if I'd ever see you anywhere other than Twenty-First Street dodging trash cans and snowdrifts."

"Free chips. That was the key. You would have found me a lot sooner."

"I'm Aaron," he says.

"I know. I'm Jane."

"I know. Can I buy you a drink?"

"Sure."

He sits down next to her and signals to the bartender, who doesn't see him.

"I cut an imposing figure," he says.

He is tall and skinny, his back bent slightly forward like he is used to talking to people much shorter than he is. He looks like he won high-school track meets and was afraid to talk to girls until he turned twenty-three.

"You really like to run," she says.

He waves his hand again. "No. Just punishing myself. You?"

"Same. Heré, let me."

Billy rushes over.

"Girls," Aaron says.

She likes the idea of it, and she doesn't want to harm this version Aaron has of her, but she figures it will become apparent in minutes how she was able to get Billy to rush over.

"He's kind of dating my friend."

"Maybe," Aaron says.

And for a second, she thinks, *Maybe,* too. As if they are in a reality-TV competition but instead of cakes or clothes, they're making up different versions of the world, and the winner is the person who believes in theirs more. She feels her version flicker at the edges.

"What can I get you?" Billy asks, and then, because it is Aaron's world now, even though Kaya is not around, he says flirtatiously, "No, wait, I have something perfect for you."

"Two," she says, holding up two fingers and wiggling them in front of her face.

Billy glances at Aaron and smiles.

"Stay out of the bathroom," he says, selecting a bottle of gin from a high shelf.

At home, she pulls on an extra-large hoodie that makes her feel like she is disappearing and finds the package of Doritos she bought at the corner store. It opens with a pop she's afraid her roommates might hear. She pulls up a show on her laptop and eats under the covers, licking the Cool Ranch powder from each chip so it's soft and quiet when her teeth bite into it. Her phone buzzes from the pile of clothes on the floor and she falls trying to find it, thudding and laughing, her nose in fabric as if she is a kitten.

Run together, maybe? Aaron has written, and it will be a terrible day to run with him, hungover, belly full.

She sends him a GIF of Lola running and throws up in the toilet, imagining for a second when she sees her hair out of the corner of her eye that it is pink. In the mirror, she looks at herself from the side, the front, over her shoulder. She eyes her stomach and takes a piece of it in her hand to see if it feels as big as it looks. But she can't tell. She wonders, as she often does, how she can be both hyper-visible and invisible to herself at the same time, which makes her think of Rita, her follower count ticking ever upward, her presence spreading over the internet as she becomes harder and harder to find.

When Jane wakes up, her throat hurts, and she reaches for the glass of water she keeps by the bed. Outside, it is dark still, and cold, and she runs fast in tight, sweat-wicking clothes and a furry band of fabric that covers her ears.

The air hits her lungs like she is breathing hand sanitizer. It is early. The streets are mostly empty; occasionally, a bundled shape walking a dog. Trash trucks with young men in dark leggings hanging from the back. No sounds except gears shifting, hydraulic cylinders compacting trash, Aaron's footsteps on the pavement. He speaks easily as they run about his siblings, because she asked him about his family. He has a younger sister who sends him music and an older sister who buys his jeans. Jane laughs but after the run, they go to his apartment, and he shows her a picture from high school. She tips over on his bed, clutching his phone to her chest, laughing at the dark wash of his jeans—so stiff they look shellacked—and admits it's better his sister buys his pants.

He cooks her breakfast, and Jane is nervous, because it suddenly seems risky to have a date that starts early on a Saturday morning, since there is no clear ending time. But after breakfast he suggests a walk in the park, and then a matinee, and then drinks, and then burritos from a place Jane has never heard of but Aaron talks about for the full twenty-five-minute walk from his apartment. The burrito is warm and heavy in her hand and comes up quickly in the restaurant bathroom, and they drink from cold bottles of beer. Then it is Sunday afternoon, and they are still together, and Kaya is texting her over and over, saying:

!!!!!!!!!!!!

So they meet Kaya and Billy for dinner. Aaron pulls on a pair of jeans his sister bought him and a pair of sneakers—the same brand he runs in, but old and gray, which suggests he is still picking out his own shoes. Jane feels a small tug on her heart she doesn't recognize but that makes her lean over and grab his hand. He looks startled, then pleased, and they sit on his floor holding hands until he has to take one back to finish tying his sneakers.

In the bathroom at the restaurant, Jane tells Kaya about her weekend while Kaya pees. It's easier, somehow, to tell her about it all with her behind the closed door.

"We've spent, like, the last thirty-six hours together."

"That's great," Kaya says. "He seems great."

"I don't know, maybe he's getting sick of me."

The toilet flushes and Kaya emerges from the stall.

"Sure seems like it," she says.

After dinner, Aaron says, "I know now is the most natural time to end our epic first date, but maybe we should lean into it and do one more thing."

"Okay," Jane says.

"What do you usually do on Sunday nights?"

"Work. What about you?"

"Watch a show, probably."

"We could start——" she begins but stops because it might imply something that continues into the future.

But Aaron is already saying yes, and they are back in her room, lying on her bed, with her laptop propped on Aaron's chest, and then they have closed the laptop and placed it on the floor and he is climbing on top of her, and then they start the show again and almost make it through this time, and then, after, they rewind a bit to the part they remember and finish the first episode.

At the elevator, Aaron says, "I'm not an episode-a-week kind of guy. You should know that about me. So I'd say Wednesday is the absolute latest we should wait to get together and watch the next episode."

"Wednesday would be okay."

"Wednesday, then?"

"Yeah."

In her room, she texts Kaya, paces. She just needs Kaya to review what happened and assure her he really is planning to see her Wednesday and that it wasn't just a ploy to get out of the goodbye without any drama.

She can't sit still so she puts her running clothes on and goes outside. It is dark and cold, and she runs fast in tight, sweat-wicking clothing and a furry band of fabric that covers her ears. The streets are mostly empty. The air hits her lungs like she is breathing hand sanitizer. She runs for an hour, is winded when she reaches the corner store. She puts on an extra-large hoodie that makes her feel like she is disappearing and scrolls the internet contrapuntally, Aaron, Jeremy, Aaron, Jeremy, pretzel, Milk Dud, pretzel, Milk Dud, Rita, Noelle, Rita, Noelle, snip-snip, bald, bald, dog shit and the way her bangs hide her too-big forehead. I feel like I need you. I feel like you need me.

When Jane wakes up, her throat hurts. She reaches for the glass of water she keeps by the bed. The glass is solid and cold from the room, and it has made the water cold. It's too harsh on her throat, which is raw and scratchy, and she wishes the water were a few degrees warmer. It is still dark outside, and cold, she knows. She can almost feel it from the color of the sky. She wants to skip her run, make coffee, sit on her bed, and read things on her phone until it's time to go to work. The coffee will feel good on her throat, and the words on her phone will float upward with the touch of her finger. But she had woken up with the feeling that something was wrong, that she had done something wrong. She waits for the shame to loose its hold on her, to realize it belonged to some dream, but then she remembers, and the dread she perceived, which felt like a heavy but lifeless presence, transforms into something restless and grasping. In her dresser, she finds clothes warm enough to run in.

Outside, the air hits her lungs like she is breathing hand sanitizer. Jane runs fast, except she slows down around corners, because she has run into too many people, and it seems to her that her body remembers now even when she forgets, as if it retains somewhere inside it the memory of slamming hard into another person, the bloody knees and the guilt, picking someone up off the sidewalk with palms torn from concrete, too tender to close properly around the outstretched hand. Though as she rounds a corner to turn toward the river, both her mind and body forget, and she has to leap out of the way of a woman and her dog. The woman glares at her, the dog barks, and Jane says sorry and runs even faster so she can reach the jogging path.

Her nose is running when she sees him.

"Oh, hi there," he says.

"Oh, hi."

They jog in place. He reaches over with his gloved hand and wipes her nose.

"Wednesday, right?"

"Yeah," Jane says, "Wednesday," and then she walks a little closer to him. It feels almost like she is being pulled, and she looks down to see if he's tugging her over, but he is not.

On the subway, she plays a word scramble, two geography puzzles, and then a mini-crossword, which she tries to finish before the train gets to her stop. When she makes it, she thinks it will be a better day than it was yesterday, that she will be better.

At the office, they meet in the conference room with mugs of coffee and a plate of croissants and fruit, because Jeremy is here.

"Jane, Jeremy," Tom says, his mouth full of apple. "You've really done something here. We have crossed into something big. You should both be really proud of what you've accomplished. Jane, you got some stuff to tell us about it?"

She smooths her skirt by rubbing her palms down her thighs three times, then she stands up, smiling. Her heels sink into the rug. She leads the team through the latest: engagement metrics, a new YouTube production.

After the clip plays, Tom says, "Who are they?"

"They go to NYU," Jane says.

Tom touches the eraser on his mechanical pencil to his lip.

"What do we do with it?" he asks.

"Leave it," Jane says.

"But it's different."

"Yeah," Miriam chimes in. "The tone is—is the tone right?"

"I'm not sure I like what they've done with Rita."

"It's not about Rita anymore," Jane says. "It's about what people do with her. We have to see what people do."

"But we want to make sure Rita stays someone people want to follow, right?" Miriam asks. "Do we want to follow that girl?"

"What do you think, Jeremy?" Tom says.

Jeremy turns his face away from the wall where the final image of the web series is stilled and finds Jane.

"Jane knows what she's doing," he says.

After the meeting, Jeremy follows her to her workspace.

"So," he says. He walks toward her, and she backs into her desk. He puts his hand on her waist, then takes it off when he remembers where they are. "Someone's making a web series, and you're writing your own characters now?"

"Well, you said no one was holding it together, right? That means I can add characters."

He laughs, shaking his head.

"Fair. More than fair. I'm impressed. I liked what you did. Well, the third time I read it, and I wasn't so pissed at you anymore."

"You did?"

"I really did, and if you want to do more like that, I'm in. But, Jane, they can't find her."

"I know. She's gone."

Jane eats salad from a Tupperware, tweets, retweets, likes, watches, edits, posts, replies, forwards. She messages Kaya, Jeremy, Aaron. She works on Rita's Tumblr:

> *Hey. Do any of your soulbonds ever ask you to do things that*
> *hurt you? I mean, Noelle is not trying to hurt me, but lately, it's*

*been a lot. I feel weak when I wake up in the morning, keep
finding bruises.*

Rita in middle school, a poem about mermaids and the rain. The effort
is painful for Jane to witness. The Brooklyn dad posts in support of an
affordable-housing development slated for their neighborhood. The ex retweets
a singer-songwriter who's playing in a local bar. The best friend, Sophie, is
organizing an event at Hunter, not a memorial, but not not a memorial either.
Rita's DMs flood in, and Jane reads them until Kaya comes for her, and they
put on their coats and gloves and walk to get coffee. Usually, she and Kaya talk
about work on their walk, but today they talk about Aaron. Jane can't look at
Kaya, because Kaya might see her. Something hot bursting at the back of her
throat. She can't stop describing the weekend, moments that have started to
look different with a little time put after them, the inscrutable tone of his texts.
And Jeremy, his hand on her waist—a relief, the words hot and streaming.
Jane's breath makes her scarf wet where she's wrapped it around her mouth.

"Just go with it," Kaya says. "You don't owe anything to either of them
yet."

"I don't know if I can do that."

"Don't feel guilty. Don't worry if they like you. Don't worry about who
you like more. It's too early for any of that stuff."

"But who do you like more?" Jane asks.

"Listen," Kaya says, pulling her hat farther down over her ears, "I don't
think you should be doing that yet. However, and for what it's worth, I like
Jeremy. But it seems like you two are always trying to impress each other."

"Is that bad, though? It's the beginning."

"I don't know. I'd be exhausted."

Kaya gets her for yoga. Amanda is teaching, and they love Amanda. She
is less earnest than the other teachers, and her classes are hard, but she never

seems like she is trying to make people fail, which they both agree Leslie does. In Amanda's class, Jane's arm balances have gotten longer and steadier. Sometimes she's sure she's never experienced progress like this before in her life. Today they have moved on to side crow, and Jane twists her abdomen and stacks her knees on her right arm. She feels sweat break out on her face like a sprinkler turning on, a few small sputters and then water everywhere. Her hair is heavy and damp where it rests on the back of her neck. Sweat drips down onto her mat, making it slick. Someone behind her falls. The sound echoes through the studio. Her arms tremble. Shake. Buckle. She comes down to child's pose. Jane loves the names of yoga poses, how simple they are, elemental. She has seen a happy baby roll with her legs in the air. She has seen a dog stretch its back, its nose pointed to the ground. She likes trying to bend her body toward animals and babies. It makes her feel connected to the earth and to something ancient, which she doesn't say out loud, because she thinks it is probably cultural appropriation and maybe offensive.

They eat at the Whole Foods salad bar with their yoga mats rolled up by their feet. Kaya buys a small bag of Mexican wedding cookies and eats them with one leg pulled up on her chair, powdered sugar on her fingers.

The couple from their yoga class is not there.

"Where are they?" Kaya asks.

"Maybe they went out to eat an unexpected day last week, so they have an extra meal still ready to prepare."

"And, what, they are just going to go shopping on Tuesday now? It would still make sense to come today; the studio is next door."

"Maybe they're going out to dinner tonight?"

"In yoga clothes?"

"We're in yoga clothes."

"Okay, yeah, fair point. Plus, they seem like the type who might wear yoga clothes almost permanently. I bet he gets turned on by her sweat."

"Jesus, just once, could you not?"

"You know, with rats," Kaya says, "they aren't supposed to come out during the day. There are enough of them to blanket the city, to cover all the people like clothes. But if you see a rat during the day, it means the whole underworld has collapsed beneath us, and it's time to get the fuck out."

"Are you comparing them to rats?"

"I'm saying, when people like that change their routine up, something big has happened."

Jane's phone buzzes, and it's Jeremy asking if she wants to come over. Blood rushes to her face, and Kaya sees it even though Jane tried to keep her face neutral.

"Jeremy or Aaron?"

"Jeremy."

"You can go if you want."

Jane wipes at spilled salad dressing with a paper napkin. "I don't think I want to."

"Well, then say no."

"Is that okay?"

"You're so weird."

It's almost ten by the time Kaya and Jane get to their neighborhood, but Jane doesn't really feel like going home, so she sits on the stairs of Kaya's building while Kaya gets her dog, and then they walk around the block together. Kaya's dog is strong, barrel-chested. He yanks Kaya toward cracks in the sidewalk, tree stumps, cockroaches, feral cats. A rat crosses their path, running nimbly over the broken sidewalk. He disappears somewhere near the stairs of a brownstone.

"Randy," Kaya says, nodding at the rat's retreating back.

"And a good evening to you, sir," Jane adds. "Give our best to your family."

At home, Jane showers and puts on an extra-large hooded sweatshirt that makes her feel like she is disappearing. Aaron texts her.

I don't think I can wait till Wednesday to watch the next episode.

What were you thinking, like, you come over now?

I could come over now.

I was kidding.

Tomorrow?

Sure. I could do tomorrow.

You know, we could watch the second episode tonight—like together, apart. We might actually watch it that way.

Jane feels her body flame, is left with the feeling of something having caught inside her.

Okay.

Okay. Let's pause. Get snacks. Do you have popcorn?

Yeah. Why?

Because if we both eat popcorn, I can type, like, "Pass the popcorn," and it will be funnier.

Jane listens to the microwave whir, standing as far away from the machine as the small kitchen will allow. The kernels begin to pop, slowly and then in rapid succession. She worries her roommates can hear it. It seems unfair that after all her hiding, they will finally hear her late-night eating when she's not even hungry. The bag is bloated. It scalds her fingers. She places it on the bed next to her and pulls her comforter up over her legs.

Pass the popcorn, he writes.

Hey! Leave some for me.

Is that your hand on my knee? I thought you really wanted to watch this.

Stop. We are not doing that.

Doing what?

Watch the show.

Want some popcorn?

No, thanks.

What are you wearing?

Stop it.

It was an innocent question.

Fine, then. A hoodie and sweatpants.

Hot.

Shut up.

Shit, do you mind if we rewind a bit? I missed the last part.

PAY ATTENTION THIS IS IMPORTANT

Stop talking about your hoodie, then.

It's green. I've washed it so many times the string came out of the hood. I kept it, but I can't get it back in.

I bet I can do it.

Oh, yeah?

I'm pretty handy. Hoodie strings, tangled necklaces. You name it.

I need to hang a shelf.

I can show you how to get TaskRabbit on your phone. Oh, shit, what happened? Why are they in France? Can we rewind?

A few hours later she is bleary-eyed and thrilled, full of a nervous pleasure that feels carbonated, tiny bubbles popping inside her. She can't stop smiling, she can't sit down, and she is so happy, she thinks to herself standing over the toilet, so unbearably happy, and when she wakes up, her throat hurts, and she reaches for a glass of water.

IT'S THE INTERNET, JESSE

1

JANE MURPHY'S BODY WAS FOUND by a New York City Department of Sanitation employee at 6:30 a.m. on Wednesday, November 6, in an alley in Alphabet City. She was wearing running clothes and was folded over on herself behind a dumpster. There was dried blood on her head and also on the dumpster, but not on the corner where she was found. It was as though whoever killed her had dragged her to this new position not out of any real desire to hide where she had died or how but to delay—at least for a few hours—anyone finding her. The medical examiner eliminated the possibility that she had died from a fall. The angle and the estimated force with which the dumpster came into contact with her head ruled out tripping. The injury was on the back of her head, and the bloodied corner of the dumpster was slightly taller than she was. To make that contact by herself, Jane would have had to leap a few inches into the air while spinning around like a ballerina. Her phone, which everyone who knew her insisted she would have carried with her, was missing and the location-finding applications had been shut off. It was ruled a homicide, and approximately one month after her body was discovered, the police arrested Jeremy Miller for her murder. He retained the law firm of Nelson, Moretti, and Green and was released on bail the same day. Nelson, Moretti, and Green engaged the litigation support department of Thorton Investigation Services—and that's how I come in.

If you're wondering how I, Jesse Haber, became a modern-day private detective, it's a story as old as boy meets girl. Except in my case, it's boy wants to be a journalist and entire enterprise of journalism implodes while he's in college. Boy does okay at freelance and even manages to break a few great stories while supporting himself until boy's mom is diagnosed with early-onset dementia at fifty-six. Boy's mother—a former high-school vice principal—earns a pension of approximately forty thousand a year, with another two hundred a month coming from the Social Security benefits of her late husband, a pit piano player who died young (also boy's dad). Due to a variety of factors boy might have written about in his former life as a journalist, around the time of boy's mom's diagnosis, her modest two-bedroom in Yonkers was suddenly supposedly worth four hundred thousand dollars, making her ineligible for Medicaid (which would have paid for extended care and nursing homes) under both income-level and asset-based requirements.

Altogether, boy's mom has access to about two thousand dollars a month and health insurance, which seems like it should be enough, except that boy learns most health-insurance plans do not cover any kind of long-term care. Indeed, while good insurance will provide a home-health aide to come to your house daily if, say, you break an ankle or have to recover from an operation, it will do this only when there is a clear end date: Until your ankle heals. Until you no longer need help using the bathroom. If someone requires permanent assistance with the activities of daily living, like boy's mom as well as one in nine people over the age of sixty-five, your only options are to pay out of pocket, break your mom's ankle once every three months, or provide the assistance yourself. The estimated value of unpaid labor performed by caregivers for family members with dementia is $257 billion a year. That's another article I might have written in my old life, but instead of writing it, I moved back to my childhood bedroom in Yonkers and took a job with Thorton Investigation Services. They pay seventy thousand a year plus benefits. Between me and a home health aide who makes slightly-above-poverty wages through a service—while still costing the entirety of my mom's income and half of mine—we get it done. There's another article in those details, if you're wondering, which is similar to the story about the gap between day-care workers' incomes and the amount of money parents need to afford childcare. I did write that article, back in the day.

If you feel like you haven't heard that story yet, don't worry, you will. It will become an archetype, like rags to riches, man chases whale. The kind of plot that, no matter how tragic in its particulars, you experience like your favorite blanket being wrapped around your shoulders. Because it is that familiar.

The transition I'm describing was not an easy one for me. First, to be back in that childhood home. The memories I bumped into getting milk from the refrigerator or climbing into my old bed. How I scooted out of the way coming around a corner to avoid knocking into my mom—not this woman losing her mind who I shared a house with, but my mom, shoving a turkey sandwich into a bag while yelling at me to get my ass in gear for school. The shadow echo of that silent piano in the corner. Sometimes I couldn't hear over it. Sometimes, when my dad was in a show, I would go with him to rehearsals and sit in the back of the house doing my math homework as the theater hummed around me—instruments warming up in the pit, the hammering and sawing of sets being built, dancers walking around half naked while costume designers pressed sheer bits of fabric against their skin.

My dad liked to play piano, and he liked to read. My mother was an

English teacher, so she liked to read too, and I think that was something they must have loved about each other. There is a lot of time in a marriage. It's nice if two people like to sit quietly directing their attention at something else. And it's nice as an only child if that thing isn't always you. When my parents got married, my mom had been told she could never have kids, and I guess that was okay with both of them, but when she was twenty-seven, technology advanced and motherhood was suddenly possible for her. I don't know what the conversations were like, if my dad was happy or disappointed with the news that the woman he'd married could suddenly have children. It's not like my dad didn't act like he loved me, but he never showed particular interest in being my father. He did not want to guide me or mold me or be my coach at Little League. He didn't even want to teach me to play piano, but he would sit and talk to me for hours.

My mom loved being a teacher. There are people like that, people who are meant to be in schools, who love everything about it. The children, yes, but it's more than that. They love the hallways and the assemblies. They love coming up with new lesson plans, decorating bulletin boards, and participating in teacher talent shows. They love that whatever happens in world history or between two kids on a playground, there is always a way to sit down and help people see what they can learn from it. That was my mom. Her coworkers were surprised when she left the classroom, but when my father died, she decided she needed to make more money. Ironically, her higher salary only fucked us in the end—too much for me to get certain kinds of financial aid but not enough to pay for college; too much for Medicaid, not enough for her actual health-care needs. I wish I could go back and tell her to stay in the classroom.

The transition to being a Thorton investigator was painful, I won't lie. I'd wanted to write news stories for as long as I could remember. My childhood attraction to this vocation was a surprise to exactly no one. I was my mother's and father's son in a hundred ways. I had a roommate at Columbia whose mother was a translator, Romance languages. My roommate was fluent in Mandarin and Arabic, but he could barely say *hola, olá, bonjour,* or *ciao.* Not in my house. There was no rebellion of any kind. I read and wrote like my mom, and I played piano in the school orchestra like my dad, though I was never as good as him. I wish you could have seen him play. No one has ever had more fun than my dad had playing the piano. Certainly not me. There is a satisfaction that comes with writing. There is a feeling I get when I write the perfect sentence, when I break a story. I have sat in front of my computer working on an article about big-box stores and tax codes, finished a paragraph, stood up, pushed the chair away with the backs of my thighs, and said, "Fuck you, then," to the computer, feeling better than I have felt in my entire life. But fun? No, writing is not fun. Not the kind of fun my dad had. Sometimes I wish I were more like him, that he had wanted to open up that part of himself and pass it on. But mostly I'm happy he had so much fun before he died.

My lack of rebellion continued with politics. I was the son of a Jewish musician and a teacher who grew up reading Freire, and it showed. When I was a kid, my parents wrote letters to the editors of various publications and read them out loud to each other sitting on the front porch. My first letter to the editor of the *Yonkers Gazette,* written when I was twelve, is still framed over the fireplace at my mom's house. It was about how we should wait for proof of weapons of mass destruction. People in town called for my mom to be fired. Someone spray-painted our door. I cried, but my dad said that was far from the worst thing that had ever happened to him, and my mom said, "That's how you know you're right."

When I got into Columbia, I could tell my mom was proud, even though her official position was that Ivies were, on balance, toxic to education. But it's hard not to be swayed by architecture. Sure, there are perfectly adequate colleges with boxy buildings of perforated concrete and mirrored glass skins. I've never looked into it, but I have no doubt that some of our greatest thinkers were taught in Brutalist buildings like that. Still, it's hard to overstate what it feels like to be on a campus like Columbia's, with all its majestic buildings and history, the weight of it all. In every class, there could be a future president, secretary of state, editor of the *New York Times*. That guy that slept through the first semester before being expelled? He could be the next Jack Dorsey. His friend who got so drunk at parties, you went and stood near your female friends every time he approached them? The next governor of New York. You have to be pretty sure of yourself not to lose who you are in a place like that. The girl who sits in the front row and always talks with her hands—did you not understand her point about *War and Peace* because she's so smart or because it was ludicrous? The debate about the Spanish Civil War you had with a political science major at Lucy's birthday party—did he win because he was right or because you had six beers? Luckily for me, I have always been pretty sure of myself.

I knew becoming my mother's live-in caregiver would be challenging but I thought it would be for reasons I could imagine: moving back to my time capsule of a bedroom and to Yonkers, taking over my mom's finances. It was the cat food that eventually broke me. If you've never known someone with dementia, one of the hardest parts—for them, surely, it is the slow, terrifying deterioration of their brains, but I mean for the family members, for me—is the denial.

Sometimes I was able to put myself in my mom's place. To imagine what it must feel like to know you are getting confused, the defense mechanisms that would rush into the fray to make you feel safe and competent. For years, my mom insisted she was fine. And at first, there was often a plausible reason for lapses. She'd missed the gas bill because she'd had to get a new debit card and forgotten the account was linked to the old one on autopay. She'd forgotten about our dinner plans because she couldn't get the new calendar app to work. The cat looked skinny because he'd almost been hit by a car and since then, he'd lost his appetite. She was trying, she told me, but you couldn't force a cat to eat. Before I moved back home, I thought it was possible that a near-death experience could make a cat anorexic. What did I know about the inner lives of cats? Of course, when I moved in, it was immediately clear he was not being fed enough. The day I came home, there was no cat food in the house.

"I ran out this morning," my mom said.

I opened the garbage can. "There's no bag in here."

"I empty the bag into a plastic container."

"Where's the container?"

"I washed it and put it away."

An impasse. Was my mom's version of events possible? Of course it was, but I knew it wasn't accurate. I don't even think she was conscious she was lying. Her brain's reaction to its deterioration was to offer up an endless supply of excuses for memory loss. Any time she felt the slightest hesitation—*Do I remember that?*—her brain assured her she did or provided a hundred reasons why, if she didn't, it didn't mean anything. Even if the narrative her brain provided had to be that I was trying to trick her.

We bought another bag of cat food at the store. At home, I went to fill the bowl, but my mother stopped me.

"I'll do it."

"Okay," I said and watched as the kibble rained down into the bowl.

The cat appeared instantly from somewhere and ate so fast he choked.

"Guess he's over his trauma," I said.

"Guess so," she said, putting the cat food—in its bag—into the pantry.

She left the room, and I retrieved the bag and poured some more. Hearing this, my mom rushed back into the room. "He doesn't need any more food. I just fed him."

"He seems really hungry."

"Well, of course he'll eat whatever you put down. But you can overfeed a cat."

"I can see his ribs."

"He's always been like that."

She picked up the bowl and dumped the food back into the bag before she left the room.

For a month, I tried to secretly feed him, but my mom would hear the bag rustling from upstairs, swoop down, and snatch it from my hands.

He seemed hungry, I would try.

Or, *I was right here, and you were upstairs.*

Or, *I accidentally kicked the water bowl, and it got his food all wet and soggy. I was only replacing it.*

At which point, she would use my own techniques against me. "Where's the soggy food?"

"What?"

"The soggy food. Where is it? It's not in the trash."

"Garbage disposal."

"Hmm."

I started buying canned food, kept it in my sock drawer, opened it outside in the backyard at midnight. I know it sounds like a comedy, but it wasn't. I was stressed all the time. The cat became the site of our battle—for my mom, to control as much of her life as she could; for me, to take that away from her. I didn't do it to be mean—the cat was actually starving—but that is what I was trying to do, and we both knew it. About a month after I started living at home, the cat came in from outside with a bleeding gash across his stomach.

"He's fine," my mom said. "Cats fight."

She refused to let me take him to the vet. By then, anything I suggested, she had to shoot down on principle. My mom wasn't trying to hurt the cat, really, but the implication that she couldn't adequately care for an animal that pretty much cared for himself was so threatening to her, she couldn't yield. I called Lucy, desperate. She volunteered to come up and take my mom to get her hair cut. Somewhere fancy in the city; they'd have lunch afterward. My mom agreed because she'd liked Lucy since college. While she was gone, I took the cat to the vet, who determined he needed stitches. I called Lucy, practically crying. What could I do? My mom would notice stitches on the cat, the telltale shaving of his tummy. We decided we'd pretend he ran away. After the cat was stitched up, I took him into the city and left him with the doorman at Lucy's building. She kept him for three weeks while my mom and I canvassed the neighbors and put signs on lampposts. When the stitches had dissolved and his fur had mostly grown back, Lucy sprayed him with a hose, threw some dirt on him, and dropped him on the front step while my mom was asleep. He weighed more than he had in a year.

When I first moved back home, I continued freelancing. The week after the "missing" cat returned home, I interviewed at Thorton. When my first check cleared, I found a home-health-care agency online. They sent Gloria, a Lithuanian woman with grown children and twenty years of experience as a home-health worker. My mom thinks I hired Gloria to do light housekeeping and cooking because she's my friend's mother who fell on hard times after her husband died.

"We're mostly helping her," I told my mom at dinner. "But she'll also help with cleaning and grocery shopping, and I know you hate that stuff."

"I do," she said.

It's not like I don't have to bring a can opener out into the backyard to feed the cat anymore, but Gloria is very good at what she does. She has this way of getting my mom to shower or eat or take her medication without insinuating anything, which I think, because I was her son, we could never really escape. One day I'd like to write an article about Gloria and how she saved us. Headline: "Person Good at Incredibly Difficult Thing Has Significant Experience and Special Skills." Subhead: "Turns Out Not Any Warm Body Can Do a Thing Just Because You Think They Can." I think my mom would like that article. It would remind her of teachers.

But for now, to afford Gloria, I work in the litigation support department of Thorton Investigation Services. And while it's hard not to be a journalist anymore—or twenty-eight anymore or anything I thought I would be—and I had no idea the million tiny ways becoming a caretaker strips your identity away, and some mornings I wake up and I have no idea who I am, at least I can say, in this new life, I helped solve the murder of Jane Murphy.

2

JEREMY MILLER CAME TO THE OFFICE with his lawyer the day after he posted bail. I saw them through the glass of the conference room. His lawyer was a man in his early forties with curly brown hair. You could guess the cadence of his voice by the way his body occupied the chair. Both Jeremy and the lawyer were sitting across the table from Phil, my boss, who was taking notes on a yellow legal pad, stopping once in a while to ask a question. I walked by them on my way to the kitchen to get some free orange juice, and on the way back, Phil saw me and waved me in.

The first impression I had of Jeremy was of a person being crushed by the weight of gravity. He started the interview mostly sitting up and ended with his head on the table. I had the feeling this was related not so much to the line of questions but to his being profoundly hungover. He looked at my orange juice with angry red eyes and answered Phil's questions with his fingers pressed hard against his temples, as if he were trying to keep his head from cracking open. The interview lasted four hours. I followed Phil to his office and wrote down the projects he assigned me in a small notebook that I kept in my back pocket, a holdover from my journalism days. I filled three pages listening to him and pulled an all-nighter in my kitchen researching online and reading Jeremy's book. I'd heard of Rita—the woman missing on the internet—before taking this case and had seen a couple of articles and tweets, but I had not followed it closely. I wanted to get the gist of it before I met with Jeremy again. At three a.m., I heard a series of strange bumps coming from my mom's room, but I was afraid to go in and see what she was doing.

My second impression of Jeremy was that he seemed like the kind of English major I had wanted to punch at Columbia. We met, just the two of us, the following day and sat on the rooftop patio on the fortieth floor of Thorton's building drinking the free coffee I'd procured from the kitchen. I'm not sure if Jeremy had gotten over the shock, if he had decided to avoid alcohol the previous evening, or if, because we met at three, the hangover had simply worn off, but he was a different person than the one I'd met the previous morning. I didn't like this person very much.

"Let's go over some basic logistics first. How long were you and Jane dating?" I asked.

"Didn't we cover all this yesterday?"

"I'd like to go over it again."

He sighed and ran his hand through his hair. For a moment, I thought he might refuse or at least compel me to show him why this exercise was useful. I could almost picture him at a seminar table with Dr. Phelps, throwing his hand in the air and asking if he could play devil's advocate.

"I wouldn't say we were dating," he said.

It was an important clarification. The police had a few possible motives for Jeremy, one of them being that Jane had tossed him over for another man. The jealous-boyfriend story would be a lot harder to spin if we could show Jeremy's feelings for Jane were negligible. Still, there was something about the way he said it that put me off, as if he'd said that same phrase many times before for different reasons.

"What would you say?"

"We were hanging out."

"And how long had you been hanging out?"

"I don't know. Six months, maybe longer."

"What season did you start hanging out? Summer?"

"Umm, yeah. No. It was cold. Spring or late winter, maybe."

"So, more like eight or nine months?"

"Sure."

"When did you break up?"

"We didn't break up."

"Because you weren't dating?"

"Because we didn't stop hanging out. Not really."

I looked down at my notes, not because I'd forgotten what was there but to give him time to elaborate. He didn't.

"Well," I went on, "she starts posting pictures of another guy around the end of June. According to the police, you stopped seeing each other about then, at least for a while."

"For a bit, yeah. We stopped seeing each other and then we started again."

"And by 'seeing each other,' you mean . . ."

"What you think I mean." He leaned back in his chair and scanned the patio as if he were at a party and wanted to see if there was someone better to talk to. "'Their confidence is based solely on ignorance.'"

I capped my pen and placed it on the notebook in front of me.

"Listen, man, you're making me work too hard to help you." He was wearing mirrored aviators. When I looked at him, I saw only two of myself reflected back at me. "Why don't you explain why they're wrong instead of quoting Kafka at me?"

He stood up and walked to the edge of the rooftop patio. After a few minutes, when it was clear he was not returning, I followed him.

"It's stupid," he said when I was standing beside him, "because I was not jealous of Aaron." He bit on one of his thumbnails, not hard enough to break it. "If anything, Aaron was jealous of me. You should be looking at that."

"We are."

"Anyway," he said, "Jane told me she and Aaron weren't seeing each other anymore."

"When did she tell you that?"

"That last time I saw her."

"Which was when?"

He looked me straight in the eye for the first time that day. Or at least, his face was pointed directly at my face. It was hard to see where his eyes were with those sunglasses.

"You know the last time I saw her," he said.

"The bar. The night before she died."

"Right. Were you hoping I'd slip up and say *At the dumpster before I killed her?*"

"Well, they do have your cell phone near her place that morning."

"I already explained that."

"I know—you were writing. At six a.m. At a diner two or three subway transfers from where you live. Because the first thing I think of when I think of New York is too bad you have to ride the train for half an hour to find a good diner."

"I'd written there the day before when I'd slept at Jane's. It had gone well. What can I say? I'm superstitious."

"Right. So the last time you saw her?"

"Was at the bar. We talked about the bar for an hour yesterday. You were there, scribbling away."

He said the word *scribbling* like I was a five-year-old pretending to write real words with a crayon.

70

"Yesterday," I said, "I didn't get to ask my questions."

He turned away from me, stubborn and quiet. Sometimes silence is a good interview technique, but with Jeremy I had the feeling that if I let the silence build, he would simply spend those minutes thinking about all the reasons I was wasting his time, so I bit my tongue—actually, I bit the inside of my cheek as hard as I could—and pressed on.

"When she told you that she and Aaron had broken it off, did you ask why?"

"No."

"And that's not what the fight was about?"

When he turned his head back in my direction, the challenging posture was gone. His shoulders dropped into something else, something like help-lessness. It wasn't my question that had done it. It was the remembering—the fight, being there again, going over what he had said and what she had said and what he could never take back or do differently.

"I told you," he said. "I didn't have a problem with her seeing Aaron."

"What was the fight about, then?"

"Nothing."

"Nothing?"

"Nothing. To know Jane was to fight about nothing." He stopped. "Are you going to tell me I shouldn't say things like that?"

"That's not really my role. I'm only here for research. Your lawyer might tell you that, though."

"Have you ever known someone who died?" he asked.

"Yes."

"Murdered?"

"No."

" 'You could say that those who die such a death die more deeply.' "

When I didn't say anything, he said, "Marías."

He was glad, I could tell, that he'd quoted something I didn't recognize. It made him feel more solid. It irked me a little, to be honest. I was still proud of myself for recognizing the Kafka, but I had to acknowledge missing this one was probably better for the interview. He talked more when he got to explain things to me.

"What Marías didn't write about," Jeremy said, "is how when you're the one accused of killing that more dead person, they die even more. They die so much it's almost as if they never existed. No," he said, "that's not right," and he tried again, because he was a writer, after all, looking for the perfect analogy, the one that would most efficiently and effectively bring one person into the experience of another. Like falling down an elevator shaft and landing in someone else's body. "It's not like she never existed—Jane— but somehow that person, the Jane I knew, has nothing to do with what's happening now. That Jane disappeared. She disappeared a little when she died, like we all do. Not only the body, not only the pulse, but the person who had the capacity to act and speak and defy whatever you've decided they are—the version of a person that exists in service to your life. When a person dies, their resistance to that service falls away. Every memory with them, every exchange—it can be exactly what you need it to be, and they can't show up to challenge it anymore. I think that's what Marías actually meant when he said those who are killed die more deeply. Because every memory, every event, has to be read through the murder, to figuring out who and why. And that portion of the person who was just herself is diminished even more in service of the mystery.

"Once you're the accused, that person—the person they were before they died—essentially ceases to be altogether. I can't even remember her, because every memory, every event, it's not something she said or did, it's something that goes in the plus or minus column: suspicious or not suspicious, cause or effect. And so I understand why we have to do this. I'm not an idiot. But what can I tell you when I can't get anywhere near the Jane you're asking about, the Jane who used to wake up in my bed and call me back when I called her?"

A gust of wind blew sharp and howling over the patio. It was colder near the ledge; my cheeks felt raw. I pulled my jacket sleeves down over my hands. In my notebook, I remembered with a pang of guilt, I'd split Jane into columns.

"Do you mind if we go back to the table?" I said.

Jeremy did not seem cold, and he was not afraid of heights. He was leaning out over the edge, his body tilted toward the streets below. At first, I thought he hadn't heard me or was ignoring me, but then he pulled himself back and walked across the roof to the table we'd been sitting at. In my chair, I sat on my hands to warm them.

"What else?" Jeremy said.

"Not that much more," I assured him. "Were you seeing anyone else besides Jane?"

"When she died? No. At any time since I met her? Yes."

"Why weren't you seeing anyone else around the time she died?"

"There wasn't anyone else I felt like sleeping with, I suppose. I was writing a lot. It's hard for me to focus on anything else when I'm writing. I'm barely in this world. Every time I have to touch back down, it feels like an interruption. That world," he continued, "the world of whatever I'm writing, I don't think it's real. I'm not delusional. But it does feel more pressing, more immediate, really, than this world."

"But you still had time to see Jane?"

"It was different with Jane."

"Nine months is a good bit of time to be not dating someone."

"I guess. Like I said, it was on and off. At least part of the time, she was with Aaron exclusively. And then she wasn't. So we started up again.

I wasn't trying to imply earlier that our relationship was casual. In many ways, it was not. *Dating* still seems like the wrong word."

"Okay. Let's switch lanes. When you said the other world felt more pressing," I asked, "did you feel that way about hashtag Searching for Rita?"

"Well, Rita was different because I wrote that with Jane. I don't usually write with other people. But yes, in some ways, Rita is more real to me than a woman I might meet at a bar. I'd often rather spend time with her too."

"Did it hurt when Rita died, then?"

"She was always dead. We came up with the idea before we came up with who Rita was going to be. She only became more and more alive. All characters do for the writer. Even if I kill them."

I watched his face twist a little with some unpleasant emotion. Sadness? Regret? I couldn't tell. "I know I told you this isn't my job, but I'm going to go ahead and advise you to avoid using the phrase *even if I kill them* with anyone but me."

"Fair enough."

"Tell me more about working on the Rita story."

"What about it?"

"It must have been nice to have so many people so into what you were working on. Everyone loves it, everyone talks about it. Different from your book."

"A lot of people liked my first book."

"Yeah, sorry, I didn't mean to be insulting." I did. He seemed like the kind of guy who did not take criticism very well. I wanted to see how he'd react. "I know it was received fairly well critically, but most people never heard of it. Of course, you've sold another book now, as you alluded to. I saw the announcement. An auction. Congratulations."

"Thank you."

"But I also saw that a lot of people are worried your second book is going to be more like your first book and less like Rita."

"A lot of people?"

"On Goodreads."

"Ahh. 'All hope abandon, ye who enter here.' I don't pay much attention to those. My second book hasn't even come out yet, so those comments are hard to take seriously."

"Still. Must have been nice with Rita. Everyone's calling you a genius instead of saying, 'I hated this book' or 'I read this because of Rita, but don't waste your time.'"

He looked at me for a long while before answering. When he finally spoke, his tone was even.

"Not every book is for everyone."

"Sure."

"It was nice to write Rita, but not for the reasons you suggest. It was fun to try to make it work, to see what it was capable of. It was fun to collaborate with Jane."

"Word around Reddit is you and Jane had a falling-out about working together."

"That wasn't real."

"You and Jane were faking that? For what—more attention for the project or something?"

"No, it simply wasn't real. From the very beginning, the bios for Rita and Joshua, the detective figure, contained a link to my website where we explained the project. This did not always stop people from thinking Rita was real, but it was right there. All the other characters—there was always something too, maybe a pinned tweet or maybe the bio would set up a little chain through Linktree or something. You would get there eventually. It was a way to cordon off Rita's world but also a little game for the readers, to see who was real and who wasn't. Later, some people even tried to blend in, link themselves to the story, so we had to adapt. But that's how it worked at first."

"It linked to you. Not Jane."

"We set it up like that—Jane and I—because in the beginning, I was the one who wrote it. I came up with the mystery, most of the characters, and I even wrote their tweets exclusively. Jane would read them and tell me why they wouldn't work or how they could be better, especially if a character was meant to be very online. Then I would go back and edit them.

"But that didn't last. It didn't make sense to do it that way; she was so much better at the internet. She was so much better at understanding how people looked for things there, how they got lost there. Also, it was a lot of work, more than even Jane anticipated. We came up with a plan of how it would go, almost like chapters or episodes. One week, we had the characters tweet X, Y, and Z in a certain order. We let that ride, and then Joshua came in with a thread to help people connect things in case they couldn't do it on their own, and he set up the next twist. But there were so many moving parts because people responded in real time. If some random on the internet called the ex-boyfriend a liar and that started trending, well, he had to respond. That's the kind of person he was, so we had to write it. If someone came up with a fan theory and it got a lot of traction, same thing, Joshua needed to take it seriously.

"We experimented with me being the lead on certain characters, Jane the lead on others, but it was all pretty collaborative. I'd think about something, I'd run it by her. Sometimes I'd write something up and send it to her, and she'd just go ahead and translate it into Twitter. Other times, it was much more back and forth.

"Eventually, people started interviewing me. At first, Jane really didn't want anyone to know about her, so I didn't tell people about her. But the minute she felt okay about it, I began talking about her in the interviews. At some point, maybe about five or six months after Rita went missing, it became like a phenomenon. It had been buzzy, culty, but all of a sudden it was everywhere. *The New Yorker* wanted to do a profile, and I convinced Jane to do it. Well, me and Tom did. After the profile came out, though, there was this public perception that I had tried to hide Jane's involvement or that I was bitter that she'd taken on a larger and larger role. But it wasn't real. It was based on nothing."

"Maybe, but that's what people think. It'd be understandable if you were mad at Jane for making you the bad guy online. Especially if it wasn't true."

"She didn't make me the bad guy online. It was one of those things the internet makes up. She tried to correct it many times, explaining how she had asked not to be named at first. People didn't believe her."

"I'm not saying it would be rational if you were angry at her for something she didn't cause, but we can't always help when we resent people."

He didn't respond.

"The angle that a lot of people are going with," I said, "and I think we can assume the prosecutor will go with, is that there was some tension there. That you were angry Jane was trying to take on a bigger role in something you believed was your creation. That you wanted to put her back in her place."

"I didn't care about that," he said.

I gave him a skeptical look.

"I know it's going to be hard to convince people I don't care if they thought Jane was the author, or the real author, or did more than I did," he said. "They're not going to believe that I really mean it, because they don't understand what I'm trying to do."

"What do you mean?"

"So some people are saying I couldn't have done it without her. Fine—she couldn't have done it without me either. That's how it worked, and I'm fine with that because I don't have ownership feelings about Rita. I don't care about that stuff. I don't view authorship like that."

"Right," I said, and I wrote down, *Tell Phil to find an angle for the Rita story*. Because if, to win his case, Jeremy had to convince a jury to believe some theoretical argument about authorship, we were in trouble. "Let's go back to the fight the night before she died."

"I don't know what we were fighting about."

"That's not going to be a satisfactory answer to a lot of people. Imagine, for a moment, there's a young woman on the jury, and she hears you say that. Maybe she starts thinking about her own boyfriend who acts like he doesn't know what the problem is when she knows for a fact she's told him a hundred times."

"I thought it wasn't your role to make me likable."

"It's not about being likable. My role is to help provide answers that a jury will accept," I said. "You know how with magnets, if you try to push like poles toward each other, they're repelled?"

He nodded.

"You don't want to give the jury an answer where it feels like that. They have your answer, and they have what they'll accept. They're pressing them toward each other, but they won't go. There's a lot of energy in that space. It breeds suspicion."

He sighed and leaned forward in his seat.

"It's not my intention to be difficult," he said. "Don't you think I've tried to figure it out? Do you have any idea how many times I've gone over that night in my head? I can't sleep anymore, but I don't know what we were fighting about. It was fine and then it wasn't."

"If I asked one of her friends, do you think they would know?"

"I don't know. Ask Kaya. If she knows, she didn't tell me."

"Kaya Mitchell?"

He nodded. "But as far as I know," he continued, "it was fine and then I asked if she wanted to leave because it was getting late, and she said she didn't want me to come over. I was annoyed, because earlier, that had been the plan. That's why I was still there, waiting for her. If I'd known, I would have left already, or I wouldn't have come at all. So I said that, and she started yelling at me."

"Was that abnormal?"

He tipped his head back and forth a few times as if he were weighing something.

"She was frequently annoyed at me about something, but it often took a more passive-aggressive track. I'd say yelling at me at a bar in front of a bunch of people was very abnormal. Not that it had never happened before, but not often."

"What was she yelling about?"

"About my writing. About how I had to grow up. I was a boy even though I was almost thirty. That my writing wasn't as original as I thought it was, that I was just copying writers fewer people had heard of. Shit like that."

"Why?"

"Because she wanted to hurt me. It was a thing she did sometimes."

"Did it hurt?"

"Yes."

"And what did you do?"

"I told her I wasn't going to let her yell at me like that, and I left."

"Did you worry about her getting home?"

"No."

"Why not? She'd been drinking. It was late."

"She didn't die walking home from the bar. She died running the next morning."

"I'm aware of that."

"Well, I hope you are also aware that there were frequently three or four nights a week I didn't see Jane. It's likely that on those days she made a variety of decisions about what to do and where to go, including what bars to go to, how much to drink, and how to get home. She didn't become incapable of doing all those things simply because I was in the same bar as her."

"Sure."

"This sounds like a likability thing again."

"Not exactly."

"People—women—go home from bars by themselves all the time."

"Yeah, but Jane died."

"But that happened in the morning. It has nothing to do with going home alone at night. Or with me."

"Maybe. But the poles, the energy there is dangerous. Some people would rather believe you did it than believe you can go for a run and not survive it."

3

THE NEXT MORNING, I was sitting on a couch in Jane's apartment. The day had gotten off to a rough start. Gloria's bus had broken down, and she'd arrived an hour later than usual. My mom, who had gotten used to her presence, was now easily thrown off with minute changes in schedule. They usually went out for coffee together first thing, and today my mom paced around the living room, looking out the window every few minutes. I took my work to my bedroom and called Jane's parents. It went badly.

"Who are you?" her mother asked again. "Dan, Dan, someone who says he works for Jeremy is on the phone."

I wanted to hang up when I heard the way she called to her husband. But I didn't. I waited for her to pass Jane's dad the phone, and I let him yell at me.

"Don't you ever call here again, do you hear me? We have nothing to say about Jeremy Miller until the judge calls us to testify at his sentencing hearing. But even then, I'm not going to talk about him. I'm going to talk about Jane and how we lost everything that mattered to us. And, son, it's your life if you want to defend murderers, but if you ever call my wife again, I will come and find you. Do you understand me?"

I was shaking slightly when I hung up. It can sometimes go like that, but it didn't make it any easier. My phone rang in my hand. When I looked down, it was the number I'd just called.

"Hello?"

"Hello," Jane's mother said. "Is it you?"

"Yes. Yes, it is."

"And the horse you came in on," she said, then hung up.

"'The horse you came in on,'" I repeated to myself, walking into the living room. My mom was peeking through the blinds to see if Gloria might be walking up the street. "I don't even know what that means."

"It means go fuck yourself."

"Thanks, Mom."

Two hours later, Gloria and my mom were probably sitting in Starbucks, and I was seated in Jane's apartment about to talk to one of her roommates, her parents' words still playing on a loop in my head. I sat stiffly on the edge of the couch and looked around. A portion of the living room had been transformed into a bedroom with dividers that didn't quite reach the ceiling. A note taped to one of the makeshift walls read *If it's after ten, get out of the den.* Despite the improvised extra bedroom, the living room was large and comfortable, with expensive-looking furniture and an improbable number of plants. Jane's room-mate Rowan had gone to the small kitchen to make coffee. I could hear her fill a kettle with water, the whirring and thwacking of the grinder as it sliced through beans. She came back in and sat in a chair across from me as she waited for the water to boil.

"Thank you for talking to me," I said.

Rowan placed her socked feet on the ottoman in front of her chair, dragging the velvet into lighter and darker blues as she sought to get comfortable. I'd arrived unannounced. Usually, I made appointments, but sometimes the element of surprise was the best bet. It seemed to have been the right choice today. Rowan had looked startled when I explained who I was, but she stepped back to let me in without many questions. After the morning's phone call, startled but amiable was a blessing.

"Do you want to get started?" I asked. "Or do you want to wait to finish the coffee?"

"We can get started," she said. "I have class at ten."

"You're in school?"

She nodded. "MFA at Columbia."

"I was an English major at Columbia. I probably had some of your professors."

"Oh, cool," she said, and her smile relaxed but then her face grew confused. I sensed she was about to ask me what I was doing there. I had told her already—an investigator, working for the defense—but I could see she was trying to make sense of that information in relation to my degree.

"That's a commute," I said.

"Yeah. My sister lives down here. I thought I wanted to live near her first and then figure out where I wanted to live."

"Good idea."

"Yeah," she said, but she looked uncomfortable.

"Who's the green thumb?" I asked.

Her smile came back. They were hers. Even talking about them calmed her.

"Oh, that's me," she said. "I was afraid they wouldn't survive the move. I came from Ohio," she explained. "I shipped all my books and clothes and rented a minivan to drive my plants here."

The kettle shrieked from the kitchen, and she rushed to finish preparing the coffee. She was gone for a few minutes, and I found myself taking stock of the room—books piled on every surface, a stack of *New Yorker*s against the wall, wire crates filled with records. I wondered if any of it was Jane's.

Rowan returned to the living room with two cups of coffee just as the front door opened and another young woman came in wheeling her bike alongside her. Two bikes were already hanging from hooks in the wall behind the couch. She hoisted hers onto a wooden mount beside them. Altogether, they looked like an art installation. When she was finished, she looked at me and my notebook.

"This is Jesse," Rowan said. "He came to talk about Jane. This is Lydia," she told me. "She'll probably be able to tell you a lot more than I can."

"I'm very sorry for your loss," I said.

Lydia was taking off her raincoat and didn't answer me. She hung it from the handlebar of her bike and took a seat on the edge of Rowan's chair, where she removed a pair of rain pants, revealing dark jeans.

"Are you a reporter?" she asked.

Not anymore, I almost said, *and if I were, I would never have appeared at your door to ask you about your dead friend without calling first.*

"I'm Jesse Haber," I said, reaching into my pocket for a card. "I'm an investigator at Thorton Investigation Services. I work for the defense."

"For Jeremy?" she asked. Her eyes were intelligent; her face was defensive. I thought I'd lucked out when Rowan opened the door and took me in so easily. *The roommates must not think Jeremy did it,* I'd thought to myself as she led me to the couch with offers of coffee. But now I wasn't so sure. I braced myself for more hostility.

"Rowan never met Jane," Lydia said.

I glanced at Rowan, and she nodded.

"I took Jane's place—well, sort of."

For a moment, I felt stupid, and I could tell Lydia could see it too. In the back of my mind, I'd imagined walking into Jane's old room, that I would learn something by seeing her space. But this was New York. She'd been dead a month. Of course they would have had to rent her room out already.

Lydia picked her rain pants up off the floor and left the room. I heard a shower curtain being pulled back. A moment later, she returned with a hand towel that she tossed on the ground. She cleaned up the water and dirt tracked in from her bike by moving the towel across the floor with her foot.

"I am truly sorry to be here," I told Lydia, "and if you don't want to talk to me, I can leave. But if you think there's a chance that Jeremy didn't do this, anything you can tell me could help him."

"I barely know Jeremy Miller," she said.

Rowan looked back and forth between us, sensing she'd made a mistake letting me in.

"Jesse went to Columbia," she told Lydia.

"Oh."

"Lydia went to Columbia too," Rowan told me.

"Nice," I said.

"But I'm at NYU now."

"For what?" I asked.

"Law."

Damn it.

"That's great," I said. "What year?"

"First."

I nodded. Having known some law students myself, I'd noticed that in their first year, many of them felt a sense of solemnity about the law. Even if before they went to law school, they believed the criminal justice system was broken or that the law was primarily a tool for the powerful, the first year tended to dilute these feelings for a time as they became distracted by the structure of opinions, the glare of procedures, polished and gleaming and made perfect by the fact that they alone could understand them. It didn't happen to everyone, but I'd assume Lydia fell into this camp until she proved otherwise.

"Do you know what you want to do when you graduate?" I asked her.

"IP. Patents."

She didn't elaborate, but I could infer she hadn't gone to law school with a bent toward abolishing the patent. What this meant about her views on prosecutorial overreach or whether she believed Jeremy was guilty or not, I didn't know.

"That's really interesting," I said. "Patents, yeah."

Rowan was nodding encouragingly at how well our conversation was going. After checking her phone, she stood.

"I have to start getting ready," she said, but I could tell she wanted to stay.

"I understand. Thanks so much for your time."

"Right." Rowan searched Lydia's face for something. I don't know if she found it, but after a moment, she ducked into the makeshift bedroom, emerged with a see-through rain slicker with white edging, took one of the bikes off the wall, and disappeared into the front hall. Lydia and I looked everywhere but at each other as Rowan struggled to maneuver her bike through the narrow entryway. After I heard the front door close and the dead bolt reengage, I turned back to Lydia and smiled.

"Do you mind if I ask you a few questions? I won't take very long."

She nodded, but I suspected she was flipping through textbooks in her mind, anticipating.

"If it helps," I said, "think of my role as balancing out the role of the police. They've talked to you, right?"

"Yes."

"The state, they have this whole apparatus at their disposal. They interview witnesses, execute search warrants. With some limitations—we can discuss how real those are—they can look at whatever they want, talk to whoever they want, threaten those who don't talk with obstruction charges or incentivize them with deals to avoid punishment. All of that in the service of proving their case. Meanwhile, the defendant has access to very few of those tools. For example, the police likely have already looked at everything in Jane's room. No problem. And we've seen their files, but Jeremy is never going to be able to do that, and maybe he would have noticed something in real life that escapes the eye in pictures and lists of belongings.

"So we talk to people. As many as we can. There are limitations on that front as well, because some people don't want to talk to us. We can't make them do it the way the police can. Plus, from here on out, Jeremy never gets to speak with anyone except from the position of suspect. And our clients are the lucky ones. There simply aren't the resources for someone to do what I do at your average public defender's office. They have investigators, sure, but how many cases are they working on at one time? Hundreds? So the way I like to think of my job is I'm leveling the playing field. Trying to, anyway."

"Your job is to get Jeremy off," she said. "Not help Jane."

Law students.

"That's true, but in this case, I do believe they're the same thing. Don't you?"

"Can I be right back?"

"Of course."

I half expected her to come back with a criminal law treatise, but she returned with the socks she'd been wearing and a blow-dryer.

"Sorry," she said. "I have to leave soon, and I haven't done laundry." She turned the blow-dryer on, aimed it at the toes. "I was telling the truth before," she yelled over the air. "I barely knew Jeremy."

"Tell me about Jane, then," I said.

But she couldn't hear me. She turned the blow-dryer off.

"What?"

"Tell me about Jane."

"What about her?"

"Did you know her well?"

She turned the blow-dryer back on while she was thinking. After about a minute, she turned it off and answered me.

"I was getting to know her better, I think. It took a long time. We lived together for almost a year and a half. She was nice, but she worked a lot, and I worked a lot. She already had a life when I moved in. I was a paralegal last year and applying to law school, so I was always busy. And then law school, especially the first year. It's consuming. But we ate together sometimes, or watched a show, went to a bar."

"Where do you think her phone is? Would she have had it with her?"

"A hundred percent."

"Does it surprise you she didn't have any location apps turned on?"

"No, not really. She could be like that. She was kind of private. She didn't like uploading things to the cloud."

"Why?"

"You know, pictures get out. All your messages."

I decided to shift away from Jane's views on privacy—no need to make Lydia reflect on how Jane would feel about her talking to me.

"How many times did you meet Jeremy?"

She turned the blow-dryer on again, thought, turned it off.

"Less than ten times, probably. And each time was basically him heading from the front door to Jane's room or vice versa. We probably exchanged a total of fifty words, half of them the sorry-dance maneuvering on the way to the bathroom."

"Did Jane ever talk to you about him?"

This time she didn't turn on the blow-dryer.

"A couple times, but only once with any depth. They'd gotten into a fight. She was a little drunk. We went out and had a guys-suck night. It was fun. But the next morning, I could tell she kind of wanted to pretend it hadn't happened. So I did."

"What were they fighting about?"

"He wanted to reschedule something they were supposed to do, and Jane was pissed. And Jeremy was pissed that she was making a big deal about it."

"When was this?"

She turned the blow-dryer on. Off.

"October, I think. At least, I was drinking pumpkin beer when we were out."

"What about Aaron? Have you met him?"

She smiled sadly. "Yeah, he's great."

"Why did you say it like that?"

"Because they broke up, and I liked him. Honestly, it seemed kind of stupid to me."

"What do you mean?"

Blow-dryer on. Off.

"Well, they had broken up once before for like a month or something, maybe longer. And she seemed pretty miserable. When they got back together, she was really happy. But then, not that long after, she broke up with him again. It happened here. I could hear it through the walls. And, I don't know, everything sounded like a pretext, like she was looking for a reason."

"But if she wanted to, why was it stupid? I think we all offer reasons in those situations that might not be one hundred percent accurate. To be kind. Better than saying, 'Look, I really tried to be into you, but I just don't feel it.'"

"I don't know. I hear what you're saying, but to me it seemed like she really liked him. Little things. The way her face looked when he texted. They spent a lot of time together. More than I saw her spend with anyone else. When they had broken up before, it was like she was focused on getting back together. And—I can't describe it well, but the night they broke up, I kept thinking that she was making up a reason for it."

"How did Aaron take the breakup—the second one?"

Lydia shot me an angry look, unplugged the blow-dryer, and wrapped the cord around the handle.

"Aaron did not do this."

It was obvious pushing this line of questioning would only harden her against me. I retreated.

"I wasn't trying to insinuate anything, really, but unless it was random, who else besides her roommates and Aaron would know Jane might be out running?"

She laughed, but then a stricken look appeared on her face. She unwound the cord on the blow-dryer and wrapped it around the handle again.

"What?" I asked.

"I don't want you to use this against her."

"I'm not working against Jane."

"I know how these trials go. Everyone does. You don't have to be in law school. She's going to be the one dissected on all fronts, and the only thing she did was get murdered."

"I—" I started, but her look stopped me. She would need more than platitudes. "That's a legitimate concern. My intention is to defend Jeremy. Who, by the way, I really don't think did it. And if it's not Jeremy, Aaron, you have to admit, is a pretty good suspect. If you know something that helps him, you should tell me. Because otherwise I'm going to spend a lot of time looking at him."

She was winding and unwinding the blow-dryer cord again. She stopped and looked at me. "Jane was always running," she said. "Anyone who knew her knew that. Anyone who lived in the neighborhood and paid attention knew she'd be running around that time. You could set your clock by it."

"She was religious about it?"

"Compulsive."

"How compulsive?"

She didn't answer.

"Like eating-disorder-compulsive?"

She stared at me. "You'll make it look like she was unstable."

"I won't."

"You will. But someone will eventually tell you."

"Thank you for telling me," I said. "How did you know?"

"It's obvious if you know what to look for."

"Did she know you knew?"

She shook her head.

"No. I was thinking about how to approach it when she died. We were more roommates than friends, but I did like her. At times, I thought we were becoming real friends. With Jane—she'd open up, and I'd think, *Oh, we crossed into a new place, we're friends now.* But then the next time I talked to her, she was closed again. With this, though, I was a little worried about her."

"Because she ran too much?"

"Yeah," she said, but she wasn't telling me something.

A door opened at the end of the hallway, and we both looked in that direction. A moment later, the bathroom door closed; someone was pissing.

"That's Wes," Lydia said. "Our other roommate."

"Oh."

He was pissing for a long time. It was hard to think about anything else.

"He sleeps in Jane's old room," she said.

"Oh, did he move in after Jane too?"

"No. He was here before. After Jane died, a few people came by to look at the apartment but didn't want to sleep in her room, so Wes said he would take it. He used to sleep over there." She pointed to Rowan's area in the corner of the living room. "It costs less than one of the bedrooms, obviously, so we each agreed to pay a little more and raised the rent for that one."

Wes entered the room shirtless and in Astros sweatpants. He looked at me, then at Lydia, then back at me, noticing the notebook on my lap.

"He's here to talk about Jane," Lydia told him. "He works for Jeremy."

"No shit." He walked past us into the kitchen and reemerged with a big glass of water and a banana. He sat on the ottoman in front of Lydia's chair. She scrunched up her legs as if she were afraid of touching him. "I always liked Jeremy," he said.

"He's easy to like," I lied.

"I told Lydia when he was arrested, 'No way. That dude is not a murderer.'"

"How do you mean?"

"He's such a writer."

"Writers don't kill people?"

He leaned down to put the water glass—now empty—on the floor. When he'd finished, he readjusted himself on the ottoman and peeled his banana. Lydia watched his back shimmying around in front of her with something akin to fear. She drew her feet off the ottoman, tucked them underneath herself on the chair.

"I'm sure some writers have killed people. But Jeremy was wound real fucking tight—and not in an 'Oh, and so he cracked one day' way. Most of what went on in that dude's life happened in his head. Some people like to exercise. Some people like to fuck. Jeremy liked to sit and think and spin out scenarios. No way he got so mad he pushed Jane into a dumpster."

Behind him, Lydia closed her eyes.

"You knew him well?" I asked.

"He would come over to see Jane. Jane would leave for work pretty early, and he'd sleep in. When he woke up, we'd hang out for a while."

"You didn't have to go to work either?"

He took a bite of his banana and shook his head. "I'm an actor. No nine-to-five."

"You make a living doing that?"

"Yeah. Been lucky."

"Good for you. Anything I might have seen?"

"Mostly theater. But you'll see me in a Kit Kat commercial real soon."

He folded the now empty banana peel in half, looked around for a place to put it, then deposited it in his empty glass. When he sat up, he leaned farther back in the chair so that his back came to rest on Lydia's knees. She moved them quickly, climbed over the armrest to get out of her seat. Wes looked at her over his shoulder.

"I have to go to work," she said.

"She babysits," he told me, sliding back in the chair to occupy the newly empty space. "You read the Rita thing?"

I nodded.

"Remember how she was a nanny and the dad was sketch?"

"Yeah."

He nodded at Lydia. "That's where that came from."

"He's fine," Lydia said.

Wes laughed.

"He wants to sleep with her real bad."

She shook her head. "It's not like that. He's very professional."

"Right," he said to Lydia. "He'll never cross the line, but if you so much as put your hand on his arm, he would detonate his entire life."

"Wes, can I talk to you for a second?" Lydia said.

She left the room without waiting for an answer. Wes shrugged at me and followed her. I heard their low voices in the hall, then Lydia came back in her rain gear, removed her bike from the wall, and wheeled it toward the front hall.

"Thanks, Lydia," I said to her back. "I really do appreciate you talking to me."

She turned around to face me. She'd zipped her rain jacket and hood so I could only see the center of her face. It made her look young.

"Yeah," she said.

Wes came back into the room with a shirt on. I wasn't going to ask what Lydia had wanted to talk to him about, but he told me.

"She wanted to remind me that you work for the defense, and your goal is not to get to the truth or get justice for Jane but to keep Jeremy out of prison whether he did it or not."

"That's true, in a sense. But I really don't think he did it."

He waved away my words. "You don't have to explain it to me. I don't think he did it either."

"Is there someone you do think did it?"

"I think it was random."

"Someone just saw her running?"

"Yeah."

"But why did they want to hurt her?"

"I don't know. Maybe they were trying to rob her and it went wrong. Maybe they wanted her to come with to … you know, and she wouldn't. I don't really like to think about it."

"Lydia said that she ran every morning, that anyone who knew her would know she'd be out running at that time?"

"Umm. I mean, whenever I woke up, Jane was already at work, but if Lydia said so, it's probably true."

"Lydia said she was pretty compulsive about it. You never noticed that?"

He shrugged.

"No. She wasn't even that thin." He stopped. "Shit, I sound like a dick. She wasn't fat or anything, but you know, you don't look at her and think, *That girl runs marathons.*"

"Right."

"I didn't mean she was overweight or anything."

"No, I get it, man."

"She was a very attractive girl. Woman."

"Why don't we change lanes?"

"I'd appreciate that."

"What did you think about Aaron?"

"What about him?"

"Did you like him?"

"He was fine. I didn't know him that well. We never clicked, but I never thought, *This guy seems like a murderer.*"

"Sure."

"He did text her a lot. Anytime her phone blew up, it was always him."

"Clingy?"

"He liked her too much. You can't like girls like Jane too much. You know what I mean?"

"Yeah, I do."

"You know I sleep in her old room?"

I nodded.

"It's kind of a mind-fuck," he continued. "The whole thing is kind of a mind-fuck. Jane's famous now. Have you ever known someone who was murdered?"

"No."

"In the beginning," he said, "when I first moved in, we slept together for a bit. She was fun and pretty, and it was an itch we scratched for a while." I thought about how Lydia had reacted to Wes sitting on the chair with her. It appeared he might scratch that itch with a number of roommates. "It was never very serious," he went on, "but when I first moved in, for the first couple months, I'd sleep in her room. And now, sometimes, when I wake up, and I'm there again, I think it's the beginning, and she's at work.

"It's weird," he continued, "because in a way, she's never been this present. Someone is always talking about her somewhere. Never before have so many people known her or known so much about her. But she's also dead, and I sleep in the room she used to sleep in, and the shower doesn't have her shampoo in it anymore. It was in there for a while. Her parents came to get her stuff, but they didn't go in the shower or anything, so it just stayed there. Then one day I went in, and it was gone."

4

WILLIAM BURROUGHS SHOT AND KILLED his wife. They were both drunk and decided to play a game called William Tell where one person tries to shoot an apple off the other person's head with a crossbow. They didn't have an apple or a crossbow, so he used a glass of water and a gun. And he missed. He was given a two-year suspended sentence. Shortly after, he published *Naked Lunch*.

Juliet Hulme spent five years in jail for killing her best friend's mother when she was a teenager. The movie *Heavenly Creatures* was based on her life. Upon her release from prison, she moved to England, changed her name to Anne Perry, and became a writer—of mystery novels. She wrote over sixty books and was selected by the *London Times* as one of the twentieth century's masters of crime.

Louis Althusser was a French philosopher and writer of over a dozen books. He strangled his wife to death. After, he claimed to have no memory of the act. He said he had been massaging her neck and when he came to, she was lifeless in his hands.

There were more, mostly people I'd never heard of, but I scrolled through the listicles and pithy stories about writers who killed while I was on the subway from Jane's old apartment to Jane's old job. There was—unsurprisingly? Surprisingly?—more than one writer of detective stories on these lists. Writers who couldn't help but publish fairly accurate accounts of murders they committed. Sometimes after they committed them, sometimes before. Jeremy, it occurred to me, wrote detective stories. About Rita, yes, but his first book was also a kind of detective story. A literary detective story, to be sure, one where it's unclear at the end whether a crime has even been committed, but a detective story nonetheless. In the book, the protagonist wakes up one day and can't find his wife. He spends the book searching the house for her. *Did he kill her?* the book wants you to ask. *Or did they kill each other living in that house, a little bit each day, until they were ghosts walking around, unable to see each other?*

More than a few writers on these lists, I noticed, killed their partners.

I don't know why my mind had decided to focus on Wes's off-the-cuff comment about writers not being killers. I was, after all, trying to prove Jeremy had not killed Jane. But it wasn't looking good. We had to get twelve people to believe that simply because a writer wrote experimental fiction about a character who might have killed his wife and a Twitter mystery where a young woman was missing and probably murdered did not mean he had anything to do with his girlfriend (of sorts) being murdered, that they shouldn't read anything into the fact that he couldn't seem to stop writing stories (of sorts) about women who disappeared.

No, not twelve people, I reminded myself. One. One could still be hard.

My notebook was in my backpack, so I made a quick note on my phone: Ask Jeremy if the husband character killed his wife. I imagined him answering with something like, *Well, that is the question, isn't it?* and using the word *metaphysical* somewhere, and twelve people on the jury wanting to punch him. I erased that and wrote: Prep Jeremy on answering questions about his first book. Not my job, strictly, but something told me I might have a better instinct on how Jeremy would answer those questions. Phil had never struck me as much of a reader. I thought of something else and added: Make sure second book isn't also about a murdered/missing woman.

I got off the subway at city hall and walked to Jane's old office. It was a pleasant day, and I unzipped my jacket after a few blocks, enjoying being outside and in the city. Between moving back to Yonkers and my new job at Thorton, I had shifted my entire way of moving through the city. I enjoyed walking among my people again. I hadn't lived in this neighborhood, but the people strolling by with their hoodies and their dogs reminded me of my old life more than the suits and golf umbrellas of midtown.

Jane's office was in an older commercial building, five stories. Her company's offices were located on the fifth floor, but when I got there, I ran into movers on the stairs bringing boxes from the fifth level to the fourth. A young woman carrying a gold clipboard was directing the movers. I approached her.

"I'm looking for Stile's offices. I was told they were on the fifth floor— are they moving?"

"Expanding," she told me, looking at the clipboard. "You can put all of those in the back room," she called to one of the movers, then she turned to me. "Who are you looking for?"

"Tom Stafford."

"Upstairs. In the conference room."

I thanked her and walked up to the fifth floor. It was mostly one open space divided by metal screens that had been painted a burnt orange. Young people were hunched over computers or scrolling through their phones in the open kitchen. A break area with couches and a Ping-Pong table and Jenga. In the corner near a big window, a woman talking on her phone was riding an exercise bike.

I'd googled the company, but I still didn't have a great idea of what they actually did. They billed themselves as a new media group. I knew that included writing Twitter mysteries and working for novelists, but their website provided no clarity about how or why. Through the modern geometric cutouts in the metal screens, I could see a bearded man about my age lean back in his chair and yawn. I felt something odd: strangled. This office could have been the workspace for any of a hundred websites— writers of various quality and commitment typing up content for the internet in some fashion. A young woman with red pigtails and fat, pillowy headphones walked by me. What was she writing? I wondered. Who was reading it? Did she write at all? It was quite possible I was going to hate this, whatever I had walked into, whatever they did here. But when I looked back at the bearded man, he was definitely writing. I could see the screen on his computer filling up, how he glanced at his pad to check his notes. I imagined he was writing something he believed mattered to the world. I wanted to sit down at the empty desk next to him and do the same, call a source to check a quote, get feedback on a piece from someone who was a better journalist than I was.

Not that I'd ever done that for very long; I'd been laid off, then laid off, then laid off again, pinging between writing at coffee shops while pitching to whoever would let me pitch to them and doing brief stints at illustrious organizations that regularly produced articles that were shared virally across the web—until the day they unexpectedly folded or laid off seventy percent of their staff. So, while a part of me wanted to pull up a chair and join the workers at Stile in whatever they were doing, I also resented everyone here. This new media group, whatever it did, was likely part of the reason I couldn't work at a newspaper and earn a good salary and a pension. I thought, as I often did, of a scene in *All the President's Men:* a large room filled with desks, a thousand phones ringing. Something that had never been available to me but that I yearned for anyway.

The conference room was at the very back of the building, a large room separated by frosted-glass walls. The door was open, and I could see a man sitting alone in front of a laptop at a long black table. I knocked lightly on the glass, and he looked up.

"Jesse?"

"Yep."

"Come in, come in," he said, waving at me.

He closed his computer and placed it on top of a file next to him.

"Thanks for speaking with me," I said. I slid into a chair a few seats from him. His face was open, his eyes very bright.

"Absolutely," he said. "Absolutely. I should tell you I want to help, but this is still really hard for me to talk about."

"I understand. I really appreciate it."

"I mean, Jane, I—I don't even know what to say, but there's no way Jeremy did this. The whole idea is absurd."

"We're in agreement, then," I said.

He stood up suddenly.

"You hungry?"

"Umm."

"Sorry. I haven't eaten in twenty hours. I haven't slept either. I can feel that shakiness coming."

My eyes flicked to his computer, the small file underneath. He did not look like someone who had pulled an all-nighter. His hair was neat, his glasses unsmudged. The table was bare except for the computer and file folder, a water bottle. I thought back to how I'd left the kitchen table last night and felt a twinge of shame that Gloria had probably cleaned up candy wrappers, half-drunk mugs of coffee, the pot from when I'd decided three a.m. seemed like a reasonable time to teach myself to poach eggs.

There was a tap on the glass—a slight young woman with black hair cut above her ears. Tom nodded, and she came in with an iPad. She showed him something on the screen but looked at me the whole time. Tom noticed, put his hand lightly on her arm, and led her out of the room.

"I'll be right back," he said at the door, and then they were beyond the frosted glass, and I couldn't see what they were doing.

I glanced around the room, but it was empty, nothing for my gaze to land on, so I pulled my phone from my pocket to check my email. There was a message from Aaron. When I'd contacted him to see if he would talk to me, he'd sounded wary and told me he was extremely busy at work for the next three days. I told him I could wait until the fourth day, and he agreed to meet me for coffee near his office. Based on the tenor of our conversation, I expected the email to be a cancellation, but instead, he'd attached a ten-page document. Bullet points, single spaced—everything he knew about Jane that might be helpful, he explained, anything she'd ever said, anywhere she'd ever been. He wasn't canceling, he said, in the email; this was in addition to, not instead of. He didn't know Jeremy Miller, and he didn't know if Jeremy had killed her, but if Jeremy didn't do it, then he wanted to know who did, and he wanted to help make sure the right person was punished.

I scrolled through the bullet points waiting for Tom to come back. Jane ran every morning, like Lydia said, always the same route, which he outlined turn by turn. She ran with headphones, and she didn't always pay attention. Sometimes, it was like she went someplace else. That's how he'd met her, actually, he wrote, the bullet-point format getting away from him as he detailed how they'd run past each other for a month before meeting, randomly, at a bar. It wasn't a bar he regularly went to, and he couldn't even remember how he'd ended up there.

After that textual excursion, Aaron seemed to remember the bullet-point structure and returned to it. Her best friend, Kaya. Yoga class and the Whole Foods salad bar. How she kept a toothbrush in a plastic case in her bag. How she used shower caps and slept hugging an old T-shirt. How he'd never seen her cry. Her boss, Tom; someone at work named Miriam. Rita. How when she was stuck on something in the Rita story, Jane worked in her Rita sweater—a thrift-shop purchase with big buttons and fat sheep. A troll who called himself @theblessing and sent her threatening messages. She saved them all, he said, in a document on her computer.

I looked up from my phone. No one had said anything about threatening messages. They had not been in any files I'd seen. The police had not mentioned them. I felt a prickling in my body, like all my limbs had fallen asleep without me realizing it, and now they were waking up.

Tom came back in with a Clif Bar hanging out of his mouth.

"Sorry about that," he said, taking a bite and making an effort to show he was chewing as fast as he could because he didn't want to waste my time by eating. "I'd told Kaya you were coming by, and I think she wanted to look at you. It's all a bit more than she can handle."

I glanced at the now closed door.

"I'd love to talk to her."

"Maybe not today," Tom said. "Maybe not at work."

"Right, sure. That makes sense."

"But you've got me," he said. "I'm not sure how I'll be able to help, but I'll try."

"Actually, you might be able to," I said. "Did Jane ever tell you she was getting threatening messages because of the Rita project?"

"What?"

"Yeah, there was a troll apparently, the Blessing. Sending DMs to the Rita account."

He shook his head.

"No," he said. "No, she never told me that." He pulled his computer over and opened it, already typing. "I wonder why she didn't tell me." A few seconds later, he was looking at Rita's DMs. He angled the computer so we could both see and ran a search on the notifications looking for @theblessing.

I wish I kept your body.

At night, the last thing I see before I fall asleep is red spreading across your cheek. I still feel it, the sting in my hand.

I only wanted to lick your forehead, from top to bottom, drag my tongue over every inch of your face.

Sometimes, I go back to the park and sit in the place where it happened. I eat a hot dog, cross-legged on the grass. People walk by with their dogs and their newspapers. If I wasn't sitting here, they'd walk right over it.

Your neck was so beautiful.

I know, when this is all over, people will say I couldn't have loved you. But this is the strongest feeling I've ever felt. If it isn't love, then love should be stronger.

They went on and on. Every once in a while, Tom would glance over at me to see if I'd finished what we could see on the screen, and he'd scroll up again. After doing this four or five times, he stopped glancing over at me or reading the messages at all and simply scrolled up waiting for them to stop. Up and up and up. Finally, he pushed the computer away.

"I feel sick," he said. "Why wouldn't she tell me about that?"

"I don't know."

He stood up and went to stand by the window. "Do the police know about those messages?"

"I don't know," I said. "Not from the information I've seen."

"Should I go tell them?"

"I think that would be a good idea."

He returned to the table and pulled his computer back to him. For about five minutes, I watched him screenshot and PDF the messages, save them to a folder, then email them to somebody. About halfway through this process, his shoulders slumped, and he put his face in his hands. Then he took a deep breath and continued. I assumed this deflation was the result of reading so many of the messages at once, but after he'd sent the email, he turned to me.

"She did tell me something," he said. "She said there was a troll. I brushed it off, told her we should expect that, but we should know about it too. We wanted to know who was reading and what they were doing, and we wouldn't know if we blocked them. We wouldn't be able to see if they were tagging us. Plus, we wanted followers generally. But she never told me they were like this. She never told me he wrote her so much. I assumed . . ."

He trailed off. I waited almost a minute for him to return to the conversation. When he didn't, I said, "I was told she kept a document on her computer with all of his messages, that she copied and pasted them there. Could I see that? Maybe she made some notes on it or was trying to figure out who this person was and got somewhere. She must have made the file for a reason."

"Who told you that?"

"Aaron."

"Is that the boyfriend who is not Jeremy?"

"Yeah. Well, ex-boyfriend, I think."

"Oh, yeah. I did hear they broke up. He said they were on her computer—from work?"

"I think so. Any way I could see her computer?"

He looked around the conference room and sighed.

"Maybe. I don't know exactly where it is right now because of the expansion, but we have it. She left it at the office that night, which was unusual for her. Generally, when someone leaves the company, we wipe the computer, give it to someone else. I figured I shouldn't do that, so I put it in a box, but I'm not sure I can lay my hands on it right now. I'll look for it. If I find it and there's anything on it, you can have it."

"Thanks."

"It might be hard to figure out who he is," Tom said. "Twitter might fight not to tell you."

"I know."

He turned back to his computer, back to Twitter, and started opening tabs quickly and efficiently. I didn't know exactly what he was doing, but the way he copied and pasted links so authoritatively made me feel sure he could find this troll before I left the room. After five minutes of this, though, I cleared my throat to remind him I was there. He looked up at me with the same open face I'd seen when I first entered the room. It was as if this level of engagement with the internet erased him somehow, his face returning to some original state.

"Sorry," he said. "Hyperfocus. A blessing and a curse."

"Right."

He had a sharp face, clean-shaven. When he smiled, everything softened.

"I've read your stuff, you know," he said. "I googled you. You were really good. Why'd you stop? Money? Or something else?"

It had been a while since someone had complimented me on my work, and the effect reminded me of when I used to smoke, the first cigarette after getting off a long plane ride. A direct hit right to my brain. I felt lightheaded.

"Mostly money."

"Sucks, man, it really sucks. This is, this is what I'm trying to do. Well, one of the things. I'm hoping to add a news division at some point. Politics. You should come work for us."

"Doing what? I haven't been able to figure out exactly what your company does. No offense."

"None taken. It didn't exist before this one, so how could you know? We have the old model, which is dead, of course, and then, what is the real alternative now? Substack? So consumers end up having to buy a thousand subscriptions like the streaming wars have turned into? And who really benefits in Substack? Someone like you? Probably not."

The rush from his compliment—along with his complaining about media models—was making me restless. I wanted to suggest we take this conversation into the outside world and walk around the city. When I imagined this—a brisk walk with cold air, insightful observations, elegant analyses of models—I realized there was a hiccup with this fantasy: The man sitting in front of me believed he already knew the answers. He was past deconstruction and diagnosis. He'd started building something.

"So what's your model?" I asked.

"Well, it's been more than one thing. That's how it always is with something new. Remember the beginning of Twitter? People didn't know what to make of it. And now? It's created a new medium and drawn to that medium people who wish to master it, or manipulate it, or profit from it. But the point is, say what you will about the internet or what gets lost in a hundred forty or two hundred eighty characters, but it has created not only an audience but new actors.

"Did you ever watch *Singin' in the Rain*?" he asked.

"Yes," I said, and I thought of my dad, which I always did whenever someone mentioned a musical.

"My mom loved that one," he said. "I must have seen it forty times when I was a kid. If you remember, the whole plot of that movie is what changes as films move from silent to sound, how the technology demands something different. In a moment, actors who had mastered one medium are thrown out because they don't have what it takes in the new one. We are meant to relate to the Debbie Reynolds character, of course—the upstart against the status quo, those baddies fighting to keep progress from happening.

"In the movie, Debbie Reynolds already has these talents, but technology is finally ready for them. What's happening now is slightly different. The technology is more aggressive. People bend to its will. Sure, there were writers and comedians before Twitter, but they bend to its constraints now. And at the same time, Twitter is creating its own supply of actors, untethered from old ideas of what it meant to be a writer or a comedian or a journalist. It's the same with TikTok, Instagram, whatever comes next. They each have their own connotations of what it means to be a master, and they create a demand for people to master them."

"Right," I said, but I still didn't see what his company actually produced or how it created value if one of those things was a free Twitter novel, unless it was just another example to share with investors of how these platforms could be used to pay writers less.

"The way it works now," he said, "is that people tweet in their spare time or make videos, all with the hope that they will build an audience and then—what? Someone will pay them somehow. Maybe they're comedians, and they'll get staffed on a show. Maybe they're dancers on TikTok, and they'll get an endorsement deal for something. It's all very diffuse, but there's this idea that putting in time on these social media sites will translate, at some point, in some way, into money."

"So like Jeremy Miller with his second book. Hashtag Searching for Rita helped him sell his book for more."

"Exactly."

"So you're a kind of publicist?"

"No. That's the thing about being in business these days. You have to be big but you also have to have octopus hands—what are those things called? Tentacles, right—going out in every direction, and you have to be flexible. Projects like hashtag Searching for Rita and clients like Jeremy, that's only one aspect of what we do. It's not the one I'm most interested in, but it's a revenue stream. And that's really the key: You have to be able to spot revenue streams—create them—where nobody else does."

"Okay, so, what other kinds of revenue streams do you produce?" I asked, but what I meant was how do the writers get paid.

"Right now at Stile, we have three primary departments. There are people, like Jane, who work for clients. Or, um, Miriam. She's actually in a different department than Jane, but what she does is eventually sold to clients. So one thing she came up with is a game similar to Two Truths and a Lie. Or Yes, Yes, No, if you've heard that podcast. She tweets out three 'answers' to a subtweet, two of which are false. The first hundred people who answer get entered in a raffle. The winner of the raffle gets a coupon for lunch."

"Oh, I've seen that. For Brother's Burritos."

"Everyone's seen it. It's been pretty successful. Miriam developed that, and then we auctioned it off. What Miriam is good at—what not everyone can do—is picking the right subtweet to appeal to the client's audience. Or to build it. Anyone can pick a random tweet or the most trending tweet, but not everyone can tell if a tweet that's trending in Black Twitter or Weird Twitter is going to stay siloed off or if it has the potential to travel. People want to learn something, and they want to be able to talk about it with their friends. It's essentially 'Did you read that article in *The New Yorker?*,' but for a subtweet, where you walk away feeling like you learned something, that some aspect about the world or humanity you didn't understand before has been bathed in light. It's a podcast where you do more than listen. But barely. The people who play the game, they don't even care about the coupon. They just want to play. But at the end, they have this ten-percent-off coupon for lunch, and they might as well use it. Even if they weren't planning to eat there before."

"So, to sell it," I said, "you have to have someone who can make up the game but who also knows the market?"

"Exactly."

"And Miriam gets paid how?"

"Well, by the client. It's just advertising, and advertising pays a lot. So much that I can pay Miriam—and the other Miriams—well, but I can do other things too, things I couldn't do without their money." His leg was shaking underneath the table, knocking the top of it. "Sorry," he said, placing his hand on his knee to steady it. "I still get excited talking about it. Like another department, something I initially called True Talent but for various reasons I now simply call Creative. Did I tell you how I started the company yet?"

"No."

"Well, I'm working as a writer initially, which may surprise you. It surprises people who think I come from a tech background, but I started as a writer at a digital media company. A content creator, I guess you would call me now. And I seem to be pretty good at making things go viral, so I get promoted and then promoted again. But I also begin to see the limitations of it all—the writers, the creators, are basically the losers in the whole thing. And so I quit, and I start Stile. And at first, it's me, and I essentially do what Jane did and what Miriam does. I sell myself to clients. And that's how I bring in money. But I also hire this guy. He makes TikTok videos. Hand-drawn illustrations. He doesn't have that many followers yet, but I have a feeling about him. So I hire him to keep doing what he's doing. And I'm right—his follower count grows and grows. And I study it, and I understand it—who they are, what they want, what they'll buy. So later, when I pitch one of his videos to a client to use as an advertisement, I have all this data about who the client's audience is and how it's their market.

"So everything is going pretty well, and I see this guy who tweets about sports, and a woman who's really funny, and a husband and wife who dress in old-timey clothes and make recipes from the 1700s, and a true-crime

TikToker. And I have a feeling about them, and I'm right again. All these creative types hustling, working for free, hoping without a real plan that one day, this thing they spend so much time on will translate into a living. So I help them. I pay them a salary. I put them on a triple-A team. And when they're playing, I'm moneyballing, and now I have a playbook filled with data. And that's where the money always is—"

"How is this not the studio system?" I interrupted.

"I'm not sure what you mean."

"Well, you brought up *Singin' in the Rain*. You're the studio, and you have everyone under contract." The hopeful feeling I'd had at the start of the conversation had worn off a bit, and I was worried that despite his protests, he was just another one of those tech guys who thought they'd invented something we already had or had stopped using for good reasons. "The golden era of Hollywood, except they made Rock Hudson get married to a woman and forced a teenage Judy Garland to take pills to stay awake to shoot and then later made her get a bunch of abortions. Which I'm sure had nothing to do with the way it all turned out for her."

"Oh. Well, for one, I'm not going to force anyone to have an abortion or enter into a beard marriage, I guess. The problem with the studio system," he rushed on, "well, I don't know much about it, so there were probably a lot of problems with it. But I don't think it was having a contract, a salary. Professional sports, they still work this way. You sign a contract with a team or you can be a free agent. There are risks either way, and people contract around the risks. But all creative people right now are essentially free agents—without even a signing bonus or a salary. They carry all the risk. What we can do here is pay a real salary to the people who otherwise would be free agents, the writers and artists and dancers, so they can write and paint and dance. These are people I think the world should know. I want to give them a chance. So I carry some of the risk, and I can, because of our other departments."

"So you're using the marketing side as a charity for starving artists out of the goodness of your heart?" I asked.

"No, of course not. The creative side does make money. Because, well, I don't hire just anyone. I'm pretty good at this. It's just that they don't *all* have to make money for this to work. Okay, I can tell you're skeptical. Example: I hired this woman, Emma Bradley. She's in the death-TikTok genre."

"I'm sorry, the what?"

Tom was my age, I figured, but he was one of those extremely online people who made me feel like I was fifty.

"She's twenty-six, and she has terminal cancer. And she's documenting it. When I found her, she didn't have that many followers, a few thousand. And maybe she would have gotten them on her own, maybe not, and maybe she would have gotten some sponcon out of it—death is a tricky one to get sponsors for, but it's not impossible. But I hire her, and her seven thousand followers become five hundred thousand. So how do we make money? Well, we could do the side-revenue streams, but, like I said, that's tougher here. So what we are doing in this case is—in addition to these videos she makes—we have her working with a documentary filmmaker. And when she dies, and we go to sell it to a streaming service, we have all this data about how many people are going to watch it."

"Isn't that a little exploitative?"

"Why? I think it might be one of the healthier things people do on the internet, let death into their lives a little bit. We spent all this time cordoning it off, and in the end, we bring it back in. But also, Emma was doing this before for free. I'm only paying her for it now."

"You're telling me this docuseries—that you have to pay for, I imagine—is going to recoup her salary and whatever you spent making sure she went from seven thousand to five hundred thousand followers?"

"Oh, yes. It is. And it's going to give her next of kin plenty of money to pay for her burial, pay off her medical bills, and then some. Because in this case, I have data that shows people will pay to sign up for a service to watch it. And the new-subscriber button, well, that's the holy grail. But if I didn't have that—that's the thing about the tentacles, remember? If it wasn't that, maybe it'd be a book of inspirational quotes sold at the cash register at Urban Outfitters. Maybe it'd be a collage of her videos set to a Sarah McLachlan song and used to sell a cell phone. It doesn't matter as long as you can come armed with the numbers to show clients what the audience is and what they want. And every time I'm right, people trust us a little more."

I was quiet, trying to see the hole, the issue. But it did seem like a net positive that at least some people could be paid for the things they wrote or created for the internet without also having to sell juice cleanses or trick their high-school friends into joining MLMs.

"Still," I said, "you must be wrong sometimes. Some of these people must cost you money."

He sat back in his chair and put his hands on his lap. "Some players don't make it to the majors," he said. "Some get sent back. Miriam, for example, I hired her first as a creative, but it didn't quite work. She couldn't create that draw. But she's still really fucking talented. So now she works for clients."

"And Jane? Did she start like that too?"

His enthusiasm as he talked about his company had made him forget why we were meeting in the first place. His smile fell away.

"No," he said. "Jane was always on the client side. She was so good." He looked at me like it was important for me to understand how good she was, that he wasn't simply saying this because she was dead. "But Jane, she didn't like being in charge that much. She liked direction. She could make any-thing better once it was there. Significantly better; levels and levels better. But she couldn't make the thing. She was too good at knowing what people wanted but not good enough at not caring if she gave it to them."

"Or maybe she got better at that," I said. "And someone didn't like it."

5

SINCE I WAS ALREADY in the city, I texted Lucy to see if she was free to do something later. She texted back that a few of our friends from college were coming over for a dinner party and that I should come. I told her I'd bring wine, then went to find a coffee shop to work for a few hours.

After ordering a red-eye and a croissant, I quickly typed up notes from my interviews and emailed them to Phil. After that, I dived into the internet to search for @theblessing. Surprisingly, it did not seem to be a burner account; @theblessing followed over a thousand accounts, and he—I think I could assume he was a he—had over a hundred followers himself. I didn't recognize any of his followers, but we did follow some of the same people. He followed the Rita accounts—her main account, @Joshtweeting, the Jeremy/detective character, the ex-boyfriend, the father of the kids she nannied, some eyewitnesses. But he did not follow Jane's personal account or Jeremy's. He also did not offer his location, contact information, website, or any identifying information of any kind. Scrolling quickly down the page, I saw he didn't post pictures of himself or of a neighborhood, a restaurant, an office, or anything I could work with to identify him. He did tweet, though. A lot.

Retweets and memes, some of which I recognized, most of which I didn't understand. Two men looking out a bus window, one happy, one sad. The happy one said, *Getting someone's password for the Criterion Collection.* The sad one: *Seeing* Freaks *isn't on here.* I opened another tab. *Freaks* was a 1932 movie referenced as a pre-code horror film. *Pre-code,* I discovered, referred to a brief time in cinematic history between the adoption of sound and the enforcement of uniform censorship guidelines. The movie in question, I learned quickly, was a controversial film on a number of levels. Was it a horror movie? Was it exploitative? Or did it carry an early anti-eugenics message? I say I realized all this quickly, but the next time I looked up—three academic papers, five blogs, countless subreddits, and infinity YouTube clips later—an hour and forty-five minutes had passed.

I returned to the tab with @theblessing's Twitter feed and scrolled past the memes and references I didn't understand, trying not to get lost in the details. When I did this, a pattern emerged: Horror. The obscure. The grotesque. Movies and images, but also links to stories at various small horror-themed publications. Leading, eventually, to

Honored to have a story up at *Emily's Rose*—my fave journal for a long time. Thanks to @charlieschaple for the edits!

When I opened the story—"Dragonfruit," by Roger Warren—the tips of my fingertips were buzzing. Suddenly, I could feel the slippery metal of the keys; I didn't remember feeling them before. The ambient noise of the coffee shop became loud and then faded away as a buzzing sound—from my head? From a light fixture?—got louder. It felt as if someone had dropped a couple Alka-Seltzer tablets into my brain, and they'd slipped into my bloodstream, fizzing. I couldn't type fast enough. I couldn't open enough tabs. *Roger Warren writer. Roger Warren NY. Roger Warren horror. Roger Warren Dragonfruit.* But no matter what I typed, it was a circle. *Roger Warren writer* led me to the *Emily's Rose* page and three other websites with three more stories, all horror-themed websites with, I guessed, a fairly small niche audience. There was a Roger Warren soccer coach (New Jersey), a Roger Warren surgeon (Albany), a Roger Warren eye doctor (Idaho), a Roger Warren sex offender (Indiana), and a Roger Warren minister (Texas). I followed them all across the country—was it likely that a registered sex offender in Indiana would have traveled to New York to find Jane? Nothing on the internet connected them. The Roger Warren surgeon had the most links of any of the Roger Warrens, but these still numbered under twenty and were mainly various medical-rating aggregation sites, a few publications. Did he—a successful thoracic surgeon—write horror stories and DM young women threatening messages in his free time? It seemed like a good plot for an *SVU* episode but unlikely in real life.

"Dragonfruit" followed a couple who moved to upstate New York, became homesteaders, and decided to explore S&M. Rather, the girlfriend decided she wanted to explore it; her boyfriend, Teddy, was reluctant. *Dragonfruit* was their safe word, chosen because they'd managed to grow one successfully in their new light-filled kitchen. Elyse, the girlfriend, overcomes Teddy's reluctance, and the couple begin to incorporate some S&M practices into their sex life. A little, at first. Elyse likes to be dominated. Teddy doesn't like his role, but he does it occasionally for Elyse. He thinks it will pass, but instead, Elyse gets more and more into it, wants to go further and further. And then:

> *Elyse lay on the bed with her wrists tied to the headboard.*

> *"Hit me," she said.*

> *"I can't," Teddy replied.*

"Please," she said. Her lips were swollen, and she jerked around on the bed.

Teddy stood over her and tapped her cheek lightly with his fingers.

"Harder."

"I don't want to."

"Harder." He was kneeling over her, and she used her knee to nudge his cock. He didn't want it to, but it grew firmer. She smiled. "See, harder."

He slapped her this time, so hard her head flew to the left, and the motion caused her bangs to slide off her face. He'd never noticed how big her forehead was before.

"Holy fuck," I said out loud.

A few people in the coffee shop looked over at me.

Sorry, I mouthed at the room.

The sex scenes became more and more violent as the story went on. The dread built with each page, whether from Warren's technical expertise or from what I knew had happened to Jane, I wasn't sure, but I had a theory. Eventually, Teddy kills Elyse accidentally. Unsure of what to do and blinded by grief, he chops up her body and buries it in their garden. In the final scene—a time jump—he fertilizes the dragonfruit with what, we presume, is Elyse.

I'd barely read the last word before I was copying and pasting the story and Aaron's document into an email to Phil. Immediately after that, I texted

Aaron: Did Jane ever mention a Roger Warren? I looked for contact info for *Emily's Rose* but couldn't find any. I returned to @theblessing's original tweet and searched for the editor tagged. I sent him a quick DM explaining who I was and linking to Thorton's website so he could verify I was who I said I was.

The sky outside the coffee-shop windows had grown dark without me noticing. When my phone buzzed, I knew it would be Lucy asking me to come early and bring an ingredient she'd forgotten for dinner. And it was.

I FORGOT POTATOES

Also please get ginger and basil (fresh!)

Come quickly, I'll pay you in gin and old-timey records!

The dinner party was technically at Lucy's parents' apartment on the Upper West Side, but they currently lived in Europe. Lucy was getting her PhD at Princeton, but she spent about half her time here since finishing her courses and beginning work on her dissertation. Twice a year, Lucy's parents descended on the States, and Lucy moved back to her apartment in New Jersey or back into her childhood bedroom, moving all her food onto one shelf in the fridge and stocking the rest with her parents' favorite snacks. She'd been having dinner parties here since college, and I'd been going to them since then, picking up whatever ingredient she'd forgotten on my way over and ending the evenings slow-dancing to albums on her grandfather's record player. Tonight's party would likely be no different—even the guests were mostly the same as when we were undergrads. That's the thing about going to college at a place like Columbia in a city like New York: a lot of people stay.

When I started working for Thorton, most of my friends were in grad school. It had been a slow transition, and as one by one they returned to school, I'd been constructing a hierarchy in my head. At the bottom were those friends and acquaintances who'd moved from college directly to grad school. I made some exceptions for doctors, but to be honest, I didn't have many friends who wanted to be doctors, so that was mostly a null set. The next level was composed of people who went to grad school two years after college. This also happened to be the biggest tranche. Like wedding season, for people like me, there is graduate-school-application season, and it happens approximately one and a half years after you get a full-time job. Then there were the back-to-school-three-or-four-years-after-college people; I put them a little higher up because they'd experienced and moved past that first discomfort at being a worker for life. Ultimately, they'd decided to head back to school anyway, but at least they'd lived with that for a while, having a job that was unfulfilling and all-consuming and underpaying. Anyone who'd waited over five years after college before going to grad school was at the top of my hierarchy. Mostly, I considered this to be a wholly different kind of person.

I'd always known I was never going to go to grad school. I wasn't going to be a fishmonger either; I never thought I couldn't write about the world if I didn't know what beer tasted like after a twelve-hour shift at the factory or how it felt to have concrete dust on my hands and in my lungs. I never put much stock in the idea that journalists couldn't write about what they hadn't experienced firsthand. I only had to be in life and listening; my job was to relay it as clearly as I could. From what I could see, grad school was not life, grad students rarely listened, and they seemed mostly allergic to writing things clearly. A large part of me didn't even want to go to Lucy's dinner party. Each day, I felt I had less and less in common with the people attending. But the only people I ever saw outside work lately were my mom and Gloria, and I couldn't remember what it was like to be young.

The guest list for tonight's party was Lucy, who was getting a PhD in Russian literature; Sarah, who was getting her master's in public policy at Columbia; Doug, NYU Law; Nate, a master's in journalism, also at Columbia. It was a place that pulled people back. I hadn't seen any of them except Lucy since I started working at Thorton, and I wasn't particularly looking forward to the conversations.

"Are you sure?" Lucy had asked me when I told her about it. I'd come to her apartment to watch a movie, and she was mixing sugar and crushed ice in a glass. Lucy didn't drink; this was not the foundation of a cocktail but a holdover from childhood—her nanny used to bring it to her before bed. "You're doing so well. There has to be some other way."

"There really isn't."

"Oh, but there has to be," she insisted.

When I got off the elevator at her building, I saw the door to her apartment was slightly ajar; music and the smell of sautéing onions wafted down the hall. I knocked anyway, calling out as I entered. Sarah and Nate were already there, sitting on the couch. They rose and we all hugged each other—me awkwardly, as I was holding a bag of potatoes.

"Jesse," Lucy called from the kitchen. "Bring it here, please, or we'll never eat."

I gave them a quick smile, which they returned with a very familiar and oft-used *When Lucy calls* smirk. When I brought the potatoes to her in the kitchen, she was pressing blue cheese into figs. There was a baking sheet of toasty French bread slices on the stovetop. I found the bruschetta mixture in the fridge and spooned the oily tomatoes over each piece. When I pulled a serving plate from the cabinet, she said, "Not that one," without looking and stopped what she was doing to retrieve a blush-pink dish from another area in the kitchen.

When I came back out to the living room, Doug had arrived and was making drinks at the bar area. I put the bruschetta on the coffee table and walked over to hug him. This time he was the one awkwardly holding something—a bottle of bitters. He patted me on the back. "Good to see you, man."

"You too, man."

The interrogation of my career change didn't happen until hours later, when—the potatoes finally ready—we sat down for dinner.

"You are probably the last person from our class I would have guessed would take a real corporate job," Sarah said. She wanted to work in education policy. I had slept with her for three breathless weeks. For a year after that, everything she said to me sounded like a question, and then it shifted to what it was now—little swipes so sharp and quick, I knew she thought nobody could see them.

"At least I'm working for the defense side."

"Corporate defense," Doug said. The previous summer he'd had an unpaid internship with an immigrants' rights organization. The summer before law school, he'd gone to a language program in Costa Rica that cost more than I made in six months.

"If you really believe innocent until proven guilty, you have to believe in it for everyone," I said. "Even rich people."

"It's about attention," Sarah said. She'd gotten her hair cut since the last time I'd seen her. Her new bangs skimmed her eyelashes. "Of course that's true, but it's not where the problem lies. You're going to spend your limited time on Earth adjacent to the problem."

"And you're going to spend your limited time on Earth at Columbia, apparently."

"That's not fair," Doug jumped in, giving Sarah a consoling look across the table.

"Academia is irrelevant," I said. "According to Alinsky."

"Well, you're hardly working for the people anymore, Jesse," Lucy said from across the table, and I felt a quick wave of shame pass through me for my last comment. It accused her Russian literature PhD the most, and Lucy was the one I'd meant to insult the least.

"I'm sorry, I didn't mean that." I looked over to try and catch her eye, but I needn't have worried, because Lucy always looked you in the eye. "All I'm saying," I said, turning to the others, "is that it's pretty easy for all of you to judge right now, since you've essentially opted out of a world where you need to have a job to survive. But mark my words, one day you too may need to work for a company. And I've got news for you about companies—there's only three of them left, and none of them are good."

"We didn't mean to offend you," Nate said.

"And one other thing," I rushed on, unwilling to be placated, "let's not romanticize these fine institutions at which you all matriculate and which some of you hope will serve as your employer in the future. At this point, every one of them is little more than a hedge fund and a real estate empire wearing a trench coat. Don't fucking kid yourself."

No one responded. The silence began to feel invasive, like it was replacing the oxygen in the room.

"We're only worried about you," Lucy said after a while. "It's a lot different than what you always said you wanted to do. It doesn't seem"—she paused, clearly looking for the right words—"to align with your values."

I could tell they'd had a conversation about me, perhaps at the last dinner party, which I'd missed because my mom had given her credit card number to someone who called pretending to work for the ASPCA. I'd gotten the credit card company to refund the charges but only after a few false starts of explaining I wasn't the credit card holder but her son. I'd tried to make the call with my mom, coaching her, but every time they asked her if she'd made a specific purchase, she said she had, perhaps afraid it was one of my tricks to catch her forgetting something. Finally, Gloria called and pretended to be my mom. After she got off the phone, she sent me a link where I could download the power-of-attorney paperwork and told me I had to make it formal. If my mother wouldn't agree to it, I had to have her declared incompetent. I spent the rest of the night trying to convince my mom to sign the forms, but she wouldn't, and the thought of starting the legal process was so overwhelming, I texted Lucy to cancel and watched *The Great British Bake Off* with my mom until we both fell asleep on the couch.

"I help people stay out of jail and defend themselves against overzealous and unscrupulous prosecutors," I answered Lucy. "We all still think prosecutors are bad, right?"

"Sure," Doug said easily. "But the kind of defendant you're likely to assist—the kind who can afford to hire a company like Thorton—is more likely to be someone who suppressed adverse data in pharmaceutical trials than a poor young kid who maybe didn't have a lot of choices."

Doug was going to make a great lawyer. He knew how to concede a point so he sounded reasonable before coming back with everything he had.

"*Allegedly* suppressed adverse data," I said, and Doug laughed. The tension cracked like glass. "Look, I'm not saying this is the most important part. Not even close, but I am still working against the carceral state, at least. The government does as much overreach in these kinds of cases as they do with marginalized communities." I didn't really believe that, of course, but no one goes to a get-together to be called an asshole. "The case I'm working on now—not a white-collar case, by the way, a murder case—I just found out the victim was getting obsessive threats from someone on Twitter. I mean, this guy wrote her multiple times a day. Very frightening stuff. And the police? Either don't know or never looked into it before arresting someone else. So, yes, maybe this guy has enough money to hire a fancy lawyer. But the police are still doing the same thing."

No one said anything. Not because I'd bested them with my superior reasoning, I knew, but because there was nothing else to say. I thought we'd moved on when Doug said, "I think I know what the case is. It's the writer and his girlfriend, right? I saw he hired Nelson, Moretti, and Green. They work with your company a lot."

I shrugged, but he smiled.

"Oh, I know who that is," Lucy added. "I've read his book."

"Is it good?" Sarah asked.

"Yes," Lucy said. "Yes, I think so. But let me say, it would not be altogether surprising to me if he didn't think of women as real people. They are frequently not real people in his writing."

"Oh, wow."

"Okay, hold on," I said. "And I'm not saying that's the case I'm working on, but if every male author who wrote one-dimensional female characters could be a killer, well, that's a lot of potential killers out there."

"Oh, Jesus," Doug said, standing up, "if we're talking about whether you can separate the art from the artist again, I'm getting more wine."

"This is so typical," I said. "You all are PIC abolitionists unless it involves a woman and her boyfriend."

"No one is talking about that," Lucy said from across the table, "so why don't you wait to have that argument with someone who is arguing it? Sarah asked if his writing was good, and I said yes, except for the fact that he doesn't treat women as real people in his fiction but uses them as either plot devices or mirrors for his main character."

"No, you implied it meant something about how he treated women in real life."

"That it might. I certainly didn't mean he was a killer or imply anything about what punishment he deserved if he was. When a writer has blind spots in fiction, it could be a blind spot in real life. I don't find that to be a particularly controversial statement."

"In this context, it is," I said, but I was beginning to remember, with some uneasiness, how Jeremy had talked about Rita. He'd said that she was more real to him than women he met at a bar, that he would rather spend time with her—a character he'd made up who did exactly what he said she should do. It would be easier to kill someone you didn't see as real, I had to admit, especially if you had a habit of doing that in your job. And wasn't Jane, in the beginning, mostly an extension of Jeremy, at least to Jeremy? Writing the story he wanted? His employee, existing to serve him in the same way Lucy was saying the female characters in his books did? He'd told me that he felt he couldn't see the real Jane anymore because of her murder—but was that true? Or had she always been a mirror for him? And what if she had wanted to be more? Or what if he hadn't liked what he saw?

"How's your mom?" Nate asked from across the table.

I was glad to see that Sarah and Doug looked momentarily chastened.

"Oh, she's okay," I said, because I had no idea what to say when people asked about my mom. Nothing I could say got anywhere close to describing what it was like. "We're getting by."

"What is she like?" Nate asked. "Is that insensitive? I apologize, but I have no idea. Does she recognize you?"

"Oh, yeah. Her short-term memory is pretty bad, though. She forgets things that happened recently. Not always, but often. It's almost like she's making fewer memories. The things that happen don't leave an impression. She also forgets to shower and eat. But mostly, besides the paranoia, it feels like she's not paying attention, like you are always talking to someone who is really distracted by something else." Nate nodded, so I continued. "She has these conversation loops that she goes back to all the time. No matter what you're talking about, she always goes there, like it's home base or something."

"Is she on medication?" Nate asked.

"Yeah, but all it does is slow it down a little. There's not really anything you can do."

"Mmm," they all said, looking down at their plates.

"It's genetic, isn't it?" asked Sarah.

When I got home, I was drunk. The train had not sobered me up, which said something I didn't want to think about involving how much I drank at Lucy's. The end of the night was a tiny bit blurry, like a phone call going in and out, when you catch individual words that don't add up to anything.

My keys fell off the hook when I hung them by the door. So did my jacket. I looked around for something else to hang up, but I didn't have anything but my phone, so I placed it on the hook by the door and it crashed to the ground, cracking the screen. When my mom came to the top of the stairs, I was sitting on the floor laughing.

"Jesse," she whispered. "He wouldn't want this."

"What?"

"Come here," she said, tightening the sash of her robe around her waist and coming down the stairs. She led me to the kitchen table and poured me a tall glass of water.

"Your father," she said, "played piano at nearly every bar and club in New York, and he never once came home this drunk. This isn't what he wanted for you."

I drank the water, but I was starting to feel more drunk. This had happened before, hadn't it? I looked at the kitchen table. The goose-shaped napkin holder a student had given my mom one Christmas was there, next to the pirate-shaped salt and pepper shakers another student had given her. The water glass, I saw, now that I looked at it more closely, was printed with a Garfield cartoon. Another student present.

"This is an important year for you," she continued. She was hunting in the fridge for something. "Colleges care about junior-year grades, and if your dad knew that he was the reason that your grades slipped and you couldn't go to any college you wanted, how do you think he would feel?"

She found what she was looking for: a package of American cheese. She unwrapped it, placed it on a plate, microwaved it. This *had* happened before—I was sixteen, my dad had just died, and I'd come home drunk from Katie Caplan's party. My mom was about to make us a traditional Haber-family snack. She was going to search through the pantry for the Snyder's hard pretzels, and then we'd dip them in the melted American cheese.

No one could quite remember how this had become a Haber-family snack, but most likely it was born out of desperation, something cobbled together from what we could find in the house. My mom really did hate to go grocery shopping. When the cheese was done, she was going to tell me to come to the couch.

"Come to the couch," she said, taking the cheese out of the microwave and walking into the living room.

I grabbed the box of pretzels off the table and followed her. She placed the cheese on the coffee table and searched through the DVDs until she found the one she was looking for: a Sondheim retrospective at Radio City Music Hall. My dad had played the piano in it. The video cut from the singers and musicians to shots of Sondheim in the audience. It was not clear who was smiling more, Sondheim or my dad.

"I know you miss him," my mom said, putting her arm around me. "But this is not the way. Look at that," she said, pausing the video on a close-up of my dad's face. "Do you see it?"

"No," I said, because when she'd asked me in high school, I hadn't, and though I knew what she was going to say now, I wanted to let her say it. There was a reason, I figured, her brain wanted her to have this moment again.

"Look at what he's holding in his body. Look what it does."

"It feels like it's going to kill me, Mom."

"I know," she said. "But it won't. I promise it won't."

I let my head fall on her shoulder, and I cried, because I had cried then, and my mom cried, and my dad played "Last Midnight," and Sondheim smiled, and I was beginning to think that time really was a circle when my phone buzzed in my pocket.

It was a message from Aaron.

I found Roger Warren.

6

THE NEXT MORNING, I was sitting outside a medium-size apartment building in Queens. Aaron was sitting next to me, drinking a hot chocolate. The hot chocolate was in a thermos he'd brought from home. It was not an impulse purchase at Starbucks. I didn't think I'd drunk hot chocolate since I graduated from middle school, especially not in the morning, but watching Aaron, I couldn't come up with a single good reason why not. We'd been waiting outside Roger Warren's apartment building for two hours, and if he didn't come out soon, I was going to head to the nearest coffee shop to purchase one for myself. I'd had the thought a number of times already, figuring I could always have Aaron text me if Roger Warren showed up while I was gone. But despite the fact that Aaron was the one who'd sent me the address and, indeed, was the only reason I knew about Roger Warren in the first place, I didn't quite trust him.

Our paths, Aaron's and mine, to @theblessing's apartment building started the same way—obsessive internet stalking that's as natural to people our age as riding bikes. We'd stumbled across the same story, the same online literary journal. While I'd written to the editor identifying myself, Aaron had taken a different tack. He'd contacted the journal, pretended he was compiling a Best of the Web list, and said he wanted to include "Dragonfruit."

Inclusion on the list, which would actually be a website hosting various stories collected from online journals, paid fifty dollars for the right to republish. Would the editor be able to give him the contact information for the author? The editor complied, and Aaron repeated the spiel in an email to Roger Warren. After Roger agreed and signed some fake paperwork, Aaron asked for an address to send the check. Which was where we were now, sitting on a bench across the street from it while Aaron drank a hot chocolate and I did not.

"I thought you were busy at work," I said casually. "I'm surprised you have time for a stakeout."

When he'd sent the address last night, I'd told him I'd check it out today, but he insisted on coming with me. I tried to dissuade him, but he was adamant, and I'd been a little drunk, so my persuasive powers were not at their strongest. At the end of our text exchange, I felt exhausted, boxed in. There was something about him that was unrelenting—as were the emails in my inbox, his ever-growing document listing anything he remembered about Jane, anything that might be helpful. I wondered what it felt like to date him. Or break up with him.

"I called in sick," Aaron said matter-of-factly.

Pretty good at lying, I noted.

"How'd you come up with the idea for the Best of the Web?" I asked.

"Just tried to think of a reason someone would give you their address without knowing you. Figured being sent a check was one."

"They didn't think that sounded fake?"

"The email explained it a little—wanted people to take horror more seriously, hoping to make this list important, prestigious, money helped do that, blah-blah-blah."

"And he believed that?"

"People believe what they want to believe. He wanted to believe his story was that good."

"What do you do, again?" I asked.

"I work for the mayor. Legislative assistant."

"Hmm." The door across the street opened, but it was an older woman and a little boy wearing a puffer jacket embossed with a Mets logo who was probably her grandson. We didn't know what Roger Warren looked like, which was a slight hiccup in our stakeout. Every time a man left the building, I got up, stood behind the bus stop structure, and yelled "Roger!" as loud as I could while Aaron checked to see if the man looked across the street toward me. It wasn't the most elegant plan, but it was the best we could do. Once, a man emerged with headphones over his ears, and I'd had to improvise. In that case, I'd crossed the street and walked directly into him.

"Roger," I said loudly. "Good to see you, man."

He shook his head at me.

"Sorry. I thought you were someone else."

Aaron was on his phone, scrolling quickly through Twitter. He flicked the screen with his index finger at a rate that seemed too rapid for him to be reading what was in front of him. After about three minutes of this, during which his finger hit the screen faster and faster, he sighed and put his phone back in his pocket.

"Find what you were looking for?" I asked.

"Never," he said.

The morning was cool and loud: Buses barreling past us or pulling up to the stop next to us with screeching, sighing brakes. People screaming down from windows at other people walking below. Police sirens. Ranchera music blasting from speakers placed outside a small market across the street. Someone was cooking meat on a grill. Around us, trash cans were overfull and wet. A homeless man pushed his shopping cart up to one and began picking through it. Aaron jumped up from the bench and handed him some cash from his wallet.

"That was cool," I said to Aaron when he returned. "I never have cash on me."

"I always have cash on me."

"Right," I said. "Remind me, how long were you and Jane seeing each other?"

"About seven months," he said. "We broke up once, but we got back together. So about seven months."

"When did you break up the second time?"

"About a month before she died."

"I'm not sure a lot of ex-boyfriends would come on a stakeout for an internet troll."

"I have no idea what other people would do," he said.

"Not sure you should be working in policy, then." He smiled but didn't laugh and didn't turn to look at me. "Why did she dump you?" I looked out of the corner of my eye to see if the phrasing stung him. It did.

"I don't know," he said, shoving his hands into his pockets. "Jane was hard to know."

"How so?"

"My therapist says some people don't give you that much to hold on to. The stuff you can hold on to—that's inside the person. And with some people, you can never get there."

"Are you saying she was superficial?"

"No," he said. "There was stuff there. She had an inner life. But she had no idea how to share it, and so there was nothing to hold on to."

Across the street, a man was hurrying up to the door of Roger Warren's apartment building. There wasn't time to disguise myself behind the bus stop, so I called out from where we were sitting. He didn't slow his stride or look up, so I turned back to Aaron.

"How much time would you say you spent discussing Jane with your shrink?"

Aaron laughed. "A lot. But, you know, she got murdered."

"Yeah. I don't know, though," I said. "She broke up with you, convinced you to take her back, and then breaks up with you again? Maybe you would've talked to your shrink about her a fair amount, even without the murder. A lot of resentment there."

He smiled with one corner of his mouth, tight and involuntary. "Statistically, it's probably your client. You're aware of that, right?"

"Or you."

"But I know it's not me. So that leaves Jeremy. At the office, we've gotten a lot of requests for extra police in the area. People are afraid to run."

"That makes sense."

"Not really. People overestimate the likelihood of something happening based on the ease with which they can bring an example to mind. Plane crashes, terrorist attacks, getting canceled. It's not irrational, per se, but it's a processing error."

"Ahh," I said. "So you do know why people do things." Or at least you think you do. "But let me ask again: How many ex-boyfriends do you think would end up stalking internet trolls who harassed girls who'd dumped them twice?"

I looked at his profile, searching for a reaction, something similar to the anguish that moved across his face before. But there was nothing this time. He'd gotten used to it.

"I don't know," he said. "How many ex-boyfriends would think it would help them feel better? That many."

"Why would it make you feel better?"

"Because I discount future time. A lot of people do."

"Another processing error?"

"Yes. Sometimes doing something—anything—is the only way to make the present bearable. But it's an illusion, a distraction from the grief that will have to be dealt with one day. In my case, I value right now more than what's coming later."

"Is that what your shrink told you?"

"Well, she doesn't know I'm doing this, but I suspect if I told her, she'd say something like that. Different metaphor, same idea."

The door of the building across the street opened and a man stepped out. He looked to be in his twenties and was wearing a leather jacket and carrying a book. I stepped behind the bus stop structure and called out, "Roger." He glanced in my direction, and I ducked down. Aaron held his phone to his ear, pretending he was talking to someone. When the man turned away from us, Aaron came to stand beside me.

"Now what?" he said.

"Now we follow him."

But the man stepped into the street and began to cross, walking directly toward us.

"Shit. Did he see you?"

"I don't think so."

The lights changed. Cars streamed toward him, and he began to run. We braced ourselves, but instead of approaching us, he veered off at the last minute, coming to a halt beside the bus stop. After checking the time, he opened his book and leaned against a faded poster of the Rock.

It felt odd to be so close to him. He was oblivious to our presence, while he was the complete focus of ours. It made the moment feel off balance, like we could all tip over.

The Q64 pulled up, groaning. We waited until Roger climbed on, then got in after him. He slid into the first open seat and we kept going, sharing a bench at the back of the bus. At each stop, Roger lifted his face from his book, looked out the window, then went back to reading. Until the fifth stop. This time, when the bus started to slow down, he glanced out the window, pushed himself up, and went to stand at the front of the bus. Aaron and I made our way to the back door and stepped out after we saw him descend the front steps. We followed him, trying to keep about half a block between us. At least I did. Aaron, afraid we might lose him, kept accelerating, and I kept touching his arm and telling him to slow down.

On 172nd Street, Roger Warren walked to the gate of a closed storefront, knelt down, unlocked the padlock, and pulled the gate up.

Warren Hardware.

Aaron started across the street, but I stopped him again.

"It's not open yet," I said. "We'll go in a little after nine. If we try to talk to him now, he'll be preoccupied with opening. We'll only annoy him."

At 9:03, Roger flipped the Open sign on the door, and we crossed the street to confront him.

Warren Hardware was small and packed. Brooms and mops hung from the ceiling in the center of each crowded aisle; a tall person would have to duck around them. Circular stools on wheels were placed randomly around the store for customers or employees to use to reach the highest shelves. Paintbrushes were stacked near sponges, PVC pipes next to snow scrapers. Roger Warren, behind the cash register, was leaning on a counter covered with so much stuff—mini-pocketknives, mini-flashlights, reusable grocery bags that could be stuffed in a sack no bigger than a fist, random glass jars of candy—there was barely any room for a customer to put down purchases. Hardy pieces of twine hung from the ceiling above Warren's head, offering more inventory: Hot Wheels, Barbies, ninety-nine-cent water guns, packets of stickers, all of them clamped on with chip clips and metal clothespins that were also for sale.

A bell rang when we entered, and Roger Warren looked up at the sound. When we made eye contact, I tried to imagine him pushing Jane into a dumpster. I did that with everyone: Jeremy, Lydia, Wes, Tom, Aaron. I don't know whether I believed in instincts like these; I don't know whether I thought it was possible to look at someone and get a feeling—not so much of evil, because I didn't believe in evil, but of guilt, that I could see the effort of carrying that secret. But I did try to imagine people killing her too, the act of it as kind of a litmus test. The truth, though, was that no matter who I picked, I could always imagine them doing it. Maybe not at first, but the more I thought about it, I could always see it. Not the motivation, not even the capability, necessarily, but the image of it in my head: That face, that body, standing close to Jane in that alley, arguing about something, and then the push. The fear hearing that crack, seeing the way she fell. With Roger Warren, though, I could see it immediately.

"Roger Warren?" Aaron asked as he approached the counter.

The man looked at Aaron warily, trying to classify him. Then his gaze fell on me and he worked out that we were together. He stood a little straighter. He was a slight man both in height and body type, but he had broad shoulders, and his chest puffed out when he pulled them back.

"Yeah?"

"We're here to talk to you about Jane Murphy," Aaron said.

Damn it. I should have known Aaron would do this, but for some reason I'd thought he'd let me take the lead. Roger's glance flicked from Aaron to me, then back to Aaron again. Slowly, he picked up his book and opened it to the bookmark.

"Don't know her."

"The hell you don't," Aaron said, taking a step closer to him. Roger put his hand below the counter.

"Okay, okay," I said, walking up to Aaron and pushing him back toward the door. I took my phone from my pocket, pulled up a picture I'd taken of Rita's DMs, and held it up so Roger could see. He looked at the screen but kept his hand under the counter.

"That you?" I asked.

He shrugged but didn't answer.

"That's your Twitter handle, isn't it?"

"So what if it is?"

"Well, you said you didn't know who Jane Murphy was. That's a lot of messages to forget."

"That's Rita Hadzic's account. Not whoever you're talking about."

I felt Aaron shift behind me, wanting to say something, so I rushed on even though I would have appreciated a moment to think through the next step.

"Are you aware that Rita's not a real person?"

"Of course I know Rita isn't real. I'm not crazy."

"Then why were you writing her?"

He took his hand out from under the counter and closed his book.

"I don't know. I liked the story. I thought the writer might appreciate it, for us to engage with it at that level. Maybe he'd even like it enough to make it a real character. Probably not the killer, because he already knew who that was before he started. But maybe a red herring. Something to throw people off."

I glanced back at Aaron. I was pretty sure his face showed what I was trying to keep off mine.

"It never occurred to you that the writer, Jane Murphy," I said, emphasizing her name, "would find those messages a little bit threatening?"

"I thought some guy wrote it."

"Not exactly."

"I think you're missing the point," he said. "They—she, whoever—wouldn't have written the thing on Twitter if they didn't want people to respond this way."

"With threatening DMs?" I said.

"They weren't threatening. They were about a character who was already dead."

"Missing," Aaron said from behind me. "Rita is missing. She might not be dead."

Roger had placed his hands on the counter. He flipped his wrists up without lifting them, a shrug with the bare minimum of physical movement. His face, I noticed, worked similarly; the muscles barely twitched. I wasn't sure I'd ever spoken to someone whose face moved so little.

"I think we all knew she was dead," Roger said.

"Did you know Jane's dead? The writer that you sent all those messages to?" Aaron said. "Murdered."

Roger looked at Aaron, then back to me, and shook his head.

"I didn't know who she was until you walked in here. She's dead?"

"Oh, come *on*," Aaron exploded. "You were so into it you wrote to Rita every day, and you expect us to believe you never looked into who was writing it?"

"I thought some guy wrote it, like I told you. I thought maybe he'd think it was interesting."

"I think the police are probably going to think it's interesting, these messages," I said.

For the first time, Roger's face betrayed some kind of emotion—not worry, but surprise.

"Why?"

"Because she was murdered, asshole," Aaron said.

"Listen—" he started, but I interrupted.

"What my colleague means is that you did write her quite a bit; obsessively, some would say. The messages can certainly be read as threatening."

"I didn't know who she was," he said. "How could I have killed her?"

"Can you prove you didn't know who she was?" I asked. "She has been publicly associated with the project for a while now, and you seem pretty invested in it."

He looked around as if for someone to corroborate what he'd said, but finding no one but us in the shop, picked up his phone and started searching for something.

"Jane Murphy, right?" he asked.

"Yes."

He was silent as he looked through his phone. He was in no rush. There was nothing in his movements that suggested he felt uncomfortable with us standing over him, waiting, or that our questions had made him nervous in any way. He swiped his finger across his screen over and over again while we watched. I took a step to the right to try to get a better view of his phone. If he noticed, he didn't care or move his phone closer to his chest to block my view. He was reading news articles about Jane. His face impassive, unchanging as he read one and moved on to the next. After the news articles, Twitter. Then the calendar app, back to Twitter, articles.

After a few minutes of this, he put his phone back in his pocket.

"First," he said, "it says she died November sixth sometime between five and six a.m. I was here doing inventory. Second, if you have my messages, you know I kept writing after November sixth. Why would I keep writing to her if I'd killed her?"

"Anyone who can vouch for you being here between five and six a.m. on November sixth?" I asked.

"Yeah," he said, smiling, "Linda and Roger Warren Senior."

"His parents," Aaron said as we walked back to the bus stop. "Are you kidding?"

"Well, it's not great," I said. "Maybe they would lie for him, maybe they wouldn't. And whether the jury believes an alibi given by his parents or not depends in part on if there's other evidence that makes Roger look suspicious."

"Well, he was creepy as fuck," Aaron said. "Don't forget to factor that in."

"Yeah." We stopped at a crossing and waited for a few cars to pass before walking against the light when the road was clear. "Do you think it's possible he really didn't know who she was? That he was so into the story he would write her hundreds of messages but never dig around a little and figure out who Jane was?"

"I don't know."

A woman was selling fruit on the side of the street, and Aaron stopped and bought a bag of sliced papayas. They were slippery in his fingers.

"Did you ever find the files I told you about?" he asked. "Maybe it would show if she ever reached out to him. Or maybe he used more than one handle, and she figured it out, and that's why she wanted to combine the messages. Maybe there are messages that show he knew who she was."

I shook my head, but I knew where he was going. If Roger was lying about knowing who Jane was, having his parents as his alibi would start to look pretty weak. At the next light, I found my phone and wrote a quick follow-up to Tom about Jane's computer. He wrote back before the light changed.

So sorry but I haven't found it yet.

Between you and me, he continued in the next text, I'm in the middle of selling the company and everything's a fucking fire drill. It's on my list for today, though. I'll let you know as soon as I find it and whether there's anything on it. If you don't hear from me by 5, text me back and remind me because it means I forgot, and I really do want to help—I just forget things.

We didn't have to wait long for the bus. It was filling up, but we found two seats across from each other and dropped down into them. Aaron let his long legs fall into the aisle but then seemed to become aware of them and pulled them back in.

"When Jane broke up with you," I said, "how many times did you ask her why?"

He pushed his knees up into the empty seat in front of him. His body looked squashed and uncomfortable.

"Look," he said. "If you want to make me come across to the jury as the guy who couldn't get over the girl, to cast some doubt on Jeremy in their minds, you probably could. I suspect you know that already. But I'll save you some time. There's no smoking gun. No email or phone call or text or altercation where I lose my shit on her. It's only drunk texts asking to come over. Emails where I try to convince her she's wrong. It's hard for me to read them now. I'm humiliated she saw that part of me. It used to be you could just be embarrassed by shit like that, but now I have to be ashamed."

"Because she died?"

"No, because that's the way it is now. You can't not get over someone. It means there's something wrong with you. If a girl can't get over a guy and keeps contacting him, she's not just clingy anymore, she's probably got some attachment or personality disorder. If it's a guy who can't get over the girl, though, it means he's abusive, or he could be. He's got that inside him because he doesn't respect boundaries."

"I didn't say that."

"You will. Unless you find someone better than me. Listen, I know what it sounds like, all right." He turned to face me across the aisle. "But it seemed like she really liked me. When we were together—not on texts, not on the phone, but together—I could feel it. It was like she was trying not to for some reason."

"Sure." I let a few blocks slide by in silence. "So, on the morning of November sixth, between five and six a.m., you were probably sleeping, with no one able to confirm or deny? Maybe some roommates who think you were home but wouldn't be able to swear to it?"

"No," he said. "I wasn't sleeping. I was running."

7

I LEFT AARON UNDERNEATH Grand Central Station. He went left to catch the 6, and I climbed up into the wide-open hall of the station. Outside, I put my sunglasses on and started walking toward the Thorton office, but after a few blocks I stopped. I really didn't want to go there. I could picture the office in my mind, the small talk in the kitchen, the hours that would pass as I wrote things or read things on my computer. I texted Jeremy to ask if Jane had ever told him about @theblessing, or Roger Warren, or the messages she was getting in Rita's DMs.

No, he wrote back.

Did you ever read Rita's DMs?

Sometimes.

Do you remember any messages from @theblessing?

Not that I recall.

It was notable, I thought, that Jane had not discussed these messages with Tom or Jeremy, only with Aaron. Maybe it could be used to help build a narrative that Jeremy and Jane were not very close. It was only Aaron she told when she was uncomfortable.

Do you know Kaya's number? I wrote Jeremy.

No.

Aaron didn't know it either. But if there was anyone who knew about Roger Warren, had any idea how much his messages disturbed Jane or if he'd ever done anything but write to her, it was Kaya. I retraced my steps, descended into the bowels of Grand Central, and took the subway to Jane's old office.

When I got there, I realized I didn't have a terrific plan on how to approach Kaya. Tom had made it clear he didn't want me to talk to her at the office. He almost seemed protective of her, now that I thought about it, and I didn't want to annoy Tom, because he was going to give me Jane's old computer, and I didn't want to jeopardize that. There was a restaurant across the street so I went in and found a table facing Stile's office with the vague notion I would see Kaya as she left for lunch. When the waiter came, I ordered a vegan bacon, lettuce, and avocado and an iced tea.

"Is it okay if I work here?" I asked him.

"Long as you pay," he said.

I set up my computer and went to Jane's Instagram page. My recollection of Kaya was more of an impression—small, dark hair, large brown eyes. I wasn't entirely sure I'd recognize her if I saw her walk out of the building, so I scrolled through pictures hoping I'd see her. But I got distracted pretty quickly by a picture of Jane in front of the Brooklyn Bridge, throwing her hat in the air; the caption *You might just make it after all.*

I felt something pinch near my chest. She was too young to know *The Mary Tyler Moore Show,* just like I was too young to know *The Mary Tyler Moore Show,* but we both did. I wondered how many people liking the photo were aware of the reference. Jane didn't work in a newsroom, but I could see how she would gravitate toward Mary's story. In the sitcom, Mary was older than she was—by only a year or two, but enough to make her feel as if she was where she was supposed to be, ahead even. A young girl in a big city, a feeling that the accumulating successes in her early career were building something solid and safe and permanent, that all her decisions about which job to take and where to live and whom to date were becoming something, that she was becoming them.

The comments on Jane's picture were a eulogy and a trial. A séance. A Ouija board with a million tiny fingers gently pushing the message toward whatever they were afraid of. It was hard to read, and I scrolled back up to the picture of Jane, smiling and scarved, her hat frozen in the sky above her head.

"Did you know Jane?" the waiter asked, setting my iced tea down on the table.

"No. Did you know Jane?"

"Yeah."

He pushed a vase of purple flowers out of the way and placed a small bottle of simple syrup on the table as well as little pots of mustard, ketchup, and some other unidentifiable condiments for my as yet unarrived meal. He leaned toward the computer, grimaced when he read her caption.

"That's brutal."

"How did you know her? Because she worked across the street?"

"Yeah, and she was best friends with my girlfriend."

"Kaya Mitchell?"

"Yeah," he said, more slowly this time. "I'm not going to talk about Jane for some article, FYI. No comment."

"Oh, I'm not a journalist," I said. "I'm an investigator. I work for Jeremy Miller. Did you know him?"

A bell rang from the kitchen, and he glanced toward it.

"That's your food," he said. "I'll be right back."

He came back with my sandwich: hearty seeded bread, bright green avocados, thick-cut tomatoes, a disproportionate amount of lettuce. French fries, thin and crunchy, a ramekin of coleslaw, and a large dill pickle I could smell from the plate. He waited until I pushed my computer out of the way, then put the plate down in front of me.

"I knew Jeremy a little," he said. "Kaya knew him better."

"Do you think he did it?"

I found it was often best to open this way, helped me know which way to proceed with the questions.

"I hope not. I mean, I don't think you ever want anyone you know to end up being a killer. There's always going to be a little part of you that wants to make that go away. But I barely knew him. Kaya doesn't think so, though."

This was good news, and I made a mental note to tell Phil: most people I'd talked to who knew Jeremy didn't think he'd done it.

"I'd love to talk to her," I said.

The door to the restaurant opened and a party of four walked in. The waiter looked them over as the hostess gathered menus. When they were pulling their chairs out at a nearby table, he turned back to me.

"I'll text her. Do you need anything else right now?"

I looked at my sandwich, my little pots of condiments, and shook my head. After I took half of the lettuce off my sandwich, I ate and read something on my phone, occasionally looking over at the waiter and trying to imagine him pushing Jane into a dumpster. But he was busy with two new tables that had come in at the same time, and the constant activity of his body prevented me from successfully placing it in another scenario. He rushed around getting drinks, putting orders in. After refilling waters at the table of four in the corner, he came back to me with the water pitcher.

"Sandwich all right?" he asked.

"Delicious."

"Yeah, it's pretty good," he said. He glanced around the restaurant to take stock of his tables. "I'm Billy, by the way."

144

"Jesse."

"Cool. So, does it look bad for Jeremy? Is he going to go to jail?"

Billy must have decided he had a few minutes.

"Well, I'm only an investigator, not a lawyer. But no, I don't think so."

He nodded, holding the water pitcher loosely at his side.

"Yeah. Yeah. It's been fucking awful, you know?"

"Of course. Did you know Jane well?" I asked.

"Yeah," he said. "They came here a lot. You know, it's right across the street, so after work, lunch. Plus she was over at Kaya's all the time."

"What was she like?"

"Like everyone, I guess. Nice, funny, smart. Quiet, especially compared to Kaya and Jeremy. She must've liked those strong personalities, now that I think about it."

"Did you know Aaron?"

He nodded. "Yeah, Aaron was a little different. Maybe that's why it didn't last."

"Was she seeing Aaron and Jeremy at the same time?"

He glanced at his other tables, and turned back to me.

"I'm not sure. One was usually more in the forefront than the other, or at least it always seemed like that."

"Was it typical for Jane to be seeing more than one person?" I worked hard to make my voice neutral, but unlike Jane's roommate Lydia, Billy did not seem worried that I might use this kind of information in the trial in a way that would make Jane look bad. Instead, he bit his lip like he had a secret. One he wasn't embarrassed about.

"Jane," he said. He stopped, started again. "Having two guys around, I'm not sure it was something she did intentionally, but it always seemed to happen."

"Really?"

"Jane liked to have guys like her. Even me sometimes. Not that there was any line crossing or anything."

"Really. What did Kaya think about that?"

"Oh, it didn't bother her. That was Jane, you know? Kaya knew nothing was ever going to happen there, on either end. I would never, and Jane, well, Jane worshipped Kaya. The flirting was something Jane couldn't help doing. It wasn't even flirting. It's hard to describe. But there was an energy. She had to turn it on."

"A look-at-me energy?" I offered.

"No," he said. "Something else."

His phone buzzed in his pocket.

"Kaya says she's in a meeting that won't end, but she'll be down as soon as she can. She said don't leave."

"As long as you don't mind me here, I'll wait all day."

He laughed, putting his phone back in his pocket. "Tom must have done an extra line this morning."

"Tom Stafford?" I asked, but the bell rang in the kitchen, and he was already walking away.

I crunched on a fry, thinking about my meeting with Tom. How he'd pulled an all-nighter and looked fresh as a daisy, the way his knee kept banging the underside of the table while we were talking, even his business with its multiple revenue streams, how much he wanted to tell me about it. How much he liked to talk. I'd thought it was him, but maybe it was cocaine.

I saw Kaya through the window. She was smaller than I remembered, as if she'd lost ten pounds since the last time I'd seen her. She saw me looking at her and hesitated. Our eyes met through the glass. I couldn't believe I'd thought I wouldn't recognize her.

I stood as she walked to the table. My napkin fell off my lap, and I left it on the floor because if I bent to get it, I'd have my head down when she got to my table.

"Did you want to get that?" she said. "Or were you waiting for someone who works here to do it?"

Her tone was much sharper than I'd expected, especially considering how chatty her boyfriend had been. He'd made it sound like Kaya was coming down as an ally.

I bent and retrieved the napkin, twisted it in my hands.

"Do you want to sit down?" I said, gesturing to the chair across from me. "Thank you for talking to me," I continued when she didn't sit. "Billy said you don't think Jeremy did it."

"Jeremy doesn't like to do anything that would limit Jeremy's ability to do whatever Jeremy wants. So, no, I don't think he'd be inclined to do something that would land him in jail."

"Well," I said, moving tentatively to sit down, "we agree on the important part." I bent slightly at the knees, waiting for her to pull out her chair before I sat. But she didn't, so I stayed half crouched.

"*An* important part," she said. "Not *the*. He could have snapped."

"Jeremy doesn't seem like the type to snap."

"I've seen him snap."

"Really?"

She smiled, finally pulled out her chair and sat down. She leaned across the table to take one of my fries.

"Really," she said. "Seems like maybe you don't know him as well as you think you do."

"You're telling me you've seen him be aggressive toward Jane?"

"Well, no. But I have seen him snap. He's not very good at feeling his feelings."

"Who is?"

"Lots of people, actually. But he's particularly bad at it. I've seen him panic."

"When?"

"Fighting with Jane." She smiled again, took another fry, dipped it in ketchup.

"I was under the impression," I said, "that you didn't think Jeremy did it."

"I don't. Jeremy's first instinct is to leave. That's what he does. That's what he did at the bar the night before she died, that's what he always did. He disappeared, then some time would pass, and they would start up again. If he went to her apartment the morning after their fight, it would be the first time he'd ever done something like that."

I couldn't think of anything to say. She was telling me that she didn't think Jeremy did it, but every time I said anything, she switched and started telling me why he did. Maybe it would be better if I said nothing. Unfortunately, I wasn't always good at that.

"That sounds right," I said.

"Unless Jane gave him some kind of ultimatum if he didn't show up," she said. "Unless he said he was leaving, and Jane held on to his arm or something. And Jeremy panicked because, for one second, he thought he might actually have to deal with her instead of just walking away."

This time I was determined to keep my mouth shut. I didn't even nod. I tried to make sure my face didn't express anything resembling agreement.

"Aren't you going to defend him?" she asked. "Isn't that your job?"

"My job——" I started.

"I know what your fucking job is."

I looked around desperately for Billy. Maybe if she saw him being nice to me, it would make her soften somehow. Her expression was, well, hostile, but I remembered the way she had looked at me when I'd been sitting in the conference room with Tom and when our eyes met through the glass of the restaurant. Like she wanted to be inside me, like she wanted to know everything I knew.

"I am actually trying to find out what happened," I said. "That's why I'm here."

"You're here to use what I know to help Jeremy."

She took the pickle off my plate. I'd been saving it for last.

"Look, I get you don't like Jeremy."

"I like Jeremy," she said. "But I'm capable of seeing his flaws, especially as many of them manifested in how he treated my best friend." She took a bite of the pickle. Some of the juice dribbled down her chin. She wiped at it with the back of her hand. When she saw me looking at her, she asked, "What? Do you not believe me?"

"I'm slightly afraid of you, actually."

"Yeah," she said.

Billy approached—a little late—with the water pitcher. He filled Kaya's glass, then mine. "Everything going all right over here?" he asked.

"Great."

"You want some fries, babe?"

"No, I can eat Jesse's—right?"

I nodded.

"Soup to go?"

"Yes, please. And extra bread."

After he left, I moved the condiments and the small jar of flowers out of the way and pushed my plate across the table to her. She reached for another fry.

"Just so we're clear, I don't trust you. But you also happen to be the only person I know who wants to hear me talk about Jane. All I want to do is talk about her and all anybody else wants is for me not to bring her up." She glanced at Billy, who was two tables away taking an order. "He's trying," she said, "but he gets this kind of frozen look on his face whenever I say her name. Which, to be fair, is something I do a hundred times a day."

"It makes sense that you would want to talk about her."

"Do you ever feel," she asked, "like something isn't real until you talk about it?"

"All the time."

"Well, it feels like that with Jane. Except about five minutes after I talk about her, it all goes back to seeming unreal again. And I really need it to feel real, because there's something terrible coming. I feel terrible now, but I know it's not it. There's something else, and I can't get there and I can't get through it until it feels real. But it won't."

"When my dad died," I said, "my mom said some losses you have to experience in pieces, because to feel them all at once would be unendurable."

"Well, I think I got fucked, because it feels both unreal and unendurable."

"That's how I felt too. Can I have a fry?"

She placed her fingers on the edge of the plate and nudged it toward me. "Okay. But don't go crazy."

We chewed our fries in silence. After a while, she took another one.

"Is there someone else you think did it?" she asked.

"Maybe. Did Jane ever mention getting threatening messages because of the Rita story?"

"Oh, the forehead messages?"

"Yeah."

"Ugh, what a freak."

"Did they scare her?"

"She didn't love them."

"To me, they're fairly disturbing."

"You'd probably be surprised to hear about the shit that got sent to Jane, or me, or any woman you know on a pretty regular basis." She dipped her fry in the small pot of ketchup. "I'm not saying it rolls off the skin. It doesn't. It leaves a film, but the upside is, it gets harder and harder for any of it to touch you. I don't think she liked being so close to the brain that came up with that shit. But it wasn't directed at her. It was about Rita."

"But she wrote Rita, right?"

"Her and Jeremy, yeah."

"Did you ever get the impression that whoever was writing those messages knew who Jane was?"

"No. Why do you think that?"

"I don't know. I'm looking into it."

"I really don't think Jeremy went to Jane's apartment that day, FYI," she said. "Is it theoretically possible that Jane called him and gave him some ultimatum to get him to come over, and he actually came? Or that he happened to see her running, and she decided to confront him? Yes, of course. But they would both have been acting fairly out of character for that to happen. And—" She stopped. "And I think she would have asked me before doing something like calling or confronting Jeremy after one of their fights. She was so in her head about Jeremy, she never knew what to do. It was like she was paralyzed."

"She could have snapped," I said. "She could have been too embarrassed to talk to you about it."

"Maybe."

"Why did you hesitate?"

"When?"

"Before, when you said you thought Jane would have asked you before she gave Jeremy an ultimatum."

She took one of the toothpicks off my plate, stabbed a rogue piece of lettuce, picked it up, looked at it to make sure the toothpick was all the way through, then stabbed another piece.

"There is one thing," she said. "I didn't want to tell the police because— well, I don't know why. But I was starting to think that Jane was seeing someone in secret."

"Someone besides Jeremy and Aaron?"

She nodded. "Jane told me everything, so for her not to tell me is really strange. After she died, I sometimes thought it would come out, but it never has. More and more I think, if it's not Jeremy, it must be connected to that."

Or completely random, I didn't say. At the wrong place at the wrong time and nothing else.

"Do you have any idea who that person could be?"

"No. But I do know that she'd recently started this email relationship with Drew Finnley."

"Drew Finnley?"

"Yeah."

"The YA author who does all the supernatural stories?"

"Yeah."

"You think she started a relationship with Drew Finnley, the writer?"

She laughed. "I know, it sounds nuts. But you know how Rita has the soulbond?"

"With Noelle?"

"Right," she said. "That's from a Drew Finnley book. So I guess he read it at some point, liked it, and got in touch with her. They started writing each other emails. A lot of them. He's famous and married and is so much older than us, so if those emails ever tipped into something else or if they ever decided to meet in person, she might not have told me. I can't think of anyone else she might have been sleeping with that she wouldn't tell me about."

I could think of someone, and he was walking over to the table. Then again, he was the one who'd told me Jane sometimes flirted with him. I wouldn't have known that without him mentioning it. And would he have done that if there was anything there? No. Not unless he was trying to get ahead of something. Now that I thought about it, he had been unusually willing to talk to a stranger representing the accused killer of his girlfriend's dead best friend.

"Soup," he said, handing Kaya a small brown bag.

"Thanks." Her phone buzzed on the table, and she looked at it and sighed. "King Tom. Gotta go back."

"Does anybody else work there?" Billy said. "Can't he go twenty minutes without you?"

She shrugged and kissed Billy on the cheek. "He's been particularly Tom-like lately. Everyone's working a ton. I think he's fighting with his wife or something. When he wants to stay away from home, he likes us all to be at the office with him."

I waited for her to continue, to say something about the sale, but she didn't and I wondered if the employees knew Tom was planning to sell the company, what it meant for them, if Kaya's job was secure. I remembered the resentment I'd felt at the bearded man I saw the first time I went to Stile, as if he were the reason for my former job insecurity when the truth was that he and Kaya and all the rest of them were as insecure as I had been.

Billy walked Kaya to the door and returned a few minutes later with the bill and a piece of dark chocolate. While I waited for him to run my card, I checked my phone. I too had received a text message from Tom.

Sorry. Someone wiped Jane's computer. I'm not sure how it happened, but I did look on the shared site we use at work. I don't see anything about that troll so far, but I'm going to download everything she wrote onto a laptop and restore all her old settings so you can look at it. Maybe there's something you'll see that I don't see.

8

WHEN I WOKE UP, I reached for the water I kept by the side of my bed, but apparently I'd finished it in the middle of the night. I staggered to the bathroom in the hall and drank water straight from the tap. I'd been drinking more alcohol since I came home, since I'd started at Thorton. A churning restlessness in the evenings as I wandered through the house I grew up in. At night I dreamed about looking for things I couldn't find. Last night—I remembered the dream as the water finally reached the desiccated crater in my brain—I was supposed to drop off a blood test, and I couldn't find the room. Why I'd taken the blood test was never revealed in the dream, but the nurse who'd drawn blood had handed me a few vials with neon-colored caps and directed me to drop them off at the main office on my way out. But I couldn't find it and I'd wandered the labyrinthine halls of the medical center with an acute and mounting panic that only dissipated about half an hour after I woke up.

I put on some workout clothes, took the train to the city, and started running Jane's run, mapped out for me so helpfully by Aaron. I'd lost weight since returning home and starting at Thorton. My pants were too big, and at the end of every block, I had to pull them back up around my waist. I turned left, straight, straight, straight, straight, left, right, straight, and there was the entrance to the alley. On any other day, she would have run past it, but that day she went in. Why? Because someone she knew called to her? Because she was trying to lose someone chasing her and couldn't run fast enough? I didn't go in; I ran past it, continuing her daily route. It was early and the streets were mainly empty, quiet save for the garbage trucks and their mechanical arms groaning. Someone in a brownstone on the next block was evidently moving. Their trash occupied eighty percent of the sidewalk, and I had to turn sideways and squeeze through it. On the other side, Aaron, jogging in place, waited for me to pass.

"Hey," I said, and he nodded and continued on.

Whether it was the result of my sunglasses and hat, the fact that he hadn't expected to see me, or because his mind was somewhere else, he hadn't recognized me. I watched his retreating back but thought of the look on his face when he passed me. Focused. Determined. It wasn't that hard to imagine him pushing Jane into a dumpster with that look on his face. But would he have left her there? I realized I had to expand my imaginative game, not only the act itself, but the walking away. Not only the flash in the pan of whatever the emotion is that leads to murder—powerlessness? Powerfulness? Rage? Fear?—but leaving her there and going on as if nothing had happened. The person who did this had to be capable of both. If Aaron had done it, could he have continued running this route? Or did he need to run it? Did he need to begin each day trying to find a different ending to that morning, one where he went on his run and didn't see her, didn't beckon her into the alley to ask her about why she'd broken up with him and everything went horribly wrong? If it were me, I probably would have altered my route whether I'd killed her or not, but then again, I was sleeping in my childhood bed, so who was I to say how easy it was to start taking different roads than the ones we were used to taking, if it was even possible.

I finished Jane's run at her apartment and I sat down and leaned back against a planter outside her building, trying to approximate the time she would have been upstairs showering and getting ready for work. Wes came out while I was sitting there.

"Hey, it's you," he said. "You find something?" He was standing directly in the sun, dressed in an orange tracksuit and big orange glasses. "It's for an audition," he explained. "Callback, actually. For this candy they sell in Russia."

"Why don't they hire a Russian actor?"

"It gets better. The commercial shoots in Singapore. They're casting it here, and after we shoot it, they'll dub it in Russian."

"Seems like there must be a more cost-effective way to do that."

He shrugged. "Not my problem. For me, it's a paid trip to Singapore. Did you find something out about Jane?"

"No. I'm—" I started and stopped. "I'm not sure what I'm doing. Walking in her footsteps, I guess."

"That makes sense," he said, coming to lean on the planter next to me. "Like the peanut butter and jelly assignment. Did you ever do that one?"

"I don't think so."

"We did it in fourth grade, I think. The assignment was to write down the steps to make a peanut butter and jelly sandwich. Then you gave your instructions to a partner, and they had to follow them—and only them—to make the sandwich. My partner couldn't even start, because I hadn't written down to pick up the knife. Honestly, sometimes I think it has something to do with me wanting to be an actor, this sense that you miss things when you're not in the body. It's part of how we learn." He glanced at his watch. "Speaking of, I got to go take a bite of a candy bar so good I start moonwalking."

He danced a few steps away from me.

"Pretty early for an audition, isn't it?" The sweat was drying cold against my skin. My quads felt tight, and I remembered Wes telling me he slept late, that he hadn't been awake during Jane's daily run, that he hadn't even been aware of it.

"They have someone in Singapore watching on video," he said. "Time difference."

"I don't understand this commercial."

"Right? Hope I get it," he said. "I thought for a second you were here to tell us it was Aaron."

"Aaron? Why?"

"Well, I've been thinking about it a little more. They live in the same neighborhood and see each other practically every day, but the first time they actually meet is when he shows up at a restaurant across the street from her office in a different neighborhood, a place she happens to go almost daily? I don't know."

"Like he followed her, you mean?"

"Like I said, dude was intense."

Dude was intense. I'd thought that too.

From Jane's apartment, I walked to her office, but instead of going upstairs, I found a coffee shop nearby and started reading things on my phone. I reread Aaron's document, looking now for something else, something beyond the information inside it, some subtext I'd missed about the day he met her at the bar. But it said just what it had said the last time, so I read the whole file again, trying to ascertain if there was any other reason he might have spent so much time creating this document. If it was meant to distract me. If I could infer from it a certain coldness, the brutal pragmatism of the policy wonk. Of someone used to making decisions about where it made sense to cut off benefits, where the risk of accidental death was outweighed by the costs of implementing the safeguards. But I didn't get anything like that; it was mostly summary, and if I could glean something from it, it would be that he was summarizing what she did without analysis, like a scientist in the first steps of a study. Whether that was for my benefit or because he'd never gotten to the next step with Jane herself, I didn't know.

From Aaron's document, I went back to Roger Warren on the internet, but even knowing more about him now yielded few results. I found a couple of pictures of Roger with his parents at the fiftieth anniversary of their hardware store. His grandparents were also there. But if I was hoping I'd be able to tell from a picture whether these parents would lie for their son and give him an alibi for murder, I was disappointed. It was just a picture of four people I didn't know standing next to a person I'd met briefly.

From Roger, I started searching for ways to contact Drew Finnley. There seemed to be a few possible routes, so I filled out a contact form on his website, wrote his publisher, then his agent. There was an official Drew Finnley fan page on Twitter, but he was not on Twitter as far as I could tell after checking approximately thirty Drew Finnley accounts. R. L. Stine was on Twitter, I realized, and there went another two hours. When I came to again, I was on an Etsy page that sold R. L. Stine–themed Christmas ornaments. I closed the browser and texted Lucy. I hadn't been my best self at her dinner party.

I'm sorry I'm an asshole.

No one's just one thing, she responded.

I felt attacked. I'm sorry. I went into defensive mode.

I didn't attack you.

Like I said, I'm an asshole.

I'm sorry it was so bad. I know it's been rough. I wanted you to have a good night.

Well, maybe next time, it can just be us. That would probably be more fun.

It probably would be.

At lunchtime, I crossed the street to Mika's, but Billy wasn't working. I ordered the same sandwich I'd had yesterday and sat at the bar, since it was busy. While I waited for my food, I opened my phone and started reading through #SearchingforRita again.

Noelle told me the strangest part of being dead was how she didn't know it. It felt like falling and then she woke up. I told

her I've felt that so many times, I have no idea if I'm alive. It's
dangerous for her to come visit me. I can feel she is unsafe and
beg her to leave, but she says she has something to tell me.

When the streets started filling up with people leaving offices, I merged into the throng and set off for Jane's yoga class. I hadn't done yoga in a year, but before that I'd done it almost daily with my then-girlfriend, and I'd found it surprisingly invigorating. During the class, my hands slipped on the mat, then my feet. We must have done forty sun salutations in a row, and my arms started to burn and shake in each successive chaturanga. While we were doing savasana, the sweat chilled on my body and someone with heated lavender-infused oil came over and rubbed my shoulders, hard. When the lights came back on, my limbs felt new.

Afterward, the Whole Foods salad bar. I watched a couple I recognized from the class buy groceries. The girlfriend pointed to a high shelf for a jar of sunflower butter, which the boyfriend retrieved. Together, they read the ingredients label, searching for what, I don't know, but there was something sweet about it. I remembered being in elementary school and my mother following me through the aisles with the cart as I dropped packages of cookies and chips inside.

"Is this cereal okay?" I'd ask, holding up a box of miniature chocolate chip cookies, a cartoon man in a prison uniform on the box for some reason.

"Sure, Jesse," my mom would say distractedly as I guided her to the ice cream section.

After Whole Foods, to Kaya's. There was a bench across the street from Kaya's apartment building, and I sat on it until it occurred to me that Kaya could come out and notice me, and I didn't want to scare her. I stood to leave, only to see Kaya and Billy coming around the corner, Kaya pulled this way and that by a large pit bull aggressively sniffing bike racks and trash cans. I turned away so they wouldn't see me.

"Billy, wait," Kaya yelled.

There was something about the tone of her voice that made me want to rush across the street to help her. I wasn't sure why the feeling came at me so powerfully, but it was hard to resist. I stepped closer to a store window and told myself it was because I knew what it felt like to lose someone you loved, and I was afraid putting anything else on top of that—a parking ticket, let alone a fight with a boyfriend—would be too much for her, like pushing a tack into an open wound.

"Billy, stop." She was almost half a block from him. He was walking fast, leaving her behind. I couldn't believe someone could walk away from the pain in that voice. "Stop."

"I don't want to talk about this anymore!" Billy yelled. "Jesus."

He didn't turn back when he said it; he stepped into the street and crossed toward me. I turned again, tucking my head deeper into my shoulder, but I'm not sure he even realized another person was around.

"Billy!" Kaya yelled. "Don't go."

But he did. He rounded the corner and was gone. I could hear Kaya crying from across the street.

"Lenny, Jesus," she said, pulling hard on his leash. The dog yelped. "Sorry," she said, crying harder now. "Sorry, I didn't mean to. I'm sorry. Come on," she said softly. "Come on," she said again, louder and more insistent, the anger creeping back in.

When I turned around, she was yanking her dog toward her building, her arms and his body straining in different directions, Kaya crying and yelling and apologizing in turn.

At home, I fell asleep on the couch watching TV. I woke up to my mom putting a comforter over me. I wasn't sure how long I'd been asleep, but it was starting to get light outside.

"Hi," she said.

I pulled my feet up to make room on the end of the couch, and she sat down and pulled my legs onto her lap.

"Jesse?"

"Yeah, Mom."

"I think I'm forgetting things."

"Like what?"

"I can't remember. Did I go to work? What time is it?"

"It's okay, Mom."

"When I was in my twenties," she said, "I stopped talking to my mother. We made up, but when she died, she'd forgotten we made up and wouldn't talk to me."

"That's not going to happen to us, Mom, because we never stopped talking."

She turned to look at me, her face going through something, then settling. She swatted me on the shoulder.

"You never stop talking," she said.

"Where do you think I got it from?"

I think about this moment a lot now, what it feels like to experience something you know you will remember forever when the other person won't even remember it in the morning. It's a terrible disease, Gloria says, and it is. But sometimes, I think about this: When the pain gets too bad, the body protects you and you black out. Maybe some people aren't meant to be there at the end, to grapple with mortality and see life taken away in pieces, to say goodbye to people they cannot say goodbye to. Or maybe more of life is like this than we think. How many moments never make a memory? How many moments do people live through together that are experienced so differently by each of them, it's almost like they didn't experience something together at all?

9

I WOKE THE NEXT MORNING determined to get more done than I'd accomplished the day before. I had that feeling of a story getting away from me as I chased it, a pressure at the back of my neck. *You are behind,* my mind kept telling me. Like Hamlet's father's ghost. Or Jane's, I suppose. *Mark me.* On the train to the office, as I reviewed my notes on the case, I could feel her presence. *I find thee apt.* I was eager, but it didn't feel very useful, that eagerness. Like a child with a sparkler, light effervescing, no heat.

At the office, I'd barely sat down with my free orange juice and bagel when Jeremy called me.

"You're up early," I said.

"I'm always up early."

"Oh." I'd pictured him still in bed at noon, the kind of guy who ate two meals a day and woke up hungover. I wondered where that came from, then I remembered. "Wes—Jane's roommate—made it sound like you two knew each other because of your shared propensity for sleeping in."

"He slept late. I wrote in Jane's room. I have to write new material first thing in the morning before I think too much. My editor voice gets stronger the longer I'm awake."

"Gotcha." I placed my phone on my desk, switched to speaker. "What's up? I'm going to be eating while we talk, by the way. You caught me at breakfast, and I hate a toasted bagel that's grown cold."

"Okay," he said. "After you asked me about Roger Warren, I remembered something."

"He did reach out to her?"

"No," he said. "Well, I don't know, I still don't know anything about him. But there was this other man that contacted her about Rita. George Kennedy."

I sucked some cream cheese off my finger, searching around on my desk for a pen.

"Okay," I said, writing the name down. "Who's that?"

"Remember how Rita wanted to be an urban planner?"

"Sure."

"She was very interested in so-called historical development; that was a personality trait—if you can call it that—which we made very visible. Before she died, Rita was quite invested in the controversy surrounding the current plans to develop Lower Manhattan around SoHo and Chinatown."

"Sure," I said. "I read something about that."

"I bet," he said. "It's pretty contentious for a lot of reasons. Displacing original residents, gentrification. But there's also pushback related to the historical nature of the neighborhood. Rita was particularly interested in facadism, where a historical building is redeveloped into luxury apartments, but the facade is kept."

"Yeah," I said. "I've seen some of those buildings. Like living on a Hollywood set and walking into a cardboard town. Terrible."

"Well, Jane and I happen to agree with you and, perhaps unsurprisingly, so did Rita. She was very vocal on Twitter about this proposed development, retweeting the opposition group, posting pictures of particularly egregious examples of facadism, et cetera. She also discovered that the brother-in-law of one of the members of the historical committee happened to be a contractor whose company just happened to specialize in facadism. And this member of the historical committee often voted for this facade redevelopment, touted its many wonderful features and the compromise it represented between preservation and development, et cetera, et cetera. Rita tweeted about this committee member quite a bit."

"Before she disappeared."

"Right."

"I don't remember her tweeting about a George Kennedy."

"Tom's a pretty careful guy. We changed his name to James Falcon and he's on the Historical Buildings Commission, which doesn't exist. We made it up. Falcon's cousin, not his brother-in-law, is the contractor. Also, we followed the small-penis rule."

"I'm sorry?"

"If you have a character that's loosely based on a real person, give him a small penis so the actual guy won't want to claim him."

"I'm wondering how you managed to work into a series of tweets about New York real estate that a member of the Historical Buildings Commission had a small penis."

"Syphilis."

"I'm sorry?" I said again.

"We made up this side story about a scandal involving James Falcon where some model accused him of giving her syphilis. See, in the story, James Falcon is like the public conception of a Kennedy: good-looking, old money, entitled, bit of a partyer. George, the real guy, is from old money, but he's not the playboy type. That was another thing we changed."

"I don't remember any of this."

"You probably didn't think it was important. Rita tweeted a lot. That's part of the game. You have to figure out what's important. Is it character building, putting in just enough that it seems real she's an urban-planning major, that she feels real, or is it a clue to who killed her?"

I was scrolling through my phone.

"So, here, she's retweeted a protest for the development originally posted by the Committee Against Development?"

"Yeah, that's real. I mean, she's retweeting a real tweet."

"And then here, she has a thread about James Falcon."

"Right, that's made up."

"But you're saying George Kennedy, the real one, knew the James Falcon character was based on him?"

"He suspected, and he wrote me, and I forwarded it to Jane."

"Was he mad?"

"Really mad. Said he was going to sue for defamation, et cetera."

"And what happened?"

"Jane made a plan to meet him."

"Why Jane?"

"Because Jane's better with people than I am in these kinds of situations. She was going to meet him so she could talk him off the ledge."

I pushed my empty bagel plate away, washed off some cream cheese stuck in my tooth with some pulpy orange juice. "You said Tom was very careful, so Jane meeting one-on-one with this guy doesn't seem like something he'd suggest."

"He didn't know," Jeremy said. "He would not have approved. Tom was very sensitive to this brand he was building, and a defamation scandal didn't fit into that, so we figured Tom would make us delete the tweets, sideline that character. We didn't want to do that."

"So Jane was going to meet him, and—what?"

"Charm him."

"That was the whole plan?"

"Listen," Jeremy said. "It's hard to describe Jane if you didn't know her. She was terribly insecure in some ways. She was fairly quiet. She often preferred to be in the background. But the truth is, Jane could be really fucking charming when she wanted to be. She was easy to flirt with, and she knew it."

It seemed like odd phrasing. Surely, *She was good at flirting* would have been the more natural way to say that. The way he said it made it sound so passive. I told him so.

"But that's exactly what I do mean," Jeremy said. "It's not a knock on her. It's the opposite. She made whoever was flirting with her feel that they were suddenly very good at it, the best in the world. People like to experience that feeling. Especially people who don't feel that way all the time." This made me think of Aaron. Maybe some people would do a lot not to lose a feeling like that. "You give that feeling to someone," Jeremy continued, "especially unexpectedly—well, you can often get your way."

"Did it work?"

"It did," Jeremy said. "In the beginning. They were emailing about some interesting directions the James Falcon character could go in. But he still wanted us to delete the tweets about the connection to the contracting company. He really wanted that gone, and we didn't want to delete that part. It's the Chinatown plot. It couldn't all be ex-boyfriends and horny dads. The city had to be in the story. We had to feel the forces running it. We had to put Rita in their crosshairs, show how they would crush her or anyone who got in their way. *Everyone* who got in their way, if it came to it, because that's what they do."

"So what happened?"

"Well, Jane was going to meet him again. Their email exchange had started to devolve. She was going to sit down with him."

"And what if that went badly—that's what you're thinking?"

"Yeah," he said. "I'm thinking what if that went badly."

"He had a lot to lose?"

"He did." Jeremy paused. "But the other thing you have to understand about Jane is, the same way she could be really charming, she could also make a person really angry. She decides something and stops listening to anything you say. It's the kind of angry that makes you feel crazy, because you only want her to acknowledge she's not listening to you. But she won't, because she really thinks she is. Don't worry, I won't go around saying that, but it's true."

10

THE NEXT DAY I WAS standing outside George Kennedy's home by seven a.m. It was unseasonably warm, which I was grateful for as the street was residential and there was nowhere to wait but outside. He lived in the West Village in a three-story brownstone that appeared on the National Register of Historic Places. Which I suppose was not surprising. Nor was any of the information I'd uncovered on the internet the night before: Horace Mann. Princeton. His wife, thin with an interior design blog and intricately highlighted hair. His kids, also at Horace Mann, left the house first with a nanny. They were sweet and young, the youngest clamoring to climb into the nanny's arms while the older boy searched in a backpack for something. George Kennedy left the house two hours after his children. He wore a blue button-down tucked into khakis, loafers with socks. I had the sense that he always wore this. At a summer barbecue, he would be wearing this. Maybe without socks. His boys would wear this, and their sons, and so on and so on, as their lives unfolded in clambakes on the Vineyard and three-course meals in restaurants with quiet waiters and starched white napkins.

When I saw George Kennedy appear on his front steps, I put my phone in my pocket and prepared to follow him. Unfortunately, he stepped straight into a waiting Uber and was gone. His office was only a ten-minute walk so I went that way, assuming that even if he had to go somewhere else first, he'd end up there eventually.

The offices of Kennedy Preservation were in another three-story brownstone. There was a large bay window on the main floor. It revealed a perfectly appointed but empty room. I had no idea if George Kennedy was inside or not. I could have walked in and introduced myself, but I wanted to watch him first. There was a small dog park on the block, and I went there and sat on a bench facing the street. I sat there for three hours enjoying the mild weather while various dogs took sniffing tours of the park before raising their legs on something. Occasionally, I'd pet the head of some pit bull or golden retriever who came to mash its face into my leg. It was not an altogether unpleasant morning, all things considered, and only a few people gave me outrightly curious stares. Most either assumed I was the owner of some dog running about or felt it was perfectly reasonable to sit outside and watch animals play. When George Kennedy came out around noon, I was taking a video of a German shepherd wrestling with a wiener dog to send to Lucy. I took only an extra fifteen seconds to make sure I got the dachshund pinning the larger dog, but as soon as I left the park, I saw him step into a waiting Uber and disappear again. With no ideas as to where he might have gone this time, I went back to my seat in the dog park.

My phone buzzed in my jacket. A new email from Drew Finnley. For a moment, I let my twelve-year-old self enjoy this. An email from Drew Finnley. Had I ever imagined this day would come? What would Samantha Peterson say if she could see me now? We'd spent fifth grade in her living room reading Drew Finnley books and holding hands. I could still taste her hair in my mouth from kissing her. Tropical shampoo.

Dear Jesse,

Thank you so much for writing me. I was devastated to hear about Jane. As you noted, we were exchanging emails for a time, and when she stopped writing back, I assumed that she had gotten bored writing letters to an old man. I did eventually learn that she had been killed, and when I did, I asked myself: Did I know? Did I notice a change in Rita? In the direction of the story in the last few months? I tell myself that I did, but who's to say if that's simply vanity. People change, characters change, stories change, that is the way of things. Maybe. But I did sense something different about Rita. A dampening. I used to tell Jane she had a real talent in making that character come so alive. To make her feel so full in a medium designed to give you only impressions.

You asked how Jane and I came to write each other. I don't spend much time on social media. It was my nephew. He was a fan of @ritahadzic and recognized her soulbond—a concept I was happy to see written about with such sincerity, though I understand it is supposed to be the sincerity of a fifteen-year-old girl. See, Noelle is a character in a book I wrote. I read what my nephew sent and kept going. I found out who the writers were, and I wrote Jane and Jeremy. Jane wrote me back. She was nervous at first. I think she worried I was angry or that I wanted her to take it down, but it was quite the opposite. I was enamored by the story. I felt invigorated seeing Noelle alive again in the hands of this agile writer, and I told her so.

I was very sad to hear of her death. I've always loved writing about and for young people. Jane was, of course, older than my usual readers and characters, but she was still young, and I saw in her such potential. And also, a person who was still making decisions with repercussions she couldn't begin to anticipate.

When I imagined being a writer as a child, I mostly envisioned writing by myself in a comfortable room, tall bookshelves, a fire, a leather chair. Even when I started writing, the young people who read my books were mostly unknown to me. Social media has changed that, and I met Jane and was able to talk to her about my books and why she wanted to use Say My Name in their story and how much it meant to her growing up.

Sometimes I think that the people who gravitate toward my books are the children who were searching for a god in the same way I was. I felt this about Jane immediately. I don't mean the Sunday-school God or a god from any particular religion. I mean Jane felt there was something missing from the way she was living, a world inside the outside of things. Something was blocking her from experiencing the kind of life where she could feel the mystery, where she could still be astonished. She was trying to find that life.

Jane was a wonderful person and a terrific talent. I'm very sorry for her family, and for the world, and for myself that she had such a short time on this Earth. I will remember her.

Drew Finnley

By the end of the letter, I felt like I might cry. My throat burned. I hoped my eyes hadn't turned red. Fucking Drew Finnley. I'd read his books in the beginning because Samantha read them, but he'd gotten me in the end, and, evidently, he could still get me.

A German shepherd loped over, concerned, and attempted to climb on my lap.

"I'm so sorry," his owner said, running up to me. "Logan, Logan, get down," she called, but he was trying to make my lap bigger, pushing his paws into my thigh.

"It's okay," I said, petting his head. "Really, it's okay."

Two hours later, George Kennedy returned to his office. He stayed inside, presumably working, until around six, when he exited and stepped directly into a waiting Uber. I walked the ten minutes to his house and parked myself outside. Thirty minutes later, he left with his wife, a blazer over his work outfit. This time, though, I was prepared. When I saw the Ford Explorer creeping slowly up the street, I ordered my own Uber. Luckily for me, George and his wife didn't come out for five minutes after their car showed up. I wondered what their rating was, but it gave my Uber enough time to get there.

I'd put Lucy's address in the app.

"Change of plans," I said. "Can you follow that car?"

"Are you serious?" the driver asked.

She was a woman who looked to be about sixty with bright red hair, a lot of lipstick.

"I'll Venmo you personally a hundred dollars right now."

I sent my expenses to Phil once a month, and though I'd never expensed Uber bribes before, I was sure it wouldn't be a problem. I knew from the free coffee and orange juice, the dinners and baseball games with various lawyers around the city, Thorton Investigation Services did not nickel-and-dime. In my opinion, whoever said that private companies could do what the government did more efficiently had never worked for a private company.

The driver twisted in her seat to face me. "A hundred and fifty."

"A hundred and fifty."

She turned back to the road, shrugging. "Buckle up, son."

Five minutes and a hundred and fifty dollars later, I saw George and his wife seated with another couple in a dark Italian restaurant. I ordered a draft beer at the bar. I was too far away to hear what they were saying, and now that I was here, I wasn't entirely sure why. Ordinarily in cases like this, I'd simply approach the guy, tell him who I was, ask my questions. But he was a politician—only a member of a historical preservation commission, sure, but still a politician. Even if he wasn't the governor, I assumed he was well practiced in telling people what they wanted to hear, remaining unrattled in situations that would rattle the average person. I wanted to observe him as much as I could before I gave him a chance to explain everything away. I ordered a gin gimlet and gnocchi, which I'd add to my expenses. It wasn't my fault the subject frequented fancy restaurants. While I waited for my food, I checked my phone. I'd set a Google alert for Jeremy Miller, and there were a number of stories about him today.

That probably wasn't good. I opened one from the NYU paper.

TISCH STUDENTS HIT
WITH A CEASE AND DESIST

NYU seniors Tim Fremont and Frankie Reed were having a great year. The two met in Professor Kittall's improv class when they were freshmen and have been friends ever since.

"We just got each other," Tim says.

"It was 'Yes, and...' from the jump," Frankie agrees. "Great things just seem to spill out of me when Tim's around."

They wrote their first web series, *Donkey Land,* their freshman year. They raised $800 on GoFundMe, cast friends from the drama department, and filmed it in one weekend on Roosevelt Island. Most NYU students will remember the heady days of spring 2017 when they released it, one episode every Thursday for six weeks.

"Everyone saw it," says NYU senior Abigail Otram. "It's a big school, but that was one thing everybody did on Thursday nights. You could bring it up to anyone, even your professors. Everyone had a theory."

The next year brought us *Amy Chicken Little,* another must-watch web series for the NYU set. The two had been working on another original piece for months when Frankie read about a girl who'd gone missing on Twitter.

"I was obsessed," Frankie said. "I talked about it so much, I thought Tim was going to stop being my friend. But instead, he said, 'Why don't we do that one?'"

Enter *The Platonic Rita,* Tim and Frankie's web series based loosely on a series of tweets related to the disappearance of fictional college student Rita Hadzic. Because they decided to focus on a whole new series, they released just two episodes at the end of their junior year. They came back senior year and released only one episode before the death of Jane Murphy, one of the creators of the source material.

"It was all so awful, we stopped. Out of respect. But when we came back after break, we realized it was still in our blood. We had one semester of college left, and we wanted to finish what we'd started," Tim said.

"Yeah," Frankie chimed in. "We wanted to do it for Jane. Plus, we had our own ideas about what would happen now, how we would end it, because, well, you know, because of Jeremy Miller."

But it was not to be. They released only one episode before they received an email from an attorney at Lincoln and Browning.

"We thought it was a joke at first," Frankie says.

But it wasn't. Turns out, Tim and Frankie didn't think much about copyright.

"We didn't think to ask. I know it sounds obvious now," says Tim, "but Frankie and I always thought of these web series as things we made for our friends in school, just like the school puts on plays every year. Now I know that the school has to pay licensing fees on those plays, but I didn't know that until recently. I just thought that you can do anything in school, because it's school."

"Sorry," Frankie says. "We're actors, not lawyers. And no one minded in the beginning."

Frankie is correct on that point. Tim and Frankie had already released three episodes of *Platonic Rita*. Maybe, if the audience had stayed primarily NYU students, they would have released their fourth episode this week. But instead, the first three have already been removed from YouTube and the scenes from the final episodes—including the new ending—are going to remain on Tim's computer.

"No one's going to know how it ends now," Frankie says. "It's just a really frustrating feeling."

There were a number of other articles on the subject: An NYU law professor discussing the copyright issues in depth. A few generic pieces reporting the basic facts. An industry article about Stile and its position as a media company to watch. And about twenty articles using a banal copyright issue that many people wouldn't have cared about as a pretext to rehash the details of Jane's death and Jeremy's arrest—the internet backlash against him and the idea that he'd tried to take credit for Jane's ideas, his propensity for writing about women who disappeared, their fight in the bar, his cell phone placing him near her apartment the morning she died, et cetera, et cetera.

The gin had gone to my head quickly, but when I glanced back to see

George Kennedy leaning over to say something into his wife's shiny hair, it struck me quite forcefully that I was being taken for a ride. *I don't care about that stuff,* Jeremy had said. To explain away the tension at the center of their project, to show he didn't care that people thought he was taking credit for Jane's work. *I don't view authorship like that.*

"The lady doth protest too much," I should have said to him. *That's Shakespeare.*

I don't think I ever really believed him, but I'd wanted to believe him, I realized now. It stung a little to see how flimsy his principles were. Maybe he did believe in it, intellectually, but eventually his ego came roaring back into play. *Mine. My way. I get to say how, because I came up with her.* Or maybe he honestly hadn't cared about owning Rita until he realized he could get more money out of it, and then all his lofty ideals crumbled away. In either case, Jeremy was lying to me and I'd spent the whole day following some random rich guy around for no other reason than because Jeremy had told me about him.

Outside, the temperature had dropped quickly. I buttoned my coat and called Jeremy.

"Riddle me this," I said when he answered. "If you believe Rita belongs to everyone, then why are you putting the screws on a couple NYU film majors who probably still have posters of Hitchcock in their dorm rooms?"

"Jesse?"

"Yeah."

"Oh, you sound—"

"Mad?"

"Drunk."

"Maybe. But don't change the subject."

"I don't know what you're talking about."

I sent him the link to one of the articles. He read it as I walked up Lexington.

"Weird," he said. "That's too bad. But I didn't do that. I couldn't. I don't own the rights to Rita."

"Who does?"

I stopped to rebutton my coat. Apparently I'd gotten it wrong on the way out of the restaurant.

"Stile," he said.

"Stile? Why?"

"It's part of our contract."

"That doesn't seem like a great deal for you."

"I told you, Jesse. I don't care about that stuff."

He was insane, I decided. We had to keep him off the stand and make sure he never spoke in public. No one was going to believe anything he said.

"You don't want to own the rights to what you write?"

"Some material, yes, but not Rita. That story was a vehicle for something else. The rate I was charged very much took into account that Stile would own the copyright—meaning it was heavily discounted. Any other publicity firms that might have been able to do what Stile did were extremely out of my price range. And I don't think they could have done what Stile did. It worked out really well for me. Professionally, I mean. With my book. Personally, it's turned out to be rather devastating. I can't sleep anymore."

With some embarrassment, I remembered Tom telling me about the TikToker and the videos he made with his hand-drawn illustrations. I hadn't thought about what the financial relationship that enabled Tom to sell those videos to an advertiser later would look like. I hadn't asked him a lot of questions. He might not be forcing anyone to get married or have abortions, but maybe I hadn't been so off with the Hollywood-studio model after all. The creators got a salary, but he owned it all in the end.

"What do you think of Tom?" I asked.

"He's fine."

"Could you be a bit more descriptive?"

"He's very good at what he does. Likes cocaine a little too much but that hasn't stopped him yet."

"He's a cokehead?" I guess this was confirmation of Billy's off-the-cuff remark. "How do you know?"

"Once you've met one, you never miss one again."

I'm not sure where I'd been walking to—some vague idea of a subway station—but I changed direction and headed back toward Stile's office. It was a long walk, but I was especially motivated to do it after watching George Kennedy Uber around the city all day.

I'm sure there are people who don't experience mistakes as life-threatening, as the first cracks in the dirt before the earth opens up and everything collapses into it. But I don't have much in common with them. Being wrong about who a person is in this job was particularly catastrophic. I was still reeling from thinking I'd been wrong about Jeremy, realizing I'd been wrong about being wrong about Jeremy, then discovering I'd been wrong about Tom. Everything felt tenuous. He'd gotten to me with his protector-of-writers spiel. Or maybe—the cringe felt physical; it shot through my body like a cramp—maybe he'd complimented my writing, and I didn't hear anything else. It was almost nine p.m. by this point, and I wasn't sure what I was expecting to find at the office. Tom, waist-deep in white powder? Predatory contracts spread out across the floor or posted on the walls of his office like in *A Beautiful Mind*? Intricate formulas written with lipstick on mirrors, the kind of calculations that win prizes and all mean the same thing: *What if I could sell the same product but make more money?* With each step, I became angrier. I'd thought Tom was different, but he was the same.

When I reached the office building, the top floor was lit up. I pressed the button for Stile, and someone immediately buzzed me in.

There were about ten people milling about on the fifth floor. Most of them looked up and, not recognizing me, looked away. The bearded man I'd seen on my last visit walked up and looked at my empty hands.

"DoorDash?" he asked.

"Jesse Haber."

Across the room, Tom raised his hand. He was standing behind Kaya, who was seated at her desk.

"Jesse," he called. "I'm glad you came in."

I glanced at Kaya. She was looking at me. Tom squeezed her shoulder and started toward the stairwell.

"Come with me," he said.

He didn't speak until the door to the stairwell had fallen shut behind us.

"Did you learn something about Jane?" he said.

"No."

The landing was narrow. We were almost touching.

"Come on." He went down the stairs. When he opened the door onto the fourth floor, we were met by a rush of cold air. It was a construction site. Piles of two-by-fours and boxes of tiles, ladders balanced against the wall. All one open room except, at the very back of the space, about where the conference room was on the fifth floor, there was an area cordoned off from the rest of the room by a heavy plastic curtain that hung from the ceiling. Behind that, the bones of a wall and a doorway. Inside, a desk and boxes piled on a bare concrete floor. A desk lamp attached to an extension cord that ran out under the sheets of plastic to the other room. Windows boarded with plywood.

A laptop resting on the small desk beeped as we walked in, and Tom went over to it, read the message, and typed something in response.

"Are you working here?" I asked.

"There was a miscommunication," he answered. "I thought it was ready."

"It's not, though."

"Yeah," he said distractedly. "I don't work here when the construction guys are here," he added, as though that explained everything.

His computer beeped, and he turned to it again.

"I read that you stopped a couple NYU students from continuing their web series about Rita."

He nodded, finished what he was typing, and looked up. "It's the sale of the company I told you about. The buyer wants Rita unencumbered."

"Why? Because they want to make their own? A guaranteed hit to make people smash that new-subscriber button?"

"I guess," he said, turning back to the computer when it chimed.

"Doesn't seem like a great deal for Jeremy, to be honest. That you own the story."

He looked up at that.

"I think he was happy with it. He sold his second book for six figures. Do you know what the average advance for a book is? Five thousand dollars."

I hadn't realized he sold his novel for that much, actually. That was quite a bit of money.

"Still," I said, "he wrote Rita. He should get to keep some of that."

"He and Jane wrote it. And it was Jane's idea."

"So why do you own it?"

"The company owns it, because Jane works here. Worked here. She developed it here, she wrote it here. I'd think as a journalist, you'd be familiar with work for hire. It's pretty standard at magazines."

"I barely ever worked for a real magazine."

"Well, websites."

"Ditto."

"I guess it is a bit different for freelance."

"It is," I said. "A lot of places let me keep the copyright. They only license first rights."

"That's because they don't think it has any value."

"Well, tell me what you really think."

"I'm not trying to be a dick, but that's why they do it that way. Not all places, of course; some of them probably keep it anyway, if they can. But the sites you are talking about, if they thought it was worth anything, they would try and keep it. But beyond that day, beyond the traffic for that article on that subject around that time, they don't care about it. That's not my model. The writing is better than that. Your writing is better than that."

He opened one of the drawers of his desk and pulled out a slim silver laptop.

"I was going to call you anyway. I downloaded everything Jane had uploaded to our shared workspace onto here. Her email and Slack are on there too; you'll be able to log in."

"Thank you," I said, stepping forward to take the laptop. He looked one more time at the computer on his desk and headed out through the plastic curtain. I guessed our conversation was over. It didn't feel over. I had that feeling I got sometimes with Lucy, where she had answered all of my questions, and I felt off balance without being able to point to exactly why. I followed him across the vast open room and into the stairwell. When we reached the landing, he turned to face me.

"I hope you find something on that. I hope it helps somehow," he said, and then he took the steps two at a time back to the fifth floor.

Outside, it felt like the temperature had dropped another fifteen degrees. Either that or the alcohol, which had kept me warm on the way over, had fully metabolized. I was underdressed because of the mild morning. The wind felt skin-stripping. I was very confused about Tom and Jeremy, and I was trying to recall if I had to turn left or right to get to the nearest subway station when a woman on the street stopped at the steps to the building and looked at me.

"Coming or going?" she asked.

"Going."

She nodded, then tilted her head, waiting for me to move away from the door. Before I could, Kaya opened it and slipped out. She was wearing a short dress, ballet shoes that laced up to her shins, and a coat longer than her dress that she hadn't bothered to button.

"I want to talk to you," she said, but then she noticed the woman waiting at the bottom of the steps. "Oh, hello, Elizabeth."

"You're working late again?" the woman said. "I hope you get to go home sometimes."

"The whole team's here," Kaya said. "We have a few more hours, probably."

"Do I need to say something to my husband?" Tom's wife, then. The woman was smiling, but there was an edge to her voice. "He shouldn't be working you this hard."

"Well, since you asked, I'm okay tonight but I'm supposed to go to my boyfriend's show in Philly this weekend, so if you could work your magic then, I think we'd all appreciate it."

Kaya was smiling widely, which made me feel slightly unsettled. I had met her under less than ideal circumstances, so I might have been more inclined to see the hostile side of her, but she was bordering on ingratiating here. It was uncomfortable to witness.

"Oh, that will be so fun," Tom's wife said. "I'll certainly see what I can do." When she brushed her hair off her shoulders, the gesture was as practiced and precise as a dancer's. "Well, I think I need to go inside. I can't believe you're not freezing in that dress."

"It has pockets. But I guess that doesn't help in this case."

Elizabeth laughed and began walking up the stairs. Kaya and I took two steps toward the edge of the landing, Kaya leaning into my chest to give Tom's wife more room to pass.

When the door had closed behind Elizabeth and we were alone, she said, "I want to talk to you."

"Okay."

"Were you outside my apartment two nights ago?" she asked.

She hadn't stepped away from me, so her face was close to my face when she asked me. I think I closed my eyes. I wanted to evaporate.

"Jesse?"

"I'm so sorry," I said, moving away from her. "I wasn't—it wasn't for you. I was doing this thing I do sometimes. Walk in Jane's shoes, follow her routine. I didn't mean to be in your space like that."

"So you saw Billy and me fighting?"

"I did. I'm sorry."

"It's not about Jane, if that's what you're thinking."

"I'm not."

"You don't think I pushed my best friend into a dumpster because she was sleeping with my boyfriend? Or maybe that Billy pushed her to keep me from finding out?"

"They were sleeping together, then?"

"No. They weren't. But that's what you think, right? Billy told me what you guys talked about."

The wind made a loud noise, rushed toward us like it was being called home. Kaya hugged herself.

"You didn't mind that Jane was flirting with your boyfriend?"

She shrugged, her arms still wrapped around her body, hands gripping her upper arms. "It didn't mean anything."

"You're nicer than I am."

"I agree, but not in the way you mean."

"How, then?"

"I'm nicer than you because you're not giving any of us any credit. I don't like to look at people that way."

"What way?"

She rubbed her hands on her upper arms, fast, a little violent.

"That's what Jane did, that's all. It was the only way she could see herself. But there's a difference between Jane wanting to know if theoretically Billy would ever sleep with her, Billy feeling like he would sleep with Jane if everything were different, and them actually sleeping together."

"It would annoy me, I think."

"Don't your friends ever do anything that you hate?"

I thought of Lucy. And Nate. And Doug. And Sarah. Our tense dinner party.

"Yes."

She shrugged again. When she lifted her shoulders, her dress rose a few inches on her thighs.

"See?" she said. "Not giving us enough credit. I'm sure I did things that Jane hated too. And she overlooked them, because she loved me. Do you get that?" she asked. "I really loved her. Please stop thinking that I could have done it."

I nodded. "I'll stop. I promise." I paused. "It could have been Billy."

"No."

"What were you and Billy fighting about that night, then?"

She pressed the button to be let back into the building.

"That's really none of your business, Jesse."

The door closed behind her. I watched her back as she climbed the stairs, her beribboned legs disappearing in pieces, first the thighs, then the shins, until all I could see were her feet in her ballet slippers and then nothing. So she thought Jane's tendency to flirt with her boyfriends was academic, theoretical. Harmless. I remembered my mother taking me aside junior year, after I'd started dating Sharon.

"Jesse," she'd said to me after a particularly humiliating day. "As a teacher, I see girls like Sharon and my heart breaks. I spend more of my life than you'd understand trying to do right by them. But as a mother, I have to tell you—insecure girls are like the scorpion in the frog story. They will always sting you in the end. They can't help it. This applies to men too, but in your case, you're not as likely to be dating them."

I took a moment to get my bearings and figure out if I had to turn left or right to get to the nearest subway station. Right, I decided, and I was about to set off when a noise made me turn. Across the road, in the shadow of a streetlamp, stood Roger Warren. He had his hands in his pockets, and he was looking straight up at the lit windows of Jane's old office.

11

THE NEXT MORNING, MY MOM had an appointment with the neurologist. Little by little, I'd been letting Gloria take on more of the medical stuff. She picked up my mom's prescriptions from the pharmacy and separated them into their respective boxes. She knew my mom's cholesterol and sugar levels, what direction they were heading in, and how she should alter her meals accordingly. She made notes about walks my mom took, days they played tennis or swam at the Y. She had a blood pressure cuff in her car, UTI tests in the bathroom, and a jar of probiotics in the fridge that I think she might have made herself. I gave it all over willingly. But I still took my mom to the big appointments: the neurologist, the yearly checkups when the doctors ran hundreds of tests and handed me thirty pages of printed information as I walked out the door. I listened carefully to everything they said, took notes on my phone, then put the papers in an expanding accordion file for Gloria.

The neurologist was in a brick building near St. Joe's Medical Center. Dr. Stahl's office was at the end of a long hall. We had an appointment at nine a.m., the first one of the day, but apparently they had also given that appointment to seven other people. The waiting room was small and most of the seats were taken, which meant I had to sit in the seat next to my mom instead of leaving one open as a buffer. Lately, she had been resisting showering or changing, even with Gloria, and she smelled sour. There was a visible red stain on the breast of her dress from when we'd had spaghetti three days ago. I was leaning as far away from my mom as I could in the small seat, which made me feel unkind, but every time I caught her smell, something rose at the back of my throat. People were looking at us. I should have made the appointment for later in the day and given Gloria a chance to at least try to get my mom to change, but I had wanted to get it out of the way and get to work. At our last appointment—in the afternoon—we'd waited for two hours. I'd hypothesized the wait was the result of the previous appointments going over and compounding throughout the day, therefore the first appointment in the morning would not have that problem. I realized my mistake now.

"It's good we're here," my mom said. "I can tell them about the water in my ear."

"Right, Mom."

This was new and incessant, her belief she had water trapped in her ear that she couldn't get out. She barely talked about anything else. Gloria had already taken her to an ear, nose, and throat doctor, who'd found nothing. My mom either didn't remember this or chose to deny it.

"If I could get it out, I think I'd feel so much better."

"Well, I hope they can do something."

"What kind of doctor is this, again?"

"A neurologist."

"Why am I seeing a neurologist? Is there something wrong with my brain?"

"No, Mom. It's just a checkup. Everyone goes when they get older."

"Oh."

It was already nine thirty and the walls of the waiting room were starting to come at me. I had the urge to stand up on the uncomfortable brown seat and yell as loud as I could.

"Maybe this doctor can do something about the water in my ear," my mom said, leaning over to me with her sour breath and body-odor-soaked dress.

"Sorry, Mom, but I have to work," I told her, pulling Jane's computer out of my bag. "Really important. Deadline," I continued, putting my headphones on.

She nodded and looked around the waiting room with a confused expression on her face. For a moment, I felt guilty and wrestled with it. *Just talk to her,* I told myself. *Who cares if she says the same thing over and over? Who cares if she smells? She doesn't remember why we're here; talk to her.* But after staring at the receptionist for a few moments, my mom took out her phone and started playing a game. I turned back to Jane's computer, absolved.

First, I searched her folders for something that might mention @the blessing or Roger Warren. Like Tom had told me, there was nothing. For a while, I simply opened random documents, scanned them, and closed them, looking for what, I wasn't sure. Then I had the idea to look for George Kennedy, and there was a folder for him. With a lot of files. Some were documents she'd downloaded from the internet—articles about him or reports from the Landmarks Preservation Commission. There were promotional materials for his brother-in-law the contractor. A glossy brochure for a recently renovated block of buildings in Brooklyn. A faded brownstone facing the street with an addition, all metal and glass, towering above the original roofline like a monster intending to menace it. Jane had collected all George Kennedy's public statements on various historical redevelopment projects across the city, his votes on the committee, his public-speaking engagements with a transcript or a YouTube link if possible. Underneath them were Jane's notes as she tried to run down if and how much he was paid for speaking.

My journalist brain turned on. The light in the waiting room started to take on texture. Background sounds moved into the foreground, demanded engrossment. I felt close to something, the way some days when the air was cold and the sun was bright, I felt more alive. My mom used to describe these kinds of days as baking-soda days—when everything was the same as it always was but your attention worked like baking soda on anything you turned it toward: There was a reaction. Things rose to meet you. I almost reminded my mom of this, then didn't, because I was afraid she might not remember. I didn't want to see the flicker of fear move across her face.

I looked more closely at Jane's document, saved simply as "Notes on George Kennedy." At first, it read more like a collection, as if she were merely putting everything she could find about him in one place. But then, as the pages went on, it became targeted, more like an argument. This argument was not articulated, but it was visible in the curation. There were more and more links to critics of facadism, examples of buildings—the London Amazon headquarters, the Carrer Pau Claris in Barcelona, the Royal Ontario Museum in Canada, a new building on Gun Street in London that had not even been attached to the facade of the historical one; there was a five-foot gap between the new structure and the facade of the demolished building. You could imagine willful English schoolboys running into the space to hide from their mothers.

There were no dates in the document so I wasn't sure if she'd done all this before she wrote the character of James Falcon. Maybe she'd begun it as a collection as she wrote the character and then the more targeted compilation of information after the real George Kennedy wrote to her. Perhaps it was an effort to say: *See, it's not libel because it's not a lie.* There was a video of him discussing the facade redevelopment and interior commercial space of the landmarks-committee-approved Tammany Hall. A lecture at the Ninety-Second Street Y where he discussed the history of the Hearst Building and the eventual addition of the Hearst Tower inside it. She wasn't accusing him of taking bribes in the document, but she was saying that facadism—as practiced in New York City, at least—was not a compromise between the old and the new. It was the city once again folding to real estate and developers at the expense of principles they pretended to care about. And George Kennedy, the document clearly argued, had chosen to side with the real estate developers, one of whom happened to be his brother-in-law.

My mom was tapping me on the shoulder. She pointed at my phone, which had slipped from the armrest of the chair onto the floor and was ringing. It was Phil, but he'd hung up by the time I reached my phone. I listened to his voice-mail message. You should check your email, he said; he'd sent me something, and he went on to describe what he had sent in exacting detail. Sometimes I wasn't sure if this was a Phil thing or a reflection of Phil's evaluation of my ability to understand emails. He had sent me some new files the lawyers had gotten through subpoenas as well as names of possible witnesses we had to vet before they got put on the stand. He'd also seen that the sale of Stile was official now, and he sent me a link to an article with this headline:

VENTURE CAPITAL BETS ON STILE FOR $50 MILLION

Fifty million dollars? For a Twitter mystery and an online game? A death TikToker and a docuseries about dying? The article had a professional picture of Tom standing in the Stile office in front of one of the metal screens, his hair smooth and blond, his glasses unsmudged and the frames gleaming. I copied the name of the venture capital group, added *Stile,* pasted them into Google, and read ten to twenty more articles about the sale. But they were all the same, the same sparse information being regurgitated by different outlets, none of them explaining the valuation except with words like *bet* and *the future of content* and *brand*. And one paragraph, sounding very much as Tom had described it to me, on Stile's ability to generate detailed information on their audiences and then use it to make accurate predictions about the all-powerful new-subscriber button. That button was worth fifty million dollars? I realized I'd started to attribute Tom's confidence and enthusiasm in our first conversation to cocaine, but I guess he was right to be excited. Or right *and* coked up. Wouldn't be the first time cocaine and confidence were used effectively to sell something to the market for enormous sums of money.

I looked at the clock. Ten. An hour past our appointment time. I spent approximately twelve minutes waiting at the front desk while the receptionist answered the phone and then helped the person in front of me, only to be told "It should be soon." I went back to poking around Jane's computer and found a document where Jane had copied and pasted all her emails with George Kennedy. So she did do that, just as Aaron had told me she'd done with her messages from Roger Warren, although I hadn't been able to locate that one yet. Why she'd copied George Kennedy's messages into a document—as opposed to saving them in her inbox and reading them as a thread—I couldn't say. Maybe she didn't like the way the email collapsed text. Maybe it made it easier to search this way. Maybe she liked a clean inbox.

As I read their correspondence, I was reminded of Jeremy's description of Jane. I could see her charm here, from his first email, hostile and accusatory, to her response when she eventually convinced him to meet her for a drink. Then, in that period after the drink, weeks where they emailed back and forth about the character of James Falcon and what might be in store for him. How she made an effort to include George, or make him feel included, in the character's direction. How she began to emphasize James Falcon's more attractive attributes both in her emails with George and also—I checked—in the Rita story by creating another character, a journalist writing a profile on James Falcon. Tweets promoting the profile included references to Falcon's charity donations, cute stories of him with his children, and his long fight to save a historical building from demolition.

But by the end of the copied-and-pasted emails, their relationship was fraying again. Although Jane was trying to humor him, as Jeremy had told me, she was unwilling to neutralize the storyline about his connection to developers. George Kennedy's emails became lightly panicked and then desperate as he realized he was losing control of how people would see James Falcon, how people would see him.

My mom was tapping me on the shoulder again so I took off my headphones.

"I'm going to go to the bathroom."

It was 10:35. I told myself not to look at the time again, as it only made me angry, but it was hard not to keep glancing down at the bottom of my screen. My mom came back, and I nodded at her but didn't take my headphones off this time. Bile flooded dangerously close to the top of my throat when she sat down, but I pushed it back. Across the room, a woman of about fifty seemed to be waving in my direction. I looked behind me, but there was no one there. When I turned back, she was still waving at me.

I got up and walked over to her. When I reached her, I pulled my headphones off so they were hanging like a necklace around my neck. I still had my laptop open in my hands. "Can I help you?"

"Is that your mom?" She pointed across the room.

"Yeah."

"I don't know how to say this, but I was waiting for the bathroom after her, and when she came out"—she looked embarrassed—"when she came out, I think she might have had a stain. On her dress. Near her bottom. That's brown."

It took a second for the implications to add up, and then my gag reflex reengaged, and I had to work pretty seriously to stop from vomiting. I looked across the room at my mother, sitting in her chair, absorbed in a game on her phone, like she was barely there.

"Oh my God," I said. The woman smiled at me, full of pity. "I don't know what to do," I told her, because I didn't know what to do. "I don't know what to do."

"You deal with the chair," she said, standing up. "I'll help your mom in the bathroom."

I felt like crying, but I couldn't speak. I watched the woman walk across the room and bend down to whisper something in my mom's ear. My mom looked confused, then scared, then followed the stranger into the bathroom while I stood rooted to the ground as though paralyzed. It was only when another person entered the office and cast about for an empty seat in the crowded room that I was able to move.

The receptionist was on the phone when I came up to her. She gestured at the sign-in sheet, but I shook my head and turned back to the waiting room to watch the man who had just entered. He walked past my mom's chair—thankfully—to stand behind me because he had to sign in. When the receptionist got off the phone, I didn't know what to say.

"There's a chair in there. It's dirty," I said, and she looked at me as though I were sending a meal back because the eggs were too runny. "My mom," I said. The man was inching closer to me, using his proximity to communicate that I should hurry up with my business so he could sign in or at least I should move my body out of the way of the sign-in sheet. But I was intentionally blocking him, because I didn't want him to try to sit down. "My mom is sick," I said, "and I think she had some trouble, um, in the bath-room, and you shouldn't let anyone sit on that chair."

The receptionist's eyes followed my arm pointing into the waiting room, and then she understood.

"We'll take care of it," she said as if I'd told her the light bulb in the bathroom didn't work, and this was something she dealt with all the time. And maybe she did. I left the desk and stood in front of the chair so no one would try to sit in it. A minute later the receptionist came into the waiting room, picked it up with gloved hands, and disappeared into the back. From the same door, a nurse appeared and called my mother's name. She and the stranger who'd offered to help her hadn't come out of the bathroom yet.

"One minute," I told the nurse. If they brought someone else in because my mom happened to be in the bathroom the exact moment they called her name, I thought I might have a nervous breakdown in the waiting room. "She's coming out right now," I said, pointing at the bathroom, but the nurse looked impatient. "We've been waiting since nine."

"Uh-huh," she said.

When the door to the bathroom opened, I waved at my mom. As she got closer, I saw that her dress was now on inside out, and the woman had tied the sweater my mom had been wearing around her waist.

"Here, Mom," I said, shaking off my hoodie so she could use it to cover her now bare arms. She swum in it. It made her look old. "They called us."

I pointed to the nurse, and my mom stepped toward her with a vaguely confused look on her face, as though she didn't know why she was going with the nurse other than because I had told her to.

"We cleaned it real good," the woman said quietly. "It's damp, but clean."

"Thank you so much," I told the woman. "I don't even know what to say."

"I had my own parents," she said.

In the exam room, we waited for another twenty minutes. I paced around the small room as my mom watched.

"Why would they bring us back here only to wait again?" I said. "Do you think they're trying to break us?"

"I'm sorry it's taking so long," she said in a way that made the guilt come at me like a wall of water.

"It's not your fault, Mom," I said, but I said it tightly. Even I could tell I sounded annoyed.

By the time the doctor entered, I was barely polite. The least she could do was apologize, but she came in like we'd kept *her* waiting. The whole thing lasted less than ten minutes, and that included the doctor administering the mini–mental state exam. Even though I knew my mom was worse in some ways than the last time we'd come here—the hygiene, the looping conversations, the way she seemed more absent sitting at the table lately—I was still shocked to hear some of her answers.

The doctor asked her what year and month it was. My mom knew the year but got the month wrong, by quite a lot.

"Can you tell me where you are?"

"Yonkers. At a doctor's office."

"What kind of doctor's office?"

She looked at me for the answer. "Just the regular kind," she said when I stayed silent. "The general one."

"I'm going to name three objects," the doctor said. "Dog, pencil, mug. Can you repeat them?" My mother repeated them, but a few questions later, when the doctor asked her to name the objects again, she could only remember the dog.

I watched the doctor tally up the score.

"Fifteen," she said. "Last time it was twenty-one."

"Is a higher or lower number better?" my mom asked.

"Higher. Fifteen is not good."

"What does fifteen mean?"

"You have dementia."

"I do?"

"Do you have any questions?" the doctor asked, turning to me.

"Talk to me," my mom said. "I'm here."

"Do you have any questions?" the doctor asked her.

"Um, no," my mom said, and the doctor turned back to me again.

"Do you have any questions?"

I couldn't think of anything to say. I hadn't really figured out how to talk to my mom about her cognitive decline yet, but I'd assumed I'd learn something about how to handle it by watching the doctor. How to be kind and make the whole thing less terrifying. But that assumption appeared to be incorrect.

"I guess—what should we do? What do you advise?"

She was typing her notes into a computer. I hated this. How could they be this behind on appointments when they typed up their notes from the appointment while we were still in the appointment?

"Well, she's already at the limit of donepezil so we can't increase that. And donepezil only slows the progression. At this point, it won't do much."

"Great."

"It looks like you were here six months ago. Why are you here again?"

"I don't know. Your office said to come back in six months, so we came back in six months."

"It's probably not necessary unless you have a specific concern," she said.

"But shouldn't we, I don't know, be tracking things, seeing if they get worse?"

"Can't you tell?" she said.

We were both mostly silent on the bus ride home. I couldn't think of anything to say. *Don't worry, Mom, dementia is not that big a deal? Going down six points in six months probably isn't a bad sign? By the time it gets really bad, you'll be too far gone to realize it's really bad?* What do you say, after all, when both people know you can't say *I'm sure it will be fine* because you both know it will only get worse? My mom was on her phone, playing a game, and I wasn't sure if she even remembered the doctor, the incident with the bathroom and the stranger, her diagnosis. I stared at the side of her face. She was looking out the window now, but she was somewhere else. With other people, if I noticed this kind of expression, I could say, *Hey, where'd you go?* and they'd come back and tell me. But my mom couldn't tell me where she'd been anymore, and increasingly, she couldn't get back.

"It's like you have a kid," my mom said.

"No," I said. "Mom, it's not like that."

"Yes, it is," she said. "You know, I was about your age when I had you."

12

I WENT DIRECTLY TO QUEENS. I wanted to confront Roger Warren. I could still sense him, a dark shadow standing right outside the light falling from a streetlamp. An unwanted presence. I was mad because of my morning, and it made me mad to think of him standing there, Kaya exiting and entering the building, her silhouette in the window upstairs. It made me mad to think of Jane receiving those messages from him at work, downplaying them to Tom for the good of the project, unburdening herself about them to Aaron, while—somewhere—she started keeping track of them. Maybe she thought she would need them someday. Maybe she could imagine some court case or restraining order. Or maybe it was all more vague than that, something she would not have been able to articulate even to herself. Select, copy, paste. To have done something in the nightmare, to compel the body toward a movement other than trembling.

Roger Warren had said he sent the messages to Jane because he thought the writer might like them, even ask to use them. No one could be that delusional, could they? That lacking in how they came off to other people? And if they could, what else were they capable of? Well, I was going to find out.

The first part of the journey was aboveground, still in neighborhoods of tract housing. I usually loved the levels of this route, houses to apartment buildings to skyscrapers, buses to elevated rails to the darkness of a tunnel. But today, I was feeling behind. We'd spent a couple of hours in the doctor's office, and the trip from Yonkers to Queens was taking too long. I pulled Jane's computer out of my bag and continued poking around. I wasn't sure what I was looking for, but when I saw her Slack account, I knew I'd found it.

Lots of messages about work and projects, but then an ongoing conversation with Kaya about—well, everything. I read the whole bus ride and then sat on a bench at 125th Street because I knew I'd lose the connection when we went underground. Work, dogs, music, a couple at their yoga class they talked about with somewhat alarming frequency. What to eat for lunch, what to eat for dinner, requests to edit emails both professional and personal, links to tweets, Instagram stories, songs on Spotify, books they were reading, protests in the city they wondered if they should go to, warehouse parties in Brooklyn they wondered if they should go to, Zillow links to apartments they maybe should rent together as well as Zillow links to million-dollar houses in the Finger Lakes and country houses in Spain with comments like *This can be our reading nook* underneath a picture of a room with floor-to-ceiling windows overlooking a gray-blue lake. There were, as one would expect, a significant amount of work-related messages—specific projects Kaya and Jane were working on, yes, but also emails related more generally to the process of it all. They were learning from each other. They were learning together. They approached each other's work with a deadly seriousness that caught me off guard each time it appeared amid the messages planning their nights or speculating about office gossip. Sometimes they were talking about work projects; sometimes they were clearly writing about personal projects.

This is so good. I was going to read it at lunch, but I opened it and couldn't stop.

Really?

Really. This is it.

Do you think the corner-store scene takes too long?

Yes and no. It's not too long, but the pacing of that part is so different from everything else, so it stutters.

Oh, shit. That's right. That's exactly right. You're so good! So if I keep that part but write it more like the scene at the school?

Yes. Do that. Hey, that part where she's at the school, is that a Veronica Mars reference?

YES! I knew you would get it.

Duh. Anyone else get it? Did Jeremy?

I haven't shown it to him yet, but I don't care if he does. I write for you.

They also discussed Aaron, Jeremy, Billy, and someone they called QB who I eventually realized was Tom. Tom was hitting on Kaya? Was that why he seemed so protective of her? And what about his wife? And what about Billy? Did he know? And if Tom was hitting on Kaya, and Kaya was not exactly discouraging it, did that mean anything with respect to the possibility that Billy and Jane might actually have crossed a line somewhere?

Kaya had told me Jane might have been seeing someone besides Aaron and Jeremy, and, reading their Slacks, I could see why she thought this. In earlier messages, Jane was usually available to do things with Kaya, and if not, she explained why: *I'm going to see Jeremy. I'm hanging out with Aaron.* But in the last month or two, she'd started being unavailable without an explanation— or her explanation was always that she had to work. A couple times, Kaya commented on it, on how much Jane was working, how unavailable she was, usually in the form of a joke. Jane answered with emojis.

Jane also complained about Aaron. A lot in the month before she died.

It's like I can't convince him I don't like him.

Just tell him to stop contacting you.

I tried that.

You told him to fuck off?

Well, no. I told him I didn't want to be friends because it was too hard. Because I was trying to be nice. But I think that just convinced him he was right.

Tell him you want him to stop emailing you. Use the word "stalker."

He's not a stalker.

I know. But he's too afraid to think of himself as a stalker. It will work. Trust.

Why are you so good at this?

Am I?

Then, a few days later:

Well, that didn't work. He sent this:

"Hi, Jane. I know I'm going to regret writing this, and I should probably keep this in the draft folder. In fact, to be honest with you, I'm supposed to send these kinds of messages to Sabrina. It's nice to have a friend who tries to save you from yourself, and I have already sent her a few of these, but this morning, my fingers only want to type 'Jane' in the To field. Does it make you uncomfortable to know there are draft emails to you somewhere? If so, I'm sorry.

"I heard everything you said yesterday, but when I saw you, I felt this thing I have felt so much since we broke up, and I knew I would regret it if I didn't say it. I'm not trying to convince you, but I have to say it out loud—and not to Sabrina—don't I? There are so many movies and TV shows and books where the plot turns on misunderstanding, whole lives ruined. When I was in high school, I had a crush on a girl in my physics class. After graduation, I found out she liked me too. I don't want that to happen again. I know this is different. We are older. We are not a hypothetical, but when I'm with you, it feels like you like me. Maybe you make everyone feel that way, and I don't know you well enough to know that. I am not like that, so I don't know what it feels like to have that connection with other people, for it to feel so easy.

"In any case, I need to say this: I think we are good together. I think there is something inside you that's trying to ruin it. I know that sounds paternalistic,

201

and I apologize for it, but it's what I believe. I think you are afraid it might be real. I think it is real. I want to try. I want to take care of you, and I want to be careful with you. Every time I'm around you, it feels like you want that too, but there's something stopping you. We already know we have fun together, that we like the same TV shows, that we can talk for hours, spend days together without getting sick of each other. I know it's hard to be vulnerable, but please, don't do this."

Kaya responded:

You saw him?

Yeah. He asked if we could hang out and, I don't know. I do miss him sometimes.

If you really want him to stop writing this kind of email, you have to stop seeing him and responding. He's not hearing what you're saying or reading what you're writing.

I know. But why can't I just tell him I only want to be friends and then we can hang out and have fun and I won't get this email the next morning?

Because you can't.

I know. I know. I'll tell him soon.

That exchange was a week before she died. Maybe she'd told him.

Roger Warren's face went through a series of contortions when I walked into his store. The lift of his eyes when he heard the bell; the brief, blank acknowledgment that two people have made eye contact without any plans to speak; the realization that he might recognize me; confusion as he tried to figure out how; the shift back to his resting impassiveness when he remembered.

"Can I help you?" he asked.

"Yeah," I said. "You can, Roger."

I leaned forward, placed my elbows on the counter, and accidentally knocked over a board displaying different kitchen magnets—Mickey Mouse, the Statue of Liberty, a tomato, all priced at $3.99. Roger looked at my elbow. I didn't right the board, and I didn't apologize. It wasn't much of an intimidation technique, but it was all I had. He didn't seem bothered.

"Well?" he said.

"Why don't you tell me why you were outside Jane Murphy's office last night, the office of a woman you said you didn't know existed?"

He pulled a pack of gum from his pocket, and slowly unwrapped a piece. When he'd finished, he held it in front of his mouth.

"I know she exists now," he said. "A little birdie told me."

He popped the gum into his mouth like punctuation. I hated when people chewed gum. The sound, bone hitting bone, the wet squish and pop of the jaw.

"So what, then," I said. "You thought, *Now that I know she exists and she's dead, I'd kind of like to see the building she used to work in late at night?*"

Even with his mouth closed, I could see him move his gum from one cheek to the other with his tongue.

"No offense, but I don't have to talk to you if I don't want to. And I don't want to."

"You don't have to, that's right. But if you don't answer my questions here, I'm going to have you answer them on the stand."

"You're a lawyer?"

I shrugged in a way that I hoped looked like *If you say so* but afforded enough plausible deniability that it could also mean *Not exactly* if I was ever called upon to explain this moment.

"I wanted to see where she worked," he said. "Idle curiosity."

"You didn't think, *Hey, I wrote these kind of scary messages to someone who was murdered. If one of her coworkers sees me hidden in the shadows staring at her building, that might freak someone out?*"

"Not really."

I laughed sharply to show my disbelief, but apparently he didn't feel like my skepticism was his problem.

"Okay," I said. "If that's all you want to say. But I wouldn't be too surprised if next week, while you're ringing up a plunger, the customer hands you a subpoena instead of his debit card. Maybe you're into that kind of thing. It'll make each day a little more exciting, wondering each time the bell tolls whether it's going to be a customer or a process server."

When I'd finished, I picked up the magnet board. I repositioned it so it was as it had been before I'd knocked it over, then turned and walked to the door. He called out as I reached it.

"It was mostly curiosity."

I stopped and turned.

"But also, I thought maybe I could talk to the new writers. See if they ever saw the character I made up. They might like it more than the girl did. Maybe they need some help."

I made sure my face stayed still as he was talking; in fact, I was trying to mimic his face. His muscles barely moved when he spoke. His words, too, seemed slow and languorous, as if he were holding each syllable just a little too long. The pause between words was also a little too long, so just as I thought he'd finished speaking, another word tumbled out from his mouth in flashes of white teeth and yellow gums.

"That seems kind of far-fetched, doesn't it?" I asked.

"I don't know. Have you been reading it lately?" he asked. "I mean, she and that guy had some issues too in how they were writing it. But at least they kept it exciting. But with her dead and him in jail or whatever, the new writers could stand to have my character show up. Maybe even be the real killer."

"How did he kill her? Your character, I mean."

"He strangled her."

"Why?"

"Why did he strangle her? It's personal, it's violent. You have to not let go for a while. You have to look at them while you're doing it."

"No, I meant why did he kill her at all?"

"Oh, because it was the strongest feeling he'd ever felt," he said. "He thought it could destroy him. Sometimes you have to choose—you or them."

By the time I left Warren Hardware, I felt raw. Being around Roger was difficult. Like sleeping on top of a cheese grater, every second with him. When I thought of going home, I remembered the doctor's appointment and called Lucy instead.

"Want company?" I asked when she picked up. "Just me, not the group."

"Sure," she said. "Where are you?"

"Queens. But I can hop on a train and be there in thirty, maybe forty-five. Text me what I need to pick up."

She laughed. "I could come to Yonkers, you know. I do leave the city."

"It's okay. My mom will just want to watch TV."

"I like your mom."

"She's not like she was anymore."

"I know."

"No, you don't, Luce. She's doing this thing now where she just talks about water in her ear over and over again, like her brain is on a loop. And she kind of smells. It can be hard to be around."

"I can handle it," she said. "Can you? It sounds like a lot."

For the second time that day, I almost cried. The world I lived in with my mom had started to feel so small and confined, I was sure no one else could fit in. It felt so small most of the time that—other than Gloria—I wasn't positive anyone could even see us.

"I'll come," Lucy said. "We'll watch a movie with your mom and then we can hang out. I'll cook. It will be nice to be in a house with a real kitchen."

"The kitchen in your parents' apartment is nicer than my mom's kitchen."

"I know," she said.

13

I WAS WALKING TO THE TRAIN STATION when I got a text message from Jane's old roommate Wes.

Hey—I found Jane's old phone. You want it?

"It was in the front closet, behind the shoes," Wes said when I arrived at his door thirty minutes later, after the train ride and a dashed-off apology to Lucy. "We had a chore wheel," Wes continued. "Well, it wasn't really a wheel, we just wrote it on a whiteboard, but it switched every week: kitchen, bathroom, den—which is what we call the room with the couch and Rowan's room inside it. Anyone cleaning up, they'd put anything they found—sunglasses, books, sweaters, whatever—in the box in the closet so you'd always know where to look for something."

He was holding Jane's phone loosely in his hand as he talked. I looked at it like a man trying to quit drinking looks at whiskey. I hadn't told Phil yet because I wanted to see if I could actually get into it. But I was imagining being able to tell him, the look on his face, the excitement in his voice.

"As soon as I found it, I called you and started charging it," Wes continued. "Jane had upgraded her phone not too long before she died, and she must have left this one in the den after she activated the new one so it got put in the box when someone cleaned. I'm not sure the cops looked in the hall closet. If they did, I guess they didn't see the box or just thought it was a box of books or something."

I offered up a quick and silent *Thank you* that Wes had found the phone instead of Lydia. "How long before she died did she switch phones?"

"Not that long. I remember, because see this?" He held the phone up, showed me the back, the case, colorful and abstract. I wasn't sure if it was a famous painting or not, but it looked vaguely familiar. "She was really pissed because the new phone was like a quarter inch bigger than the old phone, so her old case didn't fit, which meant she had to buy a new case. She wrote a little diatribe about it online. It got a lot of likes, so a few companies said they'd send her a new one for free. She was still mad, because it was the principle of the thing, and she thought Apple should do it. But I checked when she posted that thread, and it was about two weeks before she died."

Two weeks. Jane's phone—the one everyone was sure she'd taken with her when she went running the morning she died—had never been found. Since she didn't back up her phone or save anything to the cloud, whatever information that device had contained was assumed lost forever. But now—all those text messages. Emails. Pictures. Saved passwords for Twitter, Instagram, Venmo. Her bank account. I stared at the phone.

"I don't suppose you know her passcode?"

"I do, actually."

"Wait, really?"

He smiled. "Really." He handed me the phone. "Zero, seven, two, three."

I touched the numbers gently with my thumb, watched as the screen transformed into rows of colorful apps. I turned to Wes.

"Holy shit. How do you know that?"

"I don't know. We lived together for a while. We slept together for a while. She used those numbers for a lot of things."

"What do they mean?"

"No idea."

I swept through the screens on the phone. Up in the right corner, a green icon with a white text box, a little red 12. It took everything inside me not to press it and begin reading immediately.

"And you're giving this to me?" I asked. "I can take it?"

"Yeah," he said. "Fuck the police."

I'm not sure how, but I didn't look at Jane's phone until I got to the office. Every time I reached into my pocket for it, I imagined someone stealing it or the subway taking a curve too fast and it sailing out of my hand. At the office, I saw Lucy had texted me to say she'd decided to go to my house anyway. She was going to make lasagna and watch Jimmy Stewart movies with my mother.

I don't know what time I'll get home, I wrote. I'm so sorry but it's important.

That's okay. I thought it might be good for you to have a night off but still know your mom wasn't alone.

She'll probably have more fun with you anyway.

Obviously.

Jane's last text was to Kaya. Or I should say, her last text on her old phone, the one she'd used until about two weeks before her death, was to Kaya. It was hard to remember that, for some reason. I kept thinking I was looking at the evidence of a person's last hours on Earth, that the thirty-six tabs she had opened on Safari were the last things she'd googled before she died, clues as to the preoccupations of her mind hours before she was killed. But in fact, they were the preoccupations of her mind two weeks before that. Which was not nothing.

Jane's social media and work documents had allowed me to see a part of her. It was similar to what I'd learned doing interviews with her friends and colleagues. What she appeared to be. How people saw her. For some people, the filter between what they think and what they post online might be flimsy, but I'd never had that impression of Jane. She was making something, not reflecting something. The opinions of her friends and colleagues were another kind of filter or lens, Jane distorted through their perceptions. What they thought about the world. How they made decisions.

Holding her phone felt like holding her brain. The closest you could be to a person. I knew what she looked up on the internet, what she spent money on. I knew how many steps she took, how much screen time she accumulated one week compared to the week before. I knew what she couldn't stop listening to, how many emails she had to Jeremy Miller and Aaron Belatin in her draft folder. I recognized that it was dangerous to conflate the workings of the brain with the technology I happened to be most familiar with, but it was hard not to think that way. Because what is a brain besides a collection of images and information, a repository of memories and desires and remembered song lyrics, and also a hundred open tabs draining energy away from the present moment? The Jane that people saw on the internet and the Jane that people met in real life was everything she worked so hard to put together plus the rest that leaked out. But here was the source of it all. Everything no one could see.

Jane and Kaya had been texting about apartments, and then Jane had written What about this one? and linked to an apartment in Brooklyn.

I believe I've made my feelings about open shelving very clear, Kaya wrote back.

Are we in a position to be picky about shelving?

A person has to have principles. Even in New York.

What about this one?

Jane. What is this? Your opening salvo? Did you want to be roommates or enemies?

What's wrong with this one? Cabinets = closed.

They have LED lighting running underneath them. I can't live in a space designed by that kind of mind.

At your current apartment, your roommate has to walk THROUGH your room to get to his room.

It's the hell I know.

I read a week, a month, two months, three months back. Work. TV. Books. Apartments. Politics. New songs. Food. Aaron. Jeremy. Billy.

Billy.

He's acting really weird.

I hit the back button and searched for his name in Jane's contacts. When I found it, I could hear, suddenly, my heart beating, a febrile rush of something through my body. Of course it was not abnormal for a girl to have the number of her best friend's boyfriend or even to text him, but I had that particular kind of bad feeling—instantly recognizable now from years on social media—of knowing I was about to see something I didn't want to see.

We're running late.

Kaya says: U pick. No takebacks.

Winter Light?

Yes.

No.

Ha-ha

Hahahahahah

Lol

Smiley face.

Crying face.

And links—to tweets, songs on Spotify, videos on YouTube and

TikTok, Yelp reviews of bars and restaurants. I was sweeping my finger over the screen again and again, refreshing to more and more texts—they wrote each other a lot—when it occurred to me to swipe right so I could see the dates and times. One p.m. Four p.m. Three a.m. Clusters occurring on the same day and then silence for a month. And then, four months ago, at midnight,

You up?

Jane hadn't responded. Why—because it meant what it sounded like it meant, and she ignored it because she was a good friend? Then Billy, realizing it had been ignored, also ignored it and, embarrassed, stopped texting her? At least for a few weeks, and then it started again. Or because she called him, and I couldn't see that reflected here. Or maybe because it meant nothing. It was simply the time people who worked at restaurants texted their friends, and she'd been asleep, so when she got it in the morning, there was no reason to answer it. Maybe he'd known Kaya and Jane were together that night, and Kaya wasn't answering her phone. I don't know why my brain was trying so hard to make it mean nothing. It was good for us. It made Billy and Kaya look suspicious. It made Jane more unlikable.

I checked the date and switched back over to Jane's messages with Kaya. But there was nothing I could glean there. On the day Billy texted her at midnight, she was not texting Kaya and Kaya was not texting her. That's all I knew.

I wanted to keep reading her conversations with Kaya and Billy, but I searched for Jeremy and Aaron. It was more of the same. Aaron's texts could maybe help us. Jeremy's could maybe hurt us. Jeremy texts came off like Jeremy came off in person. A little arrogant, an insensitivity there that some people might consider brutal. I'd read somewhere that arrogant people were more likely to commit murder. I couldn't remember where or whether the source had been reliable, but I worried it made sense intuitively, that the jury would think so. You had to think you were better than some-one to kill them, I figured, at least on some level.

I didn't know where to go next. Read every text from Aaron since he became a contact on her phone? And Jeremy? And Kaya? Find her Gmail and read all her emails with Drew Finnley? Open her Twitter and track every DM she ever received? Go to her bank account and see what she had spent money on in the weeks before she died? See her Recently Played on Spotify? Her suggested shows in Netflix? The possibilities seemed close to endless and also, somehow, incomplete. Reading every single text and email from Aaron was probably more directly helpful to my task, but I kept wanting to check what podcasts she listened to and try to make sense of the thirty-six webpages she'd left open. I'd read that in some cultures, people did not like to get their photographs taken because they believed it stole a bit of your soul. But it seemed to me phones were made of tackier stuff. We left pieces of ourselves inside them.

In her photos app: Screenshots of websites, photos of food, of Kaya, of Aaron, of clothes laid out on her bed, a dozen or so pictures of her naked stomach, not sexual or erotic but as though she was trying to see it from different angles, understand it. Pictures of subway stations, strangers, the pink sky at dusk, Kaya's dog, Aaron again, Kaya, covers of books, some-body's baby, more food, an icy street corner, a man dressed in a Ferb cos-tume sitting on a park bench, a rat. And then a series of pictures it took me a minute to figure out: shots of her computer screen, over and over. I enlarged a picture and zoomed in. It was a conversation on Slack. She was taking pictures of it—a lot of pictures of it. I zoomed in even more to read the names.

Tom Stafford: Can I see you tonight?

Jane Murphy: Not tonight. I'm busy.

Tom Stafford: Really busy? Because I was thinking we could get a hotel room.

Jane Murphy: You don't need to go home?

Tom Stafford: I do need to go home, which means you could sleep there, all by yourself, and watch TV and take a bath with no roommates.

The room, or my body, turned suddenly cold, and I experienced that vertiginous feeling I get when I realize the world is not as I thought it was, and I'm not sure it's going to hold me anymore. Tom and Jane? Was there ever a moment I'd sensed it could be more? I ran through the memories of our conversations, but nothing appeared other than the protective way he acted around Kaya, how that had grated. Jane's computer going missing, how he'd given me what he could find on the cloud. Or perhaps the computer wasn't missing at all, and he just wanted to erase a few things. I dug around my desk until I found Jane's computer, went to her Slack account, and searched for conversations with Tom Stafford. But there weren't any. The only conversations she had with Tom were with other people.

I turned back to Jane's phone, searched for a date but couldn't find one. The pictures were all taken about five weeks before she died, but the conversations showed only time stamps. I opened another photograph.

Tom Stafford: Why are you mad?

Jane Murphy: I'm not mad.

Tom Stafford: I was not flirting with Kaya.

Jane Murphy: Okay.

Tom Stafford: I told you I've never done anything like this before.

Jane Murphy: Okay.

Tom Stafford: Do you believe me?

Jane Murphy: Okay.

Why did she take pictures of these? What happened a month before she died that made her think she needed to document them? Did she know Tom was going to erase them? I switched over to her texts and searched for Tom's name. He was there, but they'd texted only a few times. Often brief messages, like Sent you an email about the Francis project and Staff meeting canceled. I opened more of the photographs. More of the same. She was definitely documenting it. But why? I scrolled back through the photos—which might have been forward in time; I wasn't sure—and the tone began to change. Tom was talking about selling the company.

Tom Stafford: Don't tell anyone.

Jane Murphy: I won't.

Tom Stafford: Not even Kaya.

Jane Murphy: Clearly there are a lot of things I don't tell Kaya.

Tom Stafford: Or Jeremy.

Jane Murphy: I won't.

Tom Stafford: Do you still talk to him?

Jane Murphy: Sometimes.

Tom Stafford: Why?

Jane Murphy: You're married.

And then:

Tom Stafford: I wish you wouldn't be mad about this. I told you that in confidence, as my girlfriend. Not as an employee.

Jane Murphy: Well, I'm not your girlfriend because you have a wife. But I am your employee, so.

Tom Stafford: This will be good for everyone.

Jane Murphy: It sounds like it's mostly good for you.

Tom Stafford: Do you think I pay you unfairly?

Jane Murphy: Well, no. Not at the moment. But if the company is worth that much money, and we do all the writing, it seems like we should get part of it. Or, like, be a part of it more somehow, with decisions and stuff.

Tom Stafford: Everyone is getting a raise, I promise. But we'll do it after the sale.

Jane Murphy: You should tell everyone.

Tom Stafford: I can't, Jane.

Jane Murphy: They have a right to know.

Tom Stafford: I never should have told you this.

Jane Murphy: I guess not.

I looked up from Jane's phone, my office gradually coming into focus. Tom was sleeping with his employee. He was married. She was borderline threatening him that she would tell his employees about the sale so they could negotiate a percentage of a fifty-million-dollar paycheck. That was a hell of a lot of motive in pictures on Jane's phone. Messages that had already been deleted from her Slack account.

Hey, Tom, I wrote in a text. Turns out I was able to get one of Jane's old phones, and she screenshotted some Slack conversations with you. I'd love to talk to you about them. You around tomorrow?

He wrote me back immediately.

I'm free now. Can you meet me at my office?

14

UNLIKE MY LAST VISIT, the windows at Stile were mostly dark when I walked up. I could see a dim light emanating from somewhere inside, but other than that, the building looked empty. When I pressed the intercom, I half expected it to go unanswered, Tom having decided he didn't want to talk to me. But after a few moments, enough that I was about to leave, the door buzzed and clicked, and I stepped inside.

The stairwell was dim. Lighting snaking across the foot of each step was the only illumination. I climbed slowly, aware of my breath, the absence of other sounds, other people. On the fifth floor, I walked quickly through the blackness to the lit conference room at the back, but when I stepped inside, the room was empty.

"Tom?" I called out.

No one answered, and I walked more slowly back across the fifth floor, peeking into workstations, shining my phone on the couches in the break area to see if a prone body had hidden itself in the shadows. I opened the bathroom door slowly, pressed it all the way against the wall before I stepped in. But that room, too, was empty.

"Tom?" I tried again. "It's Jesse."

I went back to the stairwell and descended to the fourth floor. Since the last time I'd been there, someone had stapled thick sheets of plastic in front of the doorway. I pushed through them. They were heavy and the edges were sharp. When they fell closed behind me, the sound around me seemed off. Muffled. Construction had started in earnest. A concrete floor; a table saw, the handle raised in the air as if it had stopped mid-cut; a compressor; a tile cutter by the bathroom. Everything was still and silent, which made me think of Dorothy returning to Oz and finding that the whole world had turned to stone. The quiet there before the Wheelers appeared.

"Tom?"

I walked to the back of the building. When I got there, I pulled at the heavy plastic that separated Tom's office space from the rest of the room until I found the opening and squeezed through.

He was sitting on his desk, surrounded by boxes of what appeared to be his books and office supplies but also flooring and windows and shelving. There was one small lamp emitting a weak circle of light onto his desk. The space was so dim that I didn't notice he wasn't alone in the room until I heard something move behind me.

She leaned forward in her chair, toward the light.

"You found us," she said.

"My wife," Tom said to me. "Sorry, it's hard to hear through the plastic. I should have waited for you at the stairs."

"Elizabeth," the woman said from her chair. If she recognized me, she did not show it. "And you're the lawyer for Jeremy Miller?"

"I work for the lawyers who represent Jeremy, but I'm not a lawyer."

"Really. What are you, then?"

"An investigator."

"Well, I'll be. I didn't think I'd ever meet one of those."

She leaned back in her chair, back into the dark areas of the room. I took a step toward her, trying to see her face more clearly, but it was only shadows, sloping planes of skin. I remembered the way she had spoken to Kaya, how I'd thought there was some implication underneath her comments about Kaya working late again. She wasn't wrong to worry, but she'd been worried about the wrong person. Or, then again, maybe not.

"Did you know Jane?" I asked.

Since I couldn't see her face, I watched her body language, looking for a sudden tightness in the shoulders, a foot stopping mid-shake, something to indicate that she knew her husband was having an affair. But there was nothing. If I hadn't seen her previous interaction with Kaya, I might have assumed the lack of reaction meant she didn't know. But I couldn't unsee the tight smile, unhear the tone in her voice. She'd suspected something. She'd been communicating that to Kaya. And maybe she had to Jane as well. Maybe with more than a tone.

"I knew Jane," she said. There was something about her voice that made it sound both substantial and full of air, like cream whipped into something you could scoop up with your hands. "What a tragedy. Poor Jane. Poor Tom."

I wanted to look into her eyes—that hard-to-shake conviction that I could tell when someone was hiding something. Was that "Poor Tom" a reference to his employee being killed or his mistress? *Are you punishing him right here in front of me, and I don't know enough to know?* I looked at Tom. He was on his phone, touching the screen fast with his thumbs, not looking at his wife or at me. Elizabeth stood up. She was tall, almost as tall as her husband.

"Well, I'd better see myself off. Don't work too late." She turned to me, her face finally in the light. "He practically lives at the office."

"I've seen that," I said. "I've been trying to find out everything Jane did outside work, but from what I can tell, she practically lived here too."

"Well, I think everyone has been lately. All hands on deck for the sale, excuse the pun."

"I'll always excuse a good pun," I said to her. "I admire you for having such a good attitude about it. Tom at the office all the time. Then, even when he's not, people like Jane are writing him when he's at home."

"Well, Tom certainly inspires that kind of devotion with his employees. He's exciting. He makes exciting things happen."

There it was again. That tone, like she was keeping a secret, like she was saying something more than she was saying, and the part she wasn't saying was vibrating against the part she was, making the words land different in the air. She'd make you want to talk to her for hours, each sentence a chance to figure out how many layers of subtext she was playing with, but Tom only nodded at her.

"I'll be home soon," he said.

"Not too late, babe. Okay?"

"Yeah."

After she disappeared through the heavy plastic curtains, Tom turned back to his phone.

"Sorry," he said. "I have to finish this."

"What are you doing down here, man?"

He looked around at the plastic and the boxes like he didn't understand. "It's my office."

"It's a construction zone."

"I told you there was a miscommunication."

"So move."

"I will when they start working in here. They're mainly in the other room now."

I looked around. "It doesn't get loud down here?"

"It helps me concentrate."

"Right."

His phone buzzed. He started typing again.

"You were sleeping with Jane," I said.

A slight pause of his thumbs, a hiccup, and then he started up again.

"What makes you say that?"

"She took pictures of it. Your Slack conversations."

He looked up, stared at me for what felt like a full minute, then went back to his phone and typed something without responding.

"Did you delete that off Jane's Slack before you gave me her computer? Is that why it took so long?" I asked.

"No," he said. "I deleted those conversations a while before she died. I can do that as the administrator. Which I guess is something Jane thought I might do at some point, which I guess is why she took pictures of them."

"Why did you delete them?"

"Because I was cheating on my wife. With an employee. Using the company Slack. It's not a great look."

"Who's looking? Your wife?"

"The buyers," he said. He pulled the cord on the small desk lamp, extinguishing the last little bit of the light from the room. Normally, the lights from outside would have provided some illumination, but the windows were covered with plywood. I could hear him pull the cord again, the click, and the light came back on. "I was trying to avoid a scandal. I guess that's not going to happen anymore."

He turned the light off again. I reached into my pocket and pulled out my phone. The screen glowed in the darkness.

"Please," he said. "Don't."

"I think I'd like a little light, if you don't mind."

I turned on the phone's flashlight and shone it toward the desk. He was still sitting there, his legs hanging down, his hand on the lampstand, his eyes closed.

"I never even got to see the walls of my office up," he said. "We were going to do really cool things. I could never make her understand that."

"Jane?"

"Yeah, but you know that already, right? She took pictures." He hopped down from his desk and walked off into the darkness. I aimed my phone at him, but he was too far away for the light to catch him. I tried to remember what had been in the room when I'd seen it before, but it had all slipped away, leaving just the impression of a room taken down to its studs, heavy plastic, boxes, a dumpster against one wall. I felt in my pocket for Jane's phone to make sure it was still there. Why had I taken it with me from the office? I should have left it there, in my desk, but every time I started to leave—and I started three times—I imagined returning in the morning to find it gone. I had sent the pictures to myself. I had done something to make sure there was more than one copy in the world, but those copies were on the phone in my hand, currently being used as a pretty crappy flashlight.

"What I don't understand is why you didn't just give them a raise," I said, taking a few steps toward him in the darkness, shining the light from my phone around where I thought his hands should be. "You told me you started as a writer, that part of why you began doing this was because it seemed there was a limit as a writer in the model you were working in. So shouldn't you have wanted Jane and the others to have that too? Didn't you want to create something new for them too?"

"I did. I was going to. But part of what Jane wanted wasn't possible and for the other parts, I wanted to wait until after the sale."

I couldn't see his hands. They were not where I thought they should be. I took another step toward him, but I was so focused on where he was, I didn't notice a large box of tiles in front of me. Pain shot up through my shin, and a tile balanced on top fell off, shattering. I shone my light on the box and the broken tile on the floor, pushing some of the larger pieces aside with my foot. When I looked up again, the spot Tom had been standing in was empty.

"Jane didn't understand business."

I whirled around, trying to locate the sound of his voice. I'd been walking toward the large dumpster, but he was standing in front of a window now, staring at the plywood like he was looking out over his city. "I was trying to make her understand, that's all I meant to do. There were twelve people combing through our financials. The due diligence took months. I couldn't change the way everyone was paid all of a sudden, change how decisions were made. It would make it a different company."

"Well, so, who cares?" I said, taking a few steps toward the window. I had to keep glancing down at the floor in front of me to avoid obstacles, and every time I did, I was afraid when I looked up again, Tom would be right beside me.

"The buyers would care," Tom said. "The margins would change."

"So what, they'd pay only thirty million instead of fifty?"

"No. That's what Jane didn't understand either. That's not how it works. They'd buy something else. It wouldn't be interesting to them anymore. Later, when we proved our value, we could do anything. Do you know what it means to be valued at fifty million dollars and then actually be worth it? Everyone was going to be looking at us. We had to be perfect. We couldn't have stupid scandals about affairs or an employee revolution."

"Then just give them a raise."

"I was going to. After the sale."

"Why not before? Before you had other people to answer to?"

"Because it's my company!" he yelled. It sounded like his frustration was trying to tear through his words, become something material in the room. So there it was. The kind of anger that would make you grab someone just to make them listen. "It's my company," he rushed on. "I built it. I'm the one who got us here, and I'm going to be the one who brings us to the next place too. So I'm the one who decides when—not even if, but when—people get fucking raises. Not Jane; she wasn't in charge here."

"You told me Jane was really good."

"She was. She really was. But do you have any idea how many talented people there are in the world?"

I did. My dad used to ask me that question too when he stopped in the subway to listen to another musician before dropping some money in an instrument case or a bucket. It sounded different when Tom said it, though.

He left the window and walked to a stack of boxes that were covered with a large piece of plastic held down by bricks. When he was holding a brick in his hand, I made a split-second decision to send Jane's screenshots to Phil—why had I not done that first? Why had I sent them to myself?— instead of calling the police. Each time I pressed Send, the messages made a sound like they were slipping through space.

"What's that?" Tom asked.

"Just letting a few people know where I am. Including my uncle. Who works for the NYPD."

He looked at the brick in his hand and laughed. "I'm not going to hurt you." He turned to the pile of boxes, opened one, put it to the side, opened another. "It's over. Everything I was trying so hard to make not happen is going to happen anyway."

"Well, you did sell the company. The deal went through."

"Yeah," he said. "But someone else is going to run it now."

He stopped digging in the box. Apparently he'd found what he was looking for: a hoodie. He put it on and zipped the zipper all the way up to his chin. Then he stepped back into the darkness, and I was too far away for my phone's light to reach him. There was a loud bang—not a bullet, but as though he had thrown the brick against the wall or knocked over a file cabinet. I waited to feel something fly by my head, to feel him suddenly coming up behind me, but the next time I saw him, he was standing in the unfinished doorway.

"Good night, Jesse," he said, then he left me there in the bones of his new office with nothing but the light from my phone.

The thing about being a private detective working for a large company that works for large law firms is that sometimes cases end like this. Phil shared Jane's screenshots with the lawyer, and the lawyer shared them with the police. The police got a search warrant for Tom's home and office and sub-poenaed his cell phone company and Slack for their records, but they still made noise about not dropping the charges against Jeremy since cell-site data showed that Jeremy Miller had been near Jane's apartment on the morning she died, and he had, in their words, a lot of motive. Except the search at Stile produced Jane's missing cell phone, found inside a dumpster on the fourth floor under piles of broken tiles and old drywall. After that, the police dropped the charges against Jeremy and arrested Tom. I never saw Tom again. Or Jeremy. I wasn't in the lawyer's office when the cops called to let him off the hook. He never called me to say thank you. The day after I confronted Tom in his office, I rode the train to work, got my free orange juice, and started on a different case.

Sometimes my mom thinks I'm a lawyer now. I'm not sure how it happened, and I've tried to tell her what I actually do, but it doesn't stick. Sometimes Lucy says maybe I should just become a lawyer at this point; I'd make more money. But, like I told you when we started, I always knew I was never going to grad school. So every morning, I take the train to Thorton Investigation Services, and Gloria takes the bus to my mom's house, and we both do our work. I come home, and Gloria leaves, and if Lucy isn't in New Jersey, she often comes and cooks us dinner. Slowly, my mom's counter is accumulating fancy kitchen appliances. The miscellaneous drawer is stuffed with gadgets I've never seen before: cherry pitters, citrus peelers, fluted pasta cutters. Lately, my mom seems less interested in things. Instead of sitting with us in the kitchen while Lucy cooks, she stays on the couch with her phone. After dinner, she tells me I'm a good cook, no matter how many times I tell her Lucy is the one who made dinner. Some nights, it drives Lucy crazy, but I know it's only the path my mom's brain uses now to thank me for moving back home. After dinner, I do the dishes, and Lucy makes cocktails, choosing a recipe out of a book she has. She doesn't drink and doesn't know what they taste like, but my mom and I rate them for her, and she writes our ranking on the page. Sometimes my mom and I pour our drinks from Lucy's fancy glasses into to-go cups and walk buzzed through the neighborhood, singing show tunes and talking about my dad. After my mom falls asleep, Lucy and I go to the backyard and feed the cat.

Unless we all fall asleep watching a movie on the couch, which happens a fair amount. Like last night. I came home late from work. Lucy had put a plate for me in the fridge; a glass of wine waited on the counter, a million dishes in the sink. I warmed up the food and began rinsing dishes and placing them in the dishwasher. I filled a large pan crusted with tomato and burned cheese with soapy water and put it on the stove to soak. When I'd finished with the dishes, I took my plate and sat on the couch between Lucy and my mom, and we watched a black-and-white Jimmy Stewart look out over a black-and-white jury box. At some point, I fell asleep. I woke up hours later. The sky was still dark but lighter, the sun somewhere I couldn't see yet. My mom was staring at the TV, which was playing some kind of exercise-equipment infomercial.

"Jesse?"

"Yeah, Mom."

"I think I'm forgetting things."

"Like what?"

"I can't remember. Did I go to work? What time is it?"

"It's okay, Mom."

"When I was in my twenties," she said, "I stopped talking to my mother. We made up, but when she died, she'd forgotten we made up and wouldn't talk to me."

"That's not going to happen to us, Mom, because we never stopped talking."

She turned to look at me, her face going through something, then settling. She swatted me on the shoulder. "You never stop talking," she said.

"Where do you think I got it from?"

"Will you two shut up?" Lucy said.

She'd fallen asleep on my chest, and now she pushed herself up to look at us. When she lifted her head off my shoulder, feeling rushed back into the numb place. It hurt a little.

"Okay, Luce, we'll be quiet," I said.

I twisted on the couch to roll my eyes at my mom. But she was somewhere else, and Lucy had already fallen back asleep, and I was alone.

BOOK NINE

AN EVENING WITH
JEREMY MILLER

IN CONVERSATION WITH
DAVID HARRIS

Triangle Books, May 2023

DAVID: Can everyone hear me? Yes? We're going to get started. First of all, thank you to everyone for coming. I'm glad we kept these going. It's a testament to John, who started these conversations over three decades ago, that we managed to not only survive the pandemic, but grow. It's nice to be in this room again with you, and now with our friends from all over the country who log in every month. For those of you who are new to the Conversation series, we invite a writer down, they read some, we talk some, they read some, we talk some, repeat ad infinitum or until the beer runs out. We also have snacks. There's chips and popcorn, and Beth made brownies. Thank you, Beth.

Now, with that out of the way, it is with the greatest pleasure that I get to welcome tonight not only one of my favorite living writers but my friend, Jeremy Miller. Of Jeremy Miller's first book, Peter Boyle wrote, "Reading Miller is akin to watching a horror movie alone; for the rest of the evening, you find yourself frightened by sounds you never noticed before. With Miller, though, it's less likely to be a bump in the night than an unpleasant sensation in your body, a fractious moment with a stranger, and, instead of feeling unsettled in your house, you feel unsettled in your body, unsure of and alienated from the world."

Those of you who have read Miller know this is putting it mildly.

To read a Miller story is to know that wholeness will be deferred, resolution frustrated, and the body—well, we can never see a Miller body but askance. In his work, the human form is forever too big or too small, apart from everything or a part of everything. His narrators—twins, ghosts, missing women and the men who look for them—encounter events that cannot be integrated into a teleology of life and death, that refuse to be incorporated into a linear timeline. Because of these frequent transgressions, there is no safe space in Miller's books where we can stand apart and observe.

And yet. Despite the climate of claustrophobic threat that permeates his work—and despite Jesse Haber's now famous skepticism—Jeremy Miller has never strayed from his ultimate conviction, his true faith that art connects us all and that, in the act of writing, the author becomes conscious of his great dependence. As that other great exorcist once said, "I am not sure that I exist, actually. I am all the writers that I have read, all the people that I have met, all the women I have loved; all the cities that I have visited, all my ancestors." Like Borges, Miller is not always sure he exists. But he does believe in one ultimate body, the hallowed body of literature, from which he was born and to which he will return.

JEREMY: Wow. Wow. Thanks, David. I mean, that was mostly inaccurate, of course, and we're likely to get into the crisis of faith I had with regards to writing and how it almost killed me. But wow. Everyone should have the chance to be introduced by David once in their life. You could charge for it.

DAVID: I'm open to side hustles, but I'm not sure what the market is for that.

JEREMY: It could be like Cameo, but it's Introductions by David, where you take everything a person has done and make it sound like they have a purpose.

DAVID: I don't know what Cameo is.

JEREMY: It's a service where you pay a celebrity to send a birthday video or an inspirational message to your friends. People have told me I should be on it.

DAVID: Because of your books?

JEREMY: No.

DAVID: Oh, so, "Congratulations, the charges were dropped"?

JEREMY: I think they were trying to be helpful. A source of income, since I couldn't write anymore.

DAVID: Let's begin there because we, of course, have talked a lot about your writer's block, which started after Jane Murphy died. But let's catch everyone up. Have you written anything since Jane died?

JEREMY: Yes.

DAVID: Have you finished anything?

JEREMY: No.

DAVID: How many different projects have you started?

JEREMY: I don't know. Do you know? I think I have sent them all to you. It doesn't feel real until you have read them at this point.

DAVID: Eight, not counting what you are reading from tonight. I think you have sent me sections from eight separate books, and they've ranged from around ten pages to about five hundred, depending on the book.

JEREMY: Jesus.

DAVID: What makes you write five hundred pages of something and then abandon it? Why do you stop?

JEREMY: Well, generally, it's because it's bad.

DAVID: What does that mean?

JEREMY: David believes I escape into abstractions. This is what happens when you send someone between ten and five hundred pages of eight different and ultimately abandoned books. They start mapping your escape routes and showing them back to you.

DAVID: Do you know what else you do?

JEREMY: No. Maybe. What?

DAVID: I can say?

JEREMY: You can say.

DAVID: You don't finish things.

JEREMY: Oh, fine. I knew that one.

DAVID: Well, you say you stop them because they're bad.

JEREMY: They are bad.

DAVID: Let's talk in a way the other people in the room can understand. In these eight books, what specifically made them so bad you had to stop?

JEREMY: They didn't get anywhere close to what it felt like. For Jane to die. To be accused of her murder. To hold those in my mind.

DAVID: And in your body.

JEREMY: Yes, in my stupid body.

DAVID: What did it feel like?

JEREMY: Time works differently when you know something you can't seamlessly incorporate into your reality. When you are confused all the time. *Why do I feel like this? Why am I in this room answering these questions? Where is Jane? Why did this happen? Why can't I go back in time?* Questions that, if you had asked me the day before Jane died, I would have told you were not questions. I had this feeling—it was probably more than one feeling, but it felt like one single thing. A presence, or a pressure. It replaced me. It pushed me outside myself.

DAVID: And yet what strikes me, from what you're reading here tonight, is how close it stays to your life. Very different from your first two books, which are almost aggressively nonautobiographical.

JEREMY: If you know what is strange, you can isolate it, emphasize it by removing the elements that might be recognizable, increase the strangeness. If you, if I, don't know what is strange, I can't do that.

DAVID: Why do you use the word *strange*?

JEREMY: What other word should I use?

DAVID: Let's read a few pages so everyone else in the room can have some reference to what we're talking about. Where are you going to start for us?

JEREMY: I'm going to start at the beginning.

I began 2020 in distress. My last book had sold for six figures and then something terrible happened that made me unable to write at all. Or rather, a terrible thing happened and then, before I had a chance to

235

process the terrible thing, a substantial number of people began to believe I was responsible for the terrible thing and talked about it incessantly and publicly for months. I tried to shield myself from the chatter, but still it reached me, each time appearing unbidden like an intrusive thought. Then, for a while, everyone thought someone else had been responsible for the terrible thing, and the chatter grew less. There was more space in my mind, and I found I could go for ten minutes, even fifteen minutes at a time without remembering. Remembering called forth a sweeping emptiness that left only the terrible thing and me alone with it in the new world it had created.

In any case, it wasn't long before a large number of people stopped believing that someone else was responsible for the terrible thing. The story could not be verified either legally or by the internet, with the result that I appeared to everyone I encountered as a question. I knew I would never be myself again. To some people I was a contingent form, deferred from taking on a final shape unless there was a resolution to the terrible thing. To others, I was the terrible thing. Not that those people necessarily thought I was responsible, but to them I existed only in reference to it. While occasionally this felt unfair, I understood. I also could not think of myself without thinking of the terrible thing, and then of her. I suppose it only made sense that happened to other people as well. At some moments, I could imagine a future where it was not this way. Or my therapist would ask me to visualize this future, and I could. Some upcoming time when I went a whole day without thinking of it, or her. On those days, I would end my therapy session with a sense of peace. This could last almost twenty minutes before everything became sharp again. Then that distant day I'd been imagining—where I found myself again, where I found some way back to the life I always imagined I'd live—there would be a new book perhaps, and a review, cautiously admiring, but somewhere in the middle of that review, three paragraphs devoted to how at one point the author was affected by and thought responsible for a terrible thing, and, while he was no longer believed to be responsible, the terrible thing remained unattributable to anyone else so everything he wrote now must be read accordingly.

At night, I could never imagine anything. I could barely think. Or I thought too much. Even now, I'm not sure. I had the sense there was the thing I thought and the terrible thing on top of it, almost like a book with the answer on the last page. But to get to the thing I thought, I had to read about the terrible thing, and the reading took the whole night, and I never got to the last page, and every night I had to start over. Or sometimes, because I'd started watching old championship snooker matches on YouTube to pass the time, I imagined my brain like a table. I'd get to the point where I'd collected all my thoughts and racked them into a bright red triangle. I'd be standing over it with my cue trying to determine the angles when a rogue player was suddenly introduced, playing out of turn and sending my thoughts flying in all directions, so fast and so loud and so dispersed that I would disappear for a while until they settled. Other nights, being still was intolerable, and I had to stay in constant motion. Feelings can't kill you, my therapist would say, but I didn't understand what she was talking about. I wasn't feeling anything. I was a body that had been set in motion by a force outside myself, and I would stay in motion until another force acted to stop it.

"Maybe one of your friends can be that force," she would say. "Or maybe it's me."

By that time, though, the pandemic had started, and she was an image over Zoom, so that seemed unlikely. But it did occur to me that writing could be that force. That if I could write about the terrible thing, I could stop having to relive it every night, that if I could set out everything that had happened since I met her and since I lost her, I could get back to the thoughts I used to have and the life I used to live.

But it was harder than I'd anticipated to write without her now. I had written without her for years, and even when I knew her, I wrote without her. But on the rare days I could sit down at my desk and eke out a paragraph, when I stopped, I found myself wanting to ask her what she thought. I would look over from my desk and expect her to be there on my bed writing something on her phone, and she would not be there, and I would remember the terrible thing was real and not something I could imprison on paper if I found the right verb. Before, in fact, on the majority of days when I worked writing at my desk and she was alive on my bed, I had not turned to ask her what she thought or even shown her what I was working on. But I could have, and now I could not, and I became obsessed with this fact. It was something I could point to when my therapist or my family asked how I was doing, a way I could explain to someone what it felt like to receive a phone call with news that sets your life in a completely different direction, that makes it impossible to get back to the life you thought you were going to have. There was a feeling, also, that I started to remember, the feeling when I sat at my desk and she wrote on the bed, after I turned away from the screen, leaving there all the best things I could find in myself and composed now only of the shit left behind, and I would turn to her lying on the bed, and she would smile at me, as if that too was all right with her.

I say that I didn't turn to her on the bed to show her what I was working on, but that is not entirely accurate, because we were working on a project together, and so I frequently turned to her on the bed or sent her texts or emails asking her what she thought or wanting to discuss possible new directions. Often, we disagreed, and occasionally this was rancorous, but mostly I found it enjoyable and productive even, although I now wonder if she found it as enjoyable and productive as I did. Because if she was to me a honing tool that I used to make my thoughts sharper, she was the stone being passed over. Because of the terrible thing, however, the project we'd been working on was taken away from us before it was finished—from her because she was dead and from me because people thought I had done that. I told myself not to continue reading what the new writers produced each day, not to imagine who at her old office was responsible, but I couldn't help it.

Can you believe this? I imagined saying to her, because even though we argued over it almost daily, we both knew what it was. But of course, she didn't answer, and each day, I missed it more, the time we would spend on our project, the emails and text exchanges, the arguments over direction and plot and character, the way her brain worked against mine, and I would remember the piece I'd been working on when she died. The feeling that last month, like I couldn't write fast enough, so afraid to lose it, so sure it was good, better than anything I'd ever written. It died when she died. No matter what I did, I could not get back into the story. The words seemed to have been written by someone else. And so I started to write about what had happened. Maybe when I could contain it in a Word document, I could contain it also in a smaller part of my brain, and I could get the rest of my brain back. But each day I wrote, I became more confused, until one day, I simply stopped sitting down.

I had money and writer's block, and I took to the avenues. A few months in, I had the idea that I might walk every street in New York, but that seemed to go against the central philosophy of the flaneur and so I did not. Still, once I thought it, I couldn't get the idea out of my head. Children drawing squares with sidewalk chalk disappeared as my eyes caught sight of street names I'd never noticed before. The smell from wet cardboard and rotting fruit was overpowered by exhaust being piped out of cars as they turned toward neighborhoods I'd yet to explore. After a while, I found I couldn't walk anymore either.

I had the sense that not being able to walk around my own city was ominous. The original flaneurs may have been assaulted and overstimulated by the images of modernity, but at least they kept walking without trying to make a game out of it. Unless art is another kind of game, which I had come to suspect more and more every time I tried to write something. Even so, I encountered a second problem with my attempted flânerie: Everyone was looking at me. People followed me around the block and on Twitter. They posted screenshots of pages I'd written with words circled, or underlined, or crossed out. There was a podcast, and then two, and then four. They seemed to grow exponentially, and sometimes I dreamed up new ones, only later discovering they weren't real. Someone posted my mug shot online, and people began using it as their avatars. When they sent me messages, they came with little mes attached. When I wrote them back, as I did sometimes, I felt I was talking to myself.

Undeniably, this was bad for my walking. The part-of-the-crowd-while-also-apart-from-the-crowd vantage point of the flaneur is hard enough to manage without the surveillance. This feeling may have been exacerbated by the masks. Everywhere I went, half-faces turned to look at me. The streets were mostly empty then, and the only sounds were the sirens. One morning, traversing the empty blocks of my empty city, I passed an apartment building and thought of cartoon animals packing too-full suitcases—as if at any moment every window in the structure would explode, raining families and collared shirts down onto the street. That was when I heard someone running toward me. He was wearing a hat and gloves, a mask, a jacket with reflective stripes sewn down the arms. The material of his coat rustled with each forward stride. My sunglasses had fogged over, which made it harder to see him as he closed in on me. His breath was raggedy and loud in the silence. As, at last, the reflective stripes came back into view—the man himself still lost in the fog of my glasses—I could hear my heartbeat as if it were inside my head. His footsteps. When the first blow landed, it seemed to come from nowhere. I fell to the ground and rolled to avoid another attack. A car horn blared, followed by the shriek of skidding tires. I could smell the brake pads burning; my fingernails slid and scratched along the blacktop as I tried to stop my roll mid-turn, reverse back to the curb. I landed in a puddle. My mask took on water. I breathed the wet thing into my mouth, choking but afraid to take it off because we didn't know anything about the virus then. I ripped my sunglasses off my face instead—only to see the runner still a block away from me, and, in the building to my right, faces pressed up against the windows.

My brother had sent me an Xbox console early in the pandemic. After months of incapacitating writer's block and my failed attempts at flânerie—as well as two brief relationships that occurred entirely over Zoom and felt like trying to hold the hand of a stranger as the plane went down—I finally bought the games my brother told me to buy so we could play together online.

DAVID: So this is where you and I meet.

JEREMY: We meet on Reddit talking about video games.

DAVID: Arguing about video games.

JEREMY: Discussing. Conversations animated by the desire to challenge unquestioned assumptions.

DAVID: Assumptions like maybe one should play the game before one forms an opinion of it.

JEREMY: That was one time in a larger discussion about remakes.

DAVID: Okay, let's not relitigate this in front of all these nice people.

JEREMY: Fine. I forgot where we were.

DAVID: We meet on Reddit.

JEREMY: We meet on Reddit, only to realize we have actually met before.

DAVID: Somehow in one of our arguments—excuse me, our challenging discussions—we start talking about literature, and I mention I work at Triangle Books.

JEREMY: I had read here, because the independent press that published my first book was based in Carrboro, and they invited me to do a reading here.

DAVID: And I was at that reading.

JEREMY: You introduced me. I know I praised your introduction of me earlier, but you created extra work for yourself. You could have used what you said last time.

DAVID: I do have it. We have a folder with all our introductions, and I went back and looked at it. I would have had to add a few things.

JEREMY: "Additionally, Jeremy has written a bestselling novel, been accused of murder, and had a nervous breakdown."

DAVID: "He has started eight books he has not finished."

JEREMY: "Because I, David Harris, am the maverick czar of Triangle Books, I invited him to come down and talk about *not* writing. Readings where writers read from actual books have gotten a bit old."

DAVID: "Also, his sister asked me to invite him."

JEREMY: Is that true? That feels true.

DAVID: What is truth? Look, I know I'm the one who interrupted you, but do you mind reading the part about video games? I know we have a few gamers in the house who will appreciate it as much as I do.

JEREMY: Sure. It's the part that comes next anyway.

I hadn't played video games with my brother since we were kids. Even then, I played only at his urging. I never liked the games with guns or martial arts. I didn't like to drive, and I didn't like football. There were too many buttons to keep track of, and I didn't believe in magic. But I played with him because I had run out of ways to get through the days, and I had started to hear a voice, faint at first but more insistent over time, that asked if I was so sure I wanted to survive. We played violent multiplayer games steeped in myth and involving complicated backstories that could be distilled into revenge or survivor plots. I killed people and goblins and zombies and gargoyles and creatures whose biologic materiality was never made clear to me. I leaped on and off rooftops. I dove behind bushes. I shook off dogs who clamped their mouths to my forearms. I drove a sword into a troll's thigh. I slipped on blood. I searched locked rooms. I witnessed a man catch fire, his erratic path as he tried to outrun something that was already attached to him. I kicked my enemies in the face. I threw them off my back. I died thousands of times. I watched my brother die. I fell asleep with the controller in my hand and woke up and played again.

I told myself I was doing it for my brother, because he was my brother, and he was lonely. But one morning, he didn't want to play, so I looked around to find a game I could play by myself. I'd thought without my brother, I would gravitate toward puzzle games, but I found they couldn't hold my attention, and I ended up playing a game where I needed to go to hell to save the soul of my dead lover. The story was threaded through with the mythology of an ancient religion I was not familiar with but that I believed to be real because the game had the feel of something well researched. It felt quiet. It was true that the game was very loud and, in fact, characterized by binaural audio where the interior monologue of the main character came into my head from both ears, and her voice was a constant stream of agitated thoughts, not even one after the other but one in my right ear followed a fraction of a second later by another in my left ear, so there was no silence at all, just a flood of voiced fear rushing into my head at all times. But otherwise, it was quiet.

I could see her body on the screen, her brown tunic, the ripple in her muscles as she threw a spear at a demon, her painted face, which almost made her eyes seem two different colors. I felt like a husky running through hell. Though not exactly like that, because I knew I was myself and my body was mostly stationary, my fingers working the controller, a slight pull in my shoulders, the tension gathering somewhere along my jawline. And I knew she was an image on the screen, and the husky was a metaphor. But in the middle of that triad was a point where they all met, and while I was playing, that point was a real thing that existed in the world, and I was located in that point, even if I was also in my body and in a metaphor.

I played for days straight. I was grateful to have something to do, to be surrounded by gods and demons. I ignored my brother's calls. I didn't eat. I slept in snatches. On the fourth day, I had a meeting with my therapist, which I could not miss without triggering more serious interventions. I paused the game. In the shower, I stared at a mildew stain spreading out from the soap shelf. The mold was a black oblong shape surrounded by individual black dots as if it were growing in splotches—slowly and asymmetrically—and these new areas of blackness would eventually connect with the original oblong shape, darkening the white tile that existed in between. I couldn't understand the mechanism by which it was growing, so I left it. I walked into my room drying my hair. Something moved near the closet. I dropped the towel I was holding. My fingers sought the air for my controller. *Go back,* I heard her say in my head. *You're going to die. Go back. Why won't you run?*

I logged in five minutes after the meeting was scheduled to begin. It was agonizing. Not the talking with the therapist—who was perfectly nice and rarely asked too much of me before signing off—but the time away from the game. At one point, while the therapist was speaking, I opened a new tab and played the game trailer soundlessly. My hands felt itchy without the controller in them. I could hear her voice in my head and also another voice that sounded like *Now, now, now, now, now, now, now, now, now.* I nodded at the therapist. I looked back at her painted face, like she had divided herself into sections. I said, "Yeah, I think meditation is really helping. Sometimes I can sleep up to four hours now."

When the meeting ended, I picked up the controller. The tension dissolved from my body. For a moment, everything seemed to be working properly—breath, blood flow, the pace and intensity of thoughts slowing down. And then her voice again, breathless and heightened in both ears, and I was in hell, but I was free.

I had lied about the sleep. I hadn't slept for more than two hours for so long that I had come to the point where there was no before anymore. There was only this aching and surreal life where the streets outside my apartment were regularly empty and where I lost huge swaths of time, coming to in the bathroom with my toothbrush in my mouth and no memory of having arrived there, the bristles wet but bland so I couldn't figure out if I'd forgotten to put toothpaste on or if I'd been brushing for so long any hint of mint had long since broken down. There was only this wandering around my apartment and the hate I felt every time I looked over at my bed. And I did hate it, and I hated my whole bedroom, which meant I hated my whole apartment, because I lived in a studio. The bed and the coffee machine, and the curtains I'd put up when I moved in because the sunlight woke me—all of it still there. I started to think of myself as a hoarder. Here, this piece of furniture that took up half the square footage in my apartment, blankets and sheets taking up half the closet space, a drawer full of melatonin and sleepy-time teas, eye masks, oils, a collection of prescription medications of various strengths and legalities—all of it useless to me. I might as well have kept old newspapers or the twist ties that came on bread. At some point, I realized I must have had this exact same thought before, because, looking for a pen, I opened a drawer in the kitchen and found a collection of twist ties that I'd started keeping, unbeknownst to myself. Based on the amount in the drawer, I had been doing this for quite some time. Or I was eating extraordinary amounts of bread.

I laughed alone in my kitchen, which was also my bedroom, but which—I knew this now—was also someplace else. Because to stay up all night alone is to know there are different worlds occupying one space. I tested this by spending some of my nights drinking online with friends or meeting them to walk six feet apart from each other. Later to sit on opposite benches waiting for the sun to come up. But alone in two hundred fifty square feet, awake for twenty-four hours, and then forty-eight, and then seventy-two, and then I lost count—everything vibrated. Sounds took on texture. It was like being let into the world only bats and dogs knew. Different frequencies. Pitches. Shadows. I understood—not on an intellectual level but on a cellular level—that there is a reality the limitations of our senses prevent us from knowing. Because I could see everything now, hear everything, feel everything.

I decided I should stop playing video games. My sleep had become even worse. Every time my eyes closed, I woke up immediately with the feeling that I'd fallen asleep in a car, and the driver was crashing. I booked more appointments with the therapist. I bought a juicer and found a Zoom knife-skills class and practiced cutting carrots all the same size. Sometimes I went online and responded to people who wrote me about my novels, except for the ones who really wanted to talk about the terrible thing that had happened. Twitter had become a haunted space. Once I'd walked through it like Baudelaire walked through Paris, but after I wrote my first book, I needed it, and after I wrote my second book, people needed me, and it was never the same. Then the terrible thing happened and instead of transactional interactions with strangers, there were the hunters and ghosts. The hunters I could have dealt with, but the ghosts were something else. Someone on Twitter once said—maybe someone who could have been a real friend or maybe it was only someone who said a thing I liked once—that on the internet, you will always lose your home. And I think this is right for most of us. But not for the ghosts.

I had been reading about games on my phone. It helped to curb the craving. It made me feel stronger, like my grandfather who kept a pack of cigarettes in his car to remind himself he could smoke whenever he wanted but was choosing not to. Unfortunately, I was not made of such strong stuff as my grandfather, which was something I was used to hearing but turned out to be true.

DAVID: So you're going to be reading some more pages from this later tonight. But because we've already gotten into it, I'd like to talk more about the books you stopped writing before you got to this. Can you take us through them?

JEREMY: I'm not sure I can. Some things are a bit blurry.

DAVID: Well, when we met for the second time, you were not writing at all. You told me you'd given up and that you hadn't written anything worth anything since Jane died. But I pestered you, and you sent me a couple of things you'd started before you abandoned writing altogether. Three, I think, written in the year after she died.

JEREMY: I'm not sure those count as books. I couldn't sit down for very long. One of them, I don't even really remember writing. It might have been when the insomnia was at its peak.

DAVID: I count them, because to my mind, I see three distinct attempts. What made you stop writing after abandoning these three pieces? Why not try again?

JEREMY: It wasn't a choice. I couldn't.

DAVID: When did you start your fourth book? What changed?

JEREMY: I came out of a pretty dark period, and I wanted to understand what had happened. I was trying to make everything add up. When Jane died, I felt the bottom drop out, but it was inside me. A part of me hadn't noticed how I'd grown to depend on her, how often I thought of her, the way I felt when I was with her. At first the fact of my arrest distracted me from this. Or at least I thought that when the charges were dropped, I would start to feel better. But that didn't happen. I went through some kind of prolonged mental breakdown. When I started to come out the other side, a new kind of panic set in, because I didn't understand what had happened to me. I really cared about Jane, I missed her, but it was over a year later. It was longer than I knew her. That book— book four, as you call it—it wasn't a story. It was an algebra problem. I was trying to figure out why I felt the way I felt, what had happened to me.

DAVID: What's wrong with solving problems, puzzles? Isn't that part of why you write, to discover?

JEREMY: No, not for me. Not before this. I am not interested in solving puzzles. I'm interested in what it feels like to live inside the puzzle, how to capture that. But in this book four, everything I wrote, no matter what I did, it felt as if I kept coming back to this effort to solve.

DAVID: Her murder?

JEREMY: No, I am not interested in Jane's murder. I was interested in her. Us. Me. Life. Death. But not her murder. When I tried to write about it back then, I thought, *I'll sit down and write from the beginning.* But I couldn't, I'd get to this point—oh, I remember this day. Once I told her a story about when I was a child, and my best friend's brother died. We were doing that thing, tell me something you've never told anyone. So I told her when Eliot's brother died, I didn't know what to do so I started answering every other phone call. Then every fourth. I'd never told anyone.

In turn, Jane told me about a party she went to. At the end of the night, everyone found beds, and a boy climbed in bed with her and started to touch her. She pretended to be asleep, and all those years later, she still wasn't sure why she didn't get up and climb into the bed where her best friend was sleeping, say something. The night she told me, I remember I watched her for a while, as if I wanted to know whether I could tell if she was sleeping or faking it. Her back was to me, and she had curled up, using her arm as a pillow. Bent. It looked really uncomfortable, but I could see her breathing. It moved her back. I remember the way it moved her back.

When I was writing, though, I couldn't stay there. I was already out in front of myself, saying, *See, see, you grieve for this? That's why you found yourself, a year later, playing video games, unable to sleep.*

But then I'd remember other times. She was away for the weekend, and we were supposed to see each other Monday night. When the time came, I remember this very clear, very strong feeling: *I don't want to see her. I don't want to go.* So I didn't. All these other times we split apart from each other. The women I would meet, the excitement of them. But I couldn't write about these either because I was still using them as evidence. *This is why you should have been sleeping. This is why you don't make sense.*

So I tried writing more about the arrest and everything that came, that still comes, with it. I tried writing into that. Or maybe not my arrest, but Tom Stafford's acquittal, which I think had happened around that time. The fact that her murder is still unsolved and sometimes people email me: "I won't tell anyone, but I just want to know what it felt like when you did it." Or this writing community that embraced me for a moment became "We'd love to have you, but we don't want to distract from so-and-so's debut." I thought, *I'll start with that. The problem was starting at the beginning. I'll start at the end. It's really about the end.*

But when I tried writing about that, I immediately found myself writing about Tom and Jane. A lot, which was pretty surprising at the time, and I thought it was a breakthrough. Maybe it was finding out Jane was sleeping with Tom, that even before I lost her, I didn't have her. Not like I'd thought. Maybe I was so petty I couldn't even look at myself, and that's why I couldn't write this. You know, I wasn't sleeping with anyone else when she died. I didn't think she was. I thought we were honest about those things. At least I was.

DAVID: You were?

JEREMY: Throughout the course of our relationship, I did not go out of my way to tell her what I did when we were apart, but I was always honest about who I was. If I was sleeping with someone Jane regularly interacted with, I would have mentioned that. Or ended things.

DAVID: But you never did end things.

JEREMY: Well, I did. So did she. Those endings never lasted, which became another piece of evidence, something I could use to balance my equation. To make it make sense. Writing this way doesn't work.

DAVID: Why not?

JEREMY: It doesn't give anything back. It took a lot of things from me, and Jane, to write about it, and it didn't give anything back. It wasn't useful to anyone. It was almost a kind of fanfic.

DAVID: Fanfic can't be useful?

JEREMY: I love this about you, David, you're the most catholic reader I've ever met. You meet every book where it is, every genre on its own terms. Bad fanfic, then. And there's too much bad fanfic about Jane already. I was doing what everyone else did to her.

DAVID: It's not the same thing.

JEREMY: It is. If you can't write it well, it is.

DAVID: It could be useful to you, to write it out.

JEREMY: Writing badly is not useful to me.

DAVID: And writing well is?

JEREMY: Yes. Maybe.

DAVID: Okay, on that note, let's read a little more.

JEREMY: Sure.

DAVID: Is there anything we need to know here?

JEREMY: No. I guess the only thing to know is that after Jane died, I started buying dip.

DAVID: You mean—to clarify—the tobacco in the cans?

JEREMY: Yes. I didn't dip, but I kept buying it. I can't explain it.

DAVID: And what did you do with them?

JEREMY: Nothing. I brought them home. Stacked them on top of each other. Made towers.

DAVID: And that's where you're starting?

JEREMY: That's where I'm starting.

When my sister came to pick me up, I hadn't slept in over seventy-two hours. I'd built a small house out of the dip cans I'd purchased. Not big enough for me, but big enough for a cat, maybe, or a family of cats. There were a dozen tabs open on my computer to different pet-adoption organizations, photographs of animals with names like Smoky, Midge, and Saint Augustine.

"Come on," my sister said.

"Where?"

"You're coming home with me."

"No."

"It's either my house or a hospital."

At the time, I'd been emailing with a woman named Meg who first wrote me because she thought she'd bumped into Jane the morning she died. Or, rather, Jane had run into her coming around a corner, and Meg couldn't sleep anymore because she wondered if she could have saved her. Apparently, the collision was significant, Jane running fast, both women knocked down into the street. Jane picked herself up first, offered her hand to help Meg stand up. Jane's palms, Meg kept remembering, were scraped raw from the concrete. Meg had hurt her ankle—sprained it, actually, though she didn't know that until the next day when, still unable to put her full weight on it, she'd gone to urgent care. That morning, the morning Jane died, Meg had limped back home, waving away Jane's offers to help her, to take her somewhere, to wait, at least, so Meg could call her boyfriend to come get her.

What if I had said yes? Meg had written me the first time. And then a hundred more times, in an email thread that soon eclipsed any email thread I'd ever had with anyone. *What if I had said yes?*

We exchanged less than twenty words, she wrote me. *I was distracted. I had flown to New York to visit my boyfriend. I was supposed to stay a week, and the first night had been so different than what I was expecting, I wasn't sure how I would get through the next six days. I was trying to convince myself some initial awkwardness was expected after we hadn't seen each other for so long when something hit me in the chest. I went down hard. I didn't know it was Jane until after all the articles. She kept saying how sorry she was, but I wasn't put out by the fall. In fact, I welcomed the pain in my ankle as a substitute for the clear, stabbing feeling I thought I would experience seeing Ryan. If you knew me, you'd know there's no version of that day where I would have accepted Jane's offer to take me somewhere—I could see how much she wanted to keep running; I would have marched on broken bones rather than make her go out of her way. But what if I had said yes?*

I understood how important this question was, because I had been wondering what would have happened if I had said no. If I hadn't left the bar the night before she died. If I'd stayed.

We had been at Mika's with Billy and Kaya. Billy had worked earlier in the evening, but the kitchen was closed, and he was sitting at the bar with us, his apron and the white button-down shirt he wore while serving folded beside him. Jane was drunk. She and Kaya had come over after work and hadn't left by the time I showed up at ten thirty. I hadn't really wanted to come because I'd been writing something I was excited and scared by, but Jane's invitation had the subtext of a test.

Sure. I don't want to stay too late, though, so I can get up early to write.

Oh, she wrote back. *Well, you don't have to come.*

No, I want to. See you soon.

Billy was mixing a drink at the bar when I came in. Kaya was conducting some kind of personality test.

"Jeremy. Perfect timing. Put these four things in order: Dogmatist, king, proprietor, hopeless romantic. From most preferred to least preferred."

"Most preferred to be or most preferred to talk to?"

"Don't overthink it," Kaya said. "Just answer."

"Yeah, right," Jane said. "Billy, what are you making?"

"Patience, Jane, patience. You're going to love it."

"Jeremy." Kaya drummed her fingers on the bar. "Go."

"What about everyone else?"

"We already went," Jane said.

"Okay, fine. King. Proprietor. Hopeless Romantic. Dogmatist."

"Hmm. I would have guessed three and four would be switched," Jane said. She took a sip from the glass Billy pushed toward her, then put up her hand for a high five. "Love it. Want ten more."

"Why do you think I would have switched three and four?" I asked her, regretting that I'd come. I'd thought the invitation was a test, but now it seemed the whole night was going to be one. "They are similar to me, but at least a romantic is motivated by meaning rather than fear."

"Kinda fucked up you put king first," Billy said.

"Guys, there are still three more questions left," Kaya said. "You're not supposed to comment on it. You might change the result."

"You don't have to worry about that with Jeremy, though," Jane said. "He doesn't care what people think."

I tried to go over the previous twenty-four hours, what could have happened the day before that Jane was reacting to, but all I could remember was meeting after dinner, walking to an art exhibit one of my friends had told me about. It was cold, and we stopped to get hot apple cider at a coffee shop, taking seats at the counter along the window and watching the people rushing by. Later, falling asleep laughing about a performance piece at the art show that had inexplicably involved a game of red rover. A couple dozen twenty- and thirty-somethings running around a warehouse in Brooklyn with our cans of beer. The blob that formed as, one by one, we were picked off, a wall of flesh coming at the last people left, the cheer echoing in the empty space when they were finally absorbed. The retelling morphed into our own hybrid of red rover and strip poker, and I woke up at five ready to write. I walked to the diner down the street and wrote for three and a half hours, barely looking up. I bought bagels and coffee and walked back to Jane's. She was just home from her run, late for work, and told me she would take the bagel to eat at her desk.

But that night at Mika's, I wasn't sure what she was mad at. When I thought about the previous day, I felt calm.

At twelve, I finally suggested going.

"You just got here."

"No. No."

"It's only midnight."

"It's a Tuesday."

"Okay, I get it."

"Get what?"

"So for *your* things, like last night, we can stay for hours."

"We left by eleven last night because we met up a lot earlier. I asked you if you wanted to meet for dinner tonight, you know, but you said you were working."

"I was working."

"Okay."

"Hey, Billy." Jane threw a straw at his head. "What are you making next?"

"Are you serious?"

Billy and Kaya glanced at each other.

"I said I wanted to go," I said.

"Well, I don't want to."

"May I propose a compromise?" Billy said, standing up and making his way behind the bar. "A drink that doesn't take very long. I think some people call them shots."

Jane's and Kaya's phones buzzed at the same time, sending a vibration along the bar.

"Typical," Kaya said, glancing at the notification. "Tom's still at work."

They both turned to look out the window at their office building across the street, dark except for the fifth floor.

"Wonder why," Billy said, running his finger under his nose. "Maybe we should invite him over. That'll wake you up, Jer." He put four shot glasses down on the bar.

"I'm not tired. I want to wake up early to write."

"Oh," Kaya said. "A new book? Jane said something about that. That's exciting."

"He won't tell you," Jane said.

"I don't like to talk about my work until I have a sense of what it is."

"He doesn't want it to get infected with bad ideas."

"That's not what I said." I turned to Jane. "I'm always like this. It has nothing to do with you."

"Right, except last night with Seb. And Ricardo. You talked to them."

I was momentarily thrown. That had happened, but she hadn't acted mad the night before, or this morning.

"It wasn't like that," I said.

"Fuck off, Jeremy. I heard you. Billy, I changed my mind. I don't feel like a shot. I'd like a pint, please."

Billy looked from Jane to me and back to Jane and then pulled a beer glass off the rack.

"Okay, you're right," I said. "I did talk to them about it. But it's different."

"It's different because you think I'm not smart enough. And, like, fine, you're right, when I met you, I hadn't read a lot of the authors you like. But I've read them now, and I know you're copying

257

them. Your amused condescension about the rest of us, it comes off a little different at this point."

"Thanks. Really, this is helpful," I said. "I can't imagine why I didn't want to talk to you about this earlier. This is the kind of supportive dialogue I knew I'd get from you."

"Oh, but you get it from Seb and Ricardo?"

"You know, as fun as this is, I think I'm going to go." I started walking toward the door, but turned around and came back. "I do want to talk to you about it. But not yet. I don't understand why that's not okay with you. I would never ask you to show me something before you wanted to or to tell me something you weren't ready to tell me."

"Just stop. I may not always agree with how you do things, but at least I respect the way you do them. It doesn't go both ways, and if you think I can't see that, well, then, I don't know."

"This is exactly what I'm talking about, Jane. This is why I don't want to talk to you about it yet. Seb and Ricardo don't do this. They're not always trying to prove something. They're just listening to me."

"Oh, no, I hear you. Trust me, I hear you."

"No. You don't. Billy, Kaya, it's been a blast. Jane, it's been what it's been."

And I left. But what if I'd stayed? Or what if I'd said, *No, Jane. I've been at this bar for hours waiting for you, and it's time we went home now. If you want to talk about something, let's go home and talk about it, and not do ... whatever this is.*

For months, I replayed this scene countless times a day, analyzing it, rewriting it, revising it. It didn't help, but I couldn't stop. When I did stop, finally, it was because it wasn't working anymore. I was doing it to punish myself, but I had become numb to it. It had stopped hurting. But if I forced myself not to think about it, after a while it

258

would come back on its own with renewed strength, and I could be back in that night at Mika's watching Billy pull the tap on Jane's last beer, watching myself walk out and Jane looking at me before she turned back to Billy and said something I couldn't hear. I could be left alone with it again, a roiling unease that—slowly and unceasingly— would dredge up, turn over, dig under every aspect of that night. It was like a drug when it came on, and I spent the night in it. I liked talking to Meg, because she couldn't stop going back to the morning she met Jane either. We wrote each other hundreds of emails—it was the pandemic, after all—endeavoring to think ourselves into a different timeline or feel, if not death, then something like it. She used to send me her dreams, because after a few months, Meg began to wonder if maybe she'd seen something that day, someone follow- ing Jane, something her conscious mind would never be able to see.

There's a tree, she wrote, *and the leaves are silver. At first I think it's a trick of the light, but as I get closer, I realize the leaves are silver. They're melting. They look like raindrops as they fall to the earth. I think they'll cause gashes in the dirt, but they don't. They lie like hail on the surface. The ants come and take them down. Do you think that could mean anything?*

I thought you couldn't sleep, I responded.

I couldn't remember the last time I'd slept. I must have. Real- istically I knew the human body could not survive without sleep- ing for months, but I didn't remember sleeping. Life felt like one long day, one long night. I was resentful. Not that Meg could sleep and I could not, but that she had led me on, telling me she couldn't sleep when what she really meant was that she was having trouble sleeping. That sometimes she found it difficult to lose consciousness. That sometimes she woke in the middle of the night. I'd thought she knew how I felt, that we were the same, but we were not. To not sleep, this was not a rational choice. My body rejected it, but there was something of the siren call to it after a while. The obliteration of boundaries. Between sleep and waking, between what was real and what was not, what had happened and what could have happened.

I didn't write Meg back for a week. She continued to write, first simply as before, and then in response to my silence.

Are you okay? I'm worried about you.

And then, a week later:

Did I do something wrong? Are you mad at me?

And a week later:

Ryan asked me to marry him. I said yes.

I wrote her back after that. I forgave her her sleep. Around this time, I had come to think that if Jane was in a different world, then so was I. If Jane was a ghost, then so was I. I couldn't reach people, and they couldn't reach me. Something fundamental had shifted in what was possible between myself and others, myself and what surrounded me. And Meg. She slept. She didn't even know Jane. But she felt it, I knew she did, the edge of the old world.

It's real, I wrote her back, *the land of the dead. We're in its shadow now.*

Meg started to see a hypnotist. I started to lie in bed at night and count ants carrying orbs of silver down into the earth. Once I counted to over a hundred thousand and only later understood that days had passed.

Can I watch you sleep? I wrote Meg.

She went to bed with her fiancé, woke up at four, took her computer to the couch, and set up the video.

It was around this time that things get hazy. I'm told I started hitchhiking and that once my sister had to come pick me up at the Canadian border, where I was being held. Apparently, as I'd waited to cross, I'd stepped out of line to throw away a pen. It had started to leak in my pocket, but the border officers believed this to be a suspicious act and detained me.

DAVID: Do you mind if I interrupt you here?

JEREMY: No, please do.

DAVID: So, we have talked a few times tonight about the eight unfinished books you've sent me. But you told Jane you didn't share your work with anyone until you finished. Were you lying to her?

JEREMY: No. Not exactly.

DAVID: Not exactly.

JEREMY: You know, I admire you. You're simply one of the best readers I've ever met. But part of me sending you my work is that I cannot write without you right now. If I could, I would not send it to you. I say this even knowing that in a very real sense, talking to you about my work has been one of the best aspects of this experience. Far better than the writing of it.

So that's the *no,* because before, I could finish on my own. But I would have spoken with you about it. Many times. In terms of ideas or in terms of other books that were attempting similar things. And I did not do that with Jane. That's the *not exactly.*

DAVID: Why not?

JEREMY: Because she wouldn't have read those books. She wouldn't have liked them.

DAVID: So you were smarter than her?

JEREMY: We were different. There were things Jane was better at than I was. I really believe that, I always have. I remember once, she wrote this apology from the Brooklyn dad. We never discussed it. It was a response to a thread written by real people discussing Rita, one of his posts. And she wrote it so quickly, and it was so good. She made those people—those on the original thread—she understood what people were looking for online. She was perceptive.

DAVID: But you don't think that's as important as what you are trying to do?

JEREMY: No. I know how that sounds, but no.

DAVID: Even if she could write faster, connect to more people. She didn't throw so much away.

JEREMY: What do you want me to say? I can't help that I like some things better than other things. I couldn't say that to Jane, because it would always mean something. But Jane was the same way. She said she respected the way I worked. But she didn't. Maybe she would have in someone else. It was hard with Jane. We felt this connection that was hard to walk away from. But we weren't right for each other, I don't think. Somewhere, we both knew that. She kept testing me to see if I was there, because she knew I wasn't there. But neither was she.

Toward the beginning, we were talking on the phone every night, for hours. One night, I can't remember what we were talking about, only that I was excited. Happy. I'd gone on about something for quite a while only to realize the call had dropped, and she wasn't there. Later, I would think about that moment a lot. She could drop away, even when she was in the room with you. But I am also like that.

DAVID: It could be perfect if two people want to drop away at the same moment.

JEREMY: But it never really works out like that, does it? There's always someone dropping away when the other person is reaching out. It wears on you after a while. It might be the best conversation you've ever had with another person, but if the call keeps dropping, eventually you'll be more cautious about what you say. Both people start beginning each sentence with *Are you still there?* Every pause is a hole.

DAVID: You could hang up.

JEREMY: We didn't want to hang up.

DAVID: Let me ask you another question. Is it true that you don't remember hitchhiking?

JEREMY: That is true. Sometimes I remember things, and I'm not sure if they're real or not.

DAVID: Because you're you, and there was some interest in you—some people who picked you up took videos.

JEREMY: I'm aware of them. I've watched them.

DAVID: How does that feel?

JEREMY: Uncomfortable. To have done things I don't remember. To watch myself do them. I'm afraid, when I watch them, of what I might do.

DAVID: Mostly you quote Anne Carson.

JEREMY: Yes, I think that makes them more disturbing in some ways. That I seem so lucid, say things I normally say, have access to the part of my brain that memorizes poetry.

DAVID: Do you remember where you were trying to go when you hitchhiked?

JEREMY: No.

DAVID: No guesses? Were you trying to die, do you think?

JEREMY: No. I don't think I cared if I lived at that point, but that's not the same thing as wanting to die. The best I can answer is I wanted to surrender. I wanted to feel out of control.

DAVID: Why?

JEREMY: Because I couldn't stop trying to control everything. Jane and me. My writing. How I reacted to the world, how the world reacted to me. The criminal justice system, the internet. It was endless. There was a point, before Jane, where writing felt free to me. Where I surrendered to something. But after Jane, I realized, I picked every fucking letter in every book, obsessively edited every sentence. Of course, I knew that before, but that fact had always felt mediated by my influences. It's not only me when I write, I have always believed that. Other writers enter my work in ways I can't control. But still, I pick them. I choose who to write back to, whose advice I listen to and who I ignore. And life, sometimes you don't pick it. You become undone, and you didn't choose it. It happens to you. So here I was. I only want one thing—to render this one feeling, to make legible one state, the complete absence of choice, while at the same time I'm making all the choices. Writing felt false to me. It felt like everything I hate. It felt like a fantasy.

DAVID: But we do try to control life. That is part of life, of being human. We need to find—or create—significance out of events. We pull meaning from them one way or another.

JEREMY: But that's what I mean. I couldn't pull meaning from this. That's how it felt. It felt meaningless and painful and confusing. But I couldn't find a way to write about it. All I could see was the organizing structure. The metaphor I was aiming toward, or the plot I had to use to make it legible to anyone else. The structure changes it, see? A maze in my head, a thought flowing hits a wall, is turned back to the only path available. Ironically, it was this feeling that eventually freed me up to where I could start writing again, and I started another project.

DAVID: Ah, yes. Book five, the beginning of your internet period.

JEREMY: That was a dark time.

DAVID: For all of us.

JEREMY: In my defense, I'll say that I had gotten to this point where I'd come to distrust narrative altogether—even deconstructed narrative, even narrative that draws attention to itself as narrative. Kafka asks, "Can you know anything other than deception? If ever deception is annihilated, you must not look in that direction or you will turn into a pillar of salt." I'd become paralyzed by structure, the invisible hand massaging discrete events toward some coherent meaning—to use a dominant and obfuscatory metaphor of our time. So, I thought, I'll opt out of all that. This was my life after Jane died. These emails and direct messages and voice mails. I'll let them stand by themselves.

DAVID: But you didn't include them all. "Ten Thousand Messages" is what you were calling it for a while, I believe. You picked and chose. Curation is still a point of view, and juxtaposition is a structure. Very much a feature of the internet novel, in fact.

JEREMY: Yes, of course I see the problem now. At the time, though, I thought this might be able to show what it was like when Jane died more than anything else, better than interiority and epiphany. To juxtapose the emails I was getting and writing—to you and Meg, to my lawyers and Jesse Haber. The hundreds of strangers who wrote me, who wanted things from me. To juxtapose those emails with two hundred orders from DoorDash and emails from the city telling us how full the hospitals were.

DAVID: And there was another category of emails. We had some conversations about whether you wanted to include them.

JEREMY: Jane's emails. There was a point at which the lawyers got access to her emails, and she had a number of them to me in her draft folder. They sent them to me, because they thought maybe I would recognize something they might be able to use in trying to convince the police to drop the charges. This was before they found the other phone and arrested Tom Stafford.

DAVID: And you included them in "Ten Thousand Messages." At least some versions.

JEREMY: Yes, because even though Jane wrote them before she died— one on the night before she died, written after I left the bar—I received them after she died. And because I wrote back to them after she died.

DAVID: Saying what?

JEREMY: It depended on the email. About ten probably where the draft only said *Hey.* Or something similar. *What's up, dude? What's happening? Hola.* Almost half are along the lines of *Thought you might like this,* followed by a link to a book or song or tweet.

DAVID: Did you like the things she thought you would like?

JEREMY: It was mixed. Some things she sent, I didn't like, and I responded to her emails in kind. *Sorry, that one was not for me. Didn't care for* *that one.* But some I did like and would have enjoyed talking to her about them. Even the ones I didn't like. It was fun talking to Jane when things were good, even when we disagreed.

DAVID: Why did you write back to her draft emails?

JEREMY: I don't know. Maybe just in case.

DAVID: Why did you read them?

JEREMY: Well, because the lawyers wanted me to. But I know that's not what you're really asking. I had a feeling sometimes that Jane had been taken away before I really knew her. I was surprised by many things after she died. A lot of that was my fault. When I received these emails, there was this part of me that believed I was getting what I was supposed to get. Yes, I wasn't supposed to get them, she decidedly did not send them to me, but she wasn't supposed to die either. After a while, though, I started to think it was dangerous to believe that because I had access to thoughts she didn't want to share with me, I knew the real her now.

DAVID: Maybe not the real her, but more of her.

JEREMY: I'm not sure. We're so obsessed with data. If we can accumulate, amass, and analyze enough information, we won't have to worry about the darkness anymore. Jane didn't send me these emails, but maybe that says more about me than her. And there was one—I remember it specifically, because we had had this argument. We later made up, and she explained some things that led her to act in certain ways, certain ways I had hurt her. When we had that conversation, I expressed that it would have been helpful if she had told me all that earlier. She said she'd written me an email, but Kaya told her not to send it. So, what is the part of Jane I think I know better now? What is the real her? The email? Was that what she really thought? Or was it already altered in some way because she wanted to persuade me, appeal to me, hide from me? And then she didn't send it. So Jane, affected by me, affected by Kaya, based on what Kaya thought she should do. In the end, it all became so contingent it felt like nonsense.

DAVID: What other kinds of emails did you get?

JEREMY: The majority, by far the majority, were from people trying to get me to comment on her murder investigation. Did I think Tom Stafford did it? Had I read Jesse Haber's book? Did I think Jane had been sleeping with Billy? Did I ever get a bad vibe from Kaya? At a certain point, Jesse Haber got canceled. I hate that word, but I'll use it. The tenor of the emails I received started changing. Haber's company worked for some big corporate law firms, and while he'd stated that explicitly, people came to take offense at the way he centered his journalistic past, accused him of using it as a rhetorical device to distract from the kind of work he usually did and the kinds of people and companies he usually worked for. The internet, as it is wont to do, had looked into it—research used to discredit plaintiffs who were suing multinational corporations for polluting the groundwater, fatal side effects in pharmaceuticals. Sexual harassment, union busting.

So the book had been this massive hit, but then people turned on him. Or at least a vocal section of the internet did. People who knew him coming out to say how he'd always been obsessed with recognition. Women he'd dated telling stories. I started getting messages asking me to verify claims he'd made in his book. Was it true what he said about Jane and Billy flirting? Because Billy and Kaya denied it. Could I send my contract from Stile to a couple of lawyers so they could discuss it on a podcast? Who else would have had access to the dumpster in Tom's office? Could I be on a podcast with the YA author? He hadn't said yes yet, but if I said yes, maybe he would say yes, which was probably the same email they wrote him. In Jesse's book, Lucy said I couldn't write women, but now people are pointing out similar issues with Haber's characterization of Lucy—would I care to comment or even write an essay on this subject from a craft or a moral perspective?

DAVID: And then people like Denis, strangers who thought they knew Jane. Or you.

JEREMY: Right. Denis. He used to send me pictures from Jane's Instagram. *Doesn't she look pretty here?*

DAVID: There was one: *Is red her favorite color?* Then about twenty pictures he'd found of her wearing red.

JEREMY: I'd like to point out that you gently suggested I put this book away.

DAVID: Well, it had been over a year. A hundred versions with this email taken out or this one before this one instead of after that one.

JEREMY: You were right to do so, to be clear. I would only like to trouble the narrative that I abandon promising things. Sometimes I stay too long.

DAVID: Trust me, I did not like to do it. But you were cutting yourself off from everything you're good at. Not to mention the books you love.

JEREMY: Well, I don't think I was reading anything besides the internet at that point. Which might have been a problem.

DAVID: I want to come back to this point, but I really want to get back to your reading. Is that okay?

JEREMY: Sure.

DAVID: I'm curious. How many cans of dip do you think you'd purchased at this point?

JEREMY: Oh, I don't know. Close to a thousand, probably.

DAVID: That's, what, seven thousand dollars?

JEREMY: At least.

DAVID: What happened to it? Did you give it away?

JEREMY: I thought of that. To a rehab facility or something. But I have anxiety now about causing someone's death. What if someone got cancer from the dip I gave them? I think my sister threw them away eventually. I don't actually know what happened to all of them.

> Later, my sister will tell me that she was planning to drive into the city, yell at me, and drive home, but when she saw my apartment, she put me in the back seat of her car, buckled me in like a child, and drove upstate without any plans as to what she would do with me. The full extent of her impulsivity revealed itself shortly after we arrived at her house. She had no place to put me. Her mother-in-law lived in the third bedroom and spent ninety percent of her waking hours listening to the TV in the living room. She was nearly blind and had suffered from a series of small strokes that left her unsteady on her feet and in her language. For a week, I slept on the couch in the living room or in Joann's TV room. Rather, I lay on the couch at night for a week while everyone was sleeping. In the morning, I was supposed to fold my comforter and place it in the corner of the room with the duffel bag of clothes my sister had packed for me before we left my apartment. But one night, unable to sleep, I'd gone to a subreddit dedicated to solving Jane's murder and seen a photograph of Jane and me sitting in Central Park. I didn't remember it being taken. I had no idea

how the poster had access to the photo. In it, we are both leaning against the same tree but tilted toward each other. I have my hands in the air, like I am explaining something I believe to be important, something needing accent, and Jane has taken my hands in her hands like she wants me to shut up for a minute. We are both smiling. I have forgotten about this moment until I see the picture. I can almost hear her voice.

Jeremy. Jeremy. Jeremy. The way she is trying not to laugh. The way her hands felt on my hands. The rhythm of conversation when it was good like this. *Jeremy, Jeremy, Jeremy* and my hands being caught in the air.

There are not that many pictures of Jane and me on the internet, but I think I found them all that night. I should clarify—there are not that many photographs on the internet of Jane and me together. There are thousands of instances of our pictures put next to each other— like my author photo and a picture of her from her Instagram—and thousands of the same picture: Jane and me sitting on my bed, both with computers open on our laps. It looks to be mid-collaboration, but it's really a staged photo to go along with a profile that came out some- where around the time Rita became a sensation. There's a picture of us in the conference room at Stile. It used to be on their website but was taken down either when I got arrested or when Tom got arrested, but it had been screenshotted and shared around the web. I don't remember this moment. It doesn't do what the photo of us in Central Park does. It stays dead, behind us, inaccessible. Another one of Kaya, Jane, and me. We are at one of Billy's shows, close to the stage, and when I look at it, I remember not so much the moment the picture was taken but the time after it. We had separated from Billy and Kaya, and it was so late, the subway car we were in was empty. I remember the sound of the train on the tracks, the way we fell toward each other, the stuttering way the stations came into view. Jane didn't want to go home yet—not to mine, not to hers. She wanted more out of the night. There was something desperate about it, and it made me want to withdraw.

The experience was alienating. These memories coming back because of someone else's photographs. As if there were a part of myself that I had access to only if I chanced across certain objects. The fantasy of wholeness disturbed. I dug around the duffel bag of clothes my sister had packed, looking for the shirt I was wearing when the photograph in Central Park was taken. I had the feeling if I could find it, I could get back there. *Jeremy. Jeremy. Jeremy.* The grass was soft when I touched it.

But the shirt wasn't there, and it felt like Jane died all over again. Or rather, it felt like she died again, but this time only for me. Because the first time she died, she died for so many people. But this time, she was there, and when I couldn't find my T-shirt, it felt like she'd gone again and taken a whole world with her. When Joann came in to turn the TV on in the morning, I'd left my clothes strewn across the room, and she became tangled in a pair of sweatpants and fell. My brother-in-law seemed to appear from nowhere. She was crying and scared as he helped her to the couch.

I was moved to my niece's room. An air mattress on the floor. My sister slept in the bed with Sadie as if she thought I might wake her daughter up in the middle of the night and take her hitchhiking. Sadie had a turtle, a hamster, and mice. First, she had two mice, and then she had forty mice, walking over each other as if their paws didn't register the difference between wood shavings and the forgiving meat of their brothers and sisters. But no sooner were there forty mice than the mother began to eat her young. In the beginning, I didn't see it. I still couldn't sleep so I often took my laptop into the kitchen and would still be sitting there when the sun came up. Sadie would find the dead babies when she woke, chewed pink flesh on the shavings. My sister would bring her crying daughter to the living room, sit her down to watch cartoons with her grandmother, and return to clean the half bodies out of the cage with tissue paper. When we finished breakfast, we buried them in the backyard.

After that, I stayed in Sadie's room all night watching the mice—or the mother, really. Her red eyes. The first time I watched her eat a baby, I was mostly paralyzed. I didn't know what I was going to do when I saw her start, and so I did nothing. When it was over, I threw up in the bathroom sink. The next time, I stuck my hand in the cage, into the writhing white mass of fur, and pulled the baby away. The mother nipped my finger; a tiny prick of red bloomed near my fingernail. The baby's paws on my palm felt like they were inside me, tiny nails depressing the soft matter of my brain. I had nowhere to put it. Its tail was small and light. I found a mostly empty cereal box in the pantry, put the baby mouse inside it, and placed the box next to the cage. In the morning, the baby was dead. The second time I was more prepared. A coffee can, air holes made with a screwdriver, food piled in the corner, a yogurt container cut down to hold water. But the next baby died too. And the next one. I couldn't keep them alive. Whether they needed food from the mother, the heat of their brothers and sisters, I never figured out.

"Leave them," my sister said, cleaning out the cage in the morning.

She was blunted by the year. Her mother-in-law, her sick brother, her dyslexic daughter parked at the dining-room table watching the school year go by like a play.

"What'd you learn today, Bug?"

"Chloe wore a white shirt with a stain on it."

"Jesus Christ. Okay, let's—do you have a book or something? Oh, wait, hold on. Joann? Joann, what are you trying to get? Let me help you. Jeremy, do you think you could, I don't know, maybe you could take a shower? After that, maybe you could help Sadie. Don't you like to read or something?"

The mice didn't even faze her; she flushed chewed shoulders and half legs down the toilet when she didn't think Sadie was looking. "Just leave them, Jeremy, please."

It was easy for her to say. She could sleep. She didn't lie awake knowing it was happening. I imagined I could feel it, life ending. Not like a blast of cool air, a candle enkindled, but a strengthening in the quiet. However, I did leave them in the end, because I didn't know whether it was better to die alone in a coffee can or be eaten by your mother. When a little over half the babies were gone, she stopped.

DAVID: So I love this.

JEREMY: Thank you.

DAVID: And this is not emails.

JEREMY: No, it is not.

DAVID: I want to come back to something you said about how you were not reading anything but the internet for a while. Why was that?

JEREMY: It was a combination of things, I think. My attention wasn't very good during this time. The pandemic. Everything that was Jane was on the internet. It was hard not to want to read it.

DAVID: Did a part of you think you couldn't write about Jane without writing about the internet? Because your sixth book was also an internet book. Although a different kind.

JEREMY: I don't think it was exactly like that. I couldn't write about it. Everything has always been about: How do I write this? The problem was—depending on the minute, the problem still is—that I can't. And if I can't write this—if I can't write about this—what is the point of writing? That's all that "Ten Thousand Messages" was. An attempt to capture what it felt like to lose Jane now. To lose her, but also to experience her loss through the internet. What it means for her to die but for her story—and my story—to continue to evolve and become known by so many people.

I'd thought, with "Ten Thousand Messages," maybe I could get at that. But it didn't.

DAVID: Forgive me, but you don't even like internet novels.

JEREMY: No, I don't. It was a confusing time. When I finally put "Ten Thousand Messages" away, I'd been moving emails around in a Word document for about seven months.

DAVID: More than seven months.

JEREMY: I remember thinking that maybe Jane could do this, but I couldn't. It had begun to feel, to me, like video games, this thing I did where I lost hours of time but every once in a while, I felt as if I'd successfully released someone from hell. Then, one day, long after your first gentle suggestions, I looked down at what I was writing and felt insane. Like I was in Canada and didn't know how I'd gotten there. I was looking at something soulless and dead. Jane was nowhere, and grief was nowhere, and even though the book was dead, death was nowhere either.

DAVID: It didn't give anything back?

JEREMY: It didn't give anything back, and I didn't write again for six months.

DAVID: And then what happened?

JEREMY: I started reading again. I hadn't been reading. I realized my crisis of faith, as I might have flippantly called it earlier, was a misnomer. I had a crisis in my writing, I suppose, but I'd forgotten about books written by other people. Maybe I couldn't write about this, but other people could. And did they. It always happens. I'm lost, I read, and then I find a book. One that feels as if it avoids false plots, fake epiphanies, and it makes me want to write again. I'll start, and I'll feel for a while like a god, capable of constructing something sublime, positive that if I reach the end, I can hold it. Not that it's me, exactly, because it does feel like it comes from outside me when it's going well. Where it comes from, that feeling, eventually goes away, and I see new issues. What I thought was breaking away from convention is simply another convention; what I thought avoided artifice is simply another form of artifice I was less familiar with. What I thought exposed something important, I realize, it does, it does do that, but it hides something else, and I can no longer recognize which is more important, the part that is hidden or the part that is shown.

But before that happens, before that happens, there's nothing else like it. With the fifth book, "Ten Thousand Messages," I'd tried to take out the dominant storytelling structure I'd been raised on, but I realized I'd only replaced it with something else. A construction very rooted in the now, as you noted. Borges has this line about how we must put up with the "mythology of our time," even if it's less beautiful. And I had done that. I thought I needed to do it, but I didn't, and I didn't want to do it anymore.

DAVID: Why? Because it's not true?

JEREMY: Because it's less beautiful. Because it feels bad to me, and it did not help me get through this. There are structures, belief systems, plots and scaffolds and feedback loops that are bad for us. They lead us away from anything good. I don't want to be limited by what my brain can imagine because it keeps falling into the same stories and language—but also technologies. Another maze, new walls sending us back.

DAVID: But we are limited. In body and in mind.

JEREMY: But don't you want it to feel more expansive? I thought, in "Ten Thousand Messages," I had done that. Removed plot. Removed resolution. Removed, as much as practically possible, author. Added all these voices that were not my own. And yet, the expansiveness was not there. What I wanted, I realized, was not to remove structure, which is impossible, but to think outside the strictures of our time. I wanted to go back to the beginning. I wanted to know what people thousands of years ago thought. I wanted the chance, at least, to modify the maze in my mind, to be influenced by a more beautiful mythology.

DAVID: Because we must fasten our minds to something.

JEREMY: Yes, so I fastened mine to the Greeks. The medieval period, early modern, anything not of this time, anything that permitted a way to see something our current myths prevent us from seeing. If I am writing back to an author or a book or a tradition, there is a form there, but I'm less constrained by the kinds of plots I resist.

DAVID: And you're less trapped in your time.

JEREMY: Yes.

DAVID: And your body?

JEREMY: My stupid body.

DAVID: So you went back.

JEREMY: To Plato. He said that written words have the attitude of life, but if you ask them a question, they preserve a "solemn silence." This is the moment we realize they are dead things. He said the spoken word has a soul and that's why in his book he spoke to his dead teacher. Borges—speaking back to Plato—said that the taste of the apple is in neither the apple nor the mouth, but in the connection between the two. If words are dead things, they come alive when we read them.

So I started thinking about the internet, and Jane on the internet, which is something I'd been thinking about for almost two years at this point, longer in some ways, and gotten nowhere. Finally, a way in. The past and the present in one place. So many dead words devoted to Jane. I wrote some, and Jane wrote some, and the internet wrote the rest. Every person who read her wrote her. Everybody who read her brought her to life. Over and over again. When Borges was alive, he could only conceive of personal resurrections separated in time, place. Books opened and closed. Always the same number of words in the book. He never contemplated the internet. He never imagined someone like Jane. How many millions of words, how many millions of readers, until you can say she has been resurrected, that she is alive on the internet?

DAVID: And so this was your sixth book.

JEREMY: It turned out to be *Pet Sematary,* but online. Everyone who comes back to us from there comes back a little bit off. Except *Pet Sematary* is good, and this was not, though I had great aspirations for a while.

DAVID: Why did you focus on this metaphor of resurrection? It's a myth not of our time.

JEREMY: Some people believe in resurrection.

DAVID: But not you.

JEREMY: Not the Christian resurrection.

DAVID: And while ostensibly a part of our time—in Christianity and outside of it—resurrection is born before us.

JEREMY: Yes.

DAVID: Why would you say it was important for you to resurrect Jane?

JEREMY: I wouldn't say it was important for me to resurrect Jane. I thought it was an interesting question.

DAVID: It would seem to an outsider that you thought it was somewhat important, as you tried to write a book about it. Before Jane, did you ever think about writing in terms of resurrection?

JEREMY: No.

DAVID: When you thought of writing back to texts, or authors, you didn't think of it in terms of a kind of resurrection? Because this is something you do that predates Jane Murphy.

JEREMY: It is. For a moment, this book felt like I was coming back to myself. I was talking to Plato. I was talking to Borges. But that's never been about resurrection. It's more akin to tapping into the flow. It's always there. It doesn't have to be brought back to life.

DAVID: So why this focus now?

JEREMY: Well, I thought I knew. Because of Plato. Because of the dead words and the internet. By the time I stopped working on it, I knew it was something else.

DAVID: What?

JEREMY: "Among the tortures and devastations of life is this then—our friends are not able to finish their stories."

DAVID: To you that means what?

JEREMY: I'd accepted that Jane died, though I still resist that word *accept*. I was never in denial that Jane was dead; I did not know what that meant. In any case, while I had accepted Jane was dead, it was harder to accept that she had died the way she died.

DAVID: Young? Murdered?

JEREMY: Unhappy. It's hard to know generally, I think.

DAVID: It made you feel how to know Jane died unhappy?

JEREMY: Sad. No, it made me feel desperate. I wanted her to have had more. I know it's not my fault Jane died, but I wish I could have made the last part better for her. Her last night better. At some point I realized what I'd done: I'd created a whole book to make myself feel better. Jane alive on the internet—but not trapped by all the people who wrote about her. Taking the power of resurrection into her own slightly sinister hands. In control of all of it. Jane liked to be in control. That was a thing we had in common.

DAVID: Why did you stop writing it?

JEREMY: I stopped writing it because I hated it. It was sentimental. It was wishful thinking. This was surprising because I had written a ghost story before, and I thought that worked fairly well. But this one was terrible. I wasn't being true to the ghosts. I made them into puppets.

DAVID: Before we turn back to your reading, I have to say, because I am that guy: You said before that Borges could not have imagined the internet, but that's not true.

JEREMY: Are you thinking of "Funes"?

DAVID: Among others.

JEREMY: "I thought that each of my words (that each of my movements) would persist in his implacable memory."

DAVID: Yes, I was thinking of that line. Of course, it turns out it's not accurate—the internet remembers everything. I read the other day that almost seventy percent of links created since 2010 are dead. Movies and television shows too, dead, and no used bookstores for out-of-print streamers.

JEREMY: For someone like me, with a significant online presence, it often feels infinite. But we're not very good with time.

DAVID: No. Everything rots, it turns out, even the internet.

Okay, let's get back into it. Anything we should know about this part?

JEREMY: I wasn't sure I was going to read it, because it feels unfinished. But we're into material you haven't read, and I need to know what you think.

Joann asked me to help her find audiobooks. After some false starts with the library and its related audio apps, I sat next to her on the couch reading the synopses of various titles until she chose one, a nonfiction book about octopi. She used to listen to it for half an hour every day when she worked through the various exercises her physical therapist had left for her when he stopped coming in person. At some point, Sadie and I joined in, making it our official gym period. As soon as Sadie's teacher broke for lunch, I'd get up from wherever I'd been sitting, push the coffee table flush to the couch, and drag in some chairs from the kitchen. Sadie changed into her "gym clothes": sweatpants and a Mets hoodie, which she wore with the hood up. We each sat on a chair and stood up, which was supposed to strengthen Joann's leg muscles. Joann would stand up five times before stopping, exhausted. Sadie and I stood only when she did, waiting between her efforts. Next was pretending to put on pants, followed by some time wearing the sling and turning the TV on and off. Joann was supposed to wear this on her left arm to build back strength and control in her right. She was supposed to wear this constantly, but Sadie probably wore it more than she did, as she had invented a very involved game about hurt orphans and mice on a ship that she played every night in her room with the door closed. When we were done with the chairs, we'd move to the backyard. Sadie would run laps while Joann and I timed her. Sometimes I dragged wood from the woodpile and made hurdles or a balance beam, creating a kind of obstacle course.

"Sorry your friend," Joann said as we watched Sadie walk carefully across a log.

I wasn't sure how she knew. I hadn't told her, and my sister didn't usually bring it up in front of Sadie. But Joann jerked her head toward the kitchen, where my sister and her husband were standing by the island, and I realized Joann had likely heard them talking. We all did it. At dinner, my brother-in-law asked his mother between three and seven specific questions, my sister maybe two, myself none, and Sadie either talked at her incessantly or not at all, depending on the day. Otherwise, the conversation flowed around her.

"Hard," Joann said.

I nodded. It occurred to me later that Joann might have been the one person I could talk to, but I didn't talk to her that day. We went back to watching Sadie, who ran past us shouting, "How fast was that one?"

"Eight point six seconds. Around the tree," I said. "You have to go around the tree."

My friends, my sister, the whole country, everyone was still acting like death was bad luck or a stranger that had accidentally knocked on the wrong door. But death wasn't bad luck to Joann. Her husband, friends, a sister, her parents, her doctor, classmates, actors from movies that felt like her childhood. Like Jane and me, she was not quite in this world.

"How fast was that one?" Sadie yelled to us.

"Seven point nine. Better."

I was thinking of Jane, of this night when we were in her bed, and she'd pulled the sheet over her head so I could only see the outline of her. I pulled it from her face, but she pulled it back. Her face, when I saw her, and her voice, when she said, "No, I want to keep it like this," were neutral. I wondered if she did this often and for a moment I could see the outline of another night, another man in her bed, the Jane-shaped form under the sheet. It wasn't the beginning, but it was early enough that I didn't know what it meant or what was expected of me. I lay down next to her. I could feel her thigh through the sheet. Minutes passed and she didn't say anything.

"'The word *mute* is regarded by linguists as an onomatopoeic formation referring not to silence but to a certain fundamental opacity of human being, which likes to show the truth by allowing it to be seen hiding,'" I said.

"I think there's something wrong with me," she responded.

"What?"

"I don't know. Do you ever feel that way?"

"Yes."

"Do you think there's something wrong with me?"

"I don't know you that well. Everyone has something."

"What's yours?"

"I don't know, Jane."

She was silent again.

"I feel like maybe I can't connect to people," she said finally. "That whatever that feeling is that makes people want to be with you, I never make people feel that way."

I didn't say anything, because it wasn't the beginning, and I wasn't sure what she wanted from me.

"Never mind," she said, pulling the sheet down and rolling toward me. "Your turn."

"My turn what?"

"You have to tell me something embarrassing."

"Umm."

"Hurry," she said.

"I don't know."

"Come on, hurry. You're taking too long."

"I want to be great," I said, and for some reason, she started to cry. No sounds, just the water slipping from her eyes, leaving the skin beneath them shiny. "I'm afraid I won't be. That I'm not, and then what am I doing?"

"Thank you," she said. "Do you want to get under the sheet?"

"Sure."

She lifted it away from her body. I slid in beside her, and she drew it up over our faces. I hadn't realized I'd been wondering what it felt like until the fabric touched my forehead. I was expecting it to be cool, but it wasn't.

DAVID: Why does this feel unfinished to you? Does something happen after that?

JEREMY: No. In real life, of course, something happened after that. The scene ends here.

DAVID: Yes, the scene ends here, but I agree it's unfinished. This feels very sketched in.

JEREMY: When I think about this scene, I imagine I've walked into a room I'm afraid of for some reason. Maybe there was an unexpected noise; I come into the room, scan it to make sure no one is there, and leave. If I could go back, I could stay longer and see what was in the room instead of only investigating it for threats. But I don't want to go back. Even knowing I was reading tonight, I didn't go back.

DAVID: You don't write many scenes with Jane in them.

JEREMY: No.

DAVID: Why not?

JEREMY: I don't know. James says when we love a character, we want to protect them.

DAVID: Do you want to protect Jane?

JEREMY: I don't want to hurt her more. She was very private, in her own way. I am not sure she would like the scenes I write about her, what I show.

DAVID: The bedtime confession? The specter of her naked body?

JEREMY: That she was lonely. Really lonely. I think she wanted people to think of her a certain way. But it's what I remember. It's something we had in common.

DAVID: You know what I was thinking of when I heard this scene?

JEREMY: What?

DAVID: Maria in Silent Hill 2. He keeps running into her, and every time he does, she dies soon after.

JEREMY: Meaning what, exactly?

DAVID: Not that. What I'm trying to get at in this analogy is maybe it's still hard to meet Jane in a scene, to put her in your room, to really be there with her, because she'll die again when you finish.

JEREMY: You know in Silent Hill 2, Maria is not Mary. She looks different. She acts different.

DAVID: So?

JEREMY: So Jane when I write her is not Jane.

DAVID: Maybe I'm wrong.

JEREMY: Oh, come on, you do not think you're wrong.

DAVID: No, I don't. I've read all eight books, remember? I can see what you're doing, what you're not doing.

JEREMY: Everything I write is about Jane. I haven't written anything that isn't about Jane since she died.

DAVID: Book seven was five hundred pages and didn't mention her once.

JEREMY: It was a meditation on grief, David. Why would I write a five-hundred-page meditation on grief if not for Jane? I could write scenes with Jane in them till the end of my days, and it wouldn't solve the problem that I can't write about this. I started writing scenes about Jane, and it turned into an algebra problem.

DAVID: Nah, I read those too. I'm not sure those scenes were ever about Jane.

JEREMY: I read a long scene about Jane earlier tonight.

DAVID: The last night at the bar? That's about you.

JEREMY: Well, the seventh book was about Jane.

DAVID: I thought it was about a painting. Was the painting Jane?

JEREMY: No. The painting was the painting. It's ekphrasis, David, as you very well know.

You think I am trying to avoid it, but I am only trying to show it. I've talked a little about the dislocation I felt, but I don't think I have ever been able to render it. It almost feels like culture shock. Waking up and everyone around you is speaking a different language. You walk around jet-lagged, not knowing what anyone is saying. The texts I turned to in this seventh book, the painting, but also all the texts I used to approach it, it was like coming home to a language that made sense to me. Look at all these people who have tried to show us the grief inside them. I want to quote Kafka, even though I know what you're going to say, but he can say it so much better than I can. We do not know the griefs in each other. We cannot know them like we cannot know death, or God, or hell. And for that reason, we should worship each other, he says. And so that's what this book was to me, this attempt at a book. Worship. I read everything I could find, I took in everything I could.

DAVID: Except you didn't. You treated all the texts like lily pads so you could cross the whole lake of pain and grief without getting your feet wet.

JEREMY: I am not afraid to get my feet wet.

DAVID: What are you afraid of? Drowning?

JEREMY: No. I'm afraid I won't drown. What if I don't drown but I latch onto the wrong thing to keep from sinking?

DAVID: Like what?

JEREMY: I'll explain by discussing a work that does not do that: Anne Carson's *Nox,* written after her brother's death. The book is framed by a Latin poem that Carson translates. Each of her poems or reflections or fragments is preceded by this wall of words in the Latin translation. A page or more of possible meanings, all the ways we have ever used the word, idioms from long-dead worlds. I think she has to go through the poem to find her brother, to experience the gap we always fill in at the end. The Latin poem isn't something she is using to distance herself from her brother, it's the thing that gets her to him, or to her grief, at least. As close as it's possible to get.

DAVID: You're doing it again.

JEREMY: I'm not. That's how that book works. That's why that book works.

DAVID: Anne Carson has another line: "Do you want to go down to the pits of yourself all alone?"

JEREMY: That's exactly what I'm trying to say, though. The Latin poem helps her down into the pits. She couldn't go there without it. But it's not false, and what she finds, she gives to us.

DAVID: But she goes there. She doesn't stay on the lily pad.

JEREMY: Fuck.

DAVID: Look, I love this about you. You know I admire the hell out of the way you think about and talk to other texts. I could—and have—stayed up all night with you drinking whiskey, texting back and forth about the best way any person has ever found to say a thing. But in this context, in book seven, it felt like you were avoiding something.

Look, do you want to try something?

JEREMY: What?

DAVID: Tell us a story about Jane.

JEREMY: Any story?

DAVID: Any story. But as you'd write it. There have to be people in it, not just ideas. Things have to have smells. You have to stay in the room, in your body.

JEREMY: Fine.

DAVID: Fine?

JEREMY: Yeah, fine. I think you're wrong about this, though.

Okay, let me think—once, there was a hurricane and Jane wanted to go to Coney Island.

DAVID: She was a bit reckless?

JEREMY: No, the hurricane was landing in, I can't remember, North Carolina, maybe? In New York, it was only a storm. So she found a hotel with discounted rates, and we went out there, the subway emptying the farther out we rode. Not because anyone was evacuating exactly, but no one was going in that direction either. I realized when we got there that she had done this before. She liked the beach. She liked to wake up and run on it. She liked hotels. She had some sort of reward system that involved this specific hotel in Coney Island, but sometimes she would upend her system if there was a storm, because the hotels were cheaper, and she liked to watch it rain over the ocean.

DAVID: When was this?

JEREMY: I'm not sure. Before the night in the scene I read, but maybe not by very much.

We were working on Rita, and we'd run into this problem regarding her parents. We figured they should be part of the story, but we disagreed whether it was realistic or necessary for them to get on Twitter and start posting pleas for help, anecdotes about her childhood. So we were brainstorming. Maybe they were on Facebook, but Rita was already missing at this point, and we hadn't created Facebook accounts for them before. This didn't rule it out entirely, but it made it slightly more complicated in terms of the logistics of the project. Maybe Rita had a LiveJournal complaining about her parents when she was younger and Joshua could find it on the Wayback Machine. Maybe, on her nascent Tumblr, we could add more poems that were clearly autobiographical in that way young people think they are masking it, but they're absolutely not. It was great. We sat out on the beach for a while, watching this massive cloud move down the shore. The wind—we had to shout over it. I kept tasting salt water in my mouth. We were sitting back from the ocean, but it was in the air. The waves were concussing on the shore. Swells coming in from the horizon. The rain, when it came, dug holes in the sand. We were drenched instantly, the wet where your clothes feel like an extra ten-pound skin. Since we were that wet anyway, we decided to get food and beer and bring it back to the room.

DAVID: Not much Jane in this scene.

JEREMY: Will you hold on a minute? You said to say it like I would write it, that there have to be smells.

DAVID: No smells either.

JEREMY: The towels in the hotel room smelled like Ocean Breeze detergent, which I remember because I remember thinking they smelled nothing like the wind on the beach we'd just been sitting on. After we'd showered and changed and had our food and drinks laid out, we started to work, hashing out our Rita problem, rain lashing the window. The wind was roaring in a way that was, to me, slightly alarming but didn't seem to bother Jane at all. She spilled a beer, and it made the whole room smell beery. We placed a towel on the carpet to soak it up. It turned yellow as we worked.

DAVID: Okay, we got smells.

JEREMY: We were talking about how we would do it, what Rita's parents would say and how, and I realized that Jane didn't talk about her parents very often. I said this, and she said, "Well, you don't either." Which is true, but I do sometimes. They come up. So I asked her what they were like.

At the store, she'd purchased saltines and peanut butter, and when we came back, we realized we didn't have any silverware, so she was using her finger as a knife to make little sandwiches. She paused mid-smear but then went back to spreading. I thought she was going to ignore the question, but I guess she was deciding something, because she did start to speak.

DAVID: About her parents?

JEREMY: She said her dad had been an addict.

DAVID: That sounds hard.

JEREMY: That's what I said, but Jane mostly deflected it. He got sober when she was thirteen, her mom did the best she could, et cetera. She said the thing about having parents in recovery is that she had been to meetings with her dad for his anniversary, and she'd heard his story. His childhood was way worse than hers. Same with her mom, but she was angry at her mom. She said it in a joking way, but it was there. Something like, *Come on, Mom, how come I'm eight and I know not to go after him like that, and you don't.*

DAVID: Was she angry at her dad?

JEREMY: No, not in the same way. She said her dad often told a story about this time he had a couple job interviews lined up. He had stopped using to get a handle on things and was only drinking. He knew he couldn't be drunk or hungover at the interviews, though, so he wouldn't drink for twenty-four hours before each one. At the meetings, he pressed his hand against his chin as if he were thinking deeply about whatever the interviewer was saying, but it was for the pressure, to stop his hand from shaking. He sat on the other one, just the tips of his fingers, so the man across the desk wouldn't be able to tell what he was doing. I asked her if he got any of the jobs, and she said he got all of them. He was good at fooling people. I asked her if he fooled her, and she said, "Sometimes."

But then she said she preferred it. I didn't understand at all. Was she saying she wished her dad were still using?

DAVID: Did you ask her to clarify?

JEREMY: As I remember it, at that exact moment, there was a terrible flash of lightning, the kind where you can tell it reaches all the way down to the ground, or the ocean, in this case. I remember thinking, *I wonder if fish can get electrocuted,* and so I was a little distracted when Jane actually started speaking again. But it wasn't about her dad. She told me she grew up in Tornado Alley.

DAVID: Have you ever seen a tornado?

JEREMY: No. Only on TV. You?

DAVID: No, but I've been places where the alarm goes off, and you have to move inside.

JEREMY: That's what she was talking about. She said they used to have to get on the floor of the closet when the warnings came. The one in the middle of the house.

Once, she said, her parents weren't home. She wasn't sure where they were or how old she was, but it was the first time she was alone when a warning came in. A watch, first. She had the TV on, and she was monitoring the radar. She didn't really understand it. What the different colors meant. It all went so quickly too, the mass of greens and yellows across this area of the map that had her house in it. She didn't understand what she was supposed to be looking for exactly, what in that swirl of colors would alert her that a tornado had formed out of the atmospheric conditions necessary for a tornado to form. Her parents had a computer, she said. It was on a table in the kitchen, and she kept running to look at a map she'd pulled up on the internet, because it was hard to tell where her house was on the weather map on TV. She said when they started telling people in her area to get in the closet, she seriously considered not going, because she didn't want to leave the TV and the map. She felt safer watching it, even knowing, logically, she was safer in the closet. But then the electricity went out, and she got in the closet and waited for it to be over.

I was getting a little nervous about the storm outside, likely because we were talking about these tornadoes, but I started to wonder if we should move away from the windows. Jane was unfazed. She said she still liked to watch weather reports, the radar. How strange it was to see something bad coming toward you and to brace yourself for it. She said there weren't signs with her. Sometimes—she couldn't remember when it started—she felt a wall of pressure, and she didn't know where it came from or what it was, and all she could do was sit there looking at something else until it passed over.

DAVID: Looking at what?

JEREMY: I said, "Like the internet?" She thought I was making fun of her, but I wasn't. I knew her a little by then. I'd seen her do it. She said she loved the internet. So many people coming together to say *Have you ever noticed that?* or *Do you remember that one blanket we all had?* She liked how there were so many things to notice. She wouldn't have seen them without everyone else.

I told her I wasn't making fun of her. It sounded like depression. She said she had been to therapy a few times, but it was always the same: They would ask her how she was feeling, and she didn't know. She said, "I think everyone remembers the first time they realize no one can help them. That something is wrong, and no one can help them." I didn't say anything, and after a while she said, "Well, I remember."

She told me that sometimes she'd meet someone, and it would get better. She would feel better around them. She rushed on to say it was Kaya she was talking about. She was afraid I thought she meant me. But I never thought she meant me. She said being around Kaya made her feel better, but it never lasted. One day being around Kaya wouldn't work anymore, or she'd go to look for her, and Kaya wouldn't be there.

DAVID: What did you say?

JEREMY: I don't remember. At some point, she handed me one of the little cracker sandwiches she'd been making, and I ate it, because I didn't know what to say and I wanted to be supportive, so I thought eating the sandwich would show that. The points on the saltines scratched the inside of my mouth. My chewing sounded really loud, because I wasn't talking. Eventually, she asked me if I'd ever felt that way.

I told her I hadn't. Now I could tell her different. But at the time, I couldn't. Still, I knew she wanted something from me. I had to balance the conversation so she didn't tip over.

DAVID: What did you tell her about?

JEREMY: How sometimes I can't let things go. It can be a problem. I told her about this time I had fainted in high school. I had read something, probably something like *On the Road* that you read when you're thirteen, and I was convinced I was doing everything wrong. Missing it all. I was going to say yes to everything. I wasn't going to let anything go by. But there's this moment in my head where it switches. Instead of being, *I'm going to say yes to everything,* it's *I can't say no to anything.* I'd met my Dean Moriarty—Reed. He was a senior. He had a car. I'd sneak out of my house and meet him at the corner. There was nowhere to go, really, but he'd drive to this twenty-four-hour truck stop and we'd drink coffee and read and write in our notebooks. I was exhausted, but I didn't want to say no to him. I couldn't. I wasn't sure what would happen if I stopped. Something bad, I thought. I'm not sure what the bad thing was, but something. Anyway, eventually I fainted. It was all very dramatic because my school had this open stairwell. I stopped saying yes to everything Reed asked me. But it still happens, that switch in my head where I feel like I have to. I told her about that.

DAVID: Did that balance things?

JEREMY: I'm not sure. It was hard to tell with Jane. She started teasing me a little. She said she was picturing me being thirteen, raising my little hand in class by day, drinking black coffee in truck stops by night. The tenor of the conversation changed. I told her I couldn't picture her at thirteen, and she said, "Good." I asked her to show me a picture, that I would show her one of me, and she still said no. Then she asked if I wanted to go swimming. Outside, you couldn't see anything but rain. We could have been anywhere. "In that?" I asked her. But there was a pool in the hotel. I told her I hadn't brought a bathing suit, and she said that she'd told me to pack one. I said she hadn't, but she went to her phone and read from the text where she had, in fact, told me to bring one. I'd thought it was a joke about the storm.

Then I went swimming in my underwear. End scene.

DAVID: Well.

JEREMY: Well.

DAVID: You haven't written that scene?

JEREMY: No. But I've thought about it a lot.

DAVID: Why?

JEREMY: Because it felt like a beginning. Although I've come to know I'm not able to accurately identify beginnings. Or endings.

DAVID: What does it feel like to tell it?

JEREMY: Fine. Writing's different. There are no surprises when you tell a story.

DAVID: I don't know about that. Sometimes I remember something when I'm telling a story that I didn't remember when I started.

JEREMY: Not the same kind of surprise. When you tell a story, you tell it to relate or to illustrate, to say something about yourself. To explain. I don't want to use them that way for Jane.

DAVID: There's always a reason.

JEREMY: I don't think you're right. I'm simply trying to write it. To honor it. Jane doesn't get to pretend she's not dead. She doesn't get to redo those scenes, mine them for something. She doesn't get to pretend that her death is a metaphor or that it's the key to some puzzle. But I do believe there is a way to do it, I have to, that there's a way to write about it where it gives something back. Where it's not only something that was taken from me. A terrible thing that happened once.

DAVID: I'm getting the signal we are out of beer and we have to wrap up soon. But before you read for us for the last time, you wrote eight books to get here, and we've talked about all but one.

JEREMY: It was poetry. The only problem is I can't write poetry.

DAVID: Do you want to read us a poem?

JEREMY: I thought we were out of time.

DAVID: Poems are short.

JEREMY: Have I not humiliated myself enough for you, David?

DAVID: Why did you turn to poetry, then?

JEREMY: Well, in the previous attempt to write, and really the previous couple of attempts, I'd gone back as far as I could go, reading about death, grief. And if one goes back to the beginning, for a very long time, there were only poems. But the truth is, I've always loved poetry. I like a lot of short forms, as you know. Puzzles and paradoxes. Work that announces its incompleteness, telegraphs its humility by how it looks on the page. Writing that kneels.

And I think here it was another thing too. Grief is not a story. Death is not a story.

DAVID: How we live with it is a story.

JEREMY: Maybe. Maybe most of the stories. I know you think I'm avoiding something, and maybe I am, but all this is like the sun: It's best not to stare directly at it. Poems allowed me to get as close to something as I could, and retreat. And then do it again, and retreat again. I think that might be all we can do sometimes, this circling.

DAVID: And yet what you're reading is not a poem.

JEREMY: Because my poems are terrible. I come back to prose out of necessity, though not without a little reluctance.

DAVID: But does it feel different to you, book nine? It reads different to me.

JEREMY: Yes, but they all felt different to me in the beginning. All I can say is, I think I'm done trying to solve this. What this feeling is or where it came from or if it makes sense. If I'm bad or fearful or equal to the task of writing a hard thing without making it too easy on myself. I'm only trying to meet it.

DAVID: It reminds me of video games, in a way. You walk into a room, you have no idea why. The only way to move forward is to start engaging with what's around you.

JEREMY: It is like that. Although in a video game, someone designed it. Now it's only me picking things up and turning them over.

DAVID: Do you think you'll finish it?

JEREMY: I don't know.

DAVID: Well, on that note, do you want to take us out?

JEREMY: Sure.

DAVID: Where are you starting from?

JEREMY: Where I left off. There was another scene before this, but I reread it this morning, and I hate it.

DAVID: Why do you hate it?

JEREMY: Because it's bad, David.

DAVID: Well, this is good. What you're doing. Having you here.

JEREMY: Yes, it is good to be here. Thank you for the invitation. I guess I should thank my sister too.

DAVID: You ready, then?

JEREMY: Yes. I'm ready.

It wasn't long before Joann, Sadie, and I had formed our own kind of pack. I'd like to say that I was the alpha, but there was no question it was Sadie. Out of the three of us, she was the only one with clear ideas about what she needed at any given moment, and so Joann and I bent to her gratefully. We moved through the day en masse while my sister and brother-in-law set up their computers in various closets throughout the house and went to work. I'd get up when Sadie got up, both of us tripping out of her room in the morning to meet Joann, who had already turned the TV on in the living room. We watched the cartoons Sadie wanted. For breakfast, I poured the cereal she selected into bowls. After we ate, I helped Joann to the bathroom, opened the cap of Sadie's toothpaste for her, and we all brushed our teeth for exactly two minutes, staring at the sand spilling down out of a plastic timer Sadie had acquired from a unit on teeth before the schools shut down.

Teeth done, it was time for school. Sadie and I set up our computers, and stared at them blankly for the next two hours while Joann played a dice game on her iPad. The game was voiced, due to Joann's impaired sight, and Sadie and I could hear it; every day, we abandoned our computers earlier and earlier to play with her. Until my sister told me she couldn't talk to me anymore and my brother-in-law said, "Jeremy, she asks you for only one thing."

At night, I could hear my sister crying. My brother-in-law was more of a yeller than a crier. Thankfully, he mostly yelled at inanimate objects, but the rage directed at those objects was so pure, it affected us just the same. Sadie cowered or ignored her dad's outbursts depending on the day and how close it was to her, but Joann's and my faces took on the same blank stare, our heads turning slightly away as if it were best not to look directly at it, the anger or its object. The coffee machine. The door off the kitchen that always slid off its track. A leaking faucet. A washing machine that spun off balance if you put in more than two towels at a time. Then, in May, a tree in the backyard whose roots strangled the pipes running to the house and eventually resulted in a total loss of water. My brother-in-law rented a backhoe and replaced fifty feet of pipe himself. Because he had to go into the store to buy materials, he slept in a tent in the backyard so the rest of us, especially his mother, wouldn't get sick if he caught it.

"Daddy's not supposed to say that word. Mommy's going to be mad," Sadie told me.

We could hear him through the walls. It was day three of his camp-out and the first time I wrote something in six months.

"Sadie, today we are really going to work. If we don't, your dad might kill me."

"It's so boring, though."

"Okay, you pay attention to your class, and I'll write. And after that, we'll practice reading together."

"Can I hold Mr. Yellowpants?"

"Yes."

Mr. Yellowpants was her hamster. Slowla was the turtle. She'd named all twenty-three of the remaining mice and swore she could tell the difference between them, but I never knew whether that was true. Because it was getting nicer outside, during the first break of the day, Joann, Sadie, and I would go for a walk, often with Mr. Yellowpants or Slowla. I'd push Joann down the street in her wheelchair, and she'd hold Mr. Yellowpants in her lap, petting him with her stuttering hands, while Sadie ran this way and that way, up into the woods along the street, toward the pond and sometimes into the pond before I could stop her. Then back to school and back to writing and back to dice games. When school was officially over, Sadie would sit on my lap, and I'd help her read what I'd written that day as Joann listened.

"'Sorry. I'm a men, men—'"

"Menace."

"Menace. 'I'm not strong—'"

"Sure. 'I'm not sure.'"

"'I'm not sure what's wrap—'"

"Wrong."

301

" 'Wrong with me.' "

"Great. Okay. Let's do one more sentence. Hold on, let me find another short one. Okay, here."

" 'I saw Reg—' "

"Reggie."

" 'Reggie unplug the tick—' "

"Ticketing machine."

" 'In some kind of puh-puh—' "

"Psychotic."

" 'Cop—' "

"Coping. Psychotic coping mechanism."

Sometimes Joann clapped when Sadie read a full sentence, but sometimes I saw her grimace.

"Is that not good, Joann?"

"No."

"Which part?"

"Not good."

Sadie understood but did not fully understand why her dad slept in a tent in the backyard for two weeks or why she couldn't sleep with him in the tent, eating s'mores and playing Guess Who and falling asleep in the same sleeping bag. Joann and I tried to make it easier on her by "camping" in her room. My sister went back to her bedroom. Joann took Sadie's bed, and Sadie and I slept on the floor. We made a tent using sheets, rubber bands, and chairs pulled in from the kitchen.

"Can Mr. Yellowpants come in our tent?"

"Sure," I said.

"And Slowla?"

"Okay."

"And Mr. and Mrs. Whiskers and their children?"

This was a terrible idea, but of course we said yes. I made walls out of books, and we let everyone in: Sadie, myself, a hamster that ate toilet paper, mice that ate each other, and a turtle that would probably outlive us all. I still wasn't really sleeping, so I was able to keep an eye on them all night, but still, in the morning, three mice were missing.

"Don't tell Alex," Joann said.

"No," I agreed.

I spent the next week looking for them—I found two but not the last one, who Sadie insisted was Victoria Whiskers. Because she was sad but mostly because she continued to talk about Victoria and there was only a week left before her dad was going to take a PCR test and come back into the house, I suggested we write a story about Victoria and all the good adventures she was having.

"The way it works," I told Sadie and Joann on one of our walks, "is I say one sentence, and then, Sadie, you say one, and Joann, the next, then back to me. So, I might start, 'One day, Victoria Whiskers decided it was time to leave home.' And then you would say what, Sadie?"

" 'Because it was so boring.' "

"Okay, sure. And Joann?"

" 'Swimming.' "

"She wanted to go swimming?"

"Yes."

"Okay, so we have our first section: 'One day, Victoria Whiskers decided it was time to leave home. It was so boring, and she wanted to go swimming.' "

And so the week passed: Morning cartoons, Sadie tangled in Joann's body on the couch. Breakfast at the kitchen table, Sadie pulling the cereal box from the pantry, Joann using her hands to test the edges of cutlery to select three spoons, me on milk-pouring.

"You have to eat, Uncle Jeremy."

"I'm not that hungry."

"Breakfast is the most important meal of the day."

After breakfast, I helped Joann to the bathroom to brush her teeth, opened the toothpaste cap for Sadie.

"Like this," I said to Sadie. "You have to brush. You're just sucking on the toothbrush."

"Like this?"

"No. Hold on, let me do it," I said, pushing the toothbrush up into the corners of her mouth, massaging the gumline as she stood before me. "Feel that?"

"Uh-huh."

And then Zoom school and writing and Joann playing iPad games before it was time for a walk. I helped Joann into her wheelchair and arranged a blanket over her legs. They had begun to look wasted with disuse. Mr. Yellowpants sat on her lap, his face twitching as we meandered the back roads around my sister's house. Sadie never stopped moving, running away and back to hand her grandmother flowers, pine cones, gray rocks with pink flecks running through them. As we walked, we added to our story of Victoria Whiskers.

"After her swim, Victoria Whiskers found a stone to lie on and dry off. Sadie?"

"Her favorite color was purple."

"Joann?"

"Friend. Badger."

In the afternoon, Joann and I would read with Sadie or yell out the kitchen door to talk to her dad, the backyard crisscrossed now by trenches. This was when I thought I saw Victoria Whiskers running along a PVC pipe in a trench.

"Look," I shouted, but she was gone before the word even finished exiting my mouth. "Nothing. Sorry. Looking good, Alex."

"Come inside," Joann called out to him.

I'd brought her wheelchair to the sliding door off the kitchen.

"No, Mom. It's almost over."

"I'm sorry."

"No, forget about it. I kind of like it out here."

"Not cold."

"No, Mom. It's not too cold."

The next time I saw Victoria Whiskers was in the living room while we were watching *The Price Is Right,* skirting along the baseboard. Then hopping off the kitchen table when we walked into the room. A tail behind the shower curtain, but when I pushed it aside, there was nothing there. A scurrying in the closet. A white hair floating in my cereal.

"Are you okay, Jer?" my sister asked.

"Yeah. I'm fine. I'm fine."

A phantom paw on my hip. I jumped up from the table fully expecting a small mouse to fall to the floor. Nothing.

"I'm fine."

At night, my sister helped Joann and Sadie use the toilet, and I fixed our fort, which invariably came down throughout the day. Sadie changed into pajamas, and I helped my sister slide Joann's thin legs into a diaper and settle her in Sadie's bed. Sadie rushed around the room finding stuffed animals she thought would help her grandmother sleep better, and then we turned off the lights, and I could feel Victoria Whiskers walking up my arm. That night, she ran into my open mouth. At least I think she did. I could feel her inside me.

"Uncle Jeremy, eat your cereal."

"I don't think I can today. I feel full."

305

"You sure you're okay, Jer?" my sister said.

Finally, it was the day my brother-in-law could come back inside. Joann, Sadie, and I were at the kitchen table while my sister cooked dinner. Sadie had instructed us to illustrate our Victoria Whiskers story, and so we sat down dutifully and began to draw. No one was talking. My sister had the radio on, and there was a spitting sound from the stove, the wet slip of markers on paper, the hollow sound of eggplant being sliced.

"What's this?" my brother-in-law asked, sliding the glass door from the backyard, hugging Sadie, squeezing his mom's shoulder, walking over to my sister to kiss her on the top of her head. He nodded at me. "What are we drawing here?"

At the table, he picked up Sadie's paper: a house, a tree, a mouse bigger by a factor of ten than anything else in the picture. My stomach flipped over.

"That's Victoria Whiskers," Sadie said. "It's for our Exquisite Corpse."

"What?"

"Jesus Christ, Jeremy."

"What? That's what it's called when you make up a story and everybody does one line based on what the person before them said. That's what they're called."

"You couldn't come up with a different name? She's seven, for crying out loud."

Thus the celebratory dinner for my brother-in law's return to the house became a rather tense affair. He went to shower and change. My sister stacked slices of breaded and fried eggplant on a paper towel that turned translucent and gritty with grease. Sadie, Joann, and I drew. When my brother-in-law came back to the kitchen, he stood for a moment at the threshold touching the sides of his face and staring at the table. His daughter drawing monstrous mice and falling behind in school; his mentally unstable brother-in-law spending inordinate amounts of time with his young daughter; his dying mother, her shaking hands adding a belt to a mouse's purple dress. But then Sadie held up her paper and said, "What do you think, Grandma?" and suddenly I was looking at the table from somewhere else, I'm not sure where I was, and all I saw were two friends showing each other what it was they saw inside their heads.

ACKNOWLEDGMENTS

To my agent, Katherine Fausset—yours was my favorite email I have ever gotten in the hospital. Thank you for everything. I admire and respect you more than my frantic emails could ever convey. Thank you for believing in me and making me a better writer and helping me navigate all of this.

Liv Ryan and Josh Kendall, amazing editors—I barely even know what to say. Thank you so much for believing in this book and for working so hard to make it the best version of itself it could be. It was an incredible experience to work with you and to be read so closely by such smart, thoughtful, patient editors. I enjoyed it more than I can say, and I learned so much.

With gratitude, appreciation, and admiration for everyone who made these words into a book (with a beautiful jacket) that you can hold in your hand and buy in a store or download from somewhere or listen to on your phone or in the car. Thank you to Bruce Nichols, Craig Young, Gregg Kulick, Allison Merchant, Jeff Stiefel, Stacy Schuck, Min Lee, Ben Allen, Karen Landry, Tracy Roe, Gabrielle Leporati, Danielle Finnegan, and Melanie Schmidt.

Brendan Park—this book would not exist without you. Your name should be on the cover. In a way, I like to think it is, since you chose the title. You are, without a doubt, a prince among men and one of my favorite people in the world as well as one of my favorite writers and readers.

Kat Lewin—I likely would not make it through the week without you, let alone write a book. You are so smart and so generous. How lucky I am, and how grateful, to have you as a friend.

Amelia Furrow—thank you for being such a big and brilliant reader and for answering all sorts of insane texts. One day, we will take long walks in the countryside wearing our classic Irish capes.®

Becca Gray—for your video-game knowledge, friendship, strength, kindness, and all-around Gomma status. I will keep asking you to move to El Paso. Sorry.

Patricia Richman—for your knowledge of the rules of evidence and for being one of the strongest, smartest, most empathetic people I've ever met. Thank you for reading my work and supporting me always.

Maya Shanbhag Lang—I could not have done this without you. Once, it was a dream with an Indigo Girls soundtrack. Can you believe we've been friends for decades? To decades more.

Also, I couldn't have written this book without the following people and institutions and friendships that sustained me in multiple ways along this journey:

The University of California, Irvine—thank you for three years and all the teachers and writers and friends you brought into my life, including my cohort and the wider workshop tables. I learned so much from you all.

Michelle Latiolais—no one can write like you, no one can read like you, no one can fight like you. I'll be learning from you for the rest of my life.

And to so many other teachers, writing and otherwise, who taught me, supported me, and believed in me. At Irvine, Ron Carlson, Hugh Roberts, Glen David Gold, and Bill Kittredge; and outside Irvine, Vanessa Park, Sherry Poholchuk, Karen Parsons, Ned Parsons, Doc Falia, Peter Harris, Ira Sadoff, Wes McNair, Cedric Bryant, Kerill O'Neill, Richard Robbins, Mary Beth Mills, Catherine Besteman, and Jeffrey Anderson—I learned so much from you, and I think of you often. And to Jeff Powell, Barak Richman, and Miti Gulati—same, and thank you also for writing recommendations so I could get my MFA.

ACKNOWLEDGMENTS

Thanks to the Community of Writers, Eggtooth Editions (Will Cordeiro and M. S. Coe), *Day One* and Morgan Parker, *Mid-American Review* and Teresa Lynn Dederer, *Jellyfish Review* and Chris James, *Tin House* and Thomas Ross, *Faultline* and Kathleen MacKay, Amy Hempel and *The Best Small Fictions,* Chris Tusa and *Fiction Southeast*. Thanks also to a number of rejection letters.

To everyone in our El Paso book club past, future, and especially present—Becky Reyes, Nicky Bombara, Carol Furrow, Lauren Fenenbock, Taylor Smith, Christy Rago—what a joy and what an honor to be among readers like you.

Bernie Segura, Jerry McLain, Yuri Care, Andres Caballero, Ms. Sylvia Warren, Nacho and Vera Zumbia, Miranda Escobar, Mitzi Bose, Christine Cramer, Tristan Bouilly, Gabe Bombara, Jessie Miles, Shelby Ruff, Mague Rodriguez, Becky and Michael Griebe—our family is home because of you, and I love our home. I couldn't have written this without you.

Jason Rathod, Sandeep Vaheesan, Kiren Gopal, Benjamin Douglas, Sheetal Patel, and Geeta Bhat—the technology may change, but we are still sending shit to one another, and it means everything to me. Thank you for changing the world and for never letting a good joke die.

To 3100 Waverly—Will Litton, Albert Huber, Hilary Jay, DM Brent, and Heather Hanford—you threw me a party when I published my first ever thing; you let me set up a desk in a weird corner of the kitchen; you helped me say goodbye to Mariposa and raise Rowena. Thank you, and I think of you often.

Shanna Brownstein, Anne Kent, Jenn Ma, Julian Smith-Newman, Baskut Tuncak, Becca Worthington, Melissa Schmidt, Lisa Swaminathan, Kim Maynard, Julia DiPrete, Caroline Brownworth, Paula Harting, Melanie Gleason, and Amanda Foushee—my beautiful and brilliant friends. You mean so much to me, you inspire me, and I can't wait until I see you again.

ACKNOWLEDGMENTS

To Robert Boswell, Patrick Radden Keefe, Jacob L. Bender, Eugenie Brinkema, and Sarah Dellmann—thank you for your essays, which served as inspiration.

To everyone who read drafts of my short stories and previous novels—often multiple times—and offered advice, guidance, and recommendations for books I needed to learn from or actual recommendation letters: I would not have made it here without you. I have already mentioned many of you, but thank you also to Blake Kimzey, John Kim, Meriwether Clarke, Olga Moskvina, Ashley Farmer, Tom Barbash, Rory Cardinal, Kevin Schlottman, Rob Reynolds, Ian Tuttle, Chris Dearner, Lisa Douglas, Aaron Peters, Nicole Kelly, Vinh-Paul Ha, Zoe Vandeveer, Kendra Fish, Martina Hutchins, and Justin Jaeckels.

Kaysley Hoff, Tiffany Floyd, Nora Donatelli, and Gabby Calderon—I will never be able to thank you enough; I can only hope you know how important you are and how in awe I am of you and all that you do.

And the biggest thank you of all to my family—to my parents, for everything; to Abigail, my original partner in reading, writing, and living; and to Mary, Anna, and Steven: I love you so much. And to my extended family—Rowena and Mariposa, Joe Bradley and Joe McLaughlin, Uncle Bradley and Aunt Debbie, Judy and Al Vitolo—for welcoming me home. Marissa Vitolo, Sean Campbell, Sophia, Sylvia, and Angelo and Lisa Montague, Brandy, Brook, Misty, Horace and Ruth—life is better when we are all together; what full and lovely families I have been lucky enough to join. Nick—God only knows ♪♪. You are a true Seeker, and you make all this possible. Max and Frances—in the end, words do fail, at least mine do. But even if they let me write an acknowledgments section twice as long as this book—and I am trying—I'd still not be able to thank you for all I want to thank you for or tell you how much I love you.

REFERENCES

The following texts are explicitly quoted or referenced by the characters:

- *Nox*, Anne Carson
- *Grief Lessons: Four Plays by Euripides*, Anne Carson
- *This Craft of Verse*, Jorge Luis Borges
- *The Waves*, Virginia Woolf
- *The Trial*, Franz Kafka, translated by Breon Mitchell
- *Letters to Friends, Family, and Editors*, Franz Kafka, translated by Richard and Clara Winston
- *The Blue Octavo Notebooks*, Franz Kafka, translated by Ernst Kaiser and Eithne Wilkins
- *Funes the Memorious*, Jorge Luis Borges, translated by James E. Irby
- *Blow-Up: And Other Stories*, Julio Cortázar, translated by Paul Blackburn
- *The Infatuations*, Javier Marías, translated by Margaret Jull Costa
- *The Divine Comedy*, Dante Alighieri, translated by Henry Francis Cary

David quotes Borges in his introduction to Jeremy. This was originally published in *El País* in 1981. This is the common English translation, but I've been unable to discern if this translation was originally attributed to someone.

The characters also reference the movie *Blow-Up* (Michelangelo Antonioni), the movie *Freaks* (Tod Browning), the television show *Veronica Mars* (Rob Thomas), and the video games Silent Hill 2 (Team Silent, Konami) and Senua's Saga: Hellblade II (Ninja Theory).